CONCISE DICTIONARY OF INDIAN THEATRE

Books by M.L. Varadpande

Traditions of Indian Theatre, 1979
The Critique of Indian Theatre, 1981
Ancient Indian and Indo-Greek Theatre, 1981
Krishna Theatre in India, 1982
Religion and Theatre, 1983
Invitation to Indian Theatre, 1987
Mahabharata in Performance, 1990
History of Indian Theatre, Vol. I, II, III, 1987–2003

CONCISE DICTIONARY OF INDIAN THEATRE

M.L. Varadpande

abhinav publications
New Delhi

Cataloging in Publication Data--DK
Courtesy: D.K. Agencies (P) Ltd. <information@dkagencies.com>

Varadpande, M. L. (Manohar Laxman), 1936-
Concise dictionary of Indian theatre / M.L. Varadpande.
p. cm.
Includes bibliographical references (p.)
ISBN 81-7017-440-6

1. Theater--India--Dictionaries. 2, Theater--India--History--Dictionaries. 3. Sanskrit drama --India--Dictionaries. I. Title.

DDC 792.095 4 21

First published in India 2007

Publishers
Shakti Malik
Abhinav Publications
E-37, Hauz Khas
New Delhi-110016 (INDIA)
Phones: 26566387, 26562784, 26524658
Fax: 91-11-26857009
e-mail: shakti@nde.vsnl.net.in
website: http//www.abhinavexports.com

ISBN 81-7017-440-6

Lasertypeset by
S.R. Enterprises
Lajpat Nagar-IV
New Delhi-110024
Phone: 011-26226177

Printed at
D.K. Fine Art Press Pvt. Ltd.
Ashok Vihar, Delhi

Dedicated to
My Friend and Publisher of Several Years
Shri Shakti Malik

CONTENTS

PREFACE

History of Indian theatre is spread over several centuries. Early glimpses of its existence can be seen in prehistoric cave paintings. Archaeological findings related to Indus valley civilisation testify to its being. In Vedic and later Buddhist literature dramatic arts and drama itself is mentioned. Earliest extant dramatic works belong to fourth century B.C. In the Gupta age the Indian drama reached its zenith.

In the 15th–16th century numerous new dramatic forms emerged in different parts of the country propelled by Bhakti movement. They contributed to the richness of Indian drama.

Dramaturgists in India considered drama as an all encompassing life-size art. To quote Bharata 'there is no wise maxim, no learning, no art, no craft, no device, no action that is not found in the drama.'

Efforts are made here to cover the history of this dramatic tradition that flourished in India for several centuries. I hope the readers will find this work useful in understanding the salient features of this great tradition.

M.L. Varadpande

INTRODUCTION

Invitation to Indian Theatre

Rich and varied in its form and content Indian theatre has an eventful history spread over several centuries. By the way of this book I invite the readers to have meaningful glimpses of the theatre history of one of the oldest civilisations of the world that flourished in the Indian sub-continent.

Indian theatre tradition has its beginning in the distant past. It evolved gradually assimilating in its fold various early performative arts like dancing, singing, music and several types of enactments ritualistic and otherwise.

Pre-historic records in the form of cave paintings testify to the early stages of this process of evolution. Several theatrical performances involving dancing, singing, playing on musical instruments, stage acting, hunt dramas are depicted on the walls of cave shelters since Mesolithic period.

Five thousand years ago there flourished in India a civilization popularly known as Indus Civilization. Spread practically all over north India and extending up to Gujarat and Maharashtra in the west this civilization had two main urban centres, Harappa and Mohenjodaro, and a flourishing sea-port called Lothal. Excavations done by archaeologists revealed that the Indus people had their own forms of theatrical entertainment.

Vedic Aryans made significant contribution to the evolution of theatre. Their early book of hymns, Rig Veda, contained dialogues with story element which were known as Samvada Sukta or Akhyana Sukta. It is believed that these Suktas were enacted by Vedic priests. Several Vedic rituals were full of dramatic elements and when performed they more or less took the form of dramatic performances. Scholars believe that these performances contributed to the evolution of drama proper.

Ancient literary works are full of descriptions of different kinds of theatrical performances but the question is when exactly a literary drama or Nataka as it is called emerged on the Indian scene?

The Buddhist Jataka tales which reflect the Indian social, cultural and religious milieu of the sixth century B.C. speak of Nataka as a form of entertainment. Both the Indian epics, the Ramayana and the Mahabharata, mention the term Nataka.

Preksha, yet another term for drama, is found frequently mentioned in ancient Indian literature.

Nataka reached such an advanced stage of evolution that in the fifth century B.C. the Natasutras or Manuals for Actors were written by Acharyas. Grammarian Panini refers to Natasutras written by Shilalin and Krishasva in his Ashtadhyayi.

In the fourth century B.C. Kautilya in his Arthashastra devised code of conduct for actors and for the first time imposed entertainment tax on dramatic performances. He also introduced censorship or laws against obscenity. Kautilya was the political mentor of the Emperor Chandragupta Maurya who ruled from Pataliputra in the fourth century B.C.

The thirteen plays written around the same time by Bhasa in Sanskrit have survived the vagaries of time. Bhasa is the first known playwright of India. He borrowed his themes mainly from the epics, the Ramayana and the Mahabharata. This gave credence to the theory that drama in India emerged and evolved from the tradition of reciting the epics.

After Bhasa a number of playwrights wrote dramas but a few plays by authors such as Ashvaghosha, Kalidasa, Shudraka, Bhavabhuti, Vishakhadatta, Harsha, Bhattanarayana, Murari, Rajashekhara have survived. Apart from the plays some works on dramaturgy like Natya Shastra of Bharata written way back in the second century B.C. have survived the vagaries of time.

In India drama was considered as most exalted art. It was considered as meeting place of all arts and sciences. It was believed by ancient practitioners of this art that 'the actor who on the stage delights and amuses his audience is reborn after death among the gods of laughter.' But some opposed it saying that 'it induces sensual, misanthropic, or mentally confused states in others and causes them to lose earnestness.' It is full of mischief—bahuka hi dosa samajasa—some said.

So numerous are the references to the puppet theatre in ancient Buddhist and Brahmanical works that many scholars consider India as a Home of Puppet Play. Some scholars went up to the extent of saying that human theatre emerged in imitation of puppet theatre. A number of diverse puppet theatre forms have still survived in many parts of the country. India has also a rich tradition of folk theatre.

Since ancient times India developed the art of dancing and music. Several chapters of Bharata's Natya Shastra are devoted to the art of dancing. It was so closely associated with the dramatic art that a term 'dancing out a drama' came into vogue. Dancing performances formed part of drama and sometimes dramas were presented as ballets. In some forms of drama these two arts are beautifully integrated and blended.

This book in dictionary form takes note of these diverse trends to present before the readers the panorama of Indian theatre.

16th September, 2002 **M.L. Varadpande**

ABHIJNANA SHAKUNTALA

Most celebrated and internationally acclaimed seven-act play of Mahakavi Kalidasa based on love story of a beautiful tender aged daughter of a nymph and a king of Puru dynasty, translated in many languages and performed all over the world. When staged in Europe it became 'a rallying point of romantic taste and reaction against classical canon.'

Johann Wolfgang von Goethe, German poet, dramatist and novelist, was deeply influenced by the play to which he paid a glowing poetic tribute and said that the heaven and the earth have combined in the name of Shakuntala and by her the soul is charmed.

The play had critics too. A.K. Warder of University of Toronto, Canada wrote: 'The Abhijnanashakuntala is admired for its lyricism but its hero does nothing, things happen to him through fate, a curse or divine intervention, his character is blank. The heroine is better characterized but also the helpless plaything of supernatural powers. Thus there is no real action but only a certain depth of helpless feeling.'

V.S. Naipaul in his book *India: A Wounded Civilization* quotes Vinoba saying: 'I have never read the Shakuntala of Kalidasa, and I never shall. I do not learn the language of gods to amuse myself with love stories and literary trifles.'

It seems that the story of Shakuntala was known to Indian people centuries before the advent of Kalidasa. Vedic literature knew of the nymph Shakuntala, her son Bharata and King Dushyanta. The Shatapatha Brahmana says:

'At Nadapit, the Apsara Shakuntala conceived Bharata who after conquering the whole earth brought to Indra more than a thousand horses.

Bharata Daushyanti once performed a sacrifice and attained a whole sway now belongs to the Bharatas' (XIII, 5.4).

Aitareya Brahmana, VIII, 23, 21, also refers to Bharata Daushyanti. In the Buddhist literature a story near similar to that of Dushyanta-Shakuntala is found in the form of Katthahari Jataka. However it is in the epic Mahabharata that the love story of a beautiful girl in the hermitage and a Puru king who united with her by Gandharva rites is narrated at length.

However the most interesting and curious reference to Shakuntala story is found in the Kamasutra, Indian treatise on love, by Maharshi Vatsyayana.

In the chapter Dutikarmaprakarana Vatsyayana says that to seduce a girl for the hero the go-between or duti should tell her stories—lokavrittanta, kavikatha, paradarikakatha—of illicit relationships. Commenting on this Yashodhara defines lokavrittanta as love stories from Puranic literature, kavikatha as stories composed by poets like that of Indumati and paradarikakatha as stories of love affairs of men with the wives of others like the story of the wife of Brihaspati Tara who fell in love with Chandra and eloped with him.

Vatsyayana says the duti should tell her the love stories of Ahalya, Avimaraka and Shakuntala to incite her to form illicit relationship. He terms such stories as Anuraga katha.

Ahalya was young and extremely beautiful wife of sage Gautama who fell for handsome Indra and indulged in love affair with him behind the back of her husband. Maids of beautiful princess Kurangi smuggled in handsome youth Avimaraka in the royal harem who enjoyed her company for one full year without the knowledge of her parents. Bhasa wrote a play based on this story titled as Avimaraka with some very explicit descriptions.

Lovelorn Shakuntala too fell for handsome Dushyanta and secretly established physical relationship with him behind the back of her foster father.

These women were hailed by Vatsyayana as daring lovers whose stories could be used to incite young girls into forging illicit relationships. In the play Malati Madhava by Bhavabhuti we see heroine Malati listening to the love stories like that of Shakuntala-Dushyanta which ignited her passion just in the manner described in Kamasutra.

The Mahabharata says that once King Dushyanta on hunting expedition visited the hermitage of sage Kanva and fell in love with Kanva's beautiful daughter Shakuntala. After extracting from him the promise that if a son is born to her he will be the heir to his kingdom, she surrenders to his passion. Some years after the son is born. She along with him goes to Dushyanta's court. However Dushyanta refuses to recognise her. Angry Shakuntala subjects him to severe tongue-lashing telling him about the importance of a wife and a son in man's life. When she was about to leave the divine voice proclaims her to be the lawful wife of the king. Dushyanta promptly accepts her. Explaining his conduct he says that if he would have accepted her just like that there would have been a public scandal hence he feigned ignorance, though he recognised her at the first instant.

The Mahabharata story is much closer to its Buddhist version, the Katthahari Jataka.

Maurice Winternitz feels that the love story of Shakuntala and king Dushyanta as it appears in the Mahabharata is bowdlerised and presented in mutilated priestly form, its narrative being unattractive and inartistic. However Kalidasa turned it into sensitive love story with plethora of delicate human emotions and feelings enriching its fabric. The love scenes involving Shakuntala and Dushyanta are extremely lyrical in Kalidasa. Kalidasa portrays those with unique tenderness and provides them with most idyllic environment. He excels in the depiction of sringara in union and separation and creates delicate situations to portray its various shades with the finesse and sophistication till then unknown to Sanskrit dramatic literature. No wonder Kalidasa is described as a poet of love.

After the prologue the play opens with high action, king Dushyanta astride a speeding chariot pursuing a black deer running for life. Some critics think that this symbolises the pursuit of the heroine Shakuntala by Dushyanta which is going to take place, an innocent girl hunted by a king.

The ascetics stop him in the track saying that it is not proper for the king to kill the deer belonging to the hermitage. The king bows to their wishes. Pleased ascetics invite the king to pay a visit to the hermitage belonging to Kanva. On being asked by the king as to where the Kulapati is the inmates of the hermitage inform him that leaving the task of entertaining the guests to daughter Shakuntala he has gone to Somatirtha to propitiate the stars and heavenly bodies unfavourable to her.

The king gets down at the gate of the hermitage situated in idyllic surroundings. From a distance he sees some girls with pots filled with water coming in his direction. He hides himself behind a tree.

Enters beautiful tender aged Shakuntala, delicate in limbs like the soft bud of Navamallika creeper, wearing garment made of bark of tree along with her equally lovely female friends and starts watering the plants. She complains that her friend Priyamvada has rather firmly tied the bark around her breasts. Mischievous Priyamvada retorts that instead of blaming her why she is not blaming her youth which has made her bosoms grow giving the feeling that the costume is tight.

Laughing they continue watering the plants. Suddenly a black bumble bee attacks them. Dushyanta comes forward from behind the tree and wards it off. The king is fascinated by the beauty of Shakuntala. She too is attracted towards the handsome man. Here ends the first act.

In the second act we see the king calling off the hunting expedition and asking his soldiers to lie low. On knowing the king's love secret Vidushaka remarks that bored by constantly eating sweet dates he is now pining for sour tamarind as a change. On knowing that king Dushyanta is camping near the hermitage the ascetics approach him with the request to protect them from the demons. Taking this as a god-send opportunity to meet and seduce Shakuntala the king agrees to their request and sending back his army to the capital he decides to stay back alone.

It is interesting to note that in this act the king is shown appearing on the stage surrounded by the posse of female Yavani bodyguards with bows in their hands and garlands around their neck. It points at the practice of maintaining the female bodyguards from foreign country for the protection of the king. Yavanis in ancient India are meant the girls from Ionian island of Greece, or any Greek girl that matter.

In the third act we see love blossoming between Shakuntala and Dushyanta in the idyllic environment of the hermitage. Hit by cupid's arrow the king sees Shakuntala reclining on the soft and delicate bed of flowers, her friends fanning her with the fan made out of lotus leaves. She is suffering the painful emotions perpetuated by love. The friends ask her to write a love letter, madanalekha, addressing the king expressing her intense emotions. Shakuntala writes a verse, lalitpadabandha, and inscribes it on lotus leaf by her nail.

Kamasutra, Indian treatise on love, too advises young people in love to inscribe their special feelings on tender leaves. He also asks them to draw mithuna-chitra on leaves to communicate their feelings to each other. Explaining the term mithuna-chitra the commentator Yashodhara says that they may draw the figures of mithuna or couple of

Hansa birds to suggest love.

Dushyanta, concealed behind the tree, now comes forward overjoyed by the revelation of love by beautiful Shakuntala. Blushing profusely the girl tries to rise from her flower-bed but the gallant king prevents her from doing so. Asking the king to sit by her side the friends of Shakuntala depart. Assuring her the king says:

'Why worry dear, I, your humble attendant, am here to serve you. May I fan you with this lotus leaf sprinkled with water so that you may get cool breeze? O beautiful one, with thighs like elephant trunk, place your feet, delicate and beautiful like deep-red lotus flowers, on my lap. With pleasure I would massage them!'

A relief of fine slate, about a six and quarter feet wide, found at Bhita depicts this tender scene in a charming manner. The imaginative sculptor takes the words of the king as a theme of his depiction on stone. In the relief a man is shown fanning the lovely girl with wet lotus leaf held in his hand. The turban and the ornament worn by the man in the sculpture do indicate his being a person of high rank, a prince or king. His left hand tenderly touching the reclining maiden is expressive of his appreciation of comeliness of her thighs as also his readiness to shampoo her limbs, finally the maiden's feet are shown as placed in the lap of the man who is sitting by her side.

The sculpture is datable to first century A.D. If we agree that as suggested by Dr. Chhabra the piece depicts a love scene from Abhijnana Shakuntala we will be required to place Kalidasa before this date.

Bashful Shakuntala tries to leave the king but he speaks of Gandharva vivaha in which physical relationship is established without rituals. Dushyanta says that daughters of a number of Rajarshis have united with their lovers in the similar manner. On the pretext of consulting her friends she tries to escape. The king says if she will give him a kiss he would allow her to leave.

Suddenly senior nun Arya Gautami appears on the scene to enquire about the health of Shakuntala. The king hides himself behind the tree. Gautami asks her to return to her hut in the hermitage and leaves her. Shakuntala repents on her cowardly behaviour but on the pretext of speaking to the cluster of creepers she suggestively invites her lover for enjoying the night of love.

A Sanskrit adage says: The best form of poetry is drama, and Kalidasa's Shakuntala is the loveliest among dramatic literature and the fourth act of it is the best among all acts of the play.

The fourth act of the play describes Shakuntala's departure from the hermitage to go to her husband's house. The Indian tradition considers the moment of bride's departure from her parents' house to go to her husband's home as most poignant moment of her life. Kalidasa has beautifully described the pathos of the situation. Father Kanva's advice to departing Shakuntala about how she should behave in the house of her in-laws is still considered as the ideal piece of advice the bride should follow.

As far as the plot of the play is concerned the incidents of the king giving his own signet ring to Shakuntala while departing for his capital, Durvasa's curse that the person upon whom she is meditating will forget her and he will remember her again after seeing any piece of jewellery associated with her are part of the fourth act.

Sage Durvasa was angry as on his arrival Shakuntala who was totally engrossed in the thought of Dushyanta failed to receive him properly.

The fifth act is full of dramatic conflict and explosive action. Here we see the past lovers deprecating each other in strongest possible terms. Love turns sour and intense hate takes its place. Kalidasa is probably the only Sanskrit dramatist who has portrayed hateful dimension of love.

Pregnant Shakuntala arrives in the court of king Dushyanta of Hastinapura with a few inmates of the hermitage including ascetic Gautami and monk Sharangarava. They request the Puru king to accept Shakuntala as his lawfully wedded wife. Due to the curse of Durvasa king Dushyanta fails to remember Shakuntala and his love for her. Shakuntala says she can produce an evidence but when she looks at her finger to her dismay she finds the ring given to her by the king missing. She then tries to revive his memory by telling him some intimate details of their association in the hermitage but in vain.

Shakuntala is now angry. She calls Dushyanta anaya, kitava, his mind as a shallow pit covered with grass, he a person with honey on the tongue and poison in the heart. She is terribly angry because Dushyanta's rejection has virtually made her a woman of easy virtue, swacchandacharini.

It seems that the inmates of the hermitage never really approved of the behaviour of young Shakuntala. In the court of the king female ascetic Gautami says that the lovers did not act well in consulting the elders or speaking to relatives before uniting in hurry in the flush of the passion. Sharangarava says that things done without thinking lead to disaster. If friendship is struck with a person whose nature one does not know one day turns into enmity.

In this act Kalidasa through his characters refers to some social norms and customs. He says though of good character people speak ill of woman living in the house of her father after her marriage. He may keep her in his house or throw her out, husband has full command over his wife—tadesha bhavatah kanta tyaja vainam grihana va upapanna hi dareshu prabhuta sarvatomukhi. Husband is sole and ultimate resort of married woman. Sharangarava tells Shakuntala that if what the king is saying is true then you have no place in the pitrikula or clan of your father. If you are considering yourself pure and without blemish then you must live in the clan of your husband even as a slave.

Refusing to take her back to her father the inmates of the hermitage leave her to her fate. And a miracle occurs. From heaven a luminous figure of a woman comes down and takes away weeping Shakuntala towards Apsaratirtha or abode of heavenly nymphs. After all Shakuntala was daughter of an Apsara Menaka abandoned by her at her birth. The infant was protected and fed by Shakunta birds since she came to be known as Shakuntala. We see Shakuntala as love-child abandoned by her unwed mother at birth and discarded by her lover in the youth.

The events mentioned in next two acts of Abhijnana Shakuntala are not found mentioned either in the Mahabharata version of the story or its Buddhist recension the Katthahari Jataka. In both these versions the story ends right in the court of the king, his accepting the Nayika may be due to divine intervention or miracle of a sort.

The fifth act opens with a very interesting scene. Police chief Shyala, probably brother-in-law of the king is shown interrogating a fisherman who is found with the signet ring of the king. Harassed fisherman pleading innocence tells the police officials that he is a fisherman living in the village named Shakravatar and earns his living by killing the fish.

In ironical tone the police chief says that the fisherman has really undertaken a very noble profession indeed.

The fisherman meekly says one cannot leave the work ordained by his caste however good or bad it may be. Agreed that it is bad to kill the animals but merciful Brahmins too kill animals during Yajna rituals, he says.

Here Kalidasa has taken a dig at Brahmins.

The fisherman tells the police that he found the ring when he cut open the stomach of a fish.

He is taken to the king who returns him with a cash reward. Police chief says that after seeing the ring the king remembered someone very dear to him.

Police officials tell the fisherman that he indeed is lucky, instead of being hanged he got the reward. The fisherman offers half of the reward to police who were a few moments ago itching to adorn him with the garland of red flowers and hang him at the first instant.

A police official says that this is indeed the right of the chief to share the reward received by the fisherman implying that by doing so he is not obliging the chief.

Mighty pleased police chief says to the fisherman that now they have really become great bosom friends and to celebrate the newly found friendship he suggests that they should immediately visit the pub for drinking wine.

This small humorous piece sheds light on the character of the contemporary police administration.

In the play Durvasa's curse and the ring as a token of recognition of Shakuntala play great role. The ring virtually becomes the abhijnana of Shakuntala. In its absence the king could not recognise Shakuntala and after seeing it he remembers everything and is plunged in sorrow. In a way it is the ring which separates and ultimately unites the king with Shakuntala.

From where did Kalidasa borrow the idea of the 'ring' as abhijnana of Shakuntala? Scholars have different explanations. One explanation is that he has not borrowed it from anywhere but it is a creation of his own imagination. Another explanation is that he might have been inspired by an episode in the epic Ramayana in which Hanuman is shown carrying with him the ring of Rama as a token of recognition while going in search of Sita. On locating her in the Ashoka vana in Lanka he presents her with the same ring.

It is worth referring to the Buddhist Jataka story, the Katthahari Jataka, as a possible source of Kalidasa's ring. According to the Jataka once the king Brahmadatta of Varanasi went to the forest and there he saw a girl who was singing and collecting wood. Infatuated by her beauty the king made love to her and she got impregnated. The king gave her his ring and told her that if daughter is born to her she should sell the ring and raise her by the money thus earned and in case it is son she should bring the child to him along with the ring.

As luck would have it she gave birth to a son. After a couple of years she takes him to the king. He recognises her but due to shame he feigns ignorance even though she shows him the ring. The mother throws the son in the sky saying that if he is the son of the king he will stay put in the sky. The son miraculously stays firm up above in the sky and from there he speaks to his father about the pitridharma or duties of father. After witnessing the miracle the king accepts the child as his son and in due course he too becomes the king.

The ring as abhijnana is very clearly mentioned in the Katthahari Jataka, a Buddhist version of Shakuntala story.

However an interesting theory about the source of ring episode in Kalidasa's play is propounded by Prof. S.N. Majumdar Shastri in his article in the Journal of Bihar and Orissa Research Society, Vol. VII, 1921. He writes:

The idea of a ring as a keepsake sent by a lover to authenticate a message is to be found in the Ramayana. Hanumat, the messenger of Rama, brought the latter's signet-ring to Sita imprisoned in the 'Asoka-grove' of Ravana and took her crest-jewel to Rama [Kishkindha, xliv.12–13, Sundara, xxxvi.2–3]. And Kalidasa might have borrowed the idea from the Ramayana. But the lost ring of Shakuntala, its being dropped into the water, and its being swallowed up by a fish caught by a fisherman from whom it would pass through police officers, into the hands of the hero, have got a peculiar charm. And critics have searched, in vain, for the base metal of an old tale which the alchemy of the supreme poetic genius of Kalidasa turned into the purest gold of his 'Lost ring'. But an old tale is to be found in a strange quarter. Herodotus, the father of Greek History (484–431 B.C.), narrates a similar story in connection with Polycrates (B.C. 532), the king of Samos, one of the principal islands of the Aegean Sea off the cost of Ionia. The story runs thus: Polycrates, King of Samos, concluded with Amasis, King of Egypt, a treaty of friendship, which the two Kings cemented by mutual presents. His power and prosperity increased suddenly and he made Samos the mistress of the Aegean Sea. Being informed of the great prosperity of Polycrates, Amasis felt uneasy on that account and informed his royal friend that too much prosperity was a thing which did not always have a happy end, and advised him to test his lot by throwing away his most valuable possession. Polycrates, following the advice of his friend, searched, amongst all his rarities, for something the loss of which would be felt most by him. He fixed upon the emerald on his gold ring which he was in the habit of always wearing and which served for his seal. Having resolved to get rid of it, he embarked in a vessel. When he was far out, into the sea, from his island-home, he took the ring off his finger and threw it into the deep sea before the ship's crew and returned to his city. As soon as he reached the palace he felt uneasy on account of the loss.

After some five or six days, a fisherman having caught a very large fish, thought it to be a worthy present for the king. He brought it to the palace of Polycrates and presented it to him. The king was much pleased with the discourse of the fisherman and invited him to dinner. The fisherman returned to his house being pleased with the reception. Meantime the officers of the kitchen opened the fish, found with it the ring of Polycrates, and hastened to inform the king of it. Polycrates thought it to be a divine miracle and informed Amasis of everything.

Here we find an old legend of a king's signet-ring being dropped into water, to be swallowed up by a fish, to be caught by a fisherman and the king's recovery of the lost ring. And this legend has been recorded by Herodotus (fifth century B.C.) in connection with a king who flourished a century earlier and was an earlier contemporary of Lord Buddha himself one of whose birth-stories in the Katthahari Jataka is evidently based on the epic form of the tale of Shakuntala. Thus we have found a lost ring legend which may be the source from which Kalidasa drew his inspiration, and there is no chronological difficulty in accepting the theory. But how was it that the Aegean Sea legend reached far-off India? The clue to the solution of this question has been suggested by Kalidasa himself by his introducing Yavanis—or Greek ladies from India off the coast of Samos of Polycrates—as waiting upon king Dushyanta while on his hunting excursion. Kalidasa must have introduced them because he actually knew Yavanis as waiting maids in Indian courts, not, of course, in the time of Dushyanta, but in his own age. And there is independent testimony also. The *Periplus of the Erythraean Sea* (1st century A.D.) contains the best account of the commerce carried on from the Red Sea (Erythra) and the coast of Africa to the East Indies during the time that Egypt was a Roman Province. It mentions the articles to be presented to the rulers of the different countries to be visited by merchants; and we find, in his list, that the ruler of Barygaza (Skt. Bhrgukachchha, modern Broach), the greatest port of Western India in those days, is to be satisfied with all articles of luxury, with fine foreign wine, singing boys and *beautiful maidens for the harem*. This was the case because the country was then not under the sway of any Hindu King. Its rulers at that time were the Saka Satraps who seem to have favoured this importation of white slaves. And these Yavanis would be the fit persons to introduce folk-tales of lonia and the Aegean Sea into India. However, it is for scholars to judge whether the legend of the Lost Ring of Shakuntala is a Greek reminiscence or not.

After seeing the ring the king remembers his mistake and goes into deep depression. Suffering the pangs of separation he draws a beautiful painting of Shakuntala. At the end of the act the king receives an invitation from Indra to fight the army of demons. The king departs for heaven.

After defeating the demons king Dushyanta starts his return journey through sky. He descends on the mountain Hemakuta to visit the hermitage of Kashyapa. Here he meets his son Bharat and beloved Shakuntala.

Repentant king accepts them both and the play ends on a happy note. Thus the story which starts in Kanva's hermitage ends in the hermitage of Kashyapa in the seventh act.

Keith says that 'the Shakuntala certainly represents the perfection of Kalidasa's art.' He further says that 'he accomplished a work of such enduring merit and universal appeal' that 'it owns general recognition as a masterpiece.'

ABHINAYA

The root Abhi means to, towards, carrying towards. Abhinaya means carrying the drama to audiences in visual form.

Abhinaya is a broad term and is fourfold. The four divisions of Abhinaya are known as vachika, angika, aharya and sattvika.

Vachika means speech, verbal representation of text, recitation of dramatic literature.

Angika means physical acting, gestures, body movements done to convey the meaning of the text.

Aharya means costume, make-up, stage setting.

Sattvika is invisible aesthetic quality supporting psychological states and sentiments.

Bharata stresses the importance of Vagabhinaya in the 15th chapter of Natya Shastra. Vachika is explained by him as a body of the drama. He says gestures, costumes, make-up and acting of sattva is used to convey the meaning of the text—anganepathyasattvani vakyartham vyanjayanti hi. Text is basic to dramatic art.

ABHISHEKANATAKA

A six-act play by Bhasa based on the epic Ramayana. It covers the Rama story from Rama killing the monkey-king Vali and coronation of his brother Sugriva up to the destruction of Ravana, king of Lanka, who had abducted hero's wife Sita, and his coronation. We may say that the play is the dramatisation of Kishkindha, Sundara and Yuddha kandas.

In the Kutiyattam Sanskrit theatre of Kerala a single act from a play is taken for enactment and performed for several days. The first act of the Abhishekanataka which shows killing of monkey-king Vali is very popular with the Chakyar artists. It is staged under the title Balivadham.

In the sixth act of the play Bhasa has introduced the chorus of three Vidyadharas to describe the Rama-Ravana war. Initially all the three members of the chorus speak in unison, then they speak individually, again they speak in unison and then individually—the cycle of narration thus goes on.

Chorus as a dramatic ploy is basically found in the ancient Greek theatre. Bhasa is the one and only Sanskrit playwright who has introduced chorus in some of his plays. It seems that chorus in Bhasa's play is the relic of ancient style of ballad singing, story telling practised in ancient India.

Abhishekanataka is one of the popular plays of Bhasa.

ADBHUTADARPANA

A nine-act play based on the Ramayana story by 17th century playwright Mahadeva. Mahadeva, a Brahmin of Kaundinya gotra, was son of Krishnasuri. The name of his guru was Balakrishna. He was a resident of village Palamaraneri on the bank of river Kaveri near Tanjore.

The story of the play starts from Rama reaching Lanka in the pursuit of his wife Sita. It depicts various incidents related to Rama-Ravana conflict. Ultimately Ravana is killed and Rama accepts Sita after she performs fire-ordeal.

ADBHUTATARANGA PRAHASANA

A farce by 17th century playwright Harijivan Mishra who was the court poet of king Ramsingh of Amer. Apart from a play Vijayaparijata he wrote six farces—Prasangika, Palandumandana, Vibudhamohana, Sahridayananda, Gritakulyavali and Adbhutataranga.

King Madanankavikrama is angry with a Vaishnava named Gudharasamishra. Acharya Vidhavavidhvansaka at the instance of the king asks him to burn in kamagnikunda for self-purification. The same punishment is granted to royal physician Yamanuja. A prostitute is invited for performing the ritual of kamagnikundadahana. Wife of Acharya Vidhavavidhvansaka too is invited to witness the ritual punishment. But instead of her the Vidushaka appears on the scene in her guise and there ensues great confusion.

AGEN

In the year 326 B.C. a satyric play Agen was staged at the feast of Dionysus held in the military camp of Alexander the Great on the bank of river Hydaspes, Jhelum in Upper Punjab, during his famous India campaign. It was the first drama in Greek language ever performed on the Indian soil. Barely 18 lines of this drama have survived. A distinguished German scholar Prof. Bruno Snell who has analysed and reconstructed the drama in his book Scenes from Greek Drama feels that it was based on historical facts and performed before Alexander with specific purpose.

It was shown in the drama how the governors left behind by Alexander to look after the territory he won were misusing their position and enjoying themselves at the cost of Alexander. In the end it was shown that Agen or Alexander returns and sets the things right.

By staging this play the soldiers gave the clear message to Alexander to return home bringing to an end his ambitious campaign.

Historian W.W. Tarn writes: 'The argument that we do not know the Greek plays were acted in India is worthless. There were Greek polis, and a polis of any pretentions without a theatre is unthinkable; the one at Babylon has been excavated. And Egypt has at least taught us that whatever other works the Greeks might take with them to foreign lands they would certainly take Homer and Euripides. There is no need to doubt Plutarch's statement that Euripides and Sophocles were acted at Susa, for it is known that Sophocles reached India. On a fragment of a vase found near Peshawar and now in Punjab Museum at Lahore is depicted a scene from Antigone where Haemon begs Creon for Antigone's life. As the vase was of local manufacture it proves at the least that somebody in Gandhara was interested in Sophocles, and there is therefore no reason to doubt a knowledge of Euripides also at Pushkalavati or any other important Greek centre (*Greeks in Bactria and India*, p. xx 382).

AKHYANA

Communication of previous event, tale, story, legend. The word first occurs in the Aitareya Brahmana where it is said that at the time of Rajasuya Yajna the Hota priest tells the king the story or akhyana of Shunahshepa. In the Rig Veda there are many hymns with pronounced story element mostly in the form of dialogue and monologue. They are considered as the relic of ancient ballad poetry. These hymns are known as Samvada (RV 10.95 is called Samvada—Brihaddevata), Itihasa (Indra-Marut dialogue is called Itihasa—Brihaddevata), and even Akhyana (Samvadam iti akhyanam Nirukta, Brihaddevata).

Vedic hymns were basically composed for ritual singing, particularly at the time of various kinds of Yajnas or fire sacrifices. However no ritual use is prescribed for Samvada or Akhyana hymns by Sayana. They combine in them the elements of narrative ballad poetry and also, being in dialogue form, characteristics of dramatic composition. It is believed that the narrative element further developed into epic and dialogue element in drama.

According to one theory these hymns were initially supplemented with suitable prose portions explaining their content and context. They were really in a mixed prose and verse form. The prose portion of these ancient ballads was lost in the course of time and only verse portion remained. Probably when it came to committing the Akhyanas to writing or giving them the form of hymns in the Vedas the prose portions were deleted. When the verses were handed over to the ballad singers it would not have been difficult for them to improvise the prose narration at the time of performance.

According to yet another theory the Vedic priests used to enact these dialogue hymns at the time of fire sacrifices, probably along with dancing, singing and music, the elements which are found in Vedic rituals. These hymns, about twenty in number, are called mystery plays 'in which the priests assumed the roles of gods and sages in order to imitate on earth the events of the heaven.' They are also termed as dramas in rudimentary form. Some scholars see in them the seeds of Sanskrit drama.

Prominent among these Akhyana or Samvada Suktas are Pururava-Urvashi Samvada, Yama-Yami Samvada, Indra-Indrani-Vrishakapi Samvada, dialogue of Sarama and Panis, the monologue of the gambler, etc.

The Buddhists speak of Akhyana as a form of literary tradition, story came down by oral tradition, ballad. In the Brahmajala Sutta of Digha Nikaya along with dancing, singing, music and dramatic performances Akhyana too is mentioned. Commenting on the word Akhyana exegetists say that it refers to the recitation of Bharata and Ramayana. Both the works contain numerous Akhyanas (also see Aksha Kitava Ninda, Pururava-Urvashi Samvada, Yama Yami Samvada).

AKHYANAKAPATA

The word Akhyanakapata occurs in the Kamasutra of Vatsyayana (5.4.2) in the sense of the scroll of cloth with stories painted on it. The tradition of narrating the story visually through sculptured panels, wall paintings dates back to several centuries. We find Jataka tales sculpted at Sanchi, Bharhut and painted on the walls of Ajanta caves. Stories were painted on the cloth or pata too. One such Chitrapata is mentioned in the Bhasa's play Dutavakyam with the episode of disrobing of Draupadi in Kaurava court painted on it. Probably the stories related to illicit relationship of men and women in love, stories of public scandal or love stories written by poets—paradarikakatha, lokavrittanta, kavikatha—were the themes of Akhyanapatas mentioned by Vatsyayana. Under paradarika katha comes such stories that speak of illicit love such as the stories of Gautama and Brihaspati whose beautiful wives were seduced by Indra and Chandra respectively, says the commentator Yashodhara.

However commenting on the word Akhyanakapata Yashodhara explains it as scrolls of cloth with Akhyanas like Yama's hells, etc. painted on them. The Yamapatika is mentioned in the play Mudrarakshasa by Vishakhadatta.

An art of narrating stories by illustrating them visually with relevant paintings was developed in India which is still practised mainly in Bengal, Rajasthan, Gujarat and Maharashtra.

AKSHA KITAVA NINDA

A monologue of a rogue gambler found in the Rig Veda in the form of a hymn. In this Veda we find some hymns in monologue, dialogue and chorus form having story element. One such hymn in a monologue form is Aksha kitava ninda. It is believed that such pieces were rendered dramatically during Yajna ceremonies and rituals. They are also described as 'rudimentary dramas' from which Sanskrit theatre sprang.

Along with the gambler's monologue an interesting hymn in chorus form, a sort of frog play, is included in this entry as an illustration of dramatic chorus of Rig Veda.

In the monologue of repentant gambler we find him giving vent to his frustration caused by the loss of money in the game of dice. This beautiful dramatic speech full of conflicting emotions seems to have come from folk theatre. Mostly secular in content, it is not devised as praise of a deity. A person ruined by dicing who still cannot resist temptation of the game is well portrayed in the piece. Speaking about Bhana, Bharata says this one-act play has a knave (dhurta) as hero. The gambler certainly belongs to the knave category. In this interesting sukta entitled Aksha Kitava Ninda the gambler says:

> The large rattling dice exhilarate me as torrents borne on a precipice flowing in the desert; the exciting dice animate me as taste of Soma of Mujavat (delight of the gods).
>
> This (my wife) has not been angry (with me), nor was overcome with shame; kind was she to me and to my friends; yet for the sake of other dice, I have deserted this affectionate spouse.
>
> My mother-in-law reviles me; my wife apposes me; the beggars meet no compassionate (benefactor); I do not realise the enjoyment of the gamester any more than that of a valuable horse grown old.
>
> Others touch the wife of him whose wealth the potent dice covet; his mother, father, brothers say: "We know him not, take him away bound (wherever you will)."
>
> When I reflect (then I say): "I will play no more with them. I pay attention to my friends who desert me; and the tawny dice rattle as they are thrown; I will hasten to their accustomed place as a harlot (to an assignation)."
>
> The gamester goes to the gambling table, radiant in person and asking himself: "Shall I win?" The dice increase his passion for play as he practises the arts of (gambling) with his adversary.
>
> Dice verily are armed with hooks, with goads, pricking, paining and torturing (the gamester); to the winning (player) they are the givers of sons, they are tipped with honey; slaying him in return by taking away the gambler's (all).
>
> The aggregate 53 of them are played as the divine truth, observant Sun (travels); the dice bow not before the wrath of any, however violent; a king himself pays them homage.
>
> Now they abide below, now they palpitate on high; handless, they overpower him who has hands; cast upon the diceboard like coals from the sky, even though cold they burn the heart.

The deserted wife of the gamester is afflicted, the mother (grieves) for the son wandering wherever he likes; involved in debt, ever in fear, anxious for wealth, (the gambler) goes forth by night to the dwellings of others (to plunder).

The gamester having observed the happy wife and well-ordered home of others, suffers regret; yet in the forenoon he puts to the tawny steeds, and at night the sinner lies down by the fire.

Dice, I offer salutation to him who has been the general of your great army, the chief lord of your host; I do not provide him with wealth; I raise my ten (fingers) to the east; That (which) I speak (is) the truth.

Giving serious attention (to my advice), play not with dice, pursue agriculture, delight in wealth (so acquired), there gambler are cows, there is a wife, so has this (visible) sovereign Savitri declared to me.

Be friends with us (dice), bestow upon us happiness, approach us not in terrible wrath, let your anger light upon our enemies, let our enemy fall under the bondage of the tawny (dice).

(Rig. 10.3.5)

Nonritualistic in nature, realistic in purport, this Rig Vedic hymn in monologue form is very dramatic. It looks as if this action-packed piece is taken straight from a performer's script book. Dicing in India is as old as the Indus civilisation and in the Yajurveda the gamblers are termed Sabhasthanu, pillars of the gambling hall. Schroeder thinks that the hopping and jumping dice were represented by a retinue of dancers while Winternitz calls it a "bold fantasy" (*ISD*, p. 21). In fact one person, actor-priest, is enough to enact the piece, humorous but scathing comment on the widespread vice. Some scholars remember Nala and Yudhisthira who fell prey to gambling while reading this sukta.

The frog hymn in the seventh Mandala of the Rig Veda is yet another interesting composition, probably recited as a chorus as in the rainy season frogs sing in a chorus. This hymn is also interpreted variously. Some see in it mockery of mantra-chanting Brahmins who are compared with a bunch of frogs croaking in the rainy season, and some see it as a magic spell to cause rain. When there is no rain in the rainy season urchins tie leaves of the nimba tree and frogs around their waists and dance naked in the streets even today. There is an obvious relation between rain and croaking frogs. Winternitz says: "L. v. Schroeder cites many very precious evidences from others, especially from Indo-Germanic peoples, in support of the belief that frogs are demonic beings bringing rain and fertility. Through many ethnographic parallels he seeks to show the possibility that the hymn might have been employed in a frog mask dance, which was performed in the rain spell. This possibility—the author does not proceed further in this case—must be admitted" (*ISD*, p. 13).

In rural India various methods of inviting rain are employed. They include a procession of singing, dancing women moving from house to house with the image or symbolic representation of Indra or Shiva. The frog is invariably associated with rain rites.

Marriages of frogs are performed, when they are collected and put in a jar of water or worshipped ceremoniously as in Nepal with the belief that if the frogs are pleased rain will start falling. They are sometimes tortured by tying them to the branches of a nimba tree in the hope that their croaking will reach the sky and rain will pour in sympathy.

If we treat these beliefs as relics of Vedic rain rituals, we may also assume that in Vedic times a chorus of dancing, singing men and women might have been moving in the street as a part of the rain ritual. The frog hymn included in the *Rig Veda* might have been a snatch of the hymn song on such occasions by a moving chorus of people desiring rain. Thus runs the hymn:

> The frogs, like Brahmanas, observant of their vows, practising penance throughout the year, utter aloud praises agreeable to Parjanya.
>
> When the waters of the sky fall upon (the frogs) sleeping in the (exhausted) lake like a dry water skin, then rises together the croaking of the frogs like the lowing of cows when joined by their calves.
>
> When the rainy season arrives, and (Parjanya) has showered rain upon them, thirsty and longing (for its coming), one frog meets another croaking (his congratulations) like a child (calls to) its father with inarticulate ejaculations.
>
> One of the two congratulates the other as they are both delighted at the coming rain; the speckled frog, leaping up repeatedly (when moistened by the shower), joins greetings with the green one.
>
> When one of you imitates the croaking of another as a learner (imitates) his teacher; when crying loud you converse (leaping) on the waters, then the entire body is as were developed.
>
> One frog lows like a cow, another bleats like a goat; one of them speckled, one is green: designated by a common appellation, they are of various colours and, croaking, shew themselves in numerous places.
>
> Like the Brahmanas at the Soma libation of the Atirata sacrifice, you are now croaking around the replenished lake (throughout the night) for on that day of the year you frogs are everywhere when it is the day of rain.
>
> They utter a loud cry, like Brahmanas bearing the Soma libation, and reciting the perennial prayer: like ministrant priests with the *gharma* offering, they hid in the hot weather perspiring in their holes, but now some of them appear.
>
> The leaders of rites observe the institutes of gods, and disregard not the (appropriate) season of the twelve months: as the year revolves, and the rain returns then, scorched and heated, they obtain freedom (from their hiding places).
>
> May the cow-toned, the goat-toned, the speckled, the green frog (severally) grant us riches! May the frogs in the fertilizing season of the rain, bestowing upon us hundreds of cows prolong our lives.
>
> (Rig. 7.6.14)

AMRITA MANTHANA

According to the Natya Shastra Brahma composed a play, samvakara, named Amrita Manthana and Bharata directed and produced it. It was very much appreciated by gods and demons both of whom were familiar with the story.

The story of Amrita Manthana or Churning of the Ocean is not the part of Vedic mythology but is found mentioned in the epics and Puranas. According to it the gods and demons together churned the sea to obtain ambrosia. Several things like moon, wine, beautiful water spirits—Apsaras, Lakshmi, etc, appeared from the sea before ambrosia came up. The number of things thus produced by churning differ from book to book. The enchanting story became the theme of first drama composed by Brahma.

AMRITODAYAM

An allegorical play written by 17th century playwright Gokulnath Maithil. The play portrays clash of different schools of philosophy in which Anvikshiki is shown winning over Buddhism, Jainism, Pashupata, and similar other schools. In the first act of Bhavabhuti's play Malati Madhava there is a reference to Anvikshiki, vidya or logic. Kamandaki informs us that Devarata, the minister of king of Vidarbha, has sent his son Madhava to study Anvikshiki in the city of Padmavati. The play upholds the position of Anvikshiki in this philosophical play. Anvikshiki is respectfully mentioned by Kautilya in his Arthashastra.

ANARGHARAGHAVA

A seven-act play based on Rama legend by eighth century playwright Murari who was adorned with the title of Bal Valmiki. The play covers the Rama story from the arrival of sage Vishvamitra in Ayodhya to take Rama and Lakshmana to his hermitage to protect the Yajna he was conducting from the onslaught of demons. The play ends with the return of Rama to Ayodhya after killing Ravana along with Sita purified by fire-ordeal and his coronation as the king of Ayodhya. The play is known for its poetic beauty.

ANKA

A play is divided into acts. The act is known as anka. Number of acts vary from one dramatic form to other. For instance Bhana form of drama has only one act and Nataka can go up to having ten acts. According to rules laid down in the works of dramaturgy Hero should appear in all the acts but the number of persons appearing in it should not be very large, better if it is restricted to three or four. The time span of the segment of the story represented in an anka should not exceed beyond the period of one day. At the end of the anka all the characters present should leave the stage.

It is interesting to note that some playwrights have given sub-titles to ankas. Probably this tradition of naming individual acts has started with Shudraka's Mricchakatika. It was followed by Vishakhadatta in Mudrarakshasa, Harsha in Ratnavali, Jayadeva in Gita Govinda, etc.

ANKIA NAT

In the 16th century, as a part of neo-Vaishnava movement Mahapurusha Shankardeva (1449–1568) of Assam evolved a lyrical dance-drama based on Vaishnava mythology in one-act format. It became famous as Ankia Nat.

Ankia Nat basically takes Krishna story found in the Bhagavata Purana for enactment through dance, drama and music. It is interesting to note that ancient Assam figures in Krishna lore. Krishna slayed tribal king of Pragjyotishpur, Narakasura, to end his tyrannical rule. Usha, charming daughter of Banasura of Shonitpura, present-day Tezpur, was married to the grandson of Krishna, Aniruddha. According to a legend recorded in the Abhinaya Darpana of Nandikeshvara goddess Parvati trained Usha, daughter of Banasura, in lasya form of dance which she in turn taught to the women of Saurashtra.

Shakta goddess Kamakhya of Nilachala hill being its presiding deity, ancient Assam, that is Kamarupa, was under the sway of Tantrism. However, Vaishnavism too flourished side by side. In the sixth century Baraganga rock inscription king Mahabhuti Varman of Assam is referred to as Parama Bhagavata. Vaishnava epics, the Ramayana and the Mahabharata, were translated into Assamese in 14th century. Hayagriva Madhava temple situated on the Manikuta hill near Hajo is one of the ancient Vaishnava pithas in Assam.

But pre-Shankardeva Vaishnavism was almost Tantric in nature. Shankardeva tried to shake off tantric influence and led the purist neo-Vaishnava movement. In drama he found most convenient medium for propagating his kind of Vaishnavism.

Assam has a rich tradition of the theatrical arts. It is evident from the *Kalika Purana* that the temples would be reverberating with dance and music. *Natis* were attached to Shaiva and Vaishnava temples in the region. The tradition of temple dancers in Assam goes back to the ninth century. Another old tradition is the erotic Bihu dance which was associated with the fertility cult. *Oja Pali*, a semi-dramatic form of narrating mythical stories through dance and song, was prevalent in the region. Originally associated with the worship of the serpent goddess Manasa, it later picked up Vaishnava myths for enactment. *Vyah-gowa Oja Pali* is probably the earliest rudimentary form of Vaishnava theatre in Assam. Oja, who narrates the story through dance and *Abhinaya*, is the leader of a chorus of four or five singer-dancers known as Palis. The right hand man of Oja is called Daina Pali with whom he enters into conversation and interesting dialogues ensue. The Shankaria Ankia theatre retained many features of this semi-dramatic form. Oja was transformed into the *Sutradhar* and his associate Daina Pali became Sangi. The Pali chorus turned into the Gayan Bayan group, or the group of singers and musicians. With the synthesis of Sanskrit classical and local folk theatrical traditions, Shankardeva created Ankia theatre to narrate the story of Krishna.

His first play, *Chinha Yatra*, which scholars describe as 'dramatic representation with paintings', is not available. Out of his six available plays, one is written on the *Sita*

Swayamvara story. The other five one-act plays—*Patni Prasad Nataka, Kali Damana Yatra, Keli Gopal Nataka, Rukmini Harana Nataka* and *Prijat Harana Nataka*—are based on the Krishna theme. These operatic plays heralded an era of Krishna theatre in Assam.

Patni Prasad is based on a Bhagavata story in which vain Brahmins, proud of their Vedic learning, refuse to acknowledge the cowherd Krishna. The play depicts the Krishna *bhakti* of the simple-hearted Brahmin women and the ultimate realisation on the part of the Brahmins about the futility of their learning. The play stresses the importance of Krishna *bhakti* over other forms of ritualistic religious practices. *Kali Damana Yatra* depicts the story of how Krishna subdued the poisonous cobra Kalia and how he swallowed the great fire that broke out in the Vrindavana woods. The play suggests that Krishna protects those who have faith in him.

Keli Gopal Nataka is a lyrical play full of songs, dances and music based on the Ras Panchadhyayi of the Bhagavata Purana. In the play we hear a faint echo of the Gita Govinda.

The three plays mentioned above are based on Krishna's life in Vraja. In the next two plays episodes from the later life of Krishna are chosen for dramatization. *Rukmini Harana Nataka* depicts the story of Krishna's marriage with the Vidarbha princess Rukmini. The love and devotion of the heroine for her divine lover are very well depicted through a series of melodious songs.

Parijat Harana Nataka is also a very interesting play based on the ever popular story of the *Mana* or hurt pride of Satyabhama, the young and beautiful consort of Krishna.

Shankardeva wrote his one-act plays to describe the greatness of Krishna *bhakti* by depicting suitable episodes from Krishna's life. He uses a very simple technique of presenting a Krishna story. The *Sutradhar* relates the story with the help of actors enacting different roles. He remains on the stage throughout the performance, guiding the course of the story and commenting upon the dramatic action taking place on the stage. The play takes the form of *Kirtan* in which actors appear to speak out their dialogues or sing their songs.

Madhavdeva, disciple of Shankardeva, wrote short plays called *Jhumuras*, depicting the childhood *Leelas* of Krishna. He wrote his first play, *Arjun Bhanjan Yatra*, in 1538. His other plays are *Chor Dhara Jhumura, Bhumi Lutiya Jhumura, Bhojan Vihar Jhumura, Brahma Mohan Jhumura, Kotor Jhumura* and *Ras Jhumura.*

Gopal Ata, Daityari Thakur, Ramcharan Thakur, Dwija Bhushan and many others wrote Ankia plays in Assamese mixed with Vrajaboli, on the Krishna theme, and the tradition of staging them still continues. The plays are generally performed in the rectangular prayer hall called Namghar which is attached to Manikut where the idols of the deities are kept. At one end of the Namghar there is the *Guru Asan*, a high pedestal on which sacred works like the Bhagavata are kept. Actors present the play facing the *Guru Asan* respectfully.

Basically the Namghar is a simple structure—a rectangular hall with thatched roof supported by wooden pillars. The walls are made of bamboo mats which can be removed, if required, to accommodate a large audience. However, the big flourishing Satras have constructed majestic concrete Namghars. The outer walls are painted with various scenes depicting the Krishna story. Sometimes a pavilion called Bhaona Ghar is specially erected to stage the plays. In the Namghar there is no specially raised platform for performing the plays. The actors and the audience are on the same level. On festive occasions people assemble in large numbers to witness the Ankia plays performed there.

The performance opens with *Dhemali* by the Gayan Bayan Mandali. Clad in white *dhoti*, shirt and turban, the members of the Gayan Bayan party play on drums called Khol various types of *Dhemalis*. Then enters the *Sutradhar* wearing a white flowing skirt and a turban. He bows before the audience and sings benedictory verses while he dances. He introduces the characters, tells the audience briefly about the action to commence, maintains the link of the story and comments upon the portions enacted. Taking the cue from him, actors come on the stage. Important characters make their entry from behind the white curtain, *ar-kapor*, held before them by two persons. When Krishna makes his appearance, flowers are showered on him. Members of the assembly bow before him in reverence and in one voice chant his name: *'Hari Bola, Hari Bola'*.

The make-up room is called Cho-Ghar. Indigenous dyes are used for make-up. The colour symbolism is used to indicate the inner nature of the dramatic characters. The demonic characters are painted black. Red is used to indicate brutality and white marks the saintly character. Light blue make-up is used for Krishna who wears a yellow silken *dhoti*, 'pitambar', and in the diadem on his head a colourful peacock feather is attached. Sometimes he wears a gold embroidered velvet jacket. He has colourful and fragrant garlands around his neck, and carries a flute in his hand. In *Jhumuras* he dresses like a cowherd. Glittering jewellery is used for characters like kings, etc. Characters like Kalia, Yama, Garuda, Putana and Brahma appear in the arena wearing appropriate masks.

Ankia Nat theatre in Assam is basically operatic in form and more stress is laid on dancing and singing than on prose dialogues which are also delivered in a lyrical manner. Many melodious indigenous and classical *Ragas* are used in the play. Ankia plays are rich in musical content. Shankardeva evolved a dance style known as Satria to help the actors dance to the songs in the plays. Dances performed by Krishna are known as Krishna Bhangi. *Ras* dances in the Satria style are very popular. They are performed as a part of a play or even independently. The Gopis enter the arena dancing. They wear colourful skirts—*Ghagaras*—which swirl when the dancers move around Krishna. The Satra institutions have evolved many delightful semi-dramatic dances based on the Krishna theme. For instance the concluding song, Bhatima, of *Keli Gopal Nataka* describes the ten incarnations of Krishna. This song is independently danced out as the *Dashavatari nach*. Many delightful compositions from the plays of Shankardeva and Madhavdeva are used for solo or group dancing. As a medium of expression dance is so deeply woven into the texture of Ankia theatre that battle scenes are also choreographed and are called *Yuddhar nach*.

Ankia Nat theatre in Assam has flourished under the patronage of Satra institutions which are powerful religious, social and cultural community centres. They maintain the troupes and train the actors in the Satria style of dancing and singing. Many Satra heads have written beautiful Krishna plays. The celibate monks of the monasteries, 'Kevalia Bhagats', also participate in the performance by enacting different roles.

ANTIGONE

A fragment of vase was found near Peshawar by J.H. Marshall depicting a scene from a Greek play Antigone based on a classical myth. Antigone was daughter of Oedipus and Jocasta who defied her uncle, king Creon, by performing funeral rites over her brother, Polynices, and was condemned to be immured alive in a cave.

Writing about this vase Marshall states: '...the third piece is the most interesting of all. On it are depicted three figures, in the middle a powerfully built and bearded man, to his right a girl whom he is clutching by her garment while she tries to release herself from his grasp; to his left is a youth around whose shoulders the man's left arm is thrown and who is supplicating him with hands uplifted to his breast.

We cannot I think be wrong in recognising in this the familiar scene from Antigone where Haemon supplicates his father Creon for the life of his affianced bride Antigone.

Dramatic incidents of this kind from Greek plays were frequently depicted on Megarian vases. Perhaps it was not uncommon thing for the plays themselves to be reproduced among the Greeks of northern India (*JRAS*, 1908–9, pages 1060–61).

Though locally manufactured the vase greatly resembled the Megarian vases of the 3rd and 2nd centuries B.C. in material and design. As the vase was of local manufacture it proves at least that somebody in Gandhara was interested in Sophocles, Greek dramatist belonging to 5th century B.C.

APSARA

Water spirit, nymph, celestial woman of extraordinary beauty and charm. Apsaras are mentioned in Vedic literature. Apsara Urvashi is mentioned in the Rig Veda. Her tryst with her ex-lover king Pururava is described in one of the dialogue hymns of this Veda. Shatapatha Brahmana further elucidates this theme. In the Vajasaneyi Samhita Apsara Menaka is mentioned. Apsara Shakuntala finds mention in the Shatapatha Brahmana.

The Taittiriya Aranyaka says that Prajapati created gods, men, ancestors, Gandharvas and Apsaras from water and that Asuras, Rakshasas and Pishachas sprang from the drops that were spilled. According to later mythology found in epics and Puranas when the ocean was churned by gods and demons for ambrosia a number of things sprang from the water. Among them were beautiful Apsaras. They are also considered as daughters of Kashyapa. Ever youthful Apsaras adorned the court of Indra, the mighty king of gods, as dancers.

They are known as seductress and there are a number of stories of their sexual involvement with mortals.

In his Natya Shastra sage Bharata speaks differently about their origin. In this work a style of dramatic enactment known as Kaishiki is said to be suitable for erotic sentiment. Bharata pleaded with Lord Brahma that this style cannot be practised properly by men except with the help of women. Hence Brahma created in his mind Apsaras skilled in dramatic performance, natyalankarchatura. Their names were Manjukeshi, Sukeshi, Mishrakeshi, Sulochana, Saudamini, Devadatta, Devasena, Manorama, Sudati, Sundari, Vidagdha, Sumala, Santati, Sunanda, Sumukhi, Magadhi, Arjuni, Sarala, Kerala, Dhriti, Nanda, Supushkala and Kalabha.

Heroine of Kalidasa's celebrated play Abhijnana Shakuntalam, Shakuntala, is a charming daughter of Apsara Menaka. Apsara Urvashi is the heroine of his play Vikramorvashiyam. In Bhavabhuti's Uttararamacharita Bharata is shown staging a play with the help of Apsaras.

Apsara, Devangana or Surasundari sculptures in infinite variety of provocative postures displaying 'languid and calculated' eroticism are used in the scheme of ornamentation of the temples particularly of Orissa and Central India.

There is an inscription in lower bas relief on the outer face of the Prasenjit pillar of the Bharhut stupa which depicts a dancing scene. It reads:

> Sadika sammadam turnam devanam
> Alambusa acchara
> Misakesi acchara
> Padumavati acchara
> Subada acchara.

Acchara here means Apsara. The inscription is translated as—'a jovial, ravishing music of gods, gay with dramatic acting by Apsaras named Alambusa, Misakesi, Padumavati and Subada.' In this scene we see four Apsaras dancing while four female musicians are playing on musical instruments and yet another group of four girls singing joyfully.

According to mythology dance and drama was the vocation of Apsaras. In his Natya Shastra sage Bharata says that while living with king Pururava the Apsara Urvashi used to stage dramas in his palace harem.

ARTHOPAKSHEPAKA

The play is divided into acts, anka. Apart from anka some brief scenes, interludes, supporting scenes too are added or included in the anka. The function of these insertions or additions is to explain the context of the anka. Known as Arthopakshepaka, Explanatory Devices, they are five in number.

Bharata says: 'The Supporting Scene (vishkambhaka), the Intimating Scene (chulika), the Introductory Scene (praveshaka), the Transitional Scene (ankavatara) and the Anticipatory Scene (ankamukha) are five Explanatory Devices or Arthopakshepakas.

Vishkambhaka: The supporting scene is of two kinds, pure or shuddha and mixed or sankirna. In the pure variety middling characters appear and in the mixed inferior and middling ones. It is related to opening segment or mukhasandhi only of the Nataka, says Bharata. Its function is to provide past or future context of the anka.

Chulika: Voices from wings, tiring room or behind curtain by a superior, middling or inferior character relating to what is happening on the stage.

Praveshaka: An introductory scene in relation to Nataka and Prakarana variety of drama, placed between two acts, at the beginning of second act, etc. Only inferior characters appear in Praveshaka. Never placed at the beginning of the play. Performs similar function as that of Vishkambhaka.

Ankavatara: As suggested by characters of the previous acts the next act which comes as continuation is known as ankavatara. Bharata says it falls between two acts or within an act and relates to purpose of the seed (bija). An act follows immediately after the previous act without any interruption in action.

Ankamukha: Bharata says when the detached beginning of an act is summarized beforehand by a male or female character it is called Ankamukha. A character at the end of an act comes to announce what will open the next act.

ASHCHARYACHUDAMANI

A Ramayana based six-act play by 8th century playwright Shaktibhadra. When the play opens we see Rama, Lakshmana and Sita sojourning in Panchavati. Here demoness Shurpanakha approaches Lakshmana with marriage proposal, he in turn cuts her nose and ear. This sows the seed of discord between Rama and Ravana, king of Lanka and brother of Shurpanakha. Ravana kidnaps Sita. There ensues war and Ravana is killed. Fire-ordeal establishes the purity of Sita. After the coronation of Vibhishana Rama returns to Ayodhya.

The play is very popular on Kutiyattam stage of Kerala. The episodes derived from Ashcharyachudamani and titled as Parnashalankam, Surpanakhankam, Mayasi tankam, Jatayuvadhankam, Ashokavanikamkam and Anguliyankam are staged as independent plays on the Kutiyattam stage.

Kerala scholar D. Appukuttan Nair says that K.P. Narayana Pisharoti has published the Attaprakaram and Karmadipika, production and acting manuals, of Ashcharyachudamani. 'There is no Karmadipika for Anguliyankam, the sixth act of Ashcharyachudamani, but Attaprakaram for this act is very important. The single character Hanuman, in the form of Nirvahana, elaborately enacts from the Ramayana the episodes of Kishkindha, the crossing of the sea, Ravana's conquest of Swarga, incarnation of Vishnu as Vamana, the birth of Hanuman, and the entire action of the five acts of Ashcharyachudamani.

Sita is only an imaginary presence on the stage and the Nagiyar recites her dialogues. Anguliyankam which is performed solely through Abhinaya takes fortyone days to complete.'

Around 15th century A.D. a Kerala scholar wrote a critique of Kutiyattam theatre practices under the title Natankusha. In it he has severely criticised the style and mode of presentation of Anguliyankam episode of Ashcharyachudamani on Kutiyattam stage.

ASHTANAYIKA

Eight kinds of Nayikas in different love situations portrayed through dance, drama and poetry. See NAYIKA.

ASHVAGHOSHA

Buddhist playwright, poet, and scholar belonging to first or second century A.D. In his epic poem Saundarananda he describes himself as Mahakavi or great poet Acharya Bhadanta Ashvaghosha son of Suvarnakshi of Saketa, Aryasuvarnakshiputrasya saketasya bhikshyoracharya bhadanta Ashvaghosha. Being the resident of Saketa or Ayodhya he was well acquainted with the epic Ramayana whose profound influence is found on his poetic works, Buddhacharita and Saundarananda Mahakavya.

He was associated with king Kanishka who had his capital at Purushpur in Gandhara and ruled over large chunk of Indian territory including Kashmir, Punjab and the valley of Ganga up to Patna. According to Buddhist tradition king of Pataliputra, unable to raise large indemnity imposed on him by Kanishka, surrendered to him the alms-bowl of Buddha, the poet philosopher Ashvaghosha and a marvellous cock.

Ashvaghosha was associated with fourth Buddhist council convened for systematizing and codifying Buddhist texts. He was very much revered by the Buddhists and in some Buddhist works he is even referred to as Bodhisattva.

I-Tsing who visited India at the end of seventh century refers to Ashvaghosha as one of the great teachers of the past and asserts that his works were studied at his times. His poetic works reveal his profound knowledge of Rig Veda, Upanishadas and epic works, he being the convert from Brahmanical faith.

Fragments of three plays including Sariputraprakarana written by him were found at Turfan. At the time Buddhism was not favourably inclined towards theatre but ignoring the taboo he wrote plays on Buddhist themes, which itself was a revolutionary step. Probably this was the result of his Brahmanical background or liberal policy of Kanishka who even encouraged making of the images of Buddha in human form which too was a taboo.

ATANDRACHANDRA PRAKARANA

A seven-act play by 17th century playwright Jagannatha in Prakarana mode. It depicts the love story of two heroes, Chandra and Sagar, and two heroines, Chandrika and Chandrakala. Villain Vimudha, assisted by Yogini named Kadambini, tries to create obstacles in the way of fruitation of their love but in the end the lovers unite.

AVIMARAKA

A six-act play of Bhasa based on the popular love story of Avimaraka and Kurangi with a touch of eroticism.

Sauvira prince Avimaraka is living in the kingdom of king Kuntibhoja in exile along with his family disguised as low caste commoner, Chandala. He happens to save princess Kurangi, daughter of king Kuntibhoja, from an elephant in rut run amuck. Kurangi falls in love with her saviour.

Palace maids trace the young hero who is contemplating over the beauty of the princess, her lovely eyes, heavy bosoms and thighs and imagining how her expressions would be during the course of love-making—kathannu suratantarapprachur-avibhraman tad bhavet.

The palace maids finding the day-dreaming young man invite him to enter the royal seraglio in the night to unite with the love-lorn princess.

Disguised as a thief, rope and sword in hand, he ventures out in the city covered by darkness of night. Through the soliloquy of the hero moving in the darkness Bhasa graphically portrays the life of city by night. Avimaraka hears a girl singing in beautiful voice, her lover playing on the Veena, both enjoying music in the night, listens to the voice of woman angry with her lover, sees a girl frightened by the harsh cry of the owl embracing her lover, lover eager to meet his beloved secretly is cautioned by her attendants, a thief on the prowl, city police taking rounds of the city by night.

Scaling the walls of royal palace Avimaraka enters the women's quarter.

Encouraged by the maids of the heroine he quietly sleeps by her side and embraces her. Lovers unite in the dead of the night. Concealed in the harem Avimaraka lives there for full one year enjoying intimately the company of princess Kurangi clandestinely.

The king comes to know about the secret affair of his daughter and Avimaraka has to leave the palace. He out of frustration tries to commit suicide but is saved by a Vidyadhara who gives him a magic ring which would make him invisible and visible. And lovers reunite in the Varsha ritu the romance inducing rainy season.

Two more acts and the lovers unite for ever with the blessings of their elders by crossing some more hurdles.

Kamasutra of Vatsyayana mentions the practice of smuggling young men in the royal seraglio and keeping them there clandestinely for secret love parleys with women living therein.

In the Dutikarma Prakarana of Kamasutra Vatsyayana says that stories like that of Avimaraka should be told to girls to seduce them, to encourage them to have clandestine affairs, enjoy the company of young men at will secretly.

Avimaraka is not counted among the successful plays of Bhasa.

AYUDHA PURUSHA

Ayudha means weapons. When weapons appear in human form in drama, literature or sculpture they are known as Ayudha Purusha.

In Bhasa's play Dutavakyam when villain Duryodhana tries to capture Vasudeva Krishna standing in his court as messenger of peace his weapons like Sudarshana chakra, sword, mace, bow, conch appear before him in human form.

The tradition of describing weapons in human form dates back to the time of Mahabharata. During Chakra-musala sangram the weapons of Krishna and Balarama descended on the earth in human form. In the Anushashana Parva of the epic it is said that weapons of Shiva too used to accompany him in human form.

In the Valmiki Ramayana we are told that daughters of Daksha Prajapati, Jaya and Suprabha, gave birth to five hundred children each and they were none else but humanised form of weapons.

The tradition of showing Ayudha Purusha in Indian art dates back to Gupta period. Below the beautiful Deogarh image of Vishnu reclining on the bed of serpent coil Ayudha Purushas are carved. Some of the weapons are shown in male form and some in female.

Bharata in his Natya Shastra refers to the tradition of bringing on the stage inanimate objects in human form in suitable costumes and make-up.

BALACHARITA

A five-act play by Bhasa based on the early life of Lord Krishna he spent in the cowherd settlements in the pastoral region around Mathura on the bank of river Yamuna. The play is full of singing, dancing, music and heroic action. It is earliest known Sanskrit play based on Krishna-lila theme.

There is a brief reference to Krishna's childhood life in the epic Mahabharata. However the appendix of the epic, the Harivamsha, describes it in larger details. Conflict between Krishna and Kamsa is at the centre of the play. As is evident from the Buddhist Jataka datable to the 6th century B.C. the story was known since long time. Ghat Jataka mentions the killing of Kamsa and his two wrestlers Chanur and Mushtik by Krishna. Kautilya who lived at the time of Bhasa too mentions Krishna and Kamsa together as ones possessing great magical powers. Ancient Greeks too knew about Krishna and his cult centred around Mathura. Curtius wrote that when Paurava army marched against Alexander the Great the image of Krishna was in its vanguard.

The theme of the first act of the play is birth of Krishna and his father taking him to his cowherd friend Nanda by crossing turbulent Yamuna. An interesting feature of this act is the appearance of Vishnu-Krishna's five weapons in human form. They are known as Ayudha-purushas. Their sculptural depiction is found in late Kushana and Gupta art.

Second act is quite unique in which king Kamsa suffers from hallucinations, frightening visions and occurrence of ill-omens. He sees soot-black and fearsome Chandala girls appearing before him and asking him to marry them. Chandalas are associated with death, they are professional hangmen and work in burning grounds.

After them a Curse appears in human form, extremely dark, ferocious, displaying sharp teeth in his mouth, wearing garland of human skulls and looking at Kamsa with eyes red like those of ferocious serpents. He is joined by a band of evil spirits who drive away Rajashri, the royal splendour and glory in female form, from Kamsa's palace. Here are the seeds of later allegorical plays by authors such as Ashvaghosha and Krishnamisra.

In the same act Kamsa kills the daughter of Devaki by striking her against a stone slab and at the next moment terrible goddess Katyayani appears before him vowing the vengeance.

In the third act for the first time Krishna's Ras dance with cowherd boys and girls, Hallisaka, is shown being performed. This theme later became very popular and Bhagavata Purana went up to the extent of describing it in five chapters. Many dramatic forms later adopted this theme for stage enactment. However Bhasa does not mention Radha.

Third act relates the story of killing of demon Arishtarshabha and the fourth act depicts the story of Kaliyamardana or subduing the cobra Kaliya by Krishna. The theme of Kaliyamardana became very popular with classical dancers.

The last and fifth act shows killing of Kamsa and his wrestlers by Krishna. This theme too became very popular on Indian stage. In the second century B.C. Patanjali in his Mahabhashya mentions the enactment of the episode of Kamsa Vadha or killing of Kamsa. In Indian art sculptural representation of this episode too is found.

Bhasa's plays were preserved by the Chakyars of Kerala, the tradition of their enactment in Kutiyattam style goes back to the 10th century A.D. The Balacharita has a special significance in the sense that young trainees of Kutiyattam art are required to enact the portions of this play for their first presentation.

Explaining the ritual significance of Balacharita and why Bhasa is very popular with Chakyar community of Kerala actors Guru Ammannur Madhava Chakyar wrote:

'The Chakyars for centuries have been producing the plays of Bhasa in Kutiyattam style. Bhasa's plays are distinguished by their histrionic potential. Every line of Bhasa is rich and provides scope for elaborate imaginative interpretation. That is what endeared Bhasa to Chakyars.'

For another reason Bhasa is of particular value for them. It is even now strictly insisted that a Chakyar must act a role of Sutradhara in Bhasa's Balacharitam for his Arangettam (debut). This is a very old rule. A Chakyar boy can have his Upanayanam (ritual initiation) only after his Arangettam. Consequently even a boy who has no intention of pursuing his traditional profession (Kutiyattam) has to get trained, at least for this role (Sutradhara of Balacharita) and perform his Arangettam.

Balacharita is one of the most popular plays of Bhasa.

BALARAMA

Mighty son of Vasudeva and Rohini, elder brother of Sri Krishna, considered to be an incarnation of serpent Shesha. Of fair complexion he was fond of wearing blue clothes and ear-ornament, kundal, in one of his ears. Plough and mace were his weapons. He was considered to be an expert in mace-fight. He was fond of wine and women. The Mahabharata is the major work in which he is found portrayed basically.

He is mentioned in the Arthashastra of Kautilya by his name Sankarshana said to be having his devotees and cult. In the Naneghat (Maharashtra) inscription of a Satavahana queen belonging to the first century B.C. his name is mentioned. The inscription reads:

'(Om namo prajapati)no Dhammasa namo Idasa namo Sankarshana-Vasudevanam Chamdasutanam (mahi)ma(v)atanam...'

'(Om adoration) to Dharma (the Lord of created beings); adoration to Indra, adoration to Sankarshana and Vasudeva, descendants of the Moon, who are endowed with majesty...'

An inscription of c. 100 B.C. found at Ghosundi near Nagari in Chittorgarh district of Rajasthan refers to a stone wall constructed by a Bhagavata king around a temple of Sankarshana and Vasudeva.

Greek king Agathocles (c. 180–165 B.C.) who along with his brother Pantaleon ruled from Taxila over quite a large portion of Indian territory extending up to eastern Punjab minted coins with the images of Krishna and plough-wielding Balarama thereon.

During Shunga period worship of Balarama was prevalent in Mathura, Varanasi and Gwalior region. It became more pronounced in the Kushana period.

We start getting Balarama images since Shunga period (B.C. 184–72). Most of the Balarama sculptures are marked with a serpent spreading his hood over his head and a cup of wine in his hand.

Bharata in his Natya Shastra says that Balarama is pleased with the performance of a dance formation, pindibandha, named Hala or plough.

Before the commencement of Bhasa's play Swapnavasavadatta the Sutradhara offers prayer to Balarama. He says: May Lord Balarama having complexion like the shine of just risen moon and in beauty compares with Vasanta ritu, moving under the influence of wine, protect you. As a character Balarama appears in two of the Bhasa's dramas—Balacharita and Urubhangam.

Krishna Attam is a cycle of eight plays which are performed in the premises of Guruvayur temple of Kerala. In the seventh play titled as Vivida Vadham or killing of demon Vivida we see Balarama enjoying wine in the company of beautiful women. When Vivida disturbs him Balarama in anger kills him instantly.

Balarama finds his place in the operatic Krishnalila plays of Vraj region and locally is known as Dauji or elder brother.

In the Bhagavata Purana there is an interesting story related to Balarama. He once visited Vrindavan to revive his childhood memories. Along with beautiful cowherd girls he went for picnic and drank to his heart's content. Under the influence of liquor he ordered river Yamuna which was flowing from some distance to change her course and come to the place where he was enjoying himself with wine and cowherd girls. When Yamuna did not pay heed to him angry Balarama with his plough dragged her towards him. Thus the river was compelled to change her course to suit the wishes of mighty Balarama.

In the Vraj region there is a place called Ramghat near Shergarh. It is believed that this particular incident took place at this very spot. There is a beautiful temple of Balarama at Ramghat.

However the most famous temple of Balarama is located in the village Baldeogaon of Vraj region. It is believed that the image of Balarama in this temple is the oldest ever found in the region. There is also an image of his wife Revati in his temple. Daily the offering of Vijaya or intoxicating bhang is made to him. Dauji ki Holi is very famous and boisterous. Women strip the men of their upper garments and making whips out of them beat them ferociously. The drama goes on for hours in the premises of Balarama temple at Baldeogaon during Holi season.

BALARAMAYANA

A ten-act play based on Ramayana by the 10th century playwright Rajashekhara. The story opens with Sita Swayamvara episode and ends with return of Rama from exile and his coronation.

Interestingly it is the character of villain Ravana which dominates the play. His amorous melancholy and obsession of beautiful Sita is effectively portrayed.

Rajashekhara introduced two innovations in the play. In the third act a 'play within the play' is presented. A play Sita Swayamvara composed by Bharata and directed by Kohala is presented in the court of Ravana.

In the fifth act a puppet play is introduced. Two full sized puppets representing Sita and her maid Sindurika are brought on the stage. With speaking birds placed in their mouths they converse with Ravana. Rajashekhara uses an interesting theatrical technique—wooden puppets in conversation with living actors.

The puppets were devised by a mechanic, yantrakara, named Visharada to deceive Ravana, we are told. The puppet of Sita is referred to as Yantrajanaki. The verse says: Sutradharachala darugatreyam yantrajanaki vaktrasthasarikalapa lankendra vanchayishyati.

Rajashekhara is the first playwright who has introduced the technique of puppet play in the living theatre.

BANNING THE THEATRE

In the third century B.C. Emperor Ashoka who ruled over a vast empire with its capital at Pataliputra in Magadha promulgated a state decree banning or curbing theatrical activities in his kingdom. Emperor Ashoka ascended Mauryan throne in year 274 B.C. After the devastating Kalinga war which left many dead repentant Ashoka converted himself to Buddhism, the religion of peace and non-violence.

Buddha was not favourably inclined towards theatrical arts. In one of his sermons he declared—'Gotama the recluse refrains from being a spectator at shows, at fairs, with nauch dances, singing and music.' Probably taking cue from him Ashoka tried to curb theatrical entertainments considered to be harmful for the spiritual progress of mankind because of their sensuous nature. In one of his rock edicts Ashoka says:

'Iyam dhammalipi devanam piyena piyadasina lekhita/ hida na kichi jive alabhitu pajohitaye/ No pi ca samaje kataviya/ bahuka hi dosa samajasa devanam piye piyadasi laja dakhati/ athi pi ca ekatiya samaja sadhumata devanam piyasa piyadasisa lajine/'

'This edict on dharma has been caused to be inscribed by the command of Devanampriya Priyadarshi. Here no animal should be killed or sacrificed nor shall samaja be held because king Devanampriya Priyadarshi sees many evils in such gatherings. But there are certain samajas which are considered meritorious by king Devanampriya Priyadarshi (Rock Edict No. I).'

Samaja generally means a jovial social gathering entertained by theatrical performances. In the Hathigumpha cave inscription of Emperor Kharavela of Kalinga, well versed in music, gandharva-veda-budho, there is a description of samaja organised by him with play acting, dancing, singing, playing on musical instruments, etc. In the Kamasutra of Vatsyayana the word samaja occurs in the sense of dramatic entertainment. He enjoins the citizens to organise samaja periodically in the temple of Saraswati and arrange shows by Kushilava actors. Kautilya in his Arthashastra says that people may be granted permission to drink freely during samaja festivity. According to the Mahabharata and Harivamsha animal sacrifices were performed before erecting theatres for watching games. No wonder Ashoka saw many evils in samaja festivities—from drinking, animal sacrifices to sensuous entertainment.

However Emperor Ashoka considered some samajas as meritorious. He had no objection to take out dramatic tableaux on religious themes, to car festivals, ratha yatras, with temple idols mounted on chariots or divine representation by actors. In his yet another rock edict he says:

'Se aja devanam piyasa piyadasine lajine dhammacalanena bherighose aho dhammaghose vimanadasana hathini agikamdhani amnani diviani lupani dasayitu janesa.'

'On account of practice of dharma by king Priyadarshi, beloved of gods, there is heard in the place of sound of war drums the sound of proclamation of dharma, exhibitions to the people of vimana, chariots, elephants, illuminations and divine representations' (Rock Edict No. IV).

BHAGAVADAJJUKAM

A sparkling farce by Bodhayana full of comic situations, pithy dialogues and amusing story.

It is all about a pompous and pretentious guru Dwijashreshtha Yogeshvara Parivrajaka and his naughty disciple Shandilya, their chanced encounter with a beautiful courtesan Vasantasena and transmigration of soul leading to piquant situation.

Guru wants his indolent and naughty disciple to study arduously but he takes great delight in punching holes in the teachings of his guru and make him feel uncomfortable. Illiterate Shandilya, the disciple, was born in a poor Brahmin family always short of food. Thinking that he will be better off if he joins Buddhist order he becomes a Bhikshu. But when he came to know that the monks of the order partake food only once in a day in disgust he tore off his robes and joined the present guru who kept him burdened with donkey work and without food.

The pair enters a garden. There they see beautiful courtesan Vasantasena addressed as Ajjuka by her maid. Shandilya, the disciple, is struck by her beauty and feels jealous about rich people who have easy access to courtesans. Guru tries to dissuade the disciple from harbouring such thoughts and getting attracted to courtesans. Disciple retorts that had his guru some real money on him he too would have procured a courtesan for his pleasure. To his guru livid with anger at this remark, disciple says that it is not worthy of great souls like his guru to feel provoked and angry.

In this background Yamaduta, the attendant of the god of death Yama, appears on the scene. He causes the death of the courtesan by assuming the form of a serpent and biting her on the orders of his Master.

Disciple who was attracted by the beauty of the courtesan starts wailing. To console him guru by his yogic powers transfers his soul in the body of the courtesan. Disciple is overjoyed to see the courtesan coming back to life but he is distressed when she, having the soul of the guru, starts harassing the disciple for not studying the scriptures.

Yamaduta re-appears after being rebuked by his Master that he has targeted a wrong person. When, to his surprise, he finds the courtesan alive he puts the soul of courtesan in the body of the guru which was lying around lifeless. Guru gets up but with the soul of a courtesan in his body he starts behaving like one. Now we have a courtesan with the soul of a yogi and yogi with the soul of a courtesan. This leads to one hilarious situation to another, confusion worst confounding.

We find a number of stories related to transmigration of soul in Indian story literature. Bodhayana used the concept to create hilarious farce.

Ultimately the Yamaduta puts the right souls in right bodies and everything ends well.

This farce is very popular on Kutiyattam stage of Kerala. Chakyar actors have in their possession Attaprakara and Karmadipika—production and acting manuals of different Sanskrit plays. Attaprakara of Bhagavadajjukam is too in their collection.

The opening monologue of Shandilya who jumps from one religious sect to another for food is rendered by Chakyar actor in the guise of Vidushaka in sixteen nights exhibiting his knowledge of Hindu, Buddhist and Jain religious practices.

BHAGAVATA MELA NATAKA

A Telugu dance-drama tradition that flourished in Melattur near Tanjore in Tamil Nadu propelled by the devotional Bhagavata Bhakti movement. It is believed that this dance-drama tradition in Bharata Natyam mode originated in the 17th century under the patronage of Nayak and later Maratha rulers of Tanjore. However, it was Venkatrama Shastri who gave real boost to this tradition by writing as many as twelve plays including Prahlad Charitam and Usha Parinayam.

Every year on the occasion of Narasimha Jayanti a festival of Bhagavata Mela plays is held in the premises of local Varadaraja temple.

The festival opens with the enactment of the play Prahlad Charitam. In this play the actor playing the role of Narasimha, a man-lion incarnation of Lord Vishnu, wears ritually the sacred mask of Narasimha kept in the temple. Sometimes the actors wearing the mask enter into trance as if possessed by the deity.

When play opens the jester Konnagi appears on the scene and entertains people with his pranks. Then enter musicians under Nattuvanar and recite invocation songs. In this background an actor in the guise of Lord Ganesha appears on the scene, songs are sung in his honour. Then enters Kattiyakaran to introduce the play and the characters.

After this Purvaranga is over the play proper starts. The chorus recites the text, sings the songs and actors delineate their meaning through their abhinaya. The performance is replete with singing, dancing and music.

All the performers are male. Female roles too are performed by male actors. Bhagavata Mela Nataka is an important offshoot of theatrical tradition propelled by Bhakti movement in the country.

BHANA

One of the ten types of drama mentioned in the Natya Shastra of Bharata.

Bhana is to be acted by single character and it is of two kinds: that with one's recounting of one's own feelings and that with describing someone else's acts. The Bhana which is to include somebody else's words addressed to oneself, should be acted by means of replies in course of conversations and with an imaginary person (akashabhashita) along with the suitable movements of the limbs.

The Bhana should include characters of Dhurtas and Vitas and it is always to consist of one act, and should include many incidents which are to be acted by a Dhurta or a Vita (NS: Ghosh).

BHARATA

Celebrated author of the Natya Shastra, an ancient work on dramaturgy, ascribed to the period between second century B.C. and second century A.D.

The tradition of writing treatises on dramaturgy started much earlier. In Panini's Ashtadhyayi there is a reference to one Natasutras, manual for actors, by Shilalin and Krishashva. In Bhasa's play Avimaraka there is a reference to one Natya Shastra but the name of its author is not mentioned. Bharata himself mentions names of the authors who wrote on the subject before him.

Bharata is for the first time mentioned in Kalidasa's play Vikramorvashiya written about 4th–5th century A.D. Bhavabhuti is another playwright who in his play Uttararamacharita has referred to Bharata.

Banabhatta while describing the city of Ujjayani in his Kadambari has mentioned Bharata as an author well known to the people of the city.

A number of commentaries were written on Natya Shastra, most famous among them is Abhinavabharati by Abhinavagupta. The works such as Abhinayadarpana of Nandikeshvara, Dasharupaka of Dhananjaya mention Bharata by name.

An eighth century inscription at Virupaksha temple (IA, Vol. X, page 167) tells us about a great actor Achalan who is described as well versed in the techniques of Bharata's Natya Shastra. The inscription states that he established the superiority of Bharata Mata or the Bharata school of dramaturgy over other schools. It says: The elephant blind with rut, which is an actor of another school, is deprived of his frenzy by the lion's roar of (the rules) that are to be observed by actors framed in accordance with the arrangement of the celebrated sentences of Bharata.

In the Shiva temple at Chidambaram and Brihadeshvara temple at Tanjore the hundred and eight dance postures, karanas, described by Bharata are sculpted. The sculptures of beautiful dancing girls found adorning Indian temples display alluring dance postures described by Bharata in his Natya Shastra.

A medieval inscription (EC, Vol. V, BI 58) refers to Natya Shastra as Bharatagama. It says Queen Shantala, wife of 12th century king Vishnuvardhana of Halebid, was 'a jewelled lamp in the house of Bharatagama, a hand jewel in all manners of dancing and Saraswati in singing.' She is described as first extant Bharatanatyam dancer. Bharata and his Natya Shastra exerted tremendous influence on Sanskrit dramatic tradition.

However we know nothing about the personal life of Bharata, though hailed as all time great. Some scholars believe that the original Natya Shastra was a small treatise which grew with time due to the additions made to his text from time to time. Bharata himself says rules regarding the feelings and activities of the world, movable as well as immovable, cannot be formulated exhaustively by shastra hence playwrights and producers should take people as their ultimate authority (NS: XXVI.125-26). He asked the playwrights to transcend the limits of shastras and create their own tradition.

In the tenth century A.D. in Kerala there arose a local style of presenting Sanskrit dramas named Kutiyattam which substantially differed from the earlier tradition of drama enactment perpetuated by Bharata. The new style was virtual revolt against norms laid down by Natya Shastra. A severe critique of Kutiyattam denouncing its departure from the Natya Shastra tradition was written by a Brahmin scholar belonging to the Payyur family in North Kerala in the 15th century A.D. under the title Natankusha.

K.C. Paulose who has translated the work in English remarks: 'The author claims to be a good friend of the actors. The licentious actions of the actors have, according to him, defiled the sacred natya. He aims at regaining the prestine purity. It seems that the conflict was between two traditions—Bharataparampara and Acharyaparampara. The former, professed by the critic, traces its origin to sage Bharata. The actors on the other hand base their performance on the authority of the latter, i.e. the instructions of their preceptors. The author of Natankusha insists that the actors follow the classical tradition since it is anterior and authoritative.'

In the end of Natankusha the author says that 'the performance should strictly adhere to the precepts of Bharata.' However the practitioners of Kutiyattam, the Chakyars, stuck to their own style developed locally and continued staging Sanskrit plays according to their own tenets. Bharata's tradition thus suffered a setback.

However Bharata's tradition did not obliterate. His Natya Shastra continued to be the source book for a number of dramatic and dance-drama forms that emerged from time to time.

BHARATA NATYAM

A beautiful classical dance form that evolved in the Tamil country over two thousand years and got crystallised in Tanjore under the patronage of great Maratha ruler Raja Sarfoji II.

As is evident from Tamil Sangam literature Tamil Nadu has a rich tradition of music, dance and drama. In the Tamil epic Silappadikaram written in the second century A.D. several tribal, folk and classical dance and dance-dramas are mentioned.

Under the Chola rule magnificent temples came up in Tamil land and dancing girls, Devadasis, were consecrated to them by the rulers.

In the tenth century king Rajaraja the Great (895–1018) built a grand temple dedicated to Shiva at Tanjore. It is considered as epitome of Dravidian structural architecture in southern India. Rajaraja dedicated four hundred dancing girls to the temple as per inscription attached to the temple. It also mentions hosts of temple staff including dance-masters, musicians, drummers and singers.

It seems that Bharata's Natya Shastra reached south India certainly around the eighth century. An 8th century inscription at Virupaksha temple tells us about a great actor-dancer and guru named Achalan, well versed in the technique of Bharata's Natya Shastra. His epithet Nataseya denotes that he was revered by actor community. The inscription says he established the Bharata mata or Bharata school of dramaturgy in south India. It reads: 'The elephant blind with rut, which is an actor of another school, is deprived of his frenzy by his lion's roar of (the rules) that were to be observed by actors, framed in accordance with the arrangement of the celebrated sentences of Bharata' (IA, Vol. X, p. 167).

The 10th century dancing girls were certainly taking lessons from Bharata's Natya Shastra as the hundred and one dance postures, karanas, mentioned in the Natya Shastra are found sculpted on south Indian temples such as Brihadeshvara Shiva temple of Tanjore and Nataraja temple at Chidambaram.

The art thus evolved and preserved by temple dancing girls of Tamil Nadu and known as Dasi Attam later became famous as Bharatanatyam.

Interestingly the term Bharatagama which means Natyaveda of Bharata occurs in an inscription of medieval era. It says that Queen Shantala, wife of 12th century king Vishnuvardhana of Halebid, was a jewel lamp in the house of Bharatagama, hand jewel in all manners of dancing and Saraswati in singing.' We may say that Queen Shantala is the first Bharatanatyam dancer we know of by name.

However the four dance experts in the court of Maratha ruler of Tanjore Raja Sarfoji II, named as Chinniah, Ponniah, Vadivelu and Sivananda, crystallised Bharatanatyam tradition.

The art of Bharatanatyam suffered a setback due to movement against devadasi system in the end of the 19th century but it regained its position due to the efforts of enlightened art lovers.

Bharatanatyam is a solo art but Bhagavatamela nataka and kuravanji are considered as its dramatic form.

Bharatanatyam is comprised of pure dance and abhinaya. The mood of Sringara and Bhakti dominates the compositions taken up for enactment. A Bharatanatyam performance generally opens with a pure dance sequence Alarippu and moves on to Jatiswaram, Shabdam, Varnam, Padam and Tillana. In Shabdam, Varnam and Padam the dancer has a wide scope of interpreting song, mythological episode or a prayer to deity through abhinaya. In Varnam heroine suffering the pangs of separation pleads with her lord to come and make love to her. Tillana the concluding item is pure dance again with intricate rhythm.

Bharatanatyam is the most popular classical dance form of India.

BHASA

The first extant Sanskrit playwright ascribed to fifth-fourth century B.C. on the basis of internal evidence provided by his plays.

Nothing is known about his life. We do not find his name mentioned even in the texts of his own plays. Only information we get from some of them is that one Rajasimha was his patron king. Some scholars identify him with one of the Nanda kings and some others take him to be Emperor Chandragupta Maurya of Pataliputra. Even though Bhasa is mentioned in literary works of much earlier period some scholars went up to an extent to identify his patron king with the Pallava ruler Narasimhavarman second who had assumed the title of Rajasimha.

A very curious and unreliable verse from a work of much later poet declared that Bhasa was a washerman, dhavak, by caste, the fact which did not come in his way of receiving honours for his literary achievements and excellence.

Banabhatta in his work Harshacharita belonging to 7th–8th century A.D. referring to Bhasa said his plays start with the entry of Sutradhara, have several characters and episodes and are structured like a temple decorated with flags.

Dr. G.K. Bhat tried to glean some personal information about Bhasa by interpreting some words in Bana's verse like bahubhumika meaning many roles or characters and pataka meaning flags. He says the bahubhumika word suggests that he was an actor who has performed several roles in his own play performances. It was the practice in ancient India to give flag, pataka, as a token of honour in competitive dramatic performances to actors. Dr. Bhat feels that the word bahupataka in the verse indicates that Bhasa might have won many such flags of honour during his theatrical career.

It was Kalidasa, a playwright of Gupta era, who for the first time mentioned Bhasa along with two other playwrights, Kaviputra and Saumilla, in the prologue of his play Malavikagnimitra as a famous and successful, prathitayasha, playwright.

After Kalidasa Banabhatta, Rajashekhara, Dandin, Abhinavagupta referred to Bhasa or his plays. Jayadeva in his Prasannaraghava describes him as 'a delightful smile on the lips of the muse—Bhaso hasah.'

In his Prakrit epic Gaudavaho the poet Vakpatiraja calls him a friend of fire god or Jwalana mitra. Rajashekhara in his Kavya Mimansa refers to a fire ordeal which proclaimed his Swapnavasavadatta as the best among his plays.

Rajashekhara, a tenth century poet, dramatist, for the first time gave us a clue that Bhasa wrote many plays by using the word natakachakra in the above quoted verse about Bhasa and established the fact that he was the author of the play called Swapnavasavadatta, earlier mentioned by Vamana.

Since about tenth century A.D. some acts from Bhasa's plays were enacted in the temple theatres of Kerala but nobody knew that they belonged to Bhasa.

In 1909 the palm leaf manuscripts of ten plays were discovered at one place in Kerala by T. Ganapati Shastri. About the same time three more plays came to light. After the critical textual examination of the plays discovered scholars felt that it must have been written by the same playwright. As one of the plays in these manuscripts, the Swapnavasavadatta, was known to be of Bhasa for sure, it led to the inevitable conclusion that all the plays must have been written by him.

The plays were: Dutavakyam, Karnabharam, Dutaghatotkacham, Urubhangam, Madhyamavyayogam, Pancharatram, Balacharitam, Abhishekanatakam, Pratimanatakam, Pratijnayaugandharayanam, Swapnavasavadattam, Avimarakam and Charudattam.

Out of these plays the source of the first six is the Mahabharata, the seventh is based on Krishna lore, the next two are Ramayana based plays, the source of next two is Udayana cycle of story later found in the Brihatkatha. Avimaraka's source is Katha literature. Scholars could not locate exact source of Charudattam but it could have been based on a popular love story of his times. Shudraka later was so much enchanted by this play that he used this play for writing its new version, Mricchakatikam.

Bhasa wrote his plays in different formats—from one-act plays to the plays with several acts. All the plays are eminently stageworthy with crisp dialogues and well-knit plots. Among the Sanskrit playwrights he was most prolific. Heroic, romantic and comic sentiments dominate in his writings. He is one of the few Sanskrit playwrights who knew how to write a script for theatrical production. His plays are still enacted in the temple theatres of Kerala in Kutiyattam style.

A legend recorded in the commentary on Jayanaka's work Prithviraja Vijaya says: Once upon a time there arose a dispute between the author of Mahabharata, Maharshi Vyasa and the playwright Bhasa about who between them was a greater poet. In order to reach the conclusion both of them threw a book each in the fire. Vyasa's book went up into flames but Bhasa's work Vishnu Dharma survived the fire ordeal.

However the irony of fate is that this particular work of Bhasa is lost to posterity and his fame mainly rests on his plays based on Vyasa's famous epic, the Mahabharata.

Many of Bhasa's plays are included in the list of all time classics of Sanskrit dramatic literature.

BHATTA NARAYANA

Author of the play Venisamhara ascribed to seventh century A.D. who assumed the title of Mrigarajalakshma. Because of his very poetic description of night (nisha) the critics conferred upon him the title of Nisha-Narayana.

No biographical information about Bhatta Narayana is found in his play. According to a legend Adisura, ruler of Gauda, invited five Brahmins from Kanyakubja for the revival of Brahmanical religion, Bhatta Narayana was one of them. He came and settled in Gauda country, the modern-day Bengal. Some scholars believe that apart from the play Venisamhara he wrote a number of literary works which are lost to posterity.

It is interesting to note that Bhatta Narayana in the opening benedictory verse has mentioned cowherd girl Radha along with Krishna. The playwright says:

> Angered in sensual play,
> She lost her mood for love
> In the Rasa dance
> On the sandbanks of the Jamuna river.
> When Kamsa's foe followed Radhika
> As she left in a choking veil of tears,
> His body hairs seemed to bristle
> From his steps touching her footprints
> And from her calmed, loving looks—
> May you prosper from Krishna's innocent plea!
>
> (Miller)

Bhatta Narayana is the first playwright who had mentioned Radha in his drama. No earlier dramatic work had mentioned her. This shows that the cult of Radha-Krishna was well entrenched in Bengal at the time of the playwright which found its supreme flowering in Jayadeva's Gita Govinda.

BHAVABHUTI

Famous playwright of 7th–8th century A.D. who is known for his three plays—Malati Madhava, Uttararamacharita and Mahaviracharita. The first of the three depicts the love story of Malati and Madhava and the next two plays, inspired by the epic Ramayana, dramatize the Rama story.

In the prologues of his plays Bhavabhuti has given some information about himself and his family. He was Udumbara brahmin of Kashyapa gotra belonging to Taittiriya branch of Krishna Yajurveda. Udumbaras were worshippers of Panchagni, consumers of Somarasa and performers of various vratas or vows. These brahmins engaged themselves in the study of several shastras for tattva-nirnaya, earned wealth to perform Yajnas and for creating lakes, wells and tanks for the welfare of the people, married women for progeny and desired long life to perform penance.

Kavi Srikantha, who later became famous as Bhavabhuti, was grandson of Gopalabhatta, son of Nilakantha and Jatukarni. He was well versed in shastras including Sankhya, Yoga, Upanishadas and Mimansa. Name of his guru was Jnananidhi. His family hailed from Padmapur in Vidarbha, a southern country. According to some scholars it is the same Padmapur village situated near Amgaon in the Bhandara district of Maharashtra.

According to a legend kavi Srikantha used the word Bhavabhuti in a beautiful verse describing the profound love of Shiva and Parvati hence people started calling him as Bhavabhuti. The verse is as follows:

'Tapasvi kam gatovasthamiti smeraviva stanau / Vande Gaurighanashlesha-bhavabhuti-sitananau.'

One day Lord Shiva firmly embraced his beloved wife Parvati. Ash smeared over the body of Shiva, bhavabhuti, made Parvati's bosoms look white, as if they were saying, 'See how love made the ascetic lose his cool. I bow before that ash smeared bosoms of Parvati.'

There is yet another verse in which the word Bhavabhuti was beautifully used to describe Shiva by kavi Srikantha. Its opening line says: Samba punatu bhavabhuti pavitramurtih. This line became so famous that Srikantha came to be known as Bhavabhuti.

Yet another legend says that once Bhavabhuti went to Kalidasa and showed him his play Uttararamacharita. It is said that in one of the verses in the play Kalidasa suggested a very minor alteration of removing an anuswar on a word and that increased the profundity of its meaning.

After writing five acts of his play Mahaviracharita he took it to critics for opinion. Angered by the denouncement of the play by critics he wrote a verse stating that he has not written the play for such foolish critics. Time is infinite and earth is wide. At some time in some place a rasika would be born who would understand the merit of his play. It is said that angry Bhavabhuti did not complete the play, Mahaviracharita, deprecated by critics.

All the three plays of Bhavabhuti were staged on the occasion of annual festival, Yatra, of Bhagavan Kalapriyanatha who is identified with Mahakala of Ujjayani. However some scholars are of the opinion that Kalapriyanatha is sun god whose temple was at Kalpi in North India. In his play Malati Madhava there is a beautiful verse in the honour of the sun god.

In the Malati Madhava he is described as a close friend of the actor community to whom he himself gave his plays for enactment.

It was poet Vakpatiraj who for the first time referred to the beautiful poetry of Bhavabhuti in his work Gaudavaho. Vakpatiraja was court poet of king of Kannauj, Vashovarma. According to Rajatarangini of Kalhana poet and playwright Bhavabhuti too was in the court of the same king. In the mid-eighth century Vashovarma was defeated by king Mukhapida Lalitaditya of Kashmir. In his Kavyalankara author Vamana quotes verses from Bhavabhuti's plays. Vamana belongs to second half of the 8th century or early 9th century. Hence scholars prefer to place Bhavabhuti in late 7th century or first half of the 8th century A.D.

Evaluating his contribution Sylvain Levi says: 'Bhavabhuti asks nothing from the stage except the occasion of displaying the resources of his poetry in the various situations in which the vicissitudes of love place the hero. Seen from this point of view, the dramas of the poet called 'the Divine Throat' are certainly masterpieces. None mastered like him the inexhaustible treasures of the Sanskrit lexicon; none has exploited with an equal ease the most complicated metres; violent emotions, majestic natural scenes and poignant impressions have found in India no painter or interpreter as powerful as he. Indian critics characterise with a happy precision the manner of Kalidasa and that of Bhavabhuti: one suggests the sentiment, the other expresses it. His taste for strange and resounding words helped by his erudition has led him more than once to using obscure and archaic words; his love for grandiose explain his abuse of long and sonorous compounds. He has neither the clever animation of Shudraka nor the delicate imagination of Kalidasa, but his original quality as a writer, a painter and poet places him with them among the masters of dramatic literature' (*The Theatre of India*, Vol. 1, p. 193).

BHAVAI

Folk drama form of Gujarat full of singing, dancing and music. It is believed that one Asaita Thakur created an art of Bhavai in the 14th century. Writing about the origin of this form Govardhan Panchal said:

'Some dramatic form or forms were the common heritage of the people of the entire region and Asaita changed or added some elements to give it a local flavour. They were music dance oriented...Asaita was a Kathakara or story teller and he had acquired a name and fame for this. Thus he already had the gift of telling stories dramatically and poetically interspersed with music. And dance was all around him. He seems to have put the gift of story-telling into writing and turned out the first 'Swang' of Ramadeva, a simple narrative drama. And perhaps took the help of musicians from the neighbouring town of Vadanagara said to be abounding in musicians and thus seems to have begun a new dramatic form. He said: There are the pakhawaja player(s), two ravaja players—two making a pair or two pairs of them—tala players, and the Bhungala players, again making a pair or two pairs—and Rangalo stood in front of them (ready to begin) and thus, says Asaita, the Ramadeva was played.'

The word Bhavai as a show or spectacle occurs in literary works. Goddess Amba is the presiding deity of Bhavai. Bhavai according to some scholars is made up of two components—Bhava and Aai. Bhava means this world and Aai is mother, hence Bhavai means mother of the world—Amba: Bhavai is performed as a ritual offering to goddess Amba. In the courtyard of Ambaji temple near Mount Abu the religious Navaratri festival is celebrated with Bhavai performances.

It is believed that Asaita wrote numerous Bhavai plays known as veshas. Despite a number of mythological plays in its repertory Bhavai is particularly known for its plays with secular social content permeated with pungent humour and biting social satire. The pompous and incongruous behaviour of the high caste people is scoffed at. People belonging to different levels of social strata from king to knave are portrayed in Bhavai.

Panchal writes: 'The people of the lower rung of society, economically and socially backward, were freely portrayed. The barbers, knife-sharpeners, robbers, bangle sellers, thieves, Vanjharas, Oadas, darjis, the sadhus, fakirs—the Veshas (plays) depicting the whole gamut of life were written.'

Interestingly enough number of Muslim characters appear in the Bhavai veshas. At the end of the play Jasma Odan, a Muslim fakir, appears to whom people request to revive heroine Jasma. Miya Jhutan is the central character of yet another Vesha.

The leader of the Bhavai troupe is called Nayak. He marks the performing arena, offers kumkum to the oil-torch symbolising goddess Amba and sing prayers in her honour.

Then enters an actor covering his face with a plate, he is Lord Ganesha, the remover of obstacles. Goddess Kali is next to appear and after her departure comes the priest. After this ritual the Vesha starts rolling. Initially small Veshas are enacted and those over a long one is taken up for enactment. During the night five or six Veshas are presented in the performing arena—the chachar.

The Nayak and jester Rangalo are ever present on the stage directing the course of action with their interventions and commentary on the events taking place on the stage. Through songs, dialogues, speeches in prose and verse the story unfolds. There is lot of dancing and singing in Bhavai. Female characters are acted out by men. The traditional Bhavai is night long affair enlivened by the sound of Bhungal, a long wind instrument.

Bhavai in its localised form is popular in the Malva region of central India and Rajasthan. A Rajasthani legend says that it was Nanga Jat who evolved Bhavai. Nanga was fond of dancing, singing and music. Fellow caste-men decided to throw him out of the community. Around this time plague broke out in the village. Poor Nanga went to the temple of Shitala mata, folk goddess of epidemic diseases, to ask for her favour to stop the epidemic. Exhausted he fell asleep. Goddess Shitala mata appeared in his dream and asked him to perform Jatra at her shrine to propitiate her. Nanga told the fellow villagers about Devi's wish and from the next day started serving her with singing, dancing and music. Pleased goddess freed the villagers from the epidemic. Later Nanga Jat evolved Bhavai.

Yet another folk legend says that on breaking of a small-pox epidemic the village chiefs or Patels of five villages went to the temple of Shitala mata. She asked them to move from place to place and entertain people with khel-tamasha or dramatic performance for over a month to appease her. One of them donned female dress and others took up musical instruments such as wind pipe Bhungal, drum, dholak and cymbals, manjire. They performed all kinds of entertaining plays—swang, khyal, tamasha—to entertain the people and also exhibit their acrobatic skills. And this is how the Bhavai theatre came into being.

The Rajasthani Bhavai is full of items such as magic shows, acrobatic performances and enactment of small skits.

BHAVANA PURUSHOTTAMA

An allegorical play by 16th century writer Shrinivasa Dixit written at the instance of king Surap Naik for enacting during Vasantika festival of Venkatnatha. It portrays the love and devotion Bhavana, daughter of Jivadeva, feels for Purushottam Vishnu and their union after crossing several hurdles.

BODHAYANA

A playwright of uncertain date who wrote a sparkling farce Bhagavadajjukam, one of the best in Sanskrit dramatic literature. A few palm leaf manuscripts of the farce were found in Kerala. However the name of the author was missing in all of them. In one of the commentaries written on the play it is said that it was written by one Bodhayana.

In the prologue of the play Bodhayana, apart from the reference to unknown dramatic form, Veer, has enlisted all the ten forms of drama mentioned in the Natya Shastra and in addition one more Sanlapa which for the first time is described in 12th century work on literary criticism, Sahitya Darpana, by Vishvanatha. This places Bodhayana in a period between Bharata and Vishvanatha.

Contrary to the observation that it is sringara or erotic sentiment which dominates Sanskrit dramatic literature, Bodhayana says that in all forms of drama, he feels, it is the hasya rasa or humour which is portrayed prominently. And hence, he says, he has written a prahasana or farce.

And indeed Bodhayana very successfully wrote one at that.

BOMMALATTAM

The popular string and rod manipulated puppet theatre is known as Bommalattam in Tamil Nadu. It is particularly prevalent inTanjore district of the State. The puppet theatre tradition of Tamil country dates back to several centuries. In the Thirukkural the art of puppetry is referred to as marappavai. It is believed that puppetry originated in imitation of one of the eleven dances performed by Lakshmi, the goddess of wealth, performed to lure and destroy the demons.

The puppets are quite beautiful and made of wood. The technique of manipulation of these puppets is intricate and interesting. The elements and techniques of both string and rod puppet are used. Strings of each puppet are attached to an iron ring which fits the puppeteer's head. With the help of two rods held in his hand the puppeteer gives required movement to the hands of the puppet.

Stories from epics, Puranas and other literary works are taken up for enactment through puppets.

BRIHATKATHA

A great story book written by Gunadhya in Paishachi language in the early first century A.D. The book is lost to posterity but its three Sanskrit versions and one Tamil version, Perungadai, by Kongu-Veliar, have survived. The book in verse contains numerous stories but the story of king Udayana of Kaushambi and his son Naravahanadatta forms the core of the work. In an inscription of 875 A.D. from Cambodia author Gunadhya is mentioned respectfully.

Sanskrit dramatic literature is greatly indebted to Brihatkatha (also see GUNADHYA).

CAVE MAN'S THEATRE

Many sites showing prehistoric cave paintings, some of them belonging to mesolithic period, were discovered in India by the archaeologists. Among other things these cave paintings throw light on cultural life of aboriginal Indians. They give us some idea about cave man's theatrical activities.

Dance, the primordial unit of theatre, is predominantly portrayed in the prehistoric picture galleries located all over the country. Such is the prominence given to the depiction of dance scenes that one feels like calling the Stone Age culture a dance culture. Dance has appeared in variegated forms—as a creative aesthetic activity and medium of expression of the joys and sorrows of primitive communities, as a form of magic and significant part of ritual, as a simple recreation as well as medium of instruction. The theatricality of dance and its narrative character is also worth observing.

Various enchanting dance formations are depicted on rock surfaces with precision. We find row dancing as well as people dancing in groups but separately. Indian dramaturgy calls the first *srinkhala* (chain) and the other *gulma* (cluster). Dancing with alternate male/female partners is observed along with dancing in circles around a fire. A mesolithic painting at Lakhajoar shows a row of 17 dancers moving forward in a chainlike formation.

The most interesting is the last dancer in the row, shown tumbling and rolling while following the line. He might be doing so under the influence of wine or executing deliberate somersaults to evoke laughter. He is a precursor of the popular theatrical figure of a jester or *vidushaka* who appears on the scene to amuse the audience. Observing a group of dancers in the same painting executing difficult steps, Neumayer observes: "The S position of the dancers' bodies and the intricate positioning of the legs and arms immediately recalled to me the mating dances of the cranes I have often observed from that shelter in the fields below. A parallel which may approximate to the meaning of this dance depiction is the practice, current among many existing tribal societies, of pantomiming animal movements."

A group composition of four dancers from a mesolithic cave painting of Jaora is yet another example of an acrobatic dance pattern. Two dancers are performing by standing back to back while another balances himself on one leg. He is holding in his right hand his right leg up in the air, a typical Bharata Natyam pose. The fourth is probably bowing to the audience in anticipation of appreciation. Wakankar observes the dancers with "steps together, forward and backward, clapping along the rhythm in steps, clapping overhead and under the raised knee, dancing on the rhythm of claps by the leader at the centre." Amazed by the *angika abhinaya* of the dancers he remarks: "Dances had developed into a classical art."

Neumayer says: "Dance, music and chants are the most widely recurring cultural symbols. Mesolithic paintings show that rhythmic movements, most probably reinforced by a uniform beat, were used to forge a number of people into a unified mass sharing a homogeneous psychological condition...In the earliest rock painting style, the one in which green was used, dance scenes are almost the only theme. These pictures indicate a very complex dancing culture with uniform step and dancing pattern."

Were these dancers vocal or mute? In many paintings small circles drawn in front of the dancers' mouths are identified as "speech bubbles" by Neumayer indicating that they are singing or chanting incantations. Verbalisation of rituals in which dancing figures is a step further towards theatre proper. Were they trying to express through sound the myth about deified animals portrayed by them on the walls of cave shelters with awe or reverence? Or are they just producing sound conducive to the rhythm of their dancing?

Impersonation or imitation is yet another important element of theatre. We find dancers impersonating animals or deified animals by wearing masks. We find a person wearing an antler mask in a Mesolithic painting at Lakhajoar (Pl. 6), and equally interesting is a dancer with elephant mask from Bhimbetka (Wakankar). We also see people wearing an animal skull mask (Pl. 7) who are identified as wizards from the Mesolithic period. Wizards as we all know impersonate supernatural or mythical beings in their frenzy, a kind of dance.

Musical instruments figure in the cave paintings in the scenes depicting dancing. A Mesolithic painting from Kathotia depicts a harplike musical instrument in the hand of a human figure. According to Neumayer, some dancing and feasting is going on by the side of a dead boar where the man with musical instruments is sitting. It is a gay party with a one-piece musical accompaniment in attendance. One of a group of five dancers depicted in a Mesolithic painting from Lakhajoar is shown holding a musical instrument "composed of vibrating lines" (Pl. 9).

A round duff-like musical instrument is seen in the hand of one person accompanying the dancer from the Mesolithic painting of the same place. Chalcolithic painting from Chatur Bhoj Nath Nulla portrays a drummer among warriors. A painting from the historical period from Pachmarhi depicts a harp player and his family. Dr. Wakankar refers to horn pipes and stone drums which he located at Bhimbetka. He writes: "In several shelters cup marks on rock surfaces formed by repeated striking have been noticed. These rocks, when struck with stone or bone, produce a drumlike sound. It is possible that they were used to produce musical sounds to help rhythmic movements during dances" (Marg, Sept 75). A painting of the historic era from Bhimbetka shows drums and gongs; castanets are also seen.

Dances of course used to be performed in an open arena at a convenient place. Sometimes the dancing arena was demarcated to separate performers from members of the audience. Some scholars think that in the paintings the line drawn around the dancing group indicates a shelter, a kind of auditorium. Dr. Wakankar has come across an auditorium rock shelter at Bhimbetka which is a sort of carved out concert hall with a stone drum nearby. Tribal groups still use this hall for dancing on moonlit nights. In a painting of the Mesolithic period from Lakhajoar a high scaffolding with people dancing on it to the rhythm of musical instruments is shown. This is a kind of raised stage built for the performance.

In many paintings dancers are shown in gorgeous attire, with magnificent head-dresses and ornaments. Neumayer refers to a dancer in a Kharwai group who has an intricate head-dress painted in green, yellow and red. The dancers wear loin-cloths, a part of which flutters freely in the breeze after the graceful movements of their bodies. Dr. Wakankar observes:

> During Mesolithic epoch we find the moderation of dry climate. The luxuriant forests developed everywhere in peninsular India due to beginning of monsoon climatic conditions. Man had more vegetarian diet for him which could be stored for drier periods of the year. More cultural activity vigoured, sophisticated masks developed. Animals such as boars, deer, rhinos, monkeys were modelled for head dresses or their skulls were used for these purposes. Feathers of different birds were also used to beautify the head dresses. Arm decorations at the joint of elbows either as suspending ropes with decorated ends or certain decorative objects tied at the elbow were very common. The necklaces hanging over the chest made of bone beads or decorated bird bones were often popular. Bracelets made of reeds or some unknown materials are often observed in paintings. The hides were used as garments. Weaved garments most probably made out of palm leaves, thread made out of fibery barks must have been manufactured. The langoti was common garment for men. Women had also waist bands. The male garments in dancing were of various types. For community dancing simple langoti worked well but for ceremonial dancing masks, head dresses, skirts were essential (*The Dawn of Indian Art*).

It is also obvious from many paintings that dancers decorated their bodies with colour.

Hunting scenes dominate the walls of cave shelters. Hunt dances of tribal communities are rituals performed to ensure success in hunting, a sort of sympathetic magic. It is a complete enactment of the actual process of hunting, a drama in which we find a complete imitation of it. Dancers imitate or impersonate hunters in the field. Some of them might have acted the roles of animals by wearing animal masks. Neumayer refers to very interesting Mesolithic paintings from Lakhajoar and Jaora in which masked hunters are shown pursuing masked animals. Masks of animals and hunters are of the same design. It seems that animals here are men in guise and scenes depict dramatic enactment of hunting by members of the tribal group, one acting as hunter and another as animals hunted. Ritual connected with hunting is depicted in a Mesolithic rock painting of the earliest style from Kathotia. Here some figures are shown dancing before the severed head of an animal, a kind of magic performed to ensure success in the hunt.

Hunting dances are a kind of drama or ritualistic drama. In explaining dramatic element in tribal ritualistic hunting and war dances, Sheldon Cheney in his book *The Theatre* quotes Loomis Havemeyer's description of a Naga war dance of Northeast India:

> It commences with a review of warriors who later advance and retreat, parrying blows and throwing spears as though in actual fight. They creep along in battle array, keeping as near the ground as possible so that nothing shows but a line of shields. When they are near enough to the imaginary enemy they spring up and attack. After they have killed the opposing party they grab tufts of grass, which represent the heads, and these they sever with battle axes. Returning home, they carry the clods over their shoulders as they would the heads of real men. At the village they are met by women who join in triumphant song and dance.

A very pronounced theatrical element is clearly seen in the whole enactment. Ritual evolves into theatre. In both, many elements are common. Dramatic techniques find their origin in early religious or magical ritual. "A religious ritual is a patterned act that involves the manipulation of religious symbols. Most religious rituals use a combination of the following practices to contact and control supernatural spirits and powers: Prayer, offerings and sacrifices, manipulation of objects, telling or acting out of myths, altering the physical state of the individual (as in a trance and ecstatic experience or through drugs), music, dance and drama" (Wallace quoted in *Cultural Anthropology*: Serena Nanda). Naga ritualistic war dance contains many of the theatrical elements, nay, practically it is the theatre.

Dances with sexual overtones are not also wanting in the prehistoric picture galleries. Neumayer refers to a Mesolithic painting from Bhimbetka in which three persons are shown dancing while two copulate. Phallic dancers are shown in a chalcolithic painting from Kathotia. A chariot procession shown in a chalcolithic painting from the same place includes ithyphallic musicians and dancers. The relationship of phallic processions and theatre, particularly in the context of Greece, is well known.

Prehistoric rock paintings present a panorama of very rich dance culture. Here we observe simple, intricate and acrobatic dance postures, ballet compositions, decorative ornaments, masks and head-dresses, costumes and make-up as well as musical instruments and singing. We see here the enactment of hunting expeditions, the imitation of animals and birds, impersonation of spirits, performance of rituals reminding us of Aristotle, who said that imitation is natural to man and it is also natural for all to delight in the works of imitation. All the basic ingredients of theatre were present in primitive dancing. Hence it is called the mother of the theatre. Since its inception, dance has contained an urge to communicate an emotion, an experience, a myth in a dramatic way. Hence the history of theatre starts with dance. The actor uses masks, costumes, gestures, verbal sounds, musical instruments to communicate and entertain. All these accessories and elements of theatrical art are well recorded on the walls of ancient cave shelters in the form of paintings.

Observing the dance patterns and formations, costumes and movements of tribal dancers of India, we feel as if the figures drawn on rock surfaces have come alive through magic. The cave dwellers' civilisation has over centuries preserved their ancestral cultural heritage without much change. Traditionally, inherited dramatic dances still form a part of a tribal culture all over the world, giving a clue to the process of development of theatre from its most rudimentary form.

CENSORSHIP

Censorship relates to the rules, conventions, norms devised to suppress socially, morally objectionable contents of the dramatic performances. In ancient India efforts were made to tone down the overt display of sex and violence through visual arts and put check on the glib tongue of the actors. Certain norms were prescribed and conventions established to uphold the morality by various agencies.

The concept of state censorship was for the first time introduced by Kautilya, the political mentor of Emperor Chandragupta Maurya, in the fourth century B.C.

Kautilya prohibited the performing artists from hurting the feelings of the people and asked them to desist from speaking freely about socially and morally sensitive issues. He allowed the actors to perform at any place in the empire and entertain the people but he says they must avoid making fun of country, desha, caste, jati, family, gotra, a certain school of Vedic study, charana, and copulation of men with women. He says the same rule shall apply to other performers like dancers, dumb players and mendicants. He states that if any person is hurt by their glib tongue or obscene actions magistrate should impose a fine on them and if they fail to pay the fine they should be subjected to lashes in proportion to the fine.

For a woman it was necessary to obtain the permission of her husband to witness a dramatic performance. Kautilya says even after the refusal of husband if a wife goes to see a stage performance by female artists, stree-preksha, in the day time a fine of six panas should be imposed on her as a punishment and if she ventures to see a stage show by male artists under the same circumstances the amount of fine would go up to twelve panas. If she does the same thing in the night the fine should be doubled.

Emperor Ashoka, grandson of Chandragupta Maurya, made distinction between bad shows and good shows and virtually banned the bad ones. In the Buddhist scriptures the bad shows are described as visuka dassanam or viparita darsana and include dancing, singing, playing on musical instruments, ballad recitation and dramatic performances.

Manu in his Smriti prohibits a student of Veda living with his teacher from attending performances involving dancing, singing, playing on musical instruments—nartanam gitavadanam.

Bharata in his Natya Shastra speaks of certain moral conventions which performers were expected to follow while staging their shows. He says:

'On knowing the dramatic convention, natya dharma should not represent sleeping on the stage. But if such is necessary on some pretended need one should bring the act to a close.

If out of necessity anyone sleeps alone or with anyone, no kiss or embrace, or any other private acts such as biting, scratching with nails, loosing of Nivi, the pressing of breasts and lips, should be presented on the stage.

As a Nataka is to be witnessed by the father and the son, the mother-in-law and father-in-law all sitting together these acts should be carefully avoided.

In presenting various activities of women there should be on the stage no ascending of the bed-stead, no bath, no use of unguents and collyrium, no decoration of body and no doing of hair.

And women of the superior and middling types should not be shown as very scantily draped or wearing only one piece of garment.

Taking food or sporting in water or doing any immodest, lajjakara, act should not be presented on the stage.'

Bharata prohibits all acts which are shameful and disgraceful, lajjakara. Bharata also prohibits showing on the stage violent acts such as killing, battle, death, terrified flights. In short he has tried to restrain the artists from overt exhibition of sex and violence.

CHAITANYACHANDRODAYAM

A ten-act play by poet Karnapura based on the life of Chaitanya Mahabrabhu. It was written and staged in 1572 at the instance of Maharaja Gajapati Prataparudradeva of Orissa. The real name of kavi Karnapura was Paramanandadas. His father Shivananda Sen belonged to village Kanchanapada of Bengal. The sentiment of Bhakti dominates the play. Along with Chaitanya characters, allegorical in nature, such as Bhakti, Vairagya, Kali, Adharma appear on the scene. The play is considered historical in the sense that it throws light on the life of Chaitanya Mahaprabhu.

CHANDAKAUSHIKA

A five-act play based on the story of king Harishchandra by Kshemishvara who was in the court of king Mahipala of Kanauj. This tenth century playwright has also written one more play, Naishadhanandam, based on the love story of king Nala and princess Damayanti recorded in the Mahabharata.

CHARUDATTA

A four-act romantic play by Bhasa based on the love story of a poor Brahmin Charudatta and beautiful and rich courtesan Vasantasena. It ends abruptly giving the impression that Bhasa could not complete it. Centuries later Shudraka adopted this fragmented play and enlarging it created his own version of the story, the Mricchakatika, by adding to the original plot conceived by Bhasa a sub-plot of political revolution (see MRICCHAKATIKA).

CHARVAKA

Ancient thinker and philosopher, Charvaka belongs to materialistic school of thought who negated existence of god, exposed the futility of rituals, refuted the authority of Vedas, laid stress on rational thinking and severely opposed Brahmanical spiritualism. His brand of philosophy is known as Charvaka darshana, Lokayata or Barhaspatya-mata, and Asura-mata.

Charvaka is mentioned in the Mahabharata. After the Mahabharata war he appeared before king Yudhisthira and bluntly asked him if the victory he won by killing his brothers and shedding the blood can be termed as real victory? Krishna admitted before the startled Brahmins that he indeed was a great thinker-ascetic. He was so much hated that in the epic he is referred to as a demon in the guise of an ascetic. The epic further says that he was destroyed by angry Brahmins.

He is again mentioned in the Vishnu Purana as an atheist representing the forces of Maya-moha who instigated Asuras against Vedic way of life and spread among them the tenets of Buddhism and Jainism.

In the 11th century play Prabodha-chandrodaya by Krishnamisra Yati written to uphold Vedic ways of life and devotion to Vishnu against the evil forces of Maya, Moha, etc., the character of Charvaka appears as an atheist.

In the second act of the play Mahamoha extols Lokayata as the only worthy shastra—sarvatha lokayatameva shastram. He says that Vachaspati created this shastra and gave it to Charvaka who with the help of his disciples spread it among the people.

He further says that according to Lokayata whatever you see or perceive with senses is the only reliable evidence for formulating any opinion, the earth-water-fire-air are the basic elements, Artha and Kama are the only goals of life or purusharthas, only living has life, death is full stop to existence, there is no paraloka that is heaven or hell. When the limbs of all human beings are similar dividing them on the basis of caste is illogical.

Then Charvaka himself appears on the stage. He says judicature or dandaniti, that is administration of justice with the help of rod, is the only science. Business and agriculture, vartta, is included in it. Vedas are nothing but incoherent, confused, delirious prattle of the knaves. What is so special about the idea of heaven? If after the end of performer, the rituals he performed, and wasteful loss of material it is believed that the practitioner of Yajna reaches heaven. If this is true then burnt tree too would produce fruits. They believe that if the animals sacrificed in the Yajna beget heaven why then they did not sacrifice their own fathers? They too would reach heaven.

He says it is futile to think that dead can be satiated with nourishment by performing Shraddha ritual. If this is true then burnt-out wick would start giving light on being feeding the lamp with oil.

On hearing this the disciple asks Charvaka if eat, drink and be merry is the purushartha or goal of life why some people make themselves suffer by visiting holy places and performing troublesome rituals at the cost of earthly pleasures.

Charvaka replies that only foolish people deceived by the Vedas created by knaves indulge in such wishful thinking and believe in the efficacy of such means. There is a pleasure in embracing a young and beautiful woman with rounded breasts. Only foolish people make their bodies suffer by resorting to useless rituals like fasting, standing in scorching heat caused by sun-rays, etc.

On this the disciple asks him it is true that being mixed with sorrow sansara-sukha, worldly pleasure, is not desirable!

Charvaka laughs at his disciple and replies that is what the foolish people think. Are you going to throw away nourishing and tasty rice because it is covered with husk?

He further says that agnihotra, recitation of three Vedas, dandadharana and covering the body with ash is the way of life of people lacking in intellect and manliness.

In the Bhana play Padmaprabhrutaka by Shudraka there is a line which says—tadatvamevavekshitam nayatikam. Scholars have pointed out that the words tadatva and ayatika are the technical terms used in the Lokayata-darshana. Tadatva means thing available in present time, thing at hand. Ayatika means thing which is coming, but not immediately at hand. Two sutras of Lokayatikas convey this sense beautifully. One says the silver coin which we are getting right now is better than a gold coin whose availability is doubtful. The second sutra says today's pigeon is better than tomorrow's peacock—varamadya kapotah show mayurat.

This was the attitude of followers of Charvaka darshana.

In the Bhana play it is said that it is not wise to abandon the pleasure you are getting immediately in the hope of one you may beget in future—anagatasukhashaya pratyupsthitasukhatyago na purushartha.

A verse conveying similar meaning is found in the Shantiparva of the Mahabharata.

All this pertains to the incident in the Bhana play. Malatika, daughter of garland maker, falls in love with one Shaishilaka. She sends a young Buddhist nun to him with love-message. Without waiting for the future pleasure that is tryst with Malatika in future time he tried to seduce the Buddhist nun who was at hand.

Though Charvaka very strongly refuted the authority of Vedas by stating that they were creations of knaves, buffoons and fiends he is favourably inclined towards Gandharva Veda or Veda of music, dance, drama. He says, Arthagandharva veda veva cha vedan. According to him economics or science of wealth is real Veda, the science of dramaturgy Gandharva Veda is real Veda.

Tradition recognises dramaturgy on Veda. Bharata calls it as fifth or Panchama Veda. In the Hathigumpha cave inscription Emperor Kharavela calls himself as Gandharva Veda Budho or expert in dramatic arts and music. Charvaka extols Gandharva Veda.

As a character he appears in the 7th century play Venisamhara by Bhatta Narayana. Dr. Virendrakumar Bhattacharya wrote a play in eight acts Charvaka Tandavam in which Charvaka is shown entering into debate with the Acharyas of six Indian systems of philosophy.

CHATURBHANI

A collection of four Bhana plays translated and edited by two scholars, Dr. Motichandra and Vasudevasharana Agrawala, is known as Chaturbhani. The four plays in this collection are: Padmaprabhrutakam by Shudraka, Dhurtavitasamvada by Ishvaradatta, Ubhayabhisarika by Vararuchi and Padataditakam by Shyamilaka.

Shyamilaka in his play Padataditakam defines Bhana as a 'ekanatanataka' or one-actor drama, drama in solo performance. He further informs us about the musical instruments—Veena and Mridanga—used to provide musical score.

Though dramatic form Bhana is mentioned in the Natya Shastra the four Bhana plays mentioned above can be cited as earliest known specimen of this genre. They were written in 4th–5th century A.D. Vaishiki or harlotry is the theme of the plays which reflects the life of courtesans inhabiting two prosperous cities of the time—Pataliputra and Ujjain.

These four Bhana plays of Gupta era are known for their excellent literary qualities, sharp humour, sparkling wit and frank eroticism. A verse found at the close of the Bhana play Padmaprabhrutakam says that Kalidasa pales before Vararuchi, Ishvaradatta, Shyamilaka and Shudraka—Vararuchirishwaradattah syamilakah shudrakaschatvarah/Ete Bhanan babhanuh ka shakti Kalidasasya. And indeed it is not a vain statement.

A manuscript containing these four Bhana plays was found by M. Raikrishna

Kavi and S.K. Ramnatha Shastri at Trichur. They edited and published the collection in 1922. In 1956 Johannes Reinoud Abraham Loman translated the play Padmaprabhrutakam in English. In some research journals scholars wrote articles on some of these plays.

A scholar wrote in the Centenary Supplement of Journal of Royal Asiatic Society (1924, p. 135): 'It will, I think, be admitted that these compositions, in spite of the unedifying character of their general subject and even in spite of occasional vulgarities, have a real literary quality. They display a natural humour and a polite, intensely Indian irony which need not fear comparison with that of a Ben Jonson or a Moliere. The language is the veritable ambrosia of Sanskrit speech.'

Numerous Bhana plays were written from the 4th–5th to the 17th–18th century A.D. out of which about hundred have survived. However all of them are not of the same quality. Four Bhana plays of the Gupta era are earliest and best among the lot.

As is evident from the Arthashastra of Kautilya while planning the town a separate locality used to be marked for the courtesans to live. It was known as Vesha. From the Chaturbhani and plays like Mricchakatika it is evident that Vesha used to be located in the vicinity of Rajamarga or principal street of the city. Flower market, drinking dens and dyutashala or gambling dens were too located nearby. Vesha used to have Kamadevayatana or temple of Kama, god of love and passion, at its centre. In the Bhana Padataditakam route to reach the Vesha in Ujjain is given.

Vesha used to be most prosperous locality of the town having lofty mansions of the beautiful courtesans. The magnificent mansion of Vasantasena is described in the play Mricchakatika. In the Kuttanimata kavya it is said that most magnificent mansion of the city of Varanasi was located in the Vesha. Known as Dhavalagriha it was constructed by a Pashupata Acharya for courtesan Anangadevi.

Not only rich shresthis, prosperous citizens, royal personages but monks and ascetics too visited Veshas. Buddhist monks and nuns, Khapanakas, Pashupatas, Vaishnavas are referred to in the Bhana plays as a caricature of contemporary religious life. On temples of medieval period we find the sculptures of ascetics of different sects with women.

In the Chaturbhani we find several references to courtesans participating in dramatic performances. In the Bhana Ubhayabhisarika there is a mention of the play, Madanaradhana, which courtesans Madanasena and Narayanadatta, presented in the temple of Bhagavan Narayana. In the Bhana Padmaprabhrutakam a play Kumudvati Prakarana is mentioned in which courtesan Devasena was expected to play the role of heroine Kumudvati.

In the same Bhana drama director Natakacharya Gandharvadatta is mentioned whose disciple is one Darduraka, son of an actress or nateraka. In the Bhana Ubhayabhisarika the narrator Vita while describing the acting skill of courtesan Priyangusena uses all technical terms borrowed from the Natya Shastra. He also refers to the play Purandaravijaya which courtesans presented in the palace of Emperor Kumaragupta of Pataliputra.

In the Bhana play Padataditaka the term Preksha for dramatic entertainment is used. Preksha was held in the house of officer supervising the Vesha, Veshyadhyaksha Pratihara Draunalika.

The procedure of presenting a dance performance too is mentioned in the same play. First of all musical instruments went into action. Then Devata-mangala or prayer to gods was offered. Then with singing of the song, gitaka, dancer started performing. Dance competition between courtesan Kaverika and Mayurasena is also mentioned. One such competition was included in Kalidasa's play Malavikagnimitra.

Chaturbhani plays are rich in information about contemporary arts including dance, drama, music and painting.

CHAURAKARMA

In Sanskrit dramatic literature there are very interesting references to art of thievery, Chaurakarma. Initially in Bhasa's Charudatta and later in its elaborate version Mricchakatika there are elaborate scenes showing thief committing theft very skilfully. Sharvilaka of Mricchakatika is a skilled thief trained in the art of thievery. He carefully examines the walls, locates weak spot, decides the method of breaking it and the type of hole to be made, takes measurements. After making a hole in the wall he first inserts through it a human doll as a precaution. When he sees that nobody has attacked the doll he withdraws it and then enters through the hole.

He feels that the profession of thievery is an independent profession, better than serving some master with folded hands for livelihood.

The master thief avoids seeing woman when moving out in night to commit theft. Sight of woman was considered as bad omen.

We come to know by his speech that thief used to call himself Skandaputra. Skanda or Kartikeya is the presiding deity of thieves. Kanakashakti was the guru of thieves who had devised four methods of breaking the wall or making hole in it. Sharvilaka addresses him as Bhagavata or respectful one.

After entering the house Sharvilaka carefully observes the pattern of breathing, movements of the eye-balls apparent by the position of eye-lids, position of limbs indicative of soundness of sleep of the persons sleeping in the house.

Before committing theft Sharvilaka offers his prayers to the presiding deity of thievery, Kartikeya. Then remembers the Acharyas and gurus like Kanakashakti, Brahmanyadeva, Devavrata and Bhaskaranandin who probably wrote treatises on the art of thievery. Then he remembers his own guru Yogacharya whose first and foremost disciple he was.

In the third act of Bhasa's Avimaraka the hero Avimaraka enters the stage in the dead of night in the guise of a thief with sword and rope in his hand. He moves around in the city like a thief watching nightlife of the city.

It is very interesting to note that the hero of Shudraka's Bhana play Padmaprabhrutakam, Muladeva, is a master thief though the play is about his love affairs. In literature he is known as Karniputra and Goniputraka also. He is considered to be the Acharya of thieves and knaves. It is believed that he wrote a treatise on thievery known as Steyasutta.

In the prahasana named Mattavilasa written by the king of Kanchi, Mahendravikramavarman, there is a mention of an Acharya named Kharapata who has written Chauryashastra or treatise on thievery.

In fact the central theme of the farce is the theft of a begging bowl of Kapalika mendicant.

In the play Charudatta hero Charudatta is accused of stealing the ornaments of courtesan Vasantasena and for that he is required to face court trial.

Vatsaraja, minister of the 12th century Chandella ruler Paramardideva, wrote a farce, Hasyachudamani, which revolves round the theme of a theft of jewellery at the house of a Kuttani named Kapatakeli. In this funny farce there is a reference to Kevali-vidya or the magical power by which lost thing could be located. Kapatakeli visits an ascetic named Jnanarashi, the master of Kevali-vidya, with the hope to locate her lost jewellery. Her quest leads to several funny situations.

CHITRAKATHI

Professional story teller who uses paintings to illustrate his narration. The tradition of picture showmen dates back to the sixth century B.C.

In ancient India the picture showmen were known as Mankha. Mankhaliputra Goshala, famous apostle of Ajivaka sect and contemporary of Mahavira, was adept in this narrative style which he picked up from his father. Mankhas are frequently mentioned in Jain literature where they are defined as chitra-phalaka-hasta-bhikshaka or beggars who move around with picture scroll in their hands narrating stories.

Patanjali in his Mahabhashya has referred to the technique of illustrating the narration of stories with paintings in c. 150 B.C.

In the tenth century Kannada work Vaddaradhana we come across a picture of showman who used to entertain the merchants in the market place by his narration and found them engrossed in it he used to steal paddy from their shops.

Variants of the art of Mankha are found prevalent in different parts of the country under different names.

In Rajasthan it is known as Pabuji ka Pad. In Maharashtra the practitioners of this art are known as Chitrakathi, in Bengal and Bihar they are known as Patua and Gujarat Garoda. In Andhra and Karnataka too this art has survived. However they use different illustrative techniques and modes of narration but essentially they all are picture showmen.

In the process of making the presentation of story visual some took the help of live actors, some puppets and some painted scrolls.

In Bhasa's play Dutavakyam prince Duryodhana is shown holding a scroll of neatly painted pictures depicting series of scenes related to the episode of disrobing Draupadi. Duryodhana explains the paintings through his narration as Mankha would do.

In Bhavabhuti's play Uttararamacharita Lakshmana takes Rama and Sita to a picture gallery where paintings of an artist Arjuna depicting various scenes related to their lives were on display. Assuming the role of picture showman Lakshmana through his narrative tells the Rama story with the help of paintings on display.

In Vishakhadatta's play Mudrarakshasa there is a reference to Yamapatika.

Yamapata is a painted cloth or paper on which the god of death Yama is shown punishing sinners in different hells for their misdeeds.

Harshacharita of Banabhatta mentions Yamapatika, the carrier of Yamapata and his art of narration. He writes: '....entering the Bazar street he saw a Yamapatika surrounded by a number of eager and excited boys. He was explaining to them the fruits of other world from a painted picture scroll. In it Yama was shown sitting on a terrible buffalo. Holding a scroll in his left hand he was seen pointing with the cane in his right hand the scenes painted on it.'

The Yamapatika in Vishakhadatta's play Mudrarakshasa exhorts the people to bow at the feet of Yama, the god of death, as devotion to other deities would bear no fruit. Within a moment Yama would deprive the lives of those who would pay obeisance to deities other than him. He enters the houses of the people to show them Yamapata and sing—Yamapatam darshayan gitani gayami. He requests the guard to allow him to enter the house of Chanakya, spread the Yamapata before him and teach him the tenets of Dharma—yamapatam prasarya dharmamupadishamim!

Even today Yamapatas are sold in the market to the devouts.

CHORUS

It is believed that Greek theatre evolved out of choral singing performed as a part of Dionysian festivities. Around 560 B.C. Thespis introduced an actor impersonating a character adding new dimension to the format of choral singing and dance. This initiated the process of dramatization of chorus. Aeschylus who is considered the father of Greek tragedy, introduced the second actor and the credit of bringing a third actor on the scene in about 467 B.C. goes to Sophocles. Despite this development chorus remained a part of Greek theatre.

Probably similar development took place when drama emerged from ballad recitation in India. Chorus or narrative in choral form is found in some of the plays of Bhasa, the first extant Sanskrit dramatist. Chorus in Bhasa is the relic of the ancient style of ballad recitation or of narrating a story by a group of narrators.

DANAKELIKAUMUDI

A one-act Sanskrit play, described as Bhanika, written at the end of the 5th century A.D. by Rupa Goswami based on Radha-Krishna lore (see RUPA GOSWAMI).

DANCE IN DRAMATIC TRADITION

Earliest record of art of dancing in India is in the form of prehistoric rock paintings, oldest among whom are datable to twenty thousand years before Christian era. As Dr. V.S. Wakankar has put in upper Palaeolithic or early Mesolithic period found the beginning of Indian art. Such a rich variety of dance formations we see in the rock paintings that we are compelled to believe Dr. Wakankar who has said that during this very early period 'dances had developed into a classical art.'

Another scholar Erwin Neumayer who has studied the prehistoric rock paintings in India wrote: 'These pictures indicate a very complex dancing culture.'

As an adjunct to dance we find musical instruments, masks, ceremonial costumes drawn on the rocks by primordial artists. In one of the early rock paintings we find a lively dancer performing on the raised stage with a musician in attendance. Dance is the most recurring art symbol in the prehistoric picture galleries.

Earliest known civilization in India is known as Harappan or Indus Civilization which flourished around 3500 B.C. to 1500 B.C. A number of dance sculptures belonging to Indus era were found during excavations conducted at different sites. Prominent among them is a bronze statuette of a slender and frankly nude dancing girl.

Literary references to the art of dancing are found in sacred works composed by Aryan priests around 1500 B.C. A Vedic verse describes earth as a place 'on whom, with clamour loud, men that are mortal sing and dance.' And another refers to 'thickening cloud of dust that arose from the feet of dancers.' And yet another verse says that 'mirth and dancing prolongs the span of existence.'

The professional dancers mentioned in Vedic literature meet us frequently in the epics and Puranas. Their social status was decided by the Manusmriti and other law books—the Dharmashastras. Kautilya in the 4th century B.C. brought their activities under state administration and formulated rules and regulations regarding their social and professional conduct, even imposed entertainment tax on them. However he did not fail to provide them with state protection and speak of giving training facilities to them.

Very close and intimate association of dance and drama is there since ages. It is believed that dance is the mother of drama at the same time dance is seen as a form of drama. In India dance, song, instrumental music formed an integral part of the drama. In the Harivamsha Purana we find the term such as natakam nanrtuh or they danced a drama. In the play Karpuramanjiri it is said that the form of drama called Sattaka is to be danced out. Dance finds place in a number of Uparupakas like Kavya, Rasaka, Srigadita, Hallisa and Bhanika.

Sanskrit dramatists introduced dance performances in their plays. Bhasa has included dance performance in his plays Balacharita and Pancharatra, Kalidasa made the heroine of his play Malavikagnimitra to perform a classical dance and sing. According to Kuttanimatam kavya the first act of Sriharsha's play Ratnavali was performed in the Vishvanatha of Kashi by the local courtesans as a ballet. A number of interesting dances are included by playwright Rajashekhara in his play Karpuramanjiri.

Chinese traveller I-tsing speaking about the performance of Sriharsha's play Nagananda said:

'King Shiladitya (Harsha) versified the story of Bodhisattva Jimutavahana who surrendered himself in the place of Naga. This version was set to music. He had performed it by a band accompanied by dancing and acting and thus popularised it in his times.'

It was Bharata who codified the canons of dance in his Natya Shastra written sometime between second century B.C. and second century A.D. and gave it a classical status. A number of treatises were written with dance as a subject by later writers such as Abhinayadarpana, Nrityadhyaya, Nrityaratnakosha, Nrityaratnavali during 12th to 13th century.

Indian dance tradition was nurtured by temple-girls or Devadasis and courtesans or Ganikas.

Courtesans were educated in the techniques of dance which they preserved and developed over several centuries. Describing the gait of courtesan Vasantasena the vita says—nrityaprayogavishadau charanau kshipanti. She was a trained dancer. Also educated in the art of performing on the stage—rangapraveshana kalanam chopashikshaya.

Dance teachers were appointed to train the young prospective courtesans. They were invited to perform dance-dramas in temples as well as in royal courts.

Devadasis were proficient in dance. Classical dance styles such as Bharatanatyam and Odissi were evolved by them.

Medieval Indian temples are adorned with beautiful dance sculptures. Probably they were modelled after Devadasis and Ganikas.

In the 12th century Jayadeva composed his verse-drama, the Gita Govinda which was danced out at Jagannatha temple of Puri.

Several dance-dramas such as Krishnattam, Ramanattam, Kuchipudi, Bhagavatamela Nataka emerged on the scene.

On the popular and folk level dance-dramas like Yakshagana, Raslila and a host of dance oriented drama forms which sprang from Swang tradition were evolved around the 16th century.

Bharatanatyam, Kathak, Odissi, Kuchipudi, Manipuri, Kathakali, Mohini Attam and Satriya are considered as major classical dance styles of India today.

Rich and varied is the dance scene of India.

DANDARAS

A dance mentioned by the tenth century playwright Rajashekhara in his play Karpuramanjiri. He says thirtytwo female dancers executing variegated and amazing dance formations, vichitra-bandha, rhythmically placing their feet move in a circle whirling round.

DASHA RUPA

Bharata in his Natya Shastra says that drama is of ten types. He says that vrittis are basic to all poetic works including dramatic composition. According to him a variety of plays come into existence due to a variety of vrittis or styles (see Vritti). Vritti is mother, matrika, of these ten forms says Bharata. The distinction among the ten forms is also made on the basis of a number of acts, subject matter, type of characters that appear in them, rasas that predominate the story and the construction of the plot.

These ten forms are:

1. Bhana: One-act play in monologue form, single actor appears on the stage.
2. Vithi: One-act play with one or two characters.
3. Vyayoga, Anka and Prahasana: One-act plays with different kinds of subjects respectively and more characters.
4. Samavakara: Play with three loosely knit acts and many characters.
5. Dima and Ihamriga: Plays with four such acts and many characters.
6. Nataka and Prakarana: Plays with five to ten well-knit acts and many characters.

(NS: Ghosh)

Examples of all these forms are found in the Sanskrit dramatic literature. Bhasa is the playwright who has handled many of these forms. A number of forms other than these major forms are mentioned in the works of poetics written by other writers. They are known as Uparupakas. Sahitya Darpana has mentioned eighteen such forms. They are:

Natika
Trotaka
Goshti
Sattaka
Natyarasaka
Prasthana
Uttapya
Kavya
Prenkhana
Rasaka
Samplapaka
Srigadita
Shilpaka
Vilasika
Durmallika
Prakaranika
Hallisa
Bhanika.

DASHAVATAR

A popular folk theatre form prevalent in Konkan and Goa region. Dashavatar means ten incarnations of Lord Vishnu. They are Matsya, Kurma, Varaha, Narasimha, Vamana, Parashurama, Rama, Krishna, Buddha and Kalki. In Dashavatar drama stories related to ten incarnations are enacted.

It is believed that this form of folk drama was imported to Goa-Konkan region from neighbouring Karnataka in the early 18th century. The Yakshagana theatre of Karnataka is known as Dashavatarada Ata. Maybe it might have inspired the people of Goa-Konkan region to evolve their own dramatic form with distinct identity of its own.

Dashavatar plays are performed on the occasion of festivals of local deities, Gramadevatas, which are generally celebrated from Kartik Purnima to the end of Chaitra.

The Sabhagriha or the hall of congregation of the temple or open space in front of the temple is used for staging these plays. The play being an offering to the deity, the actors face the sanctum sanctorum of the temple wherein the deity resides. In some temple Sabhagrihas or mandapas, up above a special balcony is built where idols of the deities are placed ceremoniously during the enactment of the Dashavatari plays.

Purvaranga of the Dashavatar performance is a very elaborate affair. The Sutradhara along with his chorus appears on the stage. Then starts Dhemali, playing on the Mridanga and big brass cymbals, first in a slow and then in a fast tempo. Then enters an actor with elephant mask as Lord Ganapati with his two consorts Riddhi and Siddhi. Elaborate worship is offered to Ganapati by two priests who crack all sorts of jokes exhibiting their greedy nature.

After their departure Saraswati, goddess of learning, arrives on the stage dancing, a wooden peacock tied to her waist. After blessing the Sutradhara she departs.

And this is the end of Purvaranga.

Now the play proper opens and actors begin to enact the story of Matsyavatar or fish-incarnation of Vishnu. In this incarnation Vishnu taking the form of a fish killed the demon Shankasura and recovered the Vedas he stole from Brahmadeva.

Demon Shankasura of Dashavatar drama is an interesting character who appears on the stage in black costume with red protruding tongue made of cloth. He is at once a jester and a villain. He enters into conversation with Sutradhara, makes people laugh with his rustic jokes and regales the audience with his antics and fantastic actions.

We see Brahma immersed in deep meditation and Shankasura stealing his books, the Vedas. Great fight ensues between Shankasura and Vishnu in fish incarnation in which Shankasura gets killed.

Of remaining incarnations Kurma, Varaha, Vamana, Parashurama, Buddha and Kalki are mentioned by Sutradhara in his song. Sometimes the story of man-lion Narasimha incarnation is enacted after Matsyavatar episode is over. Sometimes skipping Narasimhavatar enactment of episodes related to Krishnavatar starts.

With this ends the Dashavatar enactment.

But the show continues. The actors then present some mythological play till the break of dawn.

Full of singing, dancing, music and dramatic action the Dashavatari shows are very popular.

DATTAKA

In Shudraka's Bhana play Padmaprabhrutakam there is a mention of Dattakasutra, a work on erotica by Dattaka. Vita humorously says that a Buddhist monk standing in the courtyard of a prostitute looks like auspicious Omkara word in the erotic Dattakasutra. In the Kamasutra of Vatsyayana we find the information that Dattaka wrote a book Vaishika Adhikarana on harlotry on the request of the courtesans of Pataliputra.

We find the name of Dattakacharya mentioned in the Kuttanimata kavya as one of the writers of Manmathatantra.

In the Bhana play Padataditakam a sutra 'apuman shabdakamah' from the work of Dattaka is quoted. It means the person who has lost the power of enjoying sex spends his time only talking about it.

DHARMAVIJAYAM

A five-act allegorical play by 16th century playwright of Gujarat, Bhupadeva Shukla. Concepts such as Adharma, Vyabhichara, Pariksha, Parasparapriti, Anachar, Panditasangati, Kavita, Vyavahara, Himsa, Ahimsa, Daya, Krodha appear on the stage in human form. The play portrays the conflict between good and evil, dharma and adharma in which good triumphs over evil, dharma over adharma.

DHURTASAMAGAMA

A prahasana or farce written by Kavishekhara Jyotirishvara in Sanskrit in the first quarter of 14th century A.D. It is available in Maithili version too. It is believed that Jyotirishvara himself translated his own Sanskrit farce in Maithili and staged it in the court of his patron king of Mithila, Harasimhadeva of Karnat dynasty.

Here is the brief synopsis of the story of the farce as related by Dr. Jayakanta Mishra:

The play opens with one ascetic called Vishvanagara who is really a fraudulent knave appearing on the stage with his equally rascal disciple Snataka. They approach a wealthy but miser man called Mritangara Thakur who refuses them food on false pretext but directs them to the house of a lady, Suratapriya.

Vishvanagara, delighted by the suggestion, approaches Suratapriya who too is a great fraud. She is willing to do anything for him because she desires to have this good looking ascetic as her lover. He asks her to cook delicious food items for midday meal.

Snataka, the disciple, expresses his desire to find out the beautiful courtesan of the town, Anangasena, as he was in love with her. Vishvanagara too goes with him and finding the courtesan very attractive he too lusts after her. Both the Guru and Shishya start quarrelling over her. Perturbed courtesan asks one Asajjati Mishra to act as arbitrator.

In the second act we see knave Asajjati Mishra finding the courtesan alluring runs away with her himself leaving the quarrelling parties high and dry. The courtesan sighs and says this is nothing but a conclave of knaves—Dhurta Samagama.

In the last scene a barber appears on the scene and asks the courtesan to pay for services rendered in the form of shaving her private parts. The courtesan asks him to realise the money from Asajjati Mishra. In lieu of money Asajjati Mishra gives the barber a little ganja, hashish, which he himself had received from Snataka for arbitrating the real owner of Anangasena.

The angry barber ties his hands and feet and leaving him unconscious goes away. However, in the end, the jester friend of Asajjati Mishra releases him.

The farce, scholars feel, reflects the social history of 14th century Mithila giving information about its caste structure, food, customs and practice of law.

Some scholars considered drama as a division of poetry or kavya. They defined drama as a visual poetry, drishya kavya, or poetry in action. Description of vibhava and anubhava is poetry or kavya, when they are portrayed through prayoga or stage representation it is drama or natya. Anubhavavibhavanam varnana kavyamucchate/ Tasmeva prayogastu natyam gitadiranjanam.

Kalidasa in his play Malavikagnimitram drops the term imitation from the definition of drama. He says three gunas, raja-tama-sattva, and the rasas or aesthetic sentiments are the basis of human nature, its portrayal is drama — Traigunyodbhavamatra lokacharitam nanarasam drishyate natyam bhinnarucherjanasya bahudhapyekam samaradhakam.

DHURTA VITA SAMVADA

A Bhana play, burlesque, by Ishvaradatta of Magadha written around 4th-5th century A.D., which basically revolves round the discussion related to Kamatantra or man-woman sexual relationship, that takes place between a Dhurta and a Vita.

Bhana is a one-actor one-act burlesque in the form of a monologue. An actor in the guise of Vita appears on the stage and describes during his wanderings the scenes, events, happenings and merrily converses with different people as if they are there in front of him.

Dhurta is knave, parasite, living off the income of prostitutes. Vita is a man of many qualities, good and bad, living in the company of citizens and courtesans, conducting liaison between them.

He is vastly experienced in harlotry. The main topic of the Bhana is dialogue, samvada, that takes place between Vita and Dhurta on the interesting topic of man-woman sexual relationship. The name of the Vita is Devalika and of Dhurta Vishvalaka. Venue is Vesha of prosperous city of Pataliputra or Kusumpura.

It is a rainy season. Vita appears on the stage and poetically describes its beauty. Rain stops. He starts thinking where to go? Gambling den or locality of harlots? Dyutasabha or Vesha? Gambling den had deprived him of everything except the cloth he is wearing hence he decides to visit Vesha, the place known for its fun and frolic, for beautiful courtesans and lovely prostitutes.

He moves out of his house and takes a look at the city of Pataliputra. He then describes the glory of the city, generosity of its art loving people and richness of its markets filled with goods of various kinds.

On his way to Vesha the first person he comes across is none but Krishnilaka, young son of the local businessman. He was coming from Vesha right after enjoying the company of his beloved, courtesan Madhavasena, sporting all signs of love-making over his body. Vita makes fun of Krishnilaka's killjoy father and remarks that father is headache personified for young men—pita nama khalu sayauvanasya purushashya murtiman shiroragah—who want to enjoy carnal pleasures of life.

When Vita comes to know that Krishnilaka's marriage was settled by his father he feels sorry for him. He compares courtesan with Mahapatha, a magnificent highway and asks him why he wants to enter the unattractive lane of kulavadhu or married woman who has a capacity to make even a happy man most unhappy one. However, says Vita, if he is happy about the decision of his father then let it be so.

Now leaving the crowded rajamarga or principal street of the city Vita enters the bylane leading to the Vesha or locality of courtesans. On reaching Vesha he elaborately describes its glory and fun filled ambience. He while loitering around sees smiling Varunika, lovely attendant of courtesan Madanasena. Looking at her lovely breasts like the pair of Chakravaka bird he asked her who really was the lucky person who first enjoyed their touch.

After speaking to Chaturika who was repairing her girdle he enters the house of

Ramadasi who was shedding tears due to separation from her lover. He sees tears falling from her lotus eyes on her hard breasts, then slipping down over thin line of hair on her soft stomach and finally disappearing into her deep navel, the place where her lover enjoyed putting his finger in during love-play.

Near similar verse is found in Kalidasa's Kumarasambhava.

Vita advises Ramadasi to venture out in rains, embrace her lover with body trembling with cool breezes of the season, kiss his lips and speak with him during the course of love-making.

When courtesan defying the rain reaches the house of her lover it is termed as Varshabhisara in the Kamasutra. The most poetic description of Varshabhisara is found in the play Mricchakatika involving two lovers courtesan Vasantasena and Charudatta.

After teasing slightly tipsy Ratisena and courtesan Pradyumnadasi who was sporting all signs of love-making on her lovely body he reaches the house of Vishvalaka, a knave or dhurta, who lives off the income of old courtesan Sunanda. After squandering all his wealth, even his cloths like Nagna Shramanaka or naked Jain monk, he took shelter in Sunanda's house. Being very popular with courtesans Sunanda gladly allowed him to stay with her.

Now Vita and Vishvalaka the knave hold long discussion about Kamatantra or various issues related to sexual relationship between men and women.

The discussion veers round several interesting topics such as—who gives more sexual pleasure—a beautiful woman or a woman who is favourable? Is there any truth in the advice of the Smritikaras like Brihaspati, Ushana that man should avoid making love to women? Etc.

Most interesting part of the play is description of various seasons including Sharada, Hemanta, Shishira, Vasanta, Grishma one after another by Vita and the effect of these seasons on the lovers. Same is the theme of Kalidasa's Ritusamhara. Who is inspired by whom is the matter of conjecture.

Both Kalidasa and Ishvaradatta have written about intense longing, autsukya, a feeling very mysterious, ethereal, extremely delicate and refined. Ishvaradatta says this mysterious longing may appear with or without any reason. Kalidasa in Abhijnana Shakuntala says that at the sight of beautiful things or hearing beautiful music the feeling of earnest longing arises in the heart and even happy person feels sad, who copied whom?

DIMA

One of the ten types of drama mentioned by Bharata in his Natya Shastra.

Dima should have well known plot, well known hero of exalted type, four acts, all sentiments except the erotic and the comic, should include incidents such as earthquake, fall of meteors, eclipse of the sun or the moon, fighting in battle, personal combat and angry conflict.

The Dima should abound in deceit, jugglery (maya and indrajala), energetic activity of many persons, dissension among themselves and it is to include sixteen characters which may be gods, Asuras, Rakshasas, Bhutas, Yakshas and Nagas, should include grand and energetic styles and many psychological states. It is full of war, fight, clash and combat.

DIONYSUS IN INDIA

A fascinating myth of the conquest of India by Dionysus, the Greek god of fertility, wine and drama, in hoary antiquity by employing Bacchic orgies, wine and dance has been recorded by ancient Greek writers like Megasthenes and Arrian. According to the myth Dionysus founded cities in India, introduced the use of wine and taught the locals how to till the land.

However the most interesting part of the myth is that it was Greek theatre god Dionysus who taught Indians the art of dancing and music. Arrian who was born towards the end of the first century A.D. and wrote a work called Indika writes: 'Indians have been particularly distinguished among the nations as lovers of dance and song ever since Dionysus and his attendant Bacchanals made their festive progress through the realms of India. He taught them the satyric dance or, as the Greeks call it, Cordax.'

Satyrs were half-human half-beast followers of Dionysus. Some scholars believe that satyr plays were the earliest form of Greek drama. Satyr plays evolved out of a chorus of these strange creatures. Satyr plays were full of vigorous dancing, boisterous action, indecent language and gesture.

Cordax is described as a dance exhibitionist in character in which body parts are uncovered intentionally.

Licht says: 'The satyrs in the satyric drama were in habit of dancing with grotesque movements and defiant stripping of the clothes. Equally indecent, or rather erotic, was the Cordax which consisted chiefly of reeling backwards and forwards, as though representing drunkenness; and to this was added a series of grotesque movements of the body, and apparently intentional denudation.'

Such dances were included in early Greek comedies. It is described as madness, full of grotesque movements, legs kicking skyhigh, exhibiting posterior, lightning whirls and twirls of limbs, tapping of belly.

Scholars believe that a Greek play Agen was staged in the military camp of Alexander the Great on the bank of river Jhelum in Upper Punjab in the year 326 B.C. Prof. Snell who wrote a critique on the play describes it as a 'Satyr play'.

In the year 1899 a papyri manuscript of a play written in Greek and Kannada languages was excavated in Egypt by the archaeologists. In the play, a farce, it is shown that a beautiful Greek girl falls in the hands of chieftain of Malpe harbour in India. The brother of the girl who rescues her is shown using the same methods as Dionysus used to conquer India such as regaling them with wine and diverting their attention to dancing.

The myth of Dionysian invasion of India insinuates that Indian theatre owes its origin to Greek god of theatre.

It is very interesting to note that at Nagarjunakonda in Andhra Pradesh during an excavation ruins of a mandapa were located. On one of the supporting pillars a figure of Dionysus was found carved. He has a small goat-like beard. He is semi-nude, carelessly holding a single piece of garment in Greco-Roman style near his waist. He is shown carrying a drinking horn and near him on the ground is placed a barrel of wine covered with an inverted drinking cup.

DRAMA CHARACTERISTICS

Bharata in his Natya Shastra defined various characteristics of drama and particularly stressed its educative and entertaining aspect by calling it repository of all arts, crafts, learning. He says:

'(In it) sometimes there is (reference to) duty, sometimes to games, sometimes to money, sometimes to peace, and sometimes laughter is found in it, sometimes fight, sometimes love-making and sometimes killing (of people).

It teaches duty to those who go against duty, love to those who are eager for its fulfilment, and it chastises those who are ill-bred and unruly, promotes self-restraint in those who are disciplined, gives courage to cowards, energy to heroic persons, enlightens men of poor intellect, and gives wisdom to learned.

It gives diversion to kings, and firmness (of mind) to persons afflicted with sorrow, and (hints of acquiring) money to those who are for earning it, and it brings composure to persons agitated in mind.

It will relate to actions of men good, bad and indifferent, and will give courage, amusement and happiness as well as counsel to them all.

It will thus be instructive to all through actions and states depicted in it and through sentiments arising out of it.

It will give relief to unlucky persons who are afflicted with sorrow and grief or over work, and will be conducive to observance to duty as well as to fame, long life, intellect and general good and educate people.

There is no wise maxim, no learning, no art or craft, no device, no action that is not found in drama.

In drama meet all departments of knowledge, different arts and various actions. Stories taken out of Vedic lore, semi-historical tales capable of giving pleasure are found in it' (Natya Shastra, Manomohan Ghosh, Chapter 1).

DRAMA DEFINITIONS

It was Bharata who tried to define drama in his Natya Shastra. Basically he considered drama as an imitation, anukarana, of spectrum of life in its totality, with people, loka, at its centre. According to various definitions provided by him drama is an imitation of

Bhava:	any state of mind (and body), feelings, sentiments, passions, emotions
Awastha:	situations, conditions
Swabhava:	emotionally rich human nature, character
Vritta:	cycle of life set in motion, actions, mode of life, occurrences, happenings, affair, conduct, behaviour, story of human life
Karma:	actions, work
Loka:	mankind, folk, people, various spheres like heaven, earth and patala or region below earth, nether world.

He says:

The Drama (natya) is an imitation (anukarana) of story of human life (lokavritta) marked by a number of situations, stages (nana avasthantaratmakam) and rich with feelings and emotions. 1.111 NS

Drama is an imitation of seven worlds (saptadwipanukaram natyam) 1.118 NS

Drama is an imitation of actions of people. 1.121 NS

He also defines drama as a depiction of human nature with its joys and sorrows (lokasya swabhava) by means of physical acting (NS 1.122). He says that when the story of the people (lokasya charitam) comprised of various situations, episodes (nana avasthantaratmaka) is presented by physical acting it is called drama (NS XXVI. 122–23). However he takes acting as a means of imitation.

The definition of drama as an imitation of things by Bharata was adopted by other dramaturgists also. For instance 10th century writer of Dasharupaka, Dhananjaya says: Imitation of states (human) is called drama (DR 1.7).

And in the Bhavaprakasha the 12th century writer Sharadatanaya says: Common characteristics of drama is an imitation of (human) states (BP, Adhikar 7).

DRAMA OF THIRTYTWO TYPES

In the Jain work Rayapaseniya Sutta thirtytwo types of drama are mentioned. It is written in the book that these dramas were performed before Lord Mahavira. In his book *Life in Ancient India as Reflected in Jain Canons* Dr. J.C. Jain has mentioned these drama types mentioned in the Rayapaseniya Sutta.

They are:

1. The first dance drama was shown to the accompaniment of orchestral music representing the eight symbols, namely sotthiya (swastika*), sirivaccha, nadiyavatta, vaddhamanaga*, bhaddasana, kalasa, maccha, dappana (swastika, vardhamana and nadiyavatta are mentioned in the Mahabharata VII, 82.20).
2. In this dance drama were shown avada, paccavada, sedhi, pasedhi, sotthiya, sovatthiya, pusa, manavaka, vaddhamanaga, macchanda, magaranda, jara, mara, phullavali, paumapatta*, sagarataranga, vasantalata, paumalayabhatticitta*.
3. In this they showed ihamiga, usabha, naraturaga, magara*, vihaga, valaga, kinnara, ruru, sarabha, camara, kunjara*, vanalaya and paumalayabhatticitta.
4. In this they showed egao, vanka, egao cakkavala, duhao, cakkavala, cakkaddhicakkavala.
5. In this were the avalis such as candavali, suravali, valiyavali, hamsavali*, egavali, travali, muttavali, kanagavali and rayanavali.
6. In this was shown the rise of the sun and the moon, canduggamana and suruggamana.
7. In this was shown the movements of sun and moon, candagamana and suragamana.
8. This showed the lunar and solar eclipse, candavarana and suravarana.
9. This showed setting of sun and moon, candatthamana and suratthamana.
10. This showed candamandala, suramandala, nagamandala, jakkhamandala, bhutamandala, rakkhasamandala, mahoragamandala, gandhavvamandala*.
11. It showed the gait of usabhamandala, sihamandala, hayavilambita, gajavilambita, hayavilasiya, gayavilasiya, mattahayavilasiya, mattagajavilasiya, mattahayavilambiya, mattagajavilambiya and duyabilambiya.
12. It showed sagarapavibhatti and nagarapavibhatti.
13. It showed the drama of Nanda and Campa.
14. It showed macchandapavibhatti, mayarandakapavibhatti, jarapavibhatti, marapavibhatti.
15. It represented the words from ka to na.
16. ca to na.
17. ta to na.
18. ta to na.
19. pa to ma.
20. It showed asoyapallavapavibhatti, ambapallavapavibhatti, jambupallavapavibhatti and kosambapallavapavibhatti.
21. It represented paumalayapavibhatti, naga, asoka, campaka, amba, vana, vasanti, kunda, atimuttaya, samalayapavibhatti.

22. Duya (druta) dance*.
23. Vila, biya dance.
24. Duyabilambiya dance.
25. Anciya dance.
26. Ribhiya dance.
27. Aciyaribhiya dance.
28. Arabhada dance*.
29. Bhasola dance*.
30. Arabhadabhasola dance.
31. Uppayanivayapavatta, sankuciya, pasariya, rayaraiya and bhantasamhanta dance.
32. In this drama the actors and actresses formed a row and represented the story of Mahavira's early life, his conception, exchange of foetus, birth, lustration, boyhood, youth, sexual sport, renunciation, penance, attainment of kevalahood, propagation of his message and finally his nirvana.

The terms with the asterisks are also found in the Natya Shastra. First 31 types seem to be dance numbers with different themes and 32nd type is obviously full-fledged opera based on the life of Bhagavan Mahavira.

DRAMA—VILE ART

Drama as an art was detested by some philosophers, law-makers, sociologists and men of religion on several counts. They found it almost amoral, lascivious, lewd, mentally disturbing, harmful to the students, hindrance in the pursuit of knowledge and spiritual attainment, even detrimental to economic activities and well-being of the society.

Though Lalitvistara describes Buddha as adept in various arts including dancing, singing, recitation, ballad singing, mimicking, even dramatic acting or natya, he severely abhorred drama. He dissuaded the shakya bhikkus from attending dramatic entertainments. According to Vinaya texts two Bhikkus living on Kita hill were expelled from the order as they went to theatre and spreading their robes asked the dancers to come and dance on it.

In the Avadanashataka there appears a story of a dancer, Kuvalaya, charming and lovely daughter of a drama director of South, Natacharya of Dakshinapatha, who was on the visit to the city of Rajagriha to attend the festival known as Girivalgusamagama. She, indeed, was very beautiful and proud of her shapely body glistening with youth and vitality.

Once singing, dancing, frankly exposing her beautiful body she performed such an overtly provocative dance that the Bhikkus of the order were greatly disturbed and stood utterly confused—sambhramitah. Angered by the mischief of the dancer he turned her into a hideous creature.

In the Thera Gatha, a Buddhist work of great antiquity, there is a story of Talaputa, a dance director, who led a dramatic troupe having five hundred actresses in it. One day, while in the city of Rajagriha, he most humbly called on the Master. Seated at one side, he said: 'I have heard it said, Your Reverence, by teachers and their teachers, when speaking of actors, that the actor who on the stage counterfeiting truth, amuses and delights his audiences will be reborn after his death among the gods of laughter. What does the Exalted One say on this point?'

Buddha rejected the question three times saying: 'Ask me not this, director!' But when asked for the fourth time he said: 'Director, those persons who induce sensual, misanthropic, or mentally confused state in others and cause them to lose earnestness, will, after death, be reborn in purgatory.' The story says thereupon Talaputa wept.

In his Smriti, law-giver Manu says that while learning at the feet of his Guru the student should remain celibate and totally shun dancing, singing, music—nartanam gitavadanam. He enjoins people to hate dramatic arts, and himself looks down upon actor community.

Kautilya, author of Arthashastra, is against the construction of recreation parks, permanent theatre buildings or buildings intended for sports and plays in the Janapada as, he feels, they are harmful to the economy of the country. If there are no facilities to perform the actors, dancers, singers, story-tellers would not be able to disturb the farmers and they would be able to concentrate upon increasing farm production.

Emperor Ashoka in his rock edict (No. I) says that Samaja or dramatic entertainment is full of vice, sinfulness, offence and mischief—bahukahi dosa samajasa.

To minimise the ill effects of dramatic entertainments on society censorship laws were promulgated by Kautilya and Bharata, author of treatise on dramaturgy, too imposed certain constraints to enhance social acceptability of drama.

DRAMA AS YAJNA

In the first act of the play Malavikagnimitram poet Kalidasa has defined drama as ocular sacrifice, Kratu chakshusam, Yajna pleasing to the gods.

Yajna is a ritual of fire sacrifice when offerings are made to appease deities. Vedic Yajnas are numerous and of different magnitudes involving many rituals.

First of all some of the gods like Indra, Maruts and Ashvini twins for whom Yajnas are performed are themselves described as dancers. Scholars inform us that generally the commonest Vedic metres Tristubh, Anustubha, Jagati and Gayatri are explained at best as modes of dance. The word chandas, that is metre, indicates according to V. Schroeder originally a dance song, since magic power is ascribed to dance in primitive cultural invocations.

Secondly, a number of Vedic rituals themselves which form the part of Yajna ceremonies are dramatic in their import and include ritual dancing, singing, playing on musical instruments and play acting. It is believed that dialogue hymns or samvada suktas found in the Rig Veda such as Pururava-Urvashi samvada were enacted by the priests associated with Yajna rituals. Louis Renou says: 'The Vedic sacrifice is presented as a kind of drama, with actors, its dialogues, its portion to be set to music, its interludes and its climaxes.'

Keith also says: 'The Vedic ritual contained within itself the germs of drama, as it is the case with practically every primitive form of worship. This ritual did not consist merely of singing songs, or recitations in honour of gods. It involved a complex round of ceremonies in some of which there was undoubtedly present the element of dramatic representations; that is performers of rites assumed for the time being personalities other than their own.'

Thirdly, major sacrifices like Rajasuya Yajna and Ashvamedha Yajna, apart from their religious and ritual significance, were social occasions with public participation. For the people assembled and also for the priests involved in the rituals various dramatic entertainments were presented.

There is a chapter in the epic Mahabharata describing the grandiose Ashvamedha Yajna conducted by the Pandava brothers in Indraprastha. The epic says that for the entertainment of the priests engaged in the arduous task of conducting complex Yajna rituals the entertainers including musicians, singers and dancers were employed—Gandharva gitakushala nrityeshu cha visharadah/ ramayanti sma tan vipran yajnakarmantareshu vai.

Also in the same epic there is a description of Rajasuya Yajna performed by the Pandavas. We are told that to entertain the people assembled on the occasion story tellers, dancers and actors were employed—kathayantah katha bahvih pasyanto natanartakan.

In the epic Ramayana's Balakanda we are told that when king Dasharatha decided to perform Ashvamedha he invited actors and dancers, tathaiva natanartakan, to entertain the guests.

In the Harivamsha Purana it is recorded that when Vasudeva, Krishna's father, performed Rajasuya Yajna the famous actor of the time, Bhadra Nata, entertained the guests with excellent dramatic performances.

A fifth century architrave from Pavaya portraying various phases of Bali's Yaga is kept in the Gwalior Museum. Describing it C. Sivaramamurti says:

'Dance is not only a pleasurable ocular sacrifice but also a popular happy adjunct to the regular sacrifice itself. Dance and music, particularly the chant of Sama hymns to the music of veena was an essential factor of yagas.'

One of the most graphic representation of Trivikrama's triumph over Bali in a Gupta architrave from Pavaya, now in Gwalior Museum, illustrates this clearly in an elaborate series of panels depicting various phases of Bali's yaga with horse stationed near the yupa post, the prince watching from the Yajnavata, the ritwik priests assembled, the musical orchestra as an accompaniment to dance.

Variations in the shape of veena are also shown there, the guitar-like kacchapi and bow shaped saptatantri. The three-fold drum, called tripushkara, is also there, and the dancer's movement is a delicate stance of angahara. The famous dance scene itself is a part of Bali's Yaga.

Ashvamedha Yajna is described by the scriptures a king among sacrifices by the Shatapatha Brahmana. The proceedings of the Yajna include a ribald ritual dialogue between the queen and the priests, a kind of drama.

A number of kings including Dasharatha, king of Ayodhya, are said to have performed the Ashvamedha or Horse Sacrifice. Senapati Pushyamitra Shunga in the second century B.C. performed Horse sacrifice which is mentioned in the play Malavikagnimitram by Kalidasa. In the fourth century A.D. Emperor Samudragupta too performed this Yajna which includes a ritual drama with ribald dialogue.

DURDINABHISARIKA

Durdina means a rainy day. Abhisarika is a young and beautiful girl who, propelled by love's intense passion, ventures out to meet her lover defying all obstacles, hindrances, hurdles. The word Durdinabhisarika, meaning a girl venturing out to meet her lover defying torrential rains, is found in the Kamasutra of Vatsyayana. Vatsyayana says that the lover should himself help the beloved changing her cloths drenched in the rain.

In the fifth act of Mricchakatika playwright Shudraka has portrayed beautifully courtesan Vasantasena as durdinabhisarika probably inspired by Kamasutra.

In the Bhana play Dhurtavitasamvada by Ishvaradatta the Vita advises courtesan Ramadasi to venture out in torrential rain and trembling with cold embrace and kiss her lover Kunjaraka.

Indian miniature painters took great delight in painting Abhisarikas including one venturing out in torrential rains to meet her lover.

DUTA GHATOTKACHA

A one-act play by Bhasa in which Ghatotkacha, as a duta or messenger of Krishna, is shown delivering a message to Kauravas that they should prepare themselves to face serious consequences of killing Arjuna's son Abhimanyu, a mere teenager, by several warriors when he was fighting alone.

Ghatotkacha, son of Bhima and demoness Hidimba, was a great warrior who played significant role in the Mahabharata war.

He was called Ghatotkacha because his hairless head looked like ghata or big rounded earthen pot kept upside down. He had a huge body and frightening appearance. With his immense strength and prowess in his very childhood he defeated many demons and pishachas.

Apart from immense strength he was endowed with magical powers and could assume any form at will. He used to dislike Brahmins and their Yajna rituals.

He promised Pandavas that he would appear before them whenever they desired. At the time of Rajasuya Yajna of Yudhisthira he was sent to Lanka which he conquered. He married a beautiful demon girl Morvi, daughter of demon Muru of Pragjyotishpur, by winning her hand in swayamvara by his wit and strength. His marriage took place in Indraprastha, capital city of Pandavas.

He made resounding entry in the Bharata war. His chariot driven by hundred horses had eight wheels and a flag having vulture, gridha, painted on it. Paulastya was the name of his terrible bow.

By his magical powers and bravery he killed numerous warriors on Kaurava side. He even defeated Kaurava prince Duryodhana. He killed the demons Alambusha and Alayudha and presented their severed heads to Duryodhana saying that one should not go to see a king like Duryodhana empty-handed.

He created havoc in Kaurava army and vowed to kill Karna, the great warrior friend of Duryodhana. Ultimately Karna was compelled to use the missile, vasavi shakti, which he had reserved to kill Arjuna to destroy the invincible demon. When he was hit by the missile Ghatotkacha who was fighting from the sky assumed huge form and fell on Kaurava army crushing to death numerous warriors under the weight of his body.

It seems that Bhasa was greatly fascinated by the character of Ghatotkacha whom he made the hero of his two plays. However the episodes on which he based his plays are not found in the Mahabharata, they seem to be invention of his own imagination.

The play moves under the shadow of Mahabharata war, particularly the killing of teenager son of Arjuna by Kauravas. Ghatotkacha appears in the Kaurava camp when they were discussing the killing. He says they were more cruel than the demons, the race to which he belonged. No demon will kill his brothers by burning them while they are asleep or kill their son in the battlefield, their form is frightening and nature harsh but they are not without mercy, says Ghatotkacha.

In the end as a messenger he delivers a chilling message of Krishna asking them to be prepared for terrible consequences of their brutal act.

DUTANGADA

A play based on Rama story by the 13th century playwright Subhatta. It is considered to be a Chaya Nataka or a play written as a text for shadow puppet theatre. It was staged in 1243 in the court of Chalukya king of Anahilapataka, Tribhuvanapala. The play is available in two recensions—one long and the other short.

Before attacking Lanka Rama sends Angada as his messenger, duta, asking Ravana to return Sita. Ravana presents before Angada an illusory Sita instead of real one who confesses her love for Ravana and asks Angada to go back. But Ravana's trick is exposed and Angada returns. Ravana's army is vanquished and Ravana is killed.

DUTAVAKYA

One of the excellent one-act Mahabharata plays written by Bhasa marked by steep dramatic tension reflected in terse dialogues, explosive central conflict, intense clash of powerful personalities and epic sweep of the theme.

According to the Mahabharata after Uttara-Abhimanyu marriage the Pandavas made serious efforts to strike peace with their impudent and crafty cousins and avert war. As a part of this move Krishna is sent to Kuru court by Yudhisthira as a duta or messenger of peace. The play revolves round the story of Krishna's arrival in Kuru court and his clash with Kuru prince Duryodhana puffed up with excessive pride and propelled by foolhardy adventurism.

In a specially erected assembly hall, mantrashala, Duryodhana is shown consulting prominent kings belonging to his side about the strategy of war and whom they should appoint as a general to lead Kuru army. Bhasa describes Duryodhana as a young man of swarthy complexion shining in the reflective glory of the diamond ornaments worn by him on his person, adorned with royal insignia like umbrella over his head. Bhasa says he was looking like a lustrous full moon shining among the stars in the firmament—nakshatramadhya eva parvagatah shashanka.

Duryodhana suggests the name of Pitamaha Bhishma to lead his army. As the consultations were going on kanchuki or attendant informs Duryodhana about the arrival of Krishna who was there as a messenger of Pandavas.

Arrogant Duryodhana orders the members of the assembly not to give Krishna a standing ovation and as a deliberate ploy to insult him he orders his attendant to bring the picture scroll depicting the incident of disrobing Draupadi and after it was brought he starts commenting on it to hurt Krishna.

But such is the impact of majestic personality of Purushottam Narayana/ Krishna that despite Duryodhana's orders all the warriors assembled there stand up and Duryodhana falls down from his throne.

In the assembly Krishna pleads for peace but haughty Duryodhana refuses to listen to reason. Conflict between two personalities intensifies and sparks start flying. Duryodhana orders the arrest of Krishna. Angry Krishna assumes his terrible universal form, vishvarupa, and his weapons start appearing one by one creating panic. On the request of Dhritarashtra, the blind and helpless Kuru king, Krishna relents. But his mission ends in disaster. The play has spectacular dimensions of Greek tragedy.

Bhasa introduced interesting dramatic ploys to enhance the appeal of the play. Duryodhana is shown spreading a chitrapata, scroll of cloth with episodes related to the incident of disrobing of Draupadi, before him and narrating the sequences verbally.

The tradition of illustrating narration with the help of paintings dates back to several centuries. In ancient times this art was known as Mankha vidha or the art of Mankhas. According to Jain literature a senior contemporary of Bhagavan Mahavira named Mankhaliputra Goshala and his father were expert in the Mankha vidha or pictorial narration. Patanjali in his

Mahabhashya also refers to the art of illustrating narration with paintings.

Bhasa has shown Duryodhana acting as a Mankha combining verbal narration and visual material in the form of painted cloth scroll, the chitrapata.

It is for the first time in the history of Indian drama Bhasa brought on stage the Ayudhapurushas or weapons of Krishna in human form. The literary references to Ayudhapurushas are found in the epics, Ramayana and Mahabharata, and their sculptural representation in Indian art is found in late Kushana and Gupta art. Bharata in his Natya Shastra says that inanimate objects can be represented on the stage in human form using adequate make-up and costumes.

Full of spectacular dramatic action, well knit plot structure with inherent dramatic tension and a grandeur of Greek tragedy showing clash of divine and human forces mark Bhasa's play.

DUTI

Female messenger, specially procuress, go-between uniting lovers. Appears more frequently in poetry than drama.

In his Natya Shastra Bharata says: A wise woman, female story teller, a female ascetic or a woman of the stage, an intelligent woman, a female neighbour, a female friend, maid-servant, an unmarried girl, a craftswoman, a foster-mother, a nun or a female fortune teller can be employed as a female messenger.

Vatsyayana in his Kamasutra has devoted one full Adhikarana to this subject. He says female messengers are of eight kinds:

1. Nishrusthartha: A go-between who takes upon herself the full burden of the business.
2. Parimitartha: A go-between who does only a limited part of the business.
3. Patrahari: A go-between who is the bearer of the letter only.
4. Swayamduti: A go-between on her own account.
5. Mudhaduti: The go-between of an innocent young woman.
6. Bharyaduti: A wife serving as go-between.
7. Mukaduti: A mute go-between.
8. Vataduti: A go-between who acts the part of the wind.

It is very interesting to note that female ascetic Kamandaki of Bhavabhuti's play Malati Madhava calls herself Nishrusthartha duti and plays major part in bringing about the union of the hero and the heroine. She virtually runs the plot.

Another interesting example of Duti is the character of Sakhi in the musical opera Gita Govinda.

In the Bhana play Padmaprabhrutakam we see Malatika, daughter of garland-maker, sending a beautiful nun to one Shaishilaka as a messenger of love. But Shaishilaka started flirting with the messenger herself.

Bharata says wise person should never engage any person who is beautiful as messenger.

ENTERTAINMENT TAX

It was Kautilya, the political mentor of Emperor Chandragupta Maurya of Pataliputra, who brought entire entertainment profession under state perview and made several laws governing their activities in the fourth century B.C. He imposed different kinds of taxes on them which were known as Durga. Kautilya says, at difficult times, to fill the royal treasury, half of the income of prostitutes, rupajiva, and actors, kushilava, should be taken away as a state tax. Kautilya was the first to introduce the concept of entertainment tax. He says that the company of performing artists from a foreign country performing in the state should pay an entertainment tax, preksha vetana, of five panas per show.

EROTIC PLAYS

It seems from the reference to the theatrical arts in the third act of the play Mricchakatika by Shudraka that there existed a class of erotic dramas, natakam sasringaram, composed for the courtesans in ancient India, though no specific example of the genre is mentioned. When the Vidushaka enters the fourth chamber of courtesan Vasantasena's magnificent mansion he sees beautiful tender aged daughters of the courtesans singing sweetly like the bees intoxicated by drinking flower-juices. He saw some of them dancing and some reading plays with erotic content—kusumarasamatta eva madhukaryoti madhuram pragita ganikadarika, nartyante, natyam pathayante sasringaram. Probably such plays were specially written for the courtesans in ancient times.

FESTIVAL OF THE RAIN GOD

Indra, the god of thunder and rain and the ruler of heaven, is one of the most important Vedic deities. About two hundred and fifty hymns of the Rig Veda are dedicated to him. He is immensely fond of dancing and singing and is himself described as a dancer in the Rig Veda. The Mahabharata says his court is adorned by beautiful apsaras and gandharvas who entertain him with dance, music, song and laughter (nrityavaditragitaischya hashyeeschya vividhairapi—Lokapal Sabhakyana Parva). One of the most important festivals of ancient India associated with dramatic entertainment is the Indra Maha which is referred to in Prakrit literature as Inda Maha. The rudiments of his festival are found in the Rig Veda itself. According to a hymn in the fourth Mandala his image was worshipped at festivals. Another hymn says: Brahmanas tva satakrata udvamsham iva yemire—O Indra, worshippers while singing songs held thee aloft as it were on a pole (1.10.1, RV).

According to tradition recorded by Bharata, at the victorious banner festival of Indra the first ever play was staged (NS: 1.55–56). Bharata says that the banner festival—Dhwajamaha sriman Mahendrasya—was the most suitable occasion for staging plays. In the fifth chapter elaborate ritual regarding the worship of the jarjara or Indra's flagstaff is prescribed to ward off evil. The following prayer used to be offered while worshipping the jarjara:

> Thou art Indra's weapon killing all the demons; thou hast been fashioned by all the gods, and thou art capable of destroying all the obstacles; bring victory to the king and defeat to the enemies, welfare to cows and Brahmins, success to dramatic undertakings (NS: III.11–13).

Jarjara demolishes obstacles—jarjaro vighnajarjarah (NS: V.83). According to the purvaranga procedure it is brought on the stage and worshipped. The well-known Tamil epic Silappadikaram also refers to the drama festival held in honour of Indra and his son Jayanta in the South. The fifth chapter of the epic describes the festival as full of singing, dancing and music. It hummed with melodies produced by flute, drum and the stringed musical instrument called yal and singing of songs by minstrels and music masters known as panar. The most interesting account of worshipping the flagstaff representing the son of Indra and planting it on the stage is given in the third canto of the epic:

> On the day (of the drama performance) this staff (representing Jayanta, son of Indra) was to be used, a dancing girl had to bathe it with holy water brought in a golden pitcher and afterwards garland it. Then it was handed over with a blessing to the state elephant already adorned with a plate of gold and other ornaments on its forehead. To the accompaniment of the drum proclaiming victory and other musical instruments the king and his five groups of advisers circumambulated the chariot and the elephant and gave the pole to the musician-poet on the top of the chariot. Then they went round the town in procession and entering the theatre placed the pole in its appointed position.

This confirms the tradition of jarjara worship recorded by Bharata in his Natya Shastra. A near similar festival used to be held in ancient Greece in honour of Dionysus. His Athenian women devotees celebrated his festival, known as Lenaia, in January. A long pole with a mask of Dionysus hoisted on it was carried in procession by masked devotees and actors to an amphitheatre, where it was planted facing the orchestra or dancing arena. Plays used to be enacted as offerings to the god of wine. A vase painting depicting the celebration has survived and gives us an idea how Dionysus was hoisted on a pole.

The Mahabharata mentions the celebration of the Indra festival started by King Uparichara Vasu. A bamboo pole decorated with garlands and various ornaments was placed on a high place and Indra, hoisted on the pole in the form of a swan, was worshipped to ensure the victory and prosperity of the nation (Anshavatarana Parva). In the Munda tribal community a festival named Inda Parab or Indi is celebrated in which a long pole buried in the earth is worshipped. Boys and girls then dance around the pole with gay abandon (Encyclopaedia Mundarica, Haufman, 1950; Bharatiya Sanskriti Kosh, Vol. 1, p. 528). Brihatsamhita (canto 43), Devi Purana (canto 12) and Kalika Purana (canto 87) also describe Indra's flag festival. The Kalika Purana describes this ritual in detail.

Canto 43, comprising 68 verses, of Varahamihira's Brihatsamhita is dedicated to the Indradhwaja festival. This flag was presented to Indra by Vishnu and was adorned with jingling bells, garlands, the royal umbrella and small boxes (pitaka). Hence kings for the prosperity of their kingdom and victory over enemies worshipped Indra's flag with adequate ritual and dramatic entertainment. The pole was made of the wood of arjun, ashvakarna, priyak, dhav, udumbar or similar trees. With much ceremony the tree used for making the pole entered the city on the auspicious occasion of Bhadrapad Shukla Ashtami hoisted on a cart. Actors, dancers, musicians crowded the streets to welcome the pole.

After performing various rituals the festival ended on the fifth day. Varahamihira also prescribes dramatic entertainments to make the festival colourful. Kalidasa's Raghuvansha mentions Indra's banner (4.3) whose vision makes people happy. Rajatarangini of Kalhana also mentions the festival of Indra (8.170–182). Indra being the god of rain the concept of his colourful flag might have been borrowed from a rainbow.

The festival of Indra is mentioned in many Jain works. The Uttaradhyayana commentary describes the celebration of this festival by King Dummuha in Kampillapur. "The banner of Indra was raised amidst loud and auspicious cries and was flagged with white banners adorned with a number of little bells, covered with beautiful wreaths and garlands, decorated with a string of jewels and decked with a pendent mass of various fruits.

"Then the dancing girls performed, poetic compositions were sung, people danced, wonderful feats were shown by jugglers, betel was served, water mixed with camphor and saffron was sprinkled, large gifts were given and drums were sounded, and thus seven days passed in great rejoicing and revelry" (*Life in Ancient India as Depicted in the Jain Canons*, J.C. Jain, p. 216).

According to Uttaradhyayana Sutra the festival in honour of Indra was celebrated on a large ground on the outskirts of the city with pomp and show. Poetry recitation, dance and drama were notable features of the festival. In verse 858 of the Gatha Saptashati reference is made to the wooden image of Indra. The practice was to worship wood, terracotta or metal images of Indra along with the festival pole on the occasion of Indradhwajamahotsava.

According to the Bhagavata Krishna opposed this festival and started in its place Govardhan puja or worship of a mountain named Govardhan, and this still continues. In Bhasa's play Madhyama Vyayoga reference is made to Indra's flag tied with rope at the annual festival (rajase rajjubhirbaddhah shakra dhwaja iyotsave 1.47). The jarjara or Indra's flagstaff was decorated with colourful ribbons of cloth. Giving details of jarjara worship on the stage Bharata says:

> (One should fasten a piece of) white cloth at the top (of the jarjara), blue cloth at the Rudra joint, yellow at the Vishnu joint, red cloth at the Skanda joint and variegated cloth at the lowest joint. And incense, garlands and unguents are offered to it in a fitting manner (NS III. 74–76).

Bharata says that when evil spirits tried to create obstacles at the first production of his play Indra beat them to a pulp with his flagstaff, hence it is worshipped as protector of actors. According to Indian theatrical tradition different deities protect different characters in a play.

Indra protects the hero, but the Indra festival has lost its significance in India. Indrajatra is, however, celebrated in the month of Bhadrapad in Nepal. Nepali dancers wearing masks of Indra worship Kalabhairava (Bharatiya Sanskriti Kosh, Vol. I, p. 533), and engage in festivities for seven days.

In the purvaranga of the Kuchipudi dance drama of Andhra Pradesh the ritual of jarjara worship still lingers. But this dance drama is also waning, and what remains of Kuchipudi is solo dance performances. In the Chaitra Parva festival at Seraikella in Bihar jarjara is hoisted and worshipped and the masked dance dramas called Chhau are performed. But here jarjara represents Shiva. In place of Indra Maha, festivals dedicated to other popular deities came into vogue, borrowing the tradition of staging plays on the occasion.

GANDHARVA

Gandharvas are celestial musicians. They are defined as ones who are blessed with the joy created by music and musical instruments—gandham sangitavadyadijanitam pramodam arvati prapnoti iti. Gandharvas are mentioned in Vedic literature. A hymn in the Rig Veda says that virgin is first enjoyed by Soma, Gandharva and Agni. Man is her fourth husband. They are handsome and fond of flowers. Apsaras are their consorts. They are mentioned in the Natya Shastra and in some plays.

GANGA AND YAMUNA

Two sacred rivers of India having their own distinct history, mythology, iconography and dramatic presence. Ganga is mentioned in the Rig Veda and subsequent epic and Puranic literature glorified her as a goddess and as an 'essential instrument of ritual purification.' Essentially a river of the heaven she was brought down on the earth by king Bhagiratha of Ishvaku dynasty. He requested Lord Shiva to receive the mighty flow of the heavenly river descending from heaven, conceding his request Shiva held her on his head, then released her. Since then she is described as consort of Shiva.

At Mahabalipuram the Pallava sculptors carved on the enormous granite boulder the magnificent scene of descent of Ganga.

According to the Mahabharata she married king Shantanu and Bhishma was one of her sons.

Yamuna is none else but twin sister of Yama, the god of death, named Yami who loved her brother passionately. In the Rig Veda there is a beautiful dialogue hymn known as Yama-Yami Samvada. Yami appeared on the earth as river Yamuna.

Particularly from Gupta era the tradition of sculpting Ganga and Yamuna in anthropomorphic form picked up. Ganga is usually shown as standing on crocodile and Yamuna on tortoise. Human size beautiful terracotta images of Ganga and Yamuna from Ahicchatra are housed in Delhi's National Museum. There was a tradition of sculpting Ganga and Yamuna on temple doors in Gupta era.

In the Bhana play of Gupta era, Padataditakam, there is a reference to the shrine of Ganga and Yamuna in the city of Ujjain, and the temple attendant Madayanti who is described as chamara-grahini and pustaka-vachika. Chamara grahini is chowrie bearer. Chamara was used to fan the images of the river goddesses. Pustaka vachika means female reader of the books, scriptures, Puranas.

In the seventh act of Bhavabhuti's Uttararamacharita we see Bharata presenting a play depicting the abandonment of Sita, a play within a play. In this play of Bharata Ganga appears as a character. In Jayadeva's Prasannaraghava both the river goddesses Ganga and Yamuna appears as characters. In his Natya Shastra Bharata says that Ganga should be shown as a woman of fair complexion. Tradition ascribes dark colour to Yamuna.

GANIKA

Courtesan par excellence. Vatsyayana in his Kamasutra says that when a beautiful prostitute, veshya, having excellent character, sheela-rupa-gunanvita, becomes adept in sixtyfour arts including dancing, singing, playing on musical instruments, play acting, painting, reading, writing she attains the position of Ganika.

Then, says Vatsyayana, she is respected by the kings, held in high esteem by society, praised by the learned people and thus becomes the centre of attraction for all.

Ganikas are found mentioned in several literary works. Ganika Amrapali, Nagaravadhu of Vaishali, is very famous in Buddhist literature. Kings vied for her favours. In the Ashokavadana there is a mention of famous Ganika of Mathura, Vasavadatta, whose fee was five hundred gold coins per night.

Kautilya in his Arthashastra wrote a full chapter, Ganikadhyaksha Prakarana, giving details of how to deal with Ganikas administratively. Vatsyayana states in his Kamasutra that on the request of Ganikas of Pataliputra Acharya Dattaka wrote a treatise on harlotry, Vaishikamadhikarana, for them. In the eighth century A.D. Damodaragupta wrote an interesting work Kuttanimata dealing with the lives of courtesans. In Bharata's Natyashastra there is a chapter on harlotry.

Vasantasena is the most famous Ganika of Sanskrit dramatic literature who is the heroine of Bhasa's Charudatta and Shudraka's Mricchakatika. In the fifth act of Charudatta we see scholars coming from different cities reading Shastras in the mansion of Vasantasena. In Mricchakatika she is referred to as Nagarashri. Splendour of her establishment too is described in detail in the fourth act of the play where the Vidushaka witnesses the daughters of Ganikas singing, dancing and reading erotic dramas. Vasantasena is shown adept in the art of theatre, expert in voice modulation and Sanskrit language. In Sanskrit plays only very elite characters speak Sanskrit.

Fragments of Buddhist scholar Ashvaghosha's plays were found in Turfan. One of the plays has Ganika as its central female character.

Ganikas are mentioned in several Bhana as well as Prahasana type of plays in Sanskrit.

Well-known Ganika of Mathura Lonasobhika is mentioned in an inscription datable to about first century B.C. now housed in the Mathura Museum. The inscription, one of the earliest to mention a Ganika by name, reads thus:

Adoration to Arhat Vardhamana. The daughter of the matron (?) courtesan (Ganika) Lonasobhika (Skr. Lavanashobhika) the disciple of the ascetics (samanasavikaye), the junior (?) courtesan Vasu (ganikaye Vasu) has erected a shrine of the Arhat (Arhato devik(u)la) a hall of homage (ayagasabha), a cistern (and) a stone slab at the sanctuary of Nirgantha Arhats, together with her mother, (her sister), her daughter, her son and her household, in honour of the Arhats.

GARUDA

Bird vehicle of Vishnu. He is described as a half-bird half-human in Puranic lore. Huge, fierce-looking, powerful he was the son of Vinita and Kashyapa. Kadru was another wife of Kashyapa and mother of serpents. She made Vinita her slave and tortured Garuda. She asked Garuda to bring for her and her serpent sons ambrosia from heaven if he wanted to free his mother from slavery. He fought with the gods and brought it for her. In a swift action Indra took it away leaving Kadru and her serpent sons high and dry. Since then Garuda became sworn enemy of serpents. In Harsha's play Nagananda Garuda plays significant role as a serpent eating bird who attacks hero Jimutavahana mistaking him for a serpent and nearly kills him.

GAULAN KALA

The oldest and most popular form of musical play depicting the childhood and adolescent life of Krishna he spent in the pastoral land of Braj bhumi on the bank of river Yamuna. As it is performed in the day time it is called Dis Kala also. Dis Kala has a format of a well knit play. In it childhood sports or lilas of Krishna are enacted. Interesting duets of Radha and Krishna, cowherd girls and Krishna in mixed prose and verse, their delightful dances enliven the Kala performance. Enacted in the temple Sabhamandapa it is presented by child actors—both boys and girls.

Gaulan Kala opens with the musical discourse by Sutradhara. Through his prayer songs he invokes various deities and underlines the importance of Krishna worship.

The task of creating humour is entrusted to two funny friends of Krishna named as Vakadya and Pendya.

On the festive occasions the beautifully decorated Sabhamandapas of the Gomantaka temples vibrate with song, dance, music inherent in Kala plays.

GHOST-MASK DANCE

In the fourth act of the play Karpuramanjiri by Rajashekhara belonging to tenth century A.D. there is a mention of Ghost-mask dance. This dance used to be performed by women wearing the masks of night-wanderer female fiends, nishachari, holding the human flesh in their hands, howling, yelling fiercely like jackals, acting like evil spirits haunting the burning grounds or doing smashanabhinaya, wearing awe-inspiring, raudra, costumes.

GOLLA KALAPAM

An interesting playlet written by Bhagavatulu Ramayya Shastri which became the part of Kuchipudi dance-drama tradition of Andhra Pradesh. Golla means cowherd. Golla Kalapam veers round the conversation of a milkmaid and a Brahmin.

Assuming superior posture the Brahmin scholar tries to impress the milkmaid with his erudition and command over Shastras. But soon he discovers that the milkmaid has not only sharp wit and the capacity for quick repartee but she too is well versed in shastric precepts. In the end the milkmaid convinces the Brahmin that Lord is supreme and all creatures being his manifestations are equal before him. This is a beautiful philosophical conversation discussing a number of topics of spiritual significance and the place of man in the universe. Golla Kalapam is a popular item in the Kuchipudi repertory, next only to the celebrated Bhama Kalapam.

GOMBEYATTA

In the Mysore region the Gombeyatta string puppetry is quite popular which imitates the local Yakshagana theatre. Highly stylised Gombeyatta puppets look like characters on Yakshagana stage. Yakshagana prasangas or dramatic texts are taken up for presentation.

GOPAL KALA

An interesting dramatic performance based on the story of demon Pralambhasura who was killed by Balarama in Vrindavana. Gopal Kala performances are staged in Gomantaka temples.

According to the legend recorded in the Bhagavata Purana Pralambhasura was sent by Kamsa, king of Mathura, to destroy Krishna. The ferocious demon mixed with friends of Krishna in the guise of cowherd boy and started playing various games with them. When he found out that it is difficult to defeat Krishna he lifted his elder brother Balarama on his shoulder and started running away. But mighty Balarama killed him by hitting his fist on his head.

The play starts with the appearance of Sutradhara. After invoking Ganesha he, along with his chorus, starts singing a song about the games Pralambha played with Krishna and got defeated every time.

It is said that in olden times all these games were actually played as a part of the performance.

The performers are divided into two groups—one led by Pralambha and other by Krishna. Facing each other they start an interesting game of riddles. One party sings a riddle-song and asks the other to supply the answer. Then other party takes its turn to sing a riddle-song challenging the opposition party to give the reply.

This goes on for an hour or two, audience immensely enjoying verbal combat. In the end

Pralambha lifts Balarama on his shoulder but Balarama kills the demon by hitting a fist on his head.

Then Sutradhara and his chorus sing song in the praise of Krishna and Balarama. Meanwhile the actors in the guise of these two brothers break an earthen pot full of milk and curd as a grand finale of the show. The contents of the pot thus broken are distributed among the members of audience as a prasad.

This interesting performance is staged as a part of temple festival in the Sabhamandapa attached to it. In it dialogues are in the form of posing riddles.

GREEK-KANNADA FARCE

An interesting farce written in Greek and Kannada languages ascribed to second century A.D., found in the archaeological excavation in Egypt.

In Egypt, in the year 1899, intensive excavation activities were undertaken under the auspices of the Biblical Archaeological Association to further Biblical research. During the excavation a large collection of ancient manuscripts inscribed on papyrus sheets were unearthed. Tall papyrus trees were common in Egypt. The thin strips cut from its plinth were used as writing material in ancient times. Scholars like P. Greenfell and Arthur S. Hunt translated the papyri material and published it as The Oxyrhynchus Papyri Part III. Among the material published is a Greek farce with passages in Indian language.

Dr. R. Shama Shastri wrote an elaborate article on the Farce in the Mysore Archaeological Report for 1926 in which he showed that the Indian language in the play is none but Kannada. Well-known historian Dr. B.A. Saletore made a thorough examination of the farce and recorded his observations in his book, *Ancient Karnataka*.

A beautiful Greek girl, Charition, falls into the hands of the Nayaka of Malpe. Malpe is the ancient sea-port of Karnataka. Probably it was a case of ship wreck or she was sold to him as a flute girl by the traders who find mention in the book the Periplus of the Erythraean Sea. Nayaka keeps her in a temple of Moon Goddess. A search party led by her brother arrives at Malpe to rescue the girl. By serving intoxicating wine to Malpe Nayaka and his friends the Greeks make them unconscious and escape with the girl.

The characters of the play are—A: Charition, B: Buffoon, All: King's people, C: Brother of Charition, D: Captain of the ship, F, G, H: Greek characters, King: Nayaka of Malpe called Basileus.

Here is the text of the play with translation of Kannada passages by Dr. Saletore.

A Tentative Reconstruction of the Greek Farce with Old Kannada Passages

B : Lady Charition, rejoice with me at my escape!

A : Great are the gods.

B : What gods, fool (?)!

A : Cease fellow.

D : Wait for me here and I will go and bring the ship to anchor.

A : Go? For see, here come their women from the chase.

B : Oh! What huge bows they have!

A Woman : Kraunou? (Shall we shoot?)[1]

Another : Lalle (Warning her).[2]

Another : Laitalianta Lalle (Lalle asks you to wait? Is it not so?)[3]

Another : Kotakos an ab, Iosara (Lo! Take the string of hemp. Give the arrow!)[4]

B : Hail!

All : Laspathia (The Buffoon! Ah!)[5]

B : Ah! Lady help!

A : Alemaka! (Alem akka—Is he (the proper) person (to be shot), Sister?)[6]

All : Alemaka (Alla emmakka—No, our sister!)[7]

B : By Athena, there is no (harm) from us.

A : Wretch, they took you for an enemy and nearly shot you.

B : I am always in misfortune. Will you them ... to the river Psolichus?

A : As you like (Drums) (B ... porade) (Against the name of A is the letter B and the word porade. If it is meant as a word spoken by B, then meaning seems to be 'Start then'. But if applied to A, the meaning probably is 'I am starting, ready!')

All : Minei (Shall we take our bath?)

F : Lady Charition, I see the wind is rising, so that we may cross the Indian Ocean and escape. So enter and fetch your property, and if you can, carry off one of the offerings to the goddess.

A : Prudence, fellow! Those in need of salvation must not accompany their petitions to the gods with sacrilege. For how will the gods listen to men who try to win mercy with wickedness?

B : Don't you touch? I will fetch it.

D : Fetch your own things then.

A : I do not need them either, but only to see my father's face.

D : Enter, then; and do you serve them ... and give them their wine strong, for here they come.

B : I think they are the daughters of swine; these too I will get rid of (Drums ...)

All : Ai Arminthi (Drums.) (Have all of you taken your bath?)

B : They also have run away to the Psolichus.

C : Yes; but let us get ready, if we are to escape.

B : Lady Charition, get ready, if you can take under your arm one of the offering to the goddess.

A : Hush! Those in need of salvation must not accompany their petitions to the gods with sacrilege. For how will they listen to the prayers of those who are about to gain mercy by wickedness? The property of the goddess must remain sacred.

B : Don't you touch; I will carry it.

A : Don't be silly, but if they come, serve them the wine neat.

B : But if they will not drink it so?

C : Fool, in these regions wine is not for sale. Consequently if they get hold of this kind of thing, they will drink it neat against their will (?)

B : I'll serve them lees and all.

C : Here they come, having bathed ... (Drums)

King : Brathis (Cause to be served in plenty.)[8]

All : Brathis.

B : What do they say?

C : Let us draw lots for the shares, he says.

B : Yes, let us.

King : Stoukepairomellokoroke (Pour a little into his hand slowly.)[9]

B : Back, accursed wretch.

King : Brathis (Drums) Bere konzei damun petrekio paktei kortames bere ialer ode pomenzi petrekiodam ut kinze paxei zebes lolo bia bradis kottos. (Give me the precious drink. Why did you put down your cup before some more was served? Take a portion! Serve a little, brother! Thinking there will be no more to be served must you have put down your cups. Is your desire for dinner so little? Would you not eat or drink? Fear! Take a little!)[10]

All : Kottos (Give a little).

B : May you be kicked by 'kottos'.

King : Zopit (Drums) (Ah! Excellent!)[11]

B : What do they say?

C : Give them a drink, quick.

B : Are you afraid to speak then? Hail, thou whose days prosper! (Drums)

King : Zeisoukormosede (Drums) (Ah! Take by deceit.)[12]

B : Ah! Not if I know it.

C : It is watery, put in some wine (Much drumming).

G : Skalmakata bapteiragoumi (The sin (of drinking) which you have not committed till now, may be ended this day only!) (In other words, empty the cups.)[13]

H : Tougoummi nekelekethro (Take once again. Why did you get up?)[14]

G : Eitou belle trachoupterugoumi [How pure (white) is the wine! Let it be finished once for all!][15]

B : Ah! None of your disgusting ways! Stop! (Drums) Ah! What are you doing?

H : Trachountermana. [It is honour to partake of the (juice of) grapes!][16]

G : Boullitikaloumbai platagouida bi ... (You will be very happy this year. Take a share lovingly.)[17]

B : Apuleukasar (Drums) (Ah! It will be sour! Get away!)

King : Chorbonorbothorba toumionaxiz despit platagoulda bi ... Sesosrachis (Drums) oradosatur ouamesare sumpsaradara ei iada ... (One shows boiled rice, another who sees the husk in it, run away out of the country. Take a share lovingly. Sesa! Protect! Show your love lovingly! Oh! Umeshvara! Is this the door of smsara?)[18]

B : Martha marithouma edmaimai maitho thamouna martha marithouma (Drums) ... tun (We have found out a medicine! Wherever the greatness of this magic spreads strongly, silence is produced. Lady! We have found out a medicine!)[19]

King : Malpinaik ouroukoukoub (n?) i karako ... ra (Take Malpe Nayaka (referring to himself) into the house.)[20]

All : Aba! (Exclamatory word)

King : Zebede za biligidoumba (Ha! Do not do so! He will order you to be shot!)[21]

All : Aba oun (Oh! Truly!) He will protect you (if you act according to his wishes!).

King : Pan oum bretikateman ouman brethououeni [Oh! Lady, how will you aspire for honour unless the drinking people (ourselves) hold you (in) high (esteem?)][22]

All : Panoumbretikate manouam brethou oueni parakoum bretikatema noum bret ouououeni olusadizaparda piskou piskate man arei man ridaou oupatei ... a (five drummings) (Oh! ... esteem? You will forfeit the happiness of this and the other world without yielding to the will of the king (i.e., if you do not yield to the will of the king) Submit! Protect us (by becoming our queen). Do you understand us? Do you not approve?)[23]

King : A boundless barbaric dance. I lead, O goddess moon. With wild measure and barbaric step; Ye Indian chiefs, bring the drum of mystic sound. The frenzied Seric step. (Much drumming and beating)

All : Orkis. (Make him lie down! (lest he should fall and hurt himself) ...)[24]

B : What do they say again?

C : He says, dance.

B : Just like living men (Drums).

C : Throw him down and bind him with the sacred girdles. (Much drumming. Finale.)

B : They are now heavy with drink.

C : Good! Charition, come out here.

A : Come, brother, quickly; is all ready?

C : Yes, all; the boat is at the anchor close by; why do you linger? Helmsman, I bid you bring this ship alongside here at once.

D : Wait till I give him the word.

B : Are you talking again you bungler? Let us leave him outside to kiss the ship's bottom.

C : Are you all aboard?

All : Aboard.

A : O unhappy me! A great trembling seizes my wretched body. Be propitious, Lady Goddess! Save thy hand maiden!

GUHYAKA

A class of Yakshas who guard treasures —guhati nidhim dhanavishesham rakshateeti. Another definition says—nidhim rakshanti te yakshaste syurguhyakasanjnaka. They live in Himalayan region and Kuber is their master. Cruel by nature they possess magical powers. Guhyakas are mentioned in the Natya Shastra of Bharata.

GUNADHYA

Author of the famous story book Brihatkatha, or Baddakaha, in Paishachi language. According to a legend he was born in Paithan in Maharashtra and became minister in the court of a Satavahana king. The legend says that due to some reason or the other he left Paithan and the Satavahana court and went to Vindhyaranya. In the dense forest on the Vindhya mountain he studied Paishachi language. Here he came in contact with a Pishacha named Kanabhuti who told him stories of seven Vidyadharas. Gunadhya wrote these stories in seven parts and returned to his native place Paithan. He sent his work to king Satavahana through his disciples but the king refused to acknowledge it. Frustrated Gunadhya started burning his book page by page. When the king came to know about it he rushed to the forest where he saw animals sitting around Gunadhya listening to his tales. The king could save only last part of the work which became famous as Brihatkatha.

A number of Sanskrit authors including Subandhu, Dandi and Banabhatta have mentioned Gunadhya and his Brihatkatha.

In the 9th century A.D. Budhaswami of Nepal prepared his version of Brihatkatha in Sanskrit under the title Brihatkatha-shloka-sangraha.

In the 11th century Kshemendra prepared his version of the work under the title Brihatkatha Manjiri and in the same century Kashmiri scholar Pandit Somadeva published his version named Kathasaritsagar.

Sanskrit drama is deeply influenced by the Brihatkatha of Gunadhya. It contains the story of Udayana king of Vatsa which is probably older than Brihatkatha. The theme of the play Nagananda of Sriharsha has been taken from Brihatkatha.

Unfortunately the original Brihatkatha is lost to posterity.

Scholars are not certain about the time of Gunadhya. However if we believe the legend about his being in the Satavahana court he might have composed his story book around the beginning of the Christian era. Some scholars contend that Gunadhya's patron king was Hal Satavahana. If so we can place him in early years of the first century A.D.

HANUMANNATAK

An interesting semi-dramatic composition said to have been written by Hanuman, now available in two recensions by Damodara Misra and Madhusudan respectively. As it is a composition with as many as fourteen acts it is also called a great drama or Mahanataka.

According to a legend recorded by Ballala Sen in his Bhoja Prabandha the play was first composed by Hanuman who engraved it on stone by his nails. When he showed it to Valmiki, the composer of the epic Ramayana, he was asked by the epic poet to drown it in the sea. Hanumannatak, the legend says, being the superior composition Valmiki thought his version of Rama story, the Ramayana, may pale into insignificance before it. Hanuman did what Valmiki asked him to do.

During the reign of king Bhoja of Dharanagari some divers recovered the stones on which the play was inscribed from the sea. King Bhoja asked his court poet Damodara Misra to read the inscription and give proper shape to the composition.

In a popular version of the legend instead of king Bhoja the name of king Vikramaditya is mentioned and the name of the poet who recast the original play is given out as Madhusudan Misra.

However it seems that a number of poets inserted extraneous material in the text by borrowing it from various works of drama and poetry including the Ramayana, Raghuvamsha, Mahavirach-arita, Uttararamacharita, Anargharaghava, Udattaraghava and Balaramayana. The process of inflating the text, it seems, continued up to the 14th century. This entry relates to the recension which came down to us as one composed by Damodara Misra and published by Chowkhamba after being edited by Pandit Jagdish Misra.

The composition has a very interesting format. This type of format is used in folk and traditional dramatic forms. A narrator stands up or sits on the stage along with musicians and narrates the story of the play. During the course of narration some actors impersonating various characters appear on the stage and speak out their dialogues as per the demand of the story and finishing their job make their exit. After that the narrator again starts his narration and takes the story further. Again at appropriate time actors reappear and play their part, after their exit, again narrator takes his turn. This goes on till the performance comes to an end.

This format is followed in Hanumannatak. The narrative passages are intercepted by dialogues of characters of the story such as Rama, Sita, Laxmana, Ravana, etc. This format of performance is seen in the Ramlila shows staged in North India in particular.

Hanumannatak is based on Rama story starting from the birth of Rama, his early life, marriage with Sita, his exile, kidnapping of Sita by Ravana, Rama killing Ravana, his victorious return to Ayodhya and ending with his coronation as a king.

In the second act of the play there is a very erotic description of the union of newly married Rama and Sita transcending all limits of dramatic conventions.

HARSHA

Great patron of arts and literature the seventh century king of Kanauj, Harshavardhana, wrote three plays in Sanskrit—Priyadarshika, Nagananda and Ratnavali, apart from two Buddhist poems Ashthtamaha-srichaitystotra and Suprabhat Stotra.

Harsha ascended the throne in 606 A.D. and ruled for about fortytwo years winning many wars and conquering many territories. The information about him and his rule is found in the account of Chinese traveller Hieun Tsang. Banabhatta wrote his biography Harshacharita which remained incomplete probably due to the death of Banabhatta.

Harsha was great patron of Buddhism. In 643 A.D. king Harsha convened a splendid assembly at Kanauj when the Ratha-yatra or chariot processions were taken out carrying in the rathas golden image of Buddha and other deities of Buddhist pantheon. A legend recorded by Hieun Tsang says that once a Buddhist monastery suddenly caught fire which automatically died down by the mere sight of the good king Harsha.

After Ashvaghosha it was Harsha who wrote a play, Nagananda, based on the life and sacrifice made by Bodhisattva Jimutavahana to save a serpent or Naga from Garuda bird. I-Tsing refers to its enactment in Buddhist monasteries.

Ratnavali too became quite popular. An eighth century work Kuttanimatam elaborately describes the performance of the portion of the play staged in the Vishvanatha temple of Kashi by the local courtesan under the guidance of a dance-master. The play is based on the love story of king Udayana and princess Ratnavali. The play became favourite with the writers of text-books of drama who often quote from its text to illustrate the technical rules.

Priyadarshika too is a romantic comedy based on the love story of king Udayana and princess Priyadarshika. It is a pleasant drama which became quite popular.

HASYACHUDAMANI

A prahasana or farce by 12th–13th century playwright Vatsaraja who was minister in the court of Chandella ruler of Kalanjara, Paramardideva, and later he held the same position in the court of his son and successor Trailokyavarmadeva.

The farce depicts the character of Jnanarashi, a pretentious and pseudo guru, who claims the knowledge of Kevali-vidya which enables him to trace stolen goods, lost articles and buried treasures.

Once a Kuttani, bawd, named Kapatakeli who was in the mood of drinking wine after getting up in the morning was informed by her maid that her jewellery has been stolen. Perturbed Kapatakeli suspects her daughter, courtesan Madanasundari, who is in love with stony-broke gambler Kalakaranda. However she decides to approach Acharya Jnanarashi to find out the real culprit.

At the time Jnanarashi was trying hard to teach his foolhardy disciple Kundinya who wanted to know nothing but how to deceive unsuspecting clients by posing as a guru having the knowledge of Kevali-vidya.

When Kapatakeli approaches him by using various tricks and fooleries of his profession the guru convinces her that her attendants Kokilaka and Paravata are the suspects. As a fee of his consultation the guru skilfully divests the Kuttani of her valuable jem-studded gold ring. Here ends act one.

In the second act we see the pair of guru and shishya entering the pleasure garden blooming with flowers. There they see beautiful Madanasundari, daughter of Kapatakeli, waiting for her lover gambler Kalakaranda. We see her maid assuring her that winning wealth in gambling he would join her to celebrate his victory by indulging in drinking wine.

The maid also reveals the secret that Kalakaranda has returned the jewellery to Kuttani which her daughter stole from her house and gave it to her lover Kalakaranda.

Disciple Kundinya gets terribly attracted towards courtesan Madanasundari. Jnanarashi too is attracted towards her but concealing his emotions he rebukes his disciple for his foetal attraction. In fact guru himself wanted the courtesan for himself.

Suddenly Kapatakeli appears on the scene. She is very happy as she got back the stolen jewellery. But she now tells the Jnanarashi that he has stolen her heart. She asks him to get rid of his yellow robes so that she could apply fragrant chandan paste over his body. When startled Jnanarashi tries to run away from the old and haggard ugly courtesan she bluntly tells him that she has made love to so many ascetics and Lord Vishnu, the progenitor of Kama, is happy with such ascetic lovers.

Angry guru lifts his stick to beat her but her attendants pounce on him. When gambler Kalakaranda appears on the scene he rescues the guru who, he thinks, is responsible for his success in gambling.

Vatsaraja successfully created hilarious situations and exposed the dealings of fake gurus with tall claims through his farce.

HERO

Principal male character in the drama around whom the plot revolves. See NAYAKA.

HUMAN SACRIFICE

The practice of ritual sacrifice of human beings is quite ancient. In the Vedic times such rituals were known as Naramedha. In this context the Vedic legend of Shunahshepa is quite well known. A lad Shunahshepa was purchased from his poor parents by king Harishchandra to sacrifice him to god Varuna.

Some esoteric tantric sects adopted this practice. It was believed that ritual sacrifice of human beings will help sacrificer acquire supernatural powers. In the play Malati Madhava by Bhavabhuti we see tantrics procuring a beautiful girl to sacrifice her in the temple of goddess Chamunda or Karala situated in the cemetery.

HUNT DRAMA

Hunting was the premier occupation of the primitive man. No wonder it became main theme of his visual presentation and performance. Hunting scenes were recreated through dance and body movements for recreation as well as a part of ritual to cast sympathetic magic on hunting expeditions to come. Such performances were in total imitation of the process of hunting or we may say its symbolic representation.

In prehistoric cave paintings hunting scenes form a major theme. In Mesolithic cave shelter paintings of Lakhajoar and Jaora we see a hunt drama depicted in which masked hunters are shown pursuing masked animals, in fact tribals in animal masks. Masks of the hunters and animals or men in the guise of animals being hunted are of the same design. Obviously this is the depiction of drama of hunt. Same is the case of tribal war dance, a dramatic recreation of actual war.

While underlining the dramatic element in such performances Sheldon Cheney in his book *The Theatre* quotes Loomis Havemeyer's description of a Naga war dance of Northeast India:

'It commences with a review of warriors who later advance and retreat, parrying blows and throwing spears as though in actual fight. They creep along in battle array, keeping as near the ground as possible so that nothing shows but a line of shields. When they are near enough to the imaginary enemy they spring up and attack. After they have killed the opposing party they grab tufts of grass which represent the heads and these they sever with their battle axes. Returning home they carry the clods over their shoulders as they would the heads of real men. At the village they are met by the women who join in triumphant song and dance.'

Recreation of hunt or war scenes through dance or dramatic movements can be described as primitive drama.

IHAMRIGA

One of the ten types of drama mentioned in the Natya Shastra of Bharata.

Ihamriga has its dramatis personae divine males who are implicated in fights about divine females. Plot should be well constructed, convincing, the plot of love is to be based on causing discord among females, carrying them off and oppressing the enemies. All that is to be made available in the Vyayoga—its male characters, styles and sentiments—should be brought in the Ihamriga, except that it is to include goddesses, divine females only, as female characters, battle should be avoided (NS: Ghosh).

INDIA IN GREEK PLAYS

Aeschylus (525–456 B.C.), one of the earliest known Greek playwrights who developed the Greek drama by introducing a second actor, mentions India by name for the first time in his play the Suppliants. The play is considered as a first extant drama in Western European literature composed about 492 B.C. E.E. Beven writes:

'We may probably infer from the long geographical passages in the plays of Aeschylus that a lively interest in far-off peoples and strange lands was generated in the Greek world of the 5th century B.C. When an ancient Argive king in the Suppliants has to express wonder at the foreign garb of the Egyptian maidens, the poet takes the opportunity to give evidence of his anthropological knowledge. The king mentions different races whose appearance might be like that, and in the course of his speculations says:

"Moreover I hear tales of Indians, of women that go roving on camels, mounted horse fashion, riding on padded saddles, them that are the citizens of the land neighbouring the Ethiopians. In the Greek books we possess this is the earliest mention of Indians by name" (*The Cambridge History of India*, Vol. I, p. 354a).'

Megasthenes, a Greek envoy in the court of Emperor Chandragupta Maurya, traced a myth about a bird included in the play of Aristophanes, The Birds of Indian Folklore. He writes:

'I hear also that the Indian hoopoe is double the size of ours, and more beautiful in appearance, and Homer says that while bridle and trappings of a horse are the delight of a Hellenic king this hoopoe is the favourite plaything of the king of Indians, who carries it on his hand and toys with it and never tires gazing in ecstasy on its splendour and the beauty with which nature has adorned it. The Brachmanes therefore even made this peculiar bird the subject of a mythic story, and the tale told of it runs thus:

To the king of Indians there was born a son. The child had elder brothers who when they came to the man's estate turned out to be very unjust and the greatest of reprobates. They despised their brother because he was youngest and they also scoffed at their father and mother, whom they despised because they were very old and grey haired. The boy and his aged parents could no longer live with these wicked men and fled from home together.

In the course of protracted journey they had then to undertake, the old couple succumbed to fatigue and died. The boy buried them in himself, having cut off his head with a sword. Then, as the Brachmanes tell us, the all seeing Sun in admiration of his surpassing act of piety, transformed the boy into most beautiful bird which lives to a very advanced age.

So on his head there grew a crest which was a memorial to what he had done at the time of his flight. The Athenians have also a fable describing marvels somewhat similar to those of the crested lark. This fable Aristophanes appears to have followed when he says in The Birds 'For thou wert ignorant, and not always bustling, nor always thumping Aesop, who spake of the crested lark, calling it first of all birds, born before even the earth was; and telling how afterwards her father became sick and died, and how that, as the earth then did not exist, he lay unburied till the fifth day, when the daughter unable to find a grave elsewhere dug one for him in her own head' (Lines 470–75).

It seems accordingly probable that the fable, though with a different bird for its subject, emanated from the Indians and spread onwards even to the Greeks. For, the Brachmanes say that a prodigious time has elapsed since the Indian hoopoe, then in human form and young in years, performed that act of piety for his parents' (*Ancient India*, McCrindle, pp. 161–63).

INDUS CIVILIZATION

Around 1925, two enterprising Indian archaeologists, R.D. Banerjee and D.R. Sahni, conducted extensive excavations at Mohenjodaro in Sind and Harappa in Punjab (part of which is now in Pakistan) and brought to light highly developed urban civilization. Described as "the first great civilization of Indian history", it became famous as Harappan or Indus Valley Civilization. Further excavations and archaeological findings proved that this civilization extended far beyond the rivers Indus and Saraswati and covered many parts of Gujarat, Uttar Pradesh and Haryana in India.

Late Harappan artefacts were found even at places like Daimabad in Maharashtra and Manda in Jammu.

After independence many Harappan sites were found in India such as Lothal, Dholavira, Surkotada in Gujarat; Banavali, Rakhigarhi, Bhagvanpura in Haryana and Kalibangan in Rajasthan. Geographical area enclosed by the Harappan civilization covered more than double the area as that by ancient civilizations elsewhere in the world.

Originating in the third millennium B.C. the Harappan civilization went through three stages of evolution—early stage (3500–2600 B.C.), developed stage (2600–2000 B.C.) and final stage (2000–1500 B.C.). Exact reasons of the decline and disappearance of this urban civilization of India are not known though scholars have speculated on the issue.

This civilization is known for its well planned cities, brick built houses, excellent drainage system and water storage tanks. Benjamin Rowland wrote: "Indeed it could be said that the population of the Indus cities lived more comfortably than did their contemporaries in the crowded and ill-built metropolises elsewhere. People were literate and had their own script. Dance and music formed essential part of their daily life."

Many objects were unearthed during the excavations at different sites which include beautiful figurines, seals, pottery, jewellery, tools, weapons, etc. About the seals found at the sites, a scholar writes: "They reveal the most consummate and delicate perfection of craftsmanship. The animal seals are among the world's greatest examples of an artist's ability to embody the essentials of a given form in artistic shape."

Beautiful ornaments were made of gold, silver, copper, bronze, stone, shell, ivory and clay. Pottery was made on potter's wheel and fired on high temperature and painted too. A number of interesting clay toys for children too have been excavated.

Harappans lived in the brick-built houses having amenities like bathroom, kitchen and drainage system of a high order. Their women wore ornaments of gold, silver, ivory, semi-precious stones, and also of bones and terracotta. Bangles, necklaces, anklets, armlets and a variety of similar ornaments were found. They used to wear cotton and woollen cloths. Cosmetics were in vogue and women knew how to do their hair artistically. They knew the art of writing though their script still remains undeciphered. Their creative mind produced sculptures and painted pottery of good quality. At Mohenjodaro a large bath with galleries and rooms around it was found. It might have been used for ritual baths. A pillared hall was excavated at the same place, presumably for public assembly. They manufactured seals and amulets and toys of many descriptions. They traded with ancient world countries like Mesopotamia and Egypt and led a cultured life.

This rich culture must have its own forms of dramatic amusements though we know little about them, but evidence shows dance was one of them. In addition to terracotta figurines of dancers we find stone and bronze dancing statuettes of great charm. A male dancing figure full of vitality sculpted in greyish limestone was found at Harappa. Art critics have described it as Nataraja the divine dancer of Indian mythology and art. Writing about it Benjamin Rowland remarks:

> This image, carved in greyish limestone, represents a dancing male figure, perhaps originally ithyphallic, four-armed and three-headed. These attributes, together with the dancing pose, make it possible that this is a prototype for the later Hindu conception of Shiva as Lord of the Dance. The modelling, again, is of an extraordinarily telling simplicity, that, in its assured establishment of form in the completely abstract plastic sense, suggests the work of a modern sculptor like Henry Moore. Even in its present fragmentary state, the figure is imbued with a vital, dynamic quality and a suggestion of movement imparted by the violent axial dislocation of the head, thorax, and hips, exactly the same device employed to suggest the violence of Shiva's dance in the great Hindu bronzes of the Chola period.

This reminds us of the Mesolithic Nataraja figures painted in a Bhimbetka cave shelter displaying the same vitality and force of movement in a majestic manner.

Another important find at Mohenjodaro is a bronze statuette of a slender, gracefully supple female dancer in an inviting posture. She is wearing nothing on her person except ornaments like bangles and a necklace with a triple pendant. Her somewhat protruding lower lip to some is indicative of Dravidian or Negroid physical traits. Her left leg, placed forward, is bent at the knee. Her right hand is placed akimbo on the hips. She looks as if she has taken a stance and is about to break into movement. This fascinating bronze figurine is not only indicative of the sculptural skill of the Harappan people but also of the rich dance culture they possessed. Katakavali, the practice of wearing a number of bangles and necklace with pendant resting in the deep cleavage between the rising bosoms, has been adopted by later sculptors who made enchanting figurines of dancing *yakshis*, *surasundaris* and *apsaras* that adorned stupas and temples in India.

Mackay, in his work *Further Excavations at Mohenjodaro*, refers to many interesting dancing figurines. Among them are statuettes of dwarfs. Writing about them he says: "Figure 13 in the plate LXXV may be an attempt to represent a dwarf or a deformed person, which suggests that perhaps dwarfs or deformed people were kept for amusement as in ancient Egypt. The figures are not unlike the achondroplastic dwarfs of ancient Egypt in disproportion between the size of the trunk and limbs.

"Dr. Rueffer has remarked that both in early Egypt and medieval Europe these dwarfs were in demand for looking after pet animals and even valuables, the latter on the principle that they could be easily identified if they ran away. From the way, however, in which the short stumpy legs are bent, the Indus Valley figurines of this type seem to have been dancers.

"The object clasped to the breast by the bandy-legged figures in the Plates LXXV, 2; LXXVI, 6 may be a drum hung around the neck...it is not unlikely that dwarfs were kept to provide amusement and they were taught to dance, as were the dwarfs and pigmies in the royal and other households of ancient Egyptians...According to Hornblower dwarfs were often associated with the worship of the Mother Goddess in Egypt.

"In two of the pyramid texts of the sixth dynasty both Pepy and Mer-en-Ra identified themselves for religious purposes with the pigmy. Dwarf figures are also sometimes associated with Shiva worship and are said to represent various *ganas*. Bandy-legged dwarfs appear on Sumerian seals in association with seated gods and worshippers or with a nude female deity, probably the Mother Goddess, and it may have been thought that they existed in Sumerian after-life as well as for the amusement of others in the temples and palaces of Sumer. The little bandy-legged figures from Mohenjodaro also (Pls. LXXIII, 1, 8; LXXV, 11, 13; LXXVI, 11) may have been associated in some way with worship of the Mother Goddess" (pp. 266, 278, 655).

Indian tradition considers a dwarf a figure of mirth. It is very interesting to note that Pramathas, dwarfish attendants of Shiva, are according to Indian dramaturgy presiding deities of *hasya rasa* or laughter. In the 5th century Shiva shrine at Bhumara these dwarf *pramatha ganas* are shown in poses evoking instant laughter. The *Shukla Yajurveda* says in the tenth verse of its 30th book that a dwarf is an object of amusement. Indian dramaturgy stipulates that a jester should be a dwarf or *vaman*. Dwarfs may also have been dancers to amuse the people.

In his book *Early Indus Civilization* further evidence regarding dance and music is quoted by Mackay. He says:

> It is still uncertain whether dancing formed part of the religious rites of the inhabitants of the Indus cities although it is an important feature of the rituals of certain sects in India today. A scene on a fragment of a faience amulet showing a man beating a drum and people dancing to music seems to suggest from its appearance on the mystical symbol that the dance was ceremonial (Pl. 40). On the amulet from Harappa a man is playing a drum before a tiger, but here again it is impossible to say whether the tiger represents a deity or whether the whole scene is simply an illustration of "music hath charm". Another amulet from the same city shows the cult object invariably associated with the urus bull, with beside it a figure which may be that of a woman dancing; if this interpretation is correct the dance must certainly be ritualistic.

Some musical instruments were also located by the archaeologists who excavated various Indus sites. Also engravings on seals and amulets give us a clue to the variety of musical instruments developed by people belonging to this culture. Dr. S.R. Rao tells us about a stringed musical instrument with bridge and a twang both made of shells found at Lothal. An arched harp probably made of a wooden bracket and metal string is seen on a seal. Castanets, drums, whistles of clay and cymbals were also popular musical instruments of Harappan people. Mackay says:

> It was suggested that dancing was perhaps included amongst the religious rituals but that it had also a secular side is very probable. That dancing was accompanied by music is certain, for an elongated drum with a skin at each end is seen on two of the amulets. Another form of drum or tambourine appears to have hung from the neck of one of the pottery male figurines. A pair of what are thought to be castanets have been found and they probably served to mark the rhythm of the dance as among strolling Arab players today. Also if we are correct in identifying certain signs in the script as harps and lyres we may surmise that at least one musical instrument of this kind was in common use as in Sumer where Wooley has succeeded in restoring remains of several specimens (*Early Indus Civilization*).

At Mohenjodaro hollowed masks with horns were found. Made of baked clay, they seem to have been moulded. Some masks are without horns. One of the masks has a beard which is shown on the chin by marking shallow incised lines. These masks are quite small but cleverly designed. Speaking about a mask with a serene expression, Mackay says: "There can be no doubt that this represents a head of the deity, and of one whose attributes seem to have been beneficent, if we may judge from the expression of the face. In fact, in none of the figures of clay or stone hereto unearthed is such dignity and repose expressed as in this mask."

Dr. Sankalia is also impressed by the peaceful expression of the mask. He remarks: "It reminds me of a similar expression on the faces of Buddhas and Bodhisattvas." These masks might have been used as votive offerings to the Indus deities and also as decorations. Though we have not as yet found a mask big enough for an actor to wear we may not deny its existence because larger terracotta masks were found at Chirand in a later period. We have already seen Mesolithic dancers using masks, and Harappan actors might also have used them. This points at rich dramatic culture of the Indus Civilization.

ISHVARADATTA

Author of the Bhana play Dhurta Vita Samvada. His Bhana finds mention in the Sringarprakasha of Bhojadeva (11th century A.D.) and Kavyanushashana of Hemachandra. In his work the glory of the city of Pataliputra is found mentioned. Probably he was the resident of the city or of Magadha, and wrote his play in the 4th–5th century A.D.

ITIHASA

It is stated in the Natya Shastra of Bharata that the fifth Veda called Natya Veda or science of dramaturgy was created with itihasa—natyakhaym panchamam vedam setihasam karomyaham.

In Vedic literature we find the word Itihasa mentioned several times along with the word Purana. The word can be explained etymologically as iti-ha-asa which means 'so indeed it was'. Hence Itihasa means a traditional account of former events or thus indeed it was according to tradition.

Itihasa contains legends as well as historical tales.

Nirukta says: iti haivamasiditi yah kathyate sa itihasa. It thus happened says the Itihasa.

In his commentary on Vishnupurana Shridharswami says: Itihasa is a compendium of tales about the past happenings, puravrittakatha, which contains lessons or advice about dharma, artha, kama and moksha. Bharata too says that itihasa is the account of the past carrying in it instructions about duty, wealth, enjoyment of pleasure, which forms the basis of Natya Veda.

The Mahabharata says that Vedas could be understood, explained and expanded with the help of Itihasa and Purana—itihasapuranabhya vedam samupambrunayet.

In the Sankhyayana Sutra, Asvalayana Sutra and the Shatapatha Brahmana we are told that a cycle of stories spread over ten days used to be recited to entertain the king performing Horse-sacrifice. On the eighth day the itihasa was narrated. Shatapatha Brahmana says:

On the eighth day he (the singer who sings to lute—vinaganaginas) tells the story which begins with Matsya Sammada. As his men were the creatures of water, as these were present, he teaches the Matsyas (fishes) or the fishermen by this story. He then says, 'The Itihasa Veda is the Veda, this is the Veda', and recites an Itihasa.

Ancient Itihasa works of Vedic times are lost to posterity. However the best surviving itihasa work is the Mahabharata. Mahabharata is called itihasa in its text. Mahabharata stories formed the thematic base of many dramatic works in Sanskrit and regional languages.

JAGANNATHAVALLABHA NATAKA

A musical Sanskrit play with five acts full of beautiful songs written by Ramananda Rai at the command of king Prataparudradeva of Puri in the 16th century A.D.

Ramananda Rai was son of Bhavananda Rai and a devotee of Krishna. He later became the disciple of Chaitanya Mahaprabhu. This play was very much liked by Mahaprabhu. It is said in the Madyalila of Chaitanya Charitamrita that Mahaprabhu was every day entertained by the recitation of works of Chandidas and Vidyapati, Jayadeva's Gita Govinda and songs from the play by Ramananda Rai.

It is said in the Chaitanya Charitamrita that Ramananda Rai trained two Devadasis of Jagannatha temple for enacting female roles in the play. It says that Ramananda Rai used to bathe and massage two young Deva Kanyas whom he kept in his house. He taught them how to dance, delineate the meaning of the songs through acting, how to express various emotions and basic sentiments through eyes and movements of body and face. Rai used to do the make-up of the girls himself.

The play is based on the romance and love of Radha and Krishna. In the fifth act there is an erotic description of physical intimacy of the lovers. The play betrays influence of Jayadeva's Gita Govinda, particularly on its beautiful songs.

JAMBAVATI KALYANAM

Written by the 16th century Vijayanagara king Krishnadevara and enacted during Chaitra Mahotsava of god Virupaksha. It portrays the story of Krishna's marriage with Jambavati and his begetting the famous jewel Syamantaka mani.

JAMBUDWIPA

Ancient India is referred to as Jambudwipa in the Puranas and Bharata's Natyashastra. It is believed that the earth is divided into seven islands surrounded by seven seas.

They are:

Jambudwipa (surrounded by salty sea—Ksharsamudra)
Lakshadwipa (surrounded by sugar-cane juice sea, Ikshurasa Samudra)
Shalmalidwipa (surrounded by sea of wine, Surasamudra)
Kushadwipa (surrounded by sea of butter, Ghritasamudra)
Kraunchadwipa (surrounded by sea of curd, Dadhisamudra)
Shakadwipa (surrounded by sea of milk, Kshirasamudra)
Pushkardwipa (surrounded by sweet water sea, Swadusamudra)

According to Puranic geography in every dwipa there are seven mountains and seven rivers. Jambudwipa is at the centre and other dwipas surround it.

JANAKIPARINAYA

A seven-act play by the 17th century playwright Ramabhadra, son of Yajnarama and worthy disciple of Balakrishna, based on Rama story. First few acts are devoted to describing Ravana's efforts to get Sita by resorting to disguises and deceptions. But Sita is in love with Rama whom she has seen in dream. She makes the portrait of Rama on the basis of his vision in the dream. Ultimately she marries Rama and furious Ravana abducts her.

In the sixth act a play-within-a-play, Sitaswayamvara, is staged in Ravana's court. It makes Ravana more furious.

Rama rescues Sita by killing Ravana and they return to Ayodhya.

JATRA

Popular musical dramatic form of Bengal. The origin of modern Jatra is traced to a musical dramatic form of the region known as Krishna Jatra of the 16th century. Krishna Jatra was essentially musical rendering of Krishna legend, particularly the Radha-Krishna lore. Gradually other mythological stories from epics, Puranas and sacred writings too were dramatised. For instance Nala-Damayanti Yatra based on the Mahabharata story became immensely popular at the beginning of the 19th century.

Another landmark was Vidyasundar Yatra based on the secular love story. For the first time in this Yatra play along with music dance too was introduced.

Jatra progressed assimilating various influences. University education and rise of English theatre in Bengal too had its impact on Jatra theatre. In imitation of Shakespearean tragedies in their Bengali rendering the Jatra theatre too started staging tragic plays.

Yatra grew under the influence of Calcutta Theatre. Its thematic base got expanded. Social, political issues were portrayed through Jatra plays. Depiction of historical legends too became popular. It was even used as a medium of propaganda of political creeds.

However Yatra retained some of its old popular features such as music and dance, as well as loud and melodramatic acting style. Initially Yatra was a male preserve but gradually women too started joining Jatra troupes.

This vibrant form full of dance, drama and music is tremendously popular in rural as well as urban Bengali masses.

JHANKI

In the Raslila plays of Braj, suddenly stopping the flow of drama, a static tableau is presented, mostly showing Krishna in his divine aspect, with the help of actors. This tableau is known as Jhanki. Jhankies can have a number of themes related to the life of Krishna. Jhanki is a dramatic scene freezed in time, a tableau, by the boys performing Ras plays. It is also described as 'group representation of the most celebrated statues of Krishna and his relatives'. Rasdharis present spectacular Jhankies inspiring awe and reverence for divine cowherd. Jhankies of Radha and Krishna in different statuesque attitudes, as seen in miniature paintings or temples, are very popular. When Jhanki is presented devout members of the audience make money offerings, the collection goes to Ras-mandali.

Jhankies are exhibited in temples and religious establishments on festive occasions such as Janmashtami independent of Raslila plays. Such Jhanki spectacles can be presented with the help of persons acting different roles in it or by arranging cardboard statues.

Jhankies or tableaux vivants of mythological and other figures are described as 'representational art where drama and image worship meet.'

JIVANMUKTI KALYANAM

An allegorical play by the 17th century dramatist Nalla Dikshit whose other name was Bhuminatha. In literary circles he was known as Abhinava-Bhojaraja. He wrote three plays—Subhadraparinaya, Chittavrittikalyanam and Jivanmukti Kalyanam—and also a Bhana named Sringarasarvasva.

In this play abstract metaphysical concepts appear in human form. It depicts attraction between Jiva and Jivanmukti who in the end get married.

JOGIMARA CAVE INSCRIPTION

On the Ramgarh hill in Madhya Pradesh there are two caves known as Sitabenga and Jogimara. In the Jogimara cave there is an interesting inscription which reads:

Sutanuka nama
devadasikyi
Sutanuka nama devadasikyi
tam kamayitha bal(a)naseye
devadinne nama lupadakhe
(Sutanuka by name a devadasi
Sutanuka by name a devadasi
The excellent among young men loved her
Devadinna by name, skilled in sculpture)

The inscription is ascribed to third century B.C. in which we find earliest inscriptional reference to Devadasi. Nearby Sitabenga cave has been described as hill-top cave theatre by the scholars. Sutanuka might have been performing in the Sitabenga cave theatre of the yore.

KALIDASA

Nothing authentic is known about Kalidasa, his life and age, though he is considered as greatest poet and dramatist of India. Some interesting fictitious tales about this literary genius are found recorded in literary works including Bhoja Prabandha by Ballala Kavi written in the 16th century.

However we know for sure that he wrote three plays—Abhijnana Shakuntalam, Malavikagnimitra and Vikramorvashiya—and works of poetry—Raghuvamsha, Kumarasambhava, Meghaduta and Ritusamhara—and one king Vikramaditya was his patron.

Scholars have speculated his time from first century B.C. to 6th century A.D.

In his play Malavikagnimitra Kalidasa has referred to Senapati Pushyamitra Shunga and his horse sacrifice. Pushyamitra was a historical figure. It was he who ended the Maurya empire by slaying king Brihadratha while he was reviewing the army and founded Shunga dynasty. A short Sanskrit inscription from Ayodhya mentions two Ashvamedhas performed by Senapati Pushyamitra and a relative of his who was perhaps ruling there as a viceroy of the Shungas. Some Buddhist works describe Pushyamitra as a veritable enemy of the Buddhist doctrine. In his play Kalidasa has depicted the love of his son Agnimitra, the viceroy of Vidisha, for Malavika, princess of Vidarbha. The play also refers to Vasumitra, the son of Agnimitra, defeating a band of Yavanas on the right bank of river Sindhu when they tried to capture the sacrificial horse of Pushyamitra (*Advanced History of India*). All this happened in the second century B.C. Hence upper limit of the date of Kalidasa can be second century B.C.

Kalidasa is for the first time mentioned by Banabhatta in his Harshacharita in A.D. 620. Aihole inscription of Pulakeshin II of A.D. 634, written by Ravikirti, refers to him by name. This means lower limit of Kalidasa's date is the seventh century A.D.

Most of the scholars agree that Vikramaditya mentioned by Kalidasa is none else but Chandragupta Vikramaditya II of Ujjayani. Hence Kalidasa can be placed at the end of the 4th and at the beginning of the 5th century A.D.

According to a popular legend Kalidasa was an illiterate but handsome lad reared by a herdsman after the death of his parents in his early childhood. A crafty minister of the king of Benares tried to marry his beautiful daughter but she outright rejected him. She wanted to marry an accomplished young man well versed in arts and literature. To avenge his insult the minister presented illiterate Kalidasa in the court of the king of Benares as a great Pundit eminently suitable for the princess.

Impressed by the handsome looks of Kalidasa princess readily married him. But on the very first day of their married life she found out that he was an absolute fool.

The princess threw him out of her palace. Kalidasa went to the temple of Kali and wept profusely. He then decided to end his life. Taking pity on him the goddess conferred all vidyas on him.

He went back to his wife and recited beautiful poems composed by him due to the grace of goddess Kali. She was immensely pleased but he did not stay with her any further.

Kalidasa continued his wayward life. Legends say he became fond of wine and women but his reputation as a literary genius started spreading all over the country.

According to Ceylonese tradition Kalidasa went to Ceylon on the invitation of his friend Kumaradasa. There he was murdered by a courtesan with whom he stayed for night. Kumaradasa, the friend of Kalidasa, is identified with the king of the same name who ruled in early part of the sixth century. The king was patron of arts and literature and author of the epic Janakiharana.

Levi terms this tradition as reliable and Keith says it is totally without value.

Tradition associates him with Ujjain where he staged his plays. Whatever may be the truth one thing is certain that Kalidasa penned literary masterpieces and his play Abhijnana Shakuntalam charmed international audiences.

KAMADEVA

Handsome god of love, passion, lust, carnal desire, youth and beauty, frequently mentioned in the dramatic literature.

He is extolled in the Vedic literature as first-born. Kamo jajne prathamo, says Atharvaveda. In the Rig Veda he is referred to as manaso retah or seed of mind. The Dharmasamhita of Shivapurana says—kamah samkalpa eva hi. Samkalpa means notion, idea, conception or desire formed in the mind. Kama is the source of samkalpa.

Also known as Madana, Ananga, Manasija, Makaradhwaja this god of love and lust was born from the mind of Lord Brahma. The name of his beautiful wife is Rati. Kama rides on parrot, carries in his hand a sugarcane bow having bowstring made of line of bees, with arrows made of fragrant flowers he shoots at men and women arousing in their hearts the feeling of love.

He is also known as Panchasayaka or one having five arrows. These arrows are made of flowers—blue lotus, jasmine, mango blossom, champak and shirisha.

Vasanta is his friend. He is most active in Vasanta ritu, say the poets.

On the request of gods once he tried to arouse passion in the mind of Shiva lost in deep meditation by shooting his arrows at him. Angry Shiva opened his third eye and burnt him to ashes. This myth about Kama is poetically depicted by Kalidasa in his long poem, Kumarasambhava. Kama was reborn as Pradyumna, son of Krishna.

In the Vishnudharmottara Purana we find information about how to make an image of Kamadeva. The book says that his beautiful image should have eight arms. His four hands should carry lotus, bow, arrow and conch respectively and other four should be shown as placed on the breasts of his four beautiful consorts Rati, Priti, Shakti and Madashakti standing by his side. His eyes should have drunken look. His flag should carry the emblem of crocodile whose face should be made of five arrows.

Brahmanda Purana says that Kama is presiding deity of Apsaras or nymphs and seasons. Hemadri enjoins courtesans to worship Kama and they should perform 'anangadana' to appease him.

Shrines were raised in the honour of Kamadeva. An interesting terracotta plaque showing Kamadeva is kept in the Mathura Museum. In this plaque one man is shown lying on the ground at the feet of the god of love as if conquered by him.

Some scholars are of the opinion that this plaque depicts the ancient love story of fisherman Shurpaka and princess Kumudvati. According to the story Kamadeva made unresponsive fisherman fall in love with the beautiful princess.

Shudraka in his Bhana play Padmaprabhrutakam mentions a play, a Prakarana, named Kumudvati Prakarana, based on the love story of princess and fisherman in which Kamadeva played a major role.

In the Bhana play Ubhayabhisarika playwright Vararuchi mentions a play Madanaradhana which courtesans performed in the temple of Bhagavan Narayana Vishnu. The title of the play clearly suggests that the story of the play must have been related to some legend of Kamadeva.

This means courtesans used to stage plays based on the mythology of Kamadeva.

Several references to the temples of Kamadeva are found in ancient and medieval literature. In the first act of Bhasa's play Charudatta there is a reference to Kamadevayatana situated in Ujjain. Shudraka in Mricchakatika says that a garden was attached to this temple.

This temple is again mentioned in the Bhana play Padataditakam. In the courtyard of the temple there was a flagstaff of Kama. It was known as makarayashti because on the flag the emblem of makara, crocodile, was painted. Courtesans used to circumambulate this makarayashti after offering worship at the temple. It seems that this temple was situated near Vesha or locality of courtesans. In the same play there is a reference to the painters who were painting the flag of the temple of Kamadeva.

Again this temple of Kamadeva, Kamadevayatana, is mentioned in the Bhana play Padmaprabhrutakam by Shudraka. In the play we see courtesans offering worship to the deity.

Madana Mahotsava, joyous festival full of singing, dancing, music celebrated by drunken men and women in the honour of Kamadeva is described elaborately in Harsha's play Ratnavali. This boisterous bacchanal festival full of drunken revelry lifts up the spirit of people to such an extent that, as Damodaragupta in his Kuttanimatam says, even women of good families, kulavadhus, start hurling obscenity at each other overcoming all their usual shyness.

This was the festival of Vasanta ritu. In the Kamasutra it is called Suvasantaka. Commentator Yashodhara says Madanotsava and Suvasantaka are the names of the same festival—suvasanto madanotsava.

In the Ratnavali entire ritual of worshipping the image of Kama placed under the Ashoka tree is described. Observing the ritual heroine Ratnavali in the guise of Sagarika exclaims that in the antahpura of her father the painting of the Kamadeva is worshipped.

In the Dashakumaracharita we are told that daughter of king of Malva, Avantisundari, worshipped Kamadeva in the form of a heap of sand under the mango tree. Bhavishya Purana says that on the day of shukla trayodashi of Vasanta ritu images of Kama and Rati should be drawn with red-lead and worshipped with great fanfare. In the night the programme of dancing, singing, play-acting should be organised at the temple of Kamadeva.

In the Bhana plays Padmaprabhrutakam and Padataditakam prayers are offered to Kamadeva. In the prologue of the play Karpuramanjiri we find Sutradhara offering prayer to the god of love.

Sten Konow in his *Indian Drama* has referred to some play woven around legends related to Kamadeva. He writes:

'Modern author, Venkataraghava Acharya, composed one Manmathavijaya (victory of Kamadeva) in five acts. The

Kama-legend became treated in five-act drama Rati-manmatha-nataka by Jagannatha. A modern legend of Kama—how he after being reduced to ashes was born again as the son of the god Sauriraja Perumal— has been treated in the anonymous five-act drama Arthapanchaka Nataka; there occurs also the six-act drama Pradyumnanandiya of Venkata Acharya, son of Raghunatha and the author of Vishvagunadarsha.

KAMALINI KALAHANSAM

A romantic play in the Natika mode by the 16th century playwright Rajachudamani Yajnanarayana Dixit. It was staged during the reign of Chola king Maharaja Raghunatha on the occasion of festival held in the honour of Lord Vishnu at Anantasanpur. It is a love story of Kalahansa and Kamalini. Kamalini lives in the harem of Kalahansa. Kalahansa's queen creates obstacles but ultimately the lovers unite.

KAMALINI RAJAHANSAM

A romantic play in five acts written by an ascetic Purnasarasvati who used to live in his monastery in Trichur in Kerala in the 14th century. It is based on the love story of Rajahansa and Kamalini.

KAMASUTRA

Extensive treatise on love, an erotica, written by a celibate ascetic Vatsyayana in the third century A.D.

The history of Kamashastric literature is given by Vatsyayana in the opening chapter of his work. He says:

'In the beginning, the Lord of Beings, Prajapati, in one hundred thousand chapters laid down rules for regulating their existence with regard to Dharma (acquisition of religious merit), Artha (acquisition of wealth and property, material things), and Kama (love, pleasure, sexual gratification).

Some of these commandments, namely those which treated of Dharma, were separately written by Swayambhu Manu; those that related to Artha were compiled by Brihaspati; and those that referred to Kama were expounded by Nandi, the follower of Mahadeva, in one thousand chapters.

Now these 'Kama Sutra' (Aphorisms on Love), written by Nandi in one thousand chapters, were reproduced by Shvetaketu, son of Uddvalaka, in an abbreviated form in five hundred chapters, and this work was again similarly reproduced in an abridged form, in one hundred and fifty chapters, by Babhravya, an inhabitant of the Punchala (South of Delhi) country. These one hundred and fifty chapters were then put together under seven heads or parts named severally

1. Sadharana (general topics)
2. Samprayogika (embrace, etc.)
3. Kanya Samprayuktaka (union of males and females)

4. Bharyadhikarika (on one's own wife)
5. Paradika (on the wives of other people)
6. Vaishika (on courtesans)
7. Aupamishadika (on the arts of seduction, tonics, medicines, etc.).

The sixth part of the last work was separately expounded by Dattaka at the request of the public women of Pataliputra, and in the same way Charayana explained the first part of it. The remaining parts, viz. the second, third, fourth, fifth and seventh were each separately expounded by Suvarnanabha, Ghotakamukha, Gonardia, Gonikaputra and Kuchumara respectively.

Thus the work being written in parts by different authors was almost unobtainable and, as the parts which were expounded by Dattaka and others treated only of the particular branches of the subject to which each part related, and moreover as the original work of Babhravya was difficult to be mastered on account of its length, Vatsyayana, therefore, composed his work in a small volume as an abstract of the whole of the works of the above named authors' (KS: Burton and Arbuthnot).

In short Vatsyayana's Kamasutra is a kind of exhaustive digest covering all the topics related to the science of love discussed by different authors in the past.

The work comprises seven Adhikaranas or chapters divided into many sub-chapters or Adhyayas.

The headings of the main chapters are—About the Shastra, Love Play and Sexual Union, Courtship and Marriage, The Wives, Seducing the Wives of Others, The Courtesans, Secret Love and Sexual Power.

Kamasutra is considered as a great classic, a masterpiece. It has deeply influenced various aspects of Indian art, literature and culture. Sexual postures described in this work are found sculpted on various temples belonging to medieval period in particular. Illustrated manuscripts of Kamasutra are also found, particularly in Orissa.

Drama along with singing, dancing, music and painting is mentioned in the list of sixtyfour arts given in this book. Kamasutra has deeply influenced the dramatic literature of India. Playwrights like Kalidasa, Shudraka, Bhavabhuti betray the influence of Kamasutra. Bhavabhuti mentions the work by name in his play Malati Madhava which he followed while writing the text of the play. Name of Dattaka, an authority on harlotry, is found mentioned in Bhana plays of Gupta era.

Characters like Ganikas, Vitas, Chetas, Vidushakas, Pithamardas found in the dramas are defined in the Kamasutra. It speaks volumes about the lives of Nagarakas or citizens of ancient India. It speaks about the tradition of organising dramatic entertainments, samaj, in the temple of Saraswati, goddess of learning and arts, on festive occasions and rewarding actors and dancers for entertaining people.

Kamasutra says that it is easy for a man to meet his beloved while attending dramatic shows. He says while watching the play he should sit by her side and try to flirt and seduce her. When audiences are engrossed in watching the play he should quietly slip away with her to make love.

Kamasutra says that girls like the men interested in dramatic arts. After marriage husband should, for three days, abstain from love making and instead should take his wife to see dramatic performances.

It also refers to the tradition of staging plays at the houses of courtesans or taking them for picnic and watch them performing plays. It also speaks of puppet theatre.

Kamasutra had a profound influence on Indian dramatic literature.

KAMSA VADHA

Lord Krishna killed tyrant king of Mathura, Kamsa, son of Ugrasena, who was son-in-law of Emperor Jarasandha of Magadha. He gave his sister Devaki in marriage to his friend Vasudeva. Frightened by the prophecy that their eighth son will kill him Kamsa put them behind bars. Krishna was born as eighth son of Devaki in prison but Vasudeva smuggled him out and entrusted the child to his friend Nanda, a cowherd chieftain. Krishna along with his brother Balarama grew in pastoral Braj and killed several demons sent by Kamsa to destroy them. As a last resort Kamsa arranged wrestling competition and invited them both with the intention of killing them. But instead Krishna killed Kamsa and his two wrestlers.

Mahabharata mentions Kamsa so also a number of Purana works. Bhasa wrote a play Balacharita based on the early life of Krishna and his killing of Kamsa. The story also finds mention in the Buddhist Ghat Jataka and Kautilya's Arthashastra.

Patanjali in the second century B.C. wrote a work on grammar, the Mahabhashya. It is believed that he was an incarnation of Shesha, a great serpent on whose coils Lord Vishnu sleeps in the ocean of milk. He was born at the place called Gonarda which possibly is Gonda in Uttar Pradesh. The legend says that Lord Shiva showed his famous Tandava dance to him at Chidambaram and asked him to write commentary on Panini's Ashtadhyayi.

In the Mahabhashya Patanjali has mentioned three ways of presenting the story of Kamsa Vadha. One is enactment of the story by actors called Shobhanika. Another by narrating it through painting, Chitra, and the third two groups of narrators, granthikas, colouring their faces with red and black, calling themselves as adherents of Kamsa and Krishna respectively, narrating the story taking turns.

Patanjali mentions interesting stages of development of theatrical art in India. The ballad singing gave rise to two modes. Out of ballad singing drama emerged and also there emerged a dramatic style of narration in which paintings were used to illustrate the narrative. All the three forms existed side by side. Granthikas were narrators, ballad singers, Shobhanikas the actors and though artists narrating the stories by showing chitras or paintings are not mentioned by name they were known as Mankhas at the time of Patanjali.

The scholars who are reluctant to place Bhasa before the commencement of Christian era consider the reference to the enactment of the story of Kamsa Vadha found in Patanjali's work as the earliest mention of drama and Ashvaghosha's plays as earliest extant Sanskrit dramatic works.

KANISHKA

Greatest of the Kushana rulers in India whose capital was Purushpura (Peshawar) in ancient Gandhara. It is believed that he ascended the throne in A.D. 78 though some scholars contend that he became the king in the second quarter of the second century. Kanishka is known for his strong inclination towards Buddhism and built a great stupa at Peshawar. Buddhists virtually consider him as a second Ashoka because of his contribution to Buddhism. According to Hieun Tsang the Fourth Buddhist Council for systematising and codifying Buddhist texts was convened during his reign. Kashmir, the whole of Punjab, the valley of Ganga up to Patna came under his rule. According to Buddhist sources the king of Pataliputra surrendered to him the alms-bowl of Buddha, the poet and philosopher Ashvaghosha and a marvellous cock.

Buddhism till his times was averse to making the images of Buddha in human form and was confined to worshipping his symbols. However during his reign the images of Buddha were made for the first time in Gandhara and Mathura. We find the icon of Buddha on his coins also.

Second revolutionary thing that happened during his reign was the beginning of Buddhist drama. Buddhism had a strong reservation about dramatic art but his court poet Ashvaghosha wrote not only a Buddhist epic, Buddhacharita, but a few dramas on Buddhist themes including the Sariputra Prakarana.

In his play Pratima Nataka Bhasa mentions a hall, Pratimagriha where the idols of the dead kings of Ishvaku dynasty were kept. The keeper of this hall was termed as Devakulik. Probably the other name of this hall was Devakula.

About fifteen kilometres from the city of Mathura there is a village named Mat. When a mound called Tokari Tila in the village was excavated a building, described in the inscription as Devakula was found. From there images of kings including Kanishka were found. His headless image exuding imperial power with an inscription which can be translated as 'The great king, king of kings, His Majesty Kanishka' cut across the bottom of the mantle he is wearing is kept in the Govt. Museum of Mathura.

KAPALIKA

An ancient tantric Shaiva sect which gained prominence during medieval period. Since early seventh century the Kapalikas started appearing in Sanskrit plays as characters. The earliest play in which Kapalika figured is a farce, Mattavilasprahasana, by Pallava king of Kanchi named Mahendravikramavarman.

In fact Kapalika Satyasoma is the central character of the play. Mattavilasprahasana is the first and only play which revolves round Kapalika.

Smearing the ash of burnt corpses, wearing around the neck the garland of bones and holding in their hands the begging bowls of human skulls the Kapalika mendicants used to roam about with their female companions. They freely indulged in kayasadhana and considered ritual drinking of wine and sexual intercourse with beautiful women as ideal means of salvation.

Satyasoma, the Kapalika of the farce Mattavilasprahasana, is shown moving with his female companion Devasoma fully drunk. He praises Pinakapani Bhagavan Shiva for showing an easy way to liberation through drinking wine from the mouth of beloved. To him drinking den is as sacred as Yajnashala.

Kapalikas were hated and feared for their association with cremation ground and terrible ritual practices. In the play Malati Madhava by the eighth century playwright Bhavabhuti we come across a terrible Kapalika named Aghoraghanta and his female consort Kapalakundala. Kapalakundala appears in fiercely blazing hideous garb wearing the garland of human skulls flying through the air in search of a beautiful woman for ritual sacrifice.

She procures such a woman and takes her to her guru Kapalika Aghoraghanta living in the temple of goddess Chamunda or Karala situated in the cremation ground filled with fiends and evil-spirits. After offering worship to the goddess they proceed to sacrifice the woman, none else but heroine of the play Malati, who is saved in the nick of time, by her lover Madhava.

Meanwhile when people come to know about the kidnapping of Malati they suspect it to be the act of Kapalika Aghoraghanta. The angry mob encircles the temple of Chamunda. Ultimately Madhava kills the Kapalika.

Again in the play Prabodhachandrodaya by the eleventh century playwright Krishnamisra Yati we meet a Kapalika Somasiddhanta. Explaining the nature of his sect he says that we, the Kapalikas, wear the garland of human skulls and bones, eat from the bowl of human skull, with eyes clear we see Ishvara or god as one and separate from the world at the same time. We perform human sacrifices, make offering of human flesh in ritual fire to appease Mahabhairava and in the end drink wine.

He further says that there is no pleasure without sensual enjoyment. By embracing his beloved, a symbol of Parvati, Kapalika freely moves around. 'The Kapalikas' ideal of salvation was to become like Shiva and enjoy the pleasures of love with consort as beautiful as Parvati.'

He criticises Jain and Buddhist monks whom he meets. After being embraced by voluptuous female Kapalika, monks of both the sects get terribly excited and ask the Kapalika to initiate them in the Mahabhairavanushashana so that they could freely enjoy wine and women.

In the play Karpuramanjiri by the tenth century poet Rajashekhara we meet a Kaula Kapalika named Bhairavananda.

Describing the Kaula tenets Dr. Devangana Desai writes: 'Kaulas believed in trikamata which consists in indulgence in drink and meat, and worship of Shiva with wine in company of a female partner sitting on the left during the rites. The Kaula worshipper played the role of Shiva as united with Parvati and exhibited the Yoni Mudra. Somadeva in his Yashastilaka and Yashapala in his Moharajaparajaya describe the free practices of Kaulacharyas. Kshemendra in the 11th century caricatures a Kaula guru who indulges in sexual practices with a Kayastha housewife amidst a midnight orgy consisting of strange characters.'

Bhairavananda says he knows not tantra, mantra or dhyana and yoga. He drinks wine, sexually enjoys women and achieves Moksha. Widows and passionate women initiated in the cult are our consorts. Drinking wine, eating meat, sleeping on the bed of animal hide is our beautiful Kaula dharma. Only Uma and her beloved husband Shiva have said that liberation can be achieved by resorting to drinking wine and performing intercourse with women—Mokshah samam sura take lisurarasai.

Bhairavananda performs many magical feats and constructs a temple of Chamunda in the garden of the queen.

We are told in the play Malati Madhava by Bhavabhuti that Sriparvata in the Andhra country was the centre of Kapalikas.

KARAYILA

A popular form of folk entertainment of Himachal Pradesh. The Karayila performance is replete with enactment of small skits, farces, revues and burlesques with social satire being its core theme, and humour its main content.

There is no written script for Karayila revues and farces. Dialogues are mostly in verse which are rendered in folk musical modes. Farces such as Churanwale ka swang, Buddha ka swang, Jogi-jogan ka swang, swang of Sahib and Mem, Pilpili saheb ka swang are very popular. Skits are based on the quarrel between husband and wife laced with rustic humour.

The performance opens with the playing on musical instruments. Next item is dance of Chandravali.

After this Sadhu ka swang is presented. Sadhu means ascetics who have relinquished the world in search of the divine. Several actors in the guise of Sadhus emerge on the scene and making their way through audiences they reach the performing arena. The Sadhus discuss many spiritual and metaphysical issues as per the tenets of their respective sects and traditions. However at times these dialogues take humorous turn due to the intervention of jester who is ever present in the performing arena.

After this swang is over other skits, farces are presented interspersed with folk songs and dances to entertain the audiences. In the centre of the performing arena a bonfire is lit which provides light and heat to endure cold winter nights of Himachal Pradesh.

KARNABHARAM

A one-act play by Bhasa based on the episode from the epic Mahabharata related to the gift of his impenetrable armour and auspicious ear ornaments, kavacha and kundala, by Karna to king of gods Indra in the guise of Brahmin.

After the fall of Guru Drona in the battlefield of Kurukshetra during Bharata war Karna, friend of prince Duryodhana, is ointed as a general of the Kaurava army.

When the play opens we see Karna and his charioteer king Shalya proceeding towards battlefield. Karna is depressed, sad and disturbed. His mind is burdened with the fact that the Pandavas with whom he was going to fight are his brothers and mother Kunti has requested him not to harm them. On his way he tells Shalya how he by using deceptive strategy acquired the knowledge of weaponry from legendary Brahmin warrior Parashurama and how, when exposed, the Guru Parashurama cursed him that his knowledge of weaponry would fail him in the battlefield.

However Karna says bravely that the efforts of the warrior in the battlefield never go waste. If victorious he gets fame and success and if defeated and has to embrace death he gets heaven. Bhasa puts the philosophy of the Gita in the mouth of Karna.

Karna asks his charioteer to take him where Arjuna, his brother and arch-enemy, is. On his way he sees Indra appearing before him in the guise of a Brahmin. Indra asks the generous Karna for his armour and ear ornaments which he gladly gives without thinking of consequences in the face of protest from Shalya. Indra pleased by his generosity gifts him shakti or powerful missile.

Thus we see Karna demoralised by the revelation of the secret of his birth, deceived by god moving towards the battlefield, his ultimate destination. In this play Karna rises to the level of tragic hero of Greek plays.

The episode related to the gift of armour to Indra occurs in the Adi and Vana Parvas of Mahabharata. The story of Parashurama's curse is found in the Shanti Parva. Bhasa brought them together in his play very effectively which has a character of Greek tragedy.

Karnabharam is one of the best plays of Bhasa.

KARNASUNDARI

A romantic play in four acts by the famous 11th-12th century poet Bilhana depicting a love story of a Chalukya king and a beautiful daughter of Vidyadhara king named Karnasundari.

Bilhana, a Brahmin of Kaushika gotra, was born to Jeshtha Kalasha and Nagadevi at Khanmukha near Pravarpur in Kashmir. He left Kashmir in his young age and wandered all over India. Ultimately he settled in the court of Chalukya king of Karnataka, Vikramanka. His works Vikramankadeva-charita, an epic, and Chaurapanchashika, erotic short poem, are very famous apart from his play Karnasundari.

The play Karnasundari was composed for staging at the Yatra Mahotsava of Anhilwad at the close of the 11th century. Probably the play was written to compliment Chalukya king Karnadeva Trailokyamalla of Anhilwad on his marriage to Miyanalladevi, daughter of Karnata king Jayakeshin.

Hero sees Karnasundari in his dream and then in a painting. He desires to marry this harem beauty but jealous queen puts obstacles in their union. Ultimately surmounting all obstacles the lovers unite in the end.

KARPURACHARITA BHANA

A humorous one act-play in Bhana form by the 12th-13th century playwright Vatsaraja who was minister of Chandella king of Kalanjara, Paramardideva, and his son Trailokyavarmadeva.

The play narrates the story or Charita of a knave and cheat (dhurta) known as Karpuraka who is a skilled gambler, in his own words, as is the style and format of Bhana plays. Defining the nature of Bhana plays the Sahitya Darpana says: Bhanah syad dhurtachari to nanavasthantartmaka. After all says Vishvanatha Bhana is a story of a dhurta!

Karpuraka appears on the stage and praises the art of cheating or Mayavidya. He says without resorting to it Rama would not have been able to kill Vali, Indra would not have been able to make love to Ahalya and Vishnu would never have succeeded in subduing Bali.

Karpuraka is in love with a beautiful courtesan Vilasavati. He is a devotee of Bhagavan Manibhadra whom he refers as one of the forms of Shiva. Manibhadra is a famous Yaksha, next to Kubera in rank. One ancient image of Yaksha Manibhadra is housed in the Gwalior Museum. This establishes the fact that in central India, where the playwright lived, Yaksha worship was prevalent at his time too. Karpuraka refers to the temple of Manibhadra—Manibhadrasya-aayatanam—situated in his city.

In the Mahabharata Manibhadra is described as dhanada or giver of wealth, money. The Dipavali is known as Yaksharatri and gambling is ritually prescribed on the day. It is also believed that Yakshas like offering of wine. Probably because of this gambler Karpuraka who was fond of wine approached Manibhadra for gaining his favours. However in his speech Karpuraka describes Manibhadra as one who vanquishes opponents of his devotees. He wanted the favour of Yaksha in vanquishing his own enemies.

However he is quite angry with Manibhadra because despite his worship and offerings—puja and upahara—the Yaksha has not in return given him what he wanted. Hence Karpuraka asks Yaksha to return the offerings earlier made by him.

But within a few days he liquidates his opponents by his clever stratagem and ascribes his success to the grace of Bhagavan Manibhadra. In his monologue gambler and cheat Karpuraka tells the story of his victory over opponents in order to reach his beloved Vilasavati without any difficulty and hindrance.

KARPURAMANJIRI

A Prakrit poetic drama written by tenth century playwright and aesthete Rajashekhara depicting the love story of king Chandrapal and princess Karpuramanjiri in four acts.

There is very little story. The play is filled with titillating and poetic description of physical charms of voluptuous heroine, Karpuramanjiri, the description of Vasanta ritu, celebration of various festivals and rituals, even regular poetry reading sessions. Karpuramanjiri is a long romantic poetic composition having the format of a drama.

Most interesting character of the play is tantric or magician, Bhairavananda, belonging to tantric Kaula-Kapalika cult. Elucidating the philosophy of his cult and its ritual practices he says that tantra, mantra, dhyana and jnana are irrelevant. Drinking of wine and intercourse with women is the only way to achieve liberation or moksha. The widows, women cruel and initiated in tantric rituals are our consorts in ritual practices. We eat meat, drink wine, beg for food and sleep on the piece of animal hide. Who would say that Kaula cult is not alluring?

His influence in the royal household increases so much that the queen Vibhramalekha becomes his disciple. In the pleasure garden of the queen, under the banyan tree, the tantric got constructed a temple of fierce goddess Chamunda who residing in turbulent fury that rages at the time of dissolution of the universe by Mahakala Shiva drinks from the skull of Brahma the wine that is blood of the living creatures.

In the first act Bhairavananda brings on the stage beautiful princess Karpuramanjiri while she was taking bath in her palace bathroom in the city of Vidarbha. The young beauty wearing only a single piece of garment, fully drenched stands on the stage exposing the contours of her shapely body through wet cloth clinging to her person. The sight inspires the king to poetically describe the charms of the bathing beauty passages after passages.

Then again in the second act there is long and quite erotic description of Karpuramanjiri enjoying the sport of swinging, hindolanalila. Due to the movement of the swing and the pleasantly blowing wind the cloth of the heroine does not quite remain in place and her limbs are exposed to the gaze of the king who describes the scene poetically.

It is believed that trees respond to quickening touch of beautiful maidens and start blooming. By embrace of beautiful woman a Kuravaka tree, by her glance a Tilaka tree and by being kicked an Ashoka tree starts blooming. In general this ritual involving women and tree is called dohada. In a number of Sanskrit plays we find this ritual of dohada being performed by the heroine. Karpuramanjiri too is no exception. In the second act we find Karpuramanjiri performing this delightful ritual in respect of Kuravaka, Tilaka and Ashoka trees and king watching it from behind the tree.

In the third act the king and Karpuramanjiri get an opportunity to meet. On knowing that angry queen is coming to rebuke the lovers Karpuramanjiri quickly enters into a secret tunnel. The queen closes the passages of the tunnel and deputes guards so that Karpuramanjiri remains confined to the tunnel.

In the fourth act we see the celebration of the Vatasavitri Vrata or Vatasavitri Mahotsava. As a part of the festival we see various dance performances including Charchari dance, Dandaras dance, tribal barbarous dance of Pulinda tribe, terrible and frightening dance of women wearing the masks of female fiends, holding in the hands human flesh, howling and yelling like jackals, and performing smashanabhinaya or acting like ghosts in cemetery, circular dance that Yoginis perform known as Yoginivalayanartanakeli.

After the dance performances are over a female attendant of the queen approaches the king and tells him that the queen wishes to perform his marriage with princess Ghanasaramanjiri, daughter of king Chandrasena of Lata country because according to the prophecy of astrologers who would marry Ghanasaramanjiri would become universal monarch or chakravarti king. Bhairavananda presents Karpuramanjiri as Ghanasaramanjiri who is married to the king.

The play is poetry, song, dance anything but a play. It is a long ode to female beauty which in the play is symbolised by princess Karpuramanjiri.

Playwright Rajashekhara was deeply in love with his beautiful wife Avantisundari born in the Chauhan family. It was a inter-caste marriage—Rajashekhara being a Yayavar Brahmin and Avantisundari a Kshatriya girl. The play, according to prologue, was staged to please Avantisundari.

KATHAK

A North Indian form of classical dance known for its technical virtuosity as well as for delineation of the moods of Bhakti and Sringar, devotion and love, in a style at once lyrical and refined.

The Kathaks are mentioned in the epic Mahabharata along with story-tellers and rhapsodists such as sutas and pauranikas in the Arjunavanavasa section of the Adiparva.

In his commentary on Patanjali's Mahabhashya the tenth century writer Kaiyata says that granthikas mentioned by Patanjali are the same as Kathakas— granthikeshv iti kathaeshva ity arthah.

In the eleventh century work Kathasaritsagara by Somadeva there is a mention of one kathaka Sangataka who entertained the king Sahasranika by telling him a long love story.

When Kathakas started using mime, body movements, gesture language there evolved a dance form named Kathak. Kathakas performed in temples and sang the songs of Krishna.

In Braj region Kathak further evolved into a dance-drama form called Raslila. It is believed that Narayana Bhatta of Chaitanya sect evolved Raslila with the help of a dancer who was nritya-gana-nipuna. Probably he belonged to the Kathak class.

During Muslim rule the art of Kathak got royal patronage and it was adopted by dancing girls as a means of entertaining their patrons. Its nritya or pure dance became more intricate and bhava darshan more refined and subtle.

Nabab Wajid Ali Shah contributed significantly in the evolution of Kathak. He composed a number of plays known as Rahas and adopted Kathak style of dance to produce them as dance-dramas. The famous operatic work Indersabha belongs to this tradition.

Lucknow, Jaipur, Banaras emerged as great centres of the art of Kathak dance flouting their own peculiar styles. It imbibed Muslim influence and achieved a beautiful synthesis. Some Kathak dancers joined the Nautanki troupes that sprang in north India and enriched its texture.

Generally Kathak is a solo performance with musical instruments Tabla and Sarangi in attendance. The beautiful lyrics and compositions in Brajbhasha, Urdu or Hindi are taken up for performance. Famous Kathak dancer Bindadin Maharaj who 'endowded the technique with new forms, variety and vitality' composed lyrics in different formats for dancers.

Kathak is a very popular classical dance form of North India.

KATHAKALI

A spectacular pageant of dance, drama and music showcasing the mystique world of sacred mythology—that is Kathakali. It evolved as a dance-drama of great visual appeal in Kerala in the 17th century A.D.

It is said that the Raja of Kottarakkara requested the Zamorin of Calicut to send his famed troupe of Krishnattam dance-drama to perform at his palace. The request was turned down because Krishnattam plays were performed only in the precincts of the Krishna temple at Guruvayur. The Raja then himself wrote a cycle of plays in people's language, Malayalam, based on the epic Ramayana. The performances of these plays became famous as Ramanattam. And this was the beginning of the dance-drama form which later became famous as Kathakali.

Kathakali evolved under the influence of earlier classical, folk as well as ritualistic dramatic forms of Kerala such as Kutiyattam, Krishnattam, Mudiyettu, Teyyam. The martial art of Kerala, Kalariyapattu, contributed significantly to the development of physical culture of actors. Kalariya techniques helped the actor to fine tune his body and gain control over his muscles. The controlled movement of facial muscles, the eyes, swift and graceful limb movements, stamina and vigour for acrobatic jumps and whirls were gifts to actors given by Kalariya exercises.

Like physical acting—mudras and dance movements—the aharya or costume and make-up is the most significant part of Kathakali performance. Kathakali theatre is known for its most decorative, elegant and imposing costumes as well as equally ornate, multi-coloured facial make-up based on carefully devised patterns of green, red, black and white in main. The Kathakali colour scheme of facial make-up relates to inner nature of the character. By merely looking at the character on the stage you can immediately know the type of person he is—good, bad or stark evil. The face to be coloured is framed in a border of rice paste or chutti creating an illusion of mask.

E. Bharata Iyer thus describes the principal types—The Paccha (green) generally speaking represents virtuous and noble characters like Krishna, Arjuna, Nala and Rama. A white chutti (rice paste) terraced and bow-like in shape is built on either side of the face running from the chin to ear close to the jaw bone; its glistening white, acting as a brilliant frame and foil to the green on the face, to deep black of the eyes and brows and to the red of the lips.

In Kathi category the prevailing green is shot with red twisted upward patch and a nose-ball attached to the tip of the nose. The type represents characters like Ravana, Shishupala and Duryodhana who, though highly accomplished and heroic, were bent on evil, arrogant and self-willed.

The Chokanna thadi, red beard, is so called because of flaming red beard worn by this type. The face is coloured red and shot with black (the colours that are expressive of fury and low passion—tamasic) acutely demarcated by brilliant white lines and dots. The tip of the nose and the forehead have snout-like protuberance imparting a beastly savagery to the face. This is an extraordinarily fierce, nevertheless, the most impressive figure on the Kathakali stage and represents characters like Dusshasana and Bakasura. Bali and Sugriva who, though not wicked, are included in this category to typify their wild animal origin and elemental strength they possessed.

The typical example of Vella thadi, white beard, is Hanuman. The colours applied to face are red, black and green; the combination is suggestive of fiery strength, animal origin and sattvic tendencies.

Kari, wholly black, represents purely tamasic beings like Shurpanakha and Simhika. Sattvic characters like Brahmins, Rishis, and women belong to the minukky type. The face is brightened with flesh-coloured paint, the eyes are deeply pencilled and lips are painted red. In every type eyes are reddened.

And there are glittering headgears, ornaments, enormous skirts and other costume material. An ordinary looking actor enters the make-up space and comes out as elegant mythological character. The transformation is stunning.

As a stage what Kathakali actors need is a level piece of land with a few stools. Locales where dramatic action takes place from palace to garden, from royal court to battlefield are created by suggestive gestures. A large brass lamp provides the light.

The Bhagavatar is the main singer. His orchestra includes two drummers who play on chende and maddalam and a cymbal player. Singers sing the story and dancer-actor delineates it through his abhinaya. He speaks only through his body-language.

The performance begins with drumming by the maddalam player. Then behind the curtain certain dances are performed, invocatory songs in the honour of various deities are sung, a song from Gita Govinda, Manjutara, is recited.

After this preliminary, purvaranga, is over the play proper starts rolling, singers singing the story and actor-dancers translating it in their action.

Kathakali started as Ramanattam or Rama plays but gradually stories from Mahabharata, Bhagavata and other Puranas, mythological and sacred works, literary classics were taken up for enactment.

KATHAPUTALI

String puppet show of Rajasthan. The torso of Kathaputali puppet is made of light wood. Hands made of cloth are attached to them. They wore medieval Rajasthani costumes, particularly flowing skirts. Rajasthani puppets are quite colourful and small in size. The strings are attached to different parts of the puppet which the puppeteer standing above them manipulates with skill giving them desired movement.

Court scenes, fights, dances dominate the show. Amarsingh Rathore is a popular play performed by the puppeteers.

In the beginning prayers are offered to Shiva, Hari and other deities. First to enter is drummer, dugdugiwala, who plays on drum and departs. After him comes sweeper who sweeps the floor and then the waterman Bhisti who sprinkles water on the floor. Then enter different interesting characters and depart after enacting some humorous dialogues. Then the play of Amarsingh Rathore unfolds which is full of sword fights and war scenes in which Amarsingh is killed by treachery. However in the end son of Amarsingh avenges his father's death by killing Arjun Gaud who had killed brave Amarsingh.

KIRTANIYA

A class of Brahmins who used to perform Krishnalila plays with the help of child actors. Abul Fazl, courtier of Emperor Akbar, wrote an encyclopaedic work named Ain-i-Akbari in the year 1597. Writing about classes of singers he said: 'The Kirtaniyas are Brahmans, whose instruments are such as were in use among ancients. They dress up smooth-faced boys as women and make them perform, singing the praises of Krishna and reciting his acts.' Scholars believe that these Kirtaniya performances represent the formative phase of the modern day Raslila theatre of Braj.

KOOTHAMPALAM

Temple theatres of Kerala built to stage Sanskrit plays in Kutiyattam style. According to Shastric injunctions the Koothampalam should be constructed in front of the sanctum of the temple, on the right hand side.

It is believed that once all the temples in Kerala had such theatres, but according to one estimation about twenty have survived. The Koothampalam in the premises of Vadakunnatha temple of Trichur is in the best state of preservation.

Its architecture mostly follows the model of rectangular theatre building described by Bharata in his Natya Shastra.

Auditorium, stage and make-up room are the main components of the Koothampalam. Stage is a rectangular platform in the auditorium. There is a roof supported by the pillars above the stage. For staging plays the stage is beautifully decorated with bunches of plantains, coconut fronds, clusters of tender coconuts, coloured cloths, etc. An oil lamp is placed on the stage to illuminate it.

Behind the stage is the make-up room. Two doors connect make-up room with stage. In the name of stage property there are a few small wooden stools.

The Koothampalams with their imposing roofs are used to stage Koothu and Kutiyattam performances on festive occasions.

KRISHNA

The great epic hero worshipped as divinity. Krishna is mentioned in the Vedic literature. In the Chandogya Upanishada one Krishna Devakiputra, disciple of Ghora Angirasa, is mentioned. However scholars dispute his identification with Devakiputra Krishna, the great Yadava hero of the epic Mahabharata.

He is at the centre of the epic Mahabharata in which his life is described at great length for the first time. The epic itself starts with a benedictory verse in his honour—Narayanam namaskritya. A twelfth century inscription refers to him as Mahabharata sutradhara, the string holder of the Mahabharata. Later Puranas like Vishnu, Harivamsha, Bhagavata and Brahmavaivarta elaborated upon colourful Krishna lore. He is mentioned in Buddhist and Jain literature too. In the Buddhist Ghat Jataka he is referred to as a son of Devagarbha and Upasagara and slayer of Kamsa.

Temples were raised in his honour at least since second century B.C. as is evident from the relic of Garuda Stambha or pillar with Garuda emblem erected in front of his now extinct temple at Vidisha by Dion's son Heliodorus, Greek ambassador to the court of Kaustiputra Bhagabhadra, around 126 B.C. The distinguished Greek called himself Bhagavata, the devotee of Krishna.

Krishna was worshipped by Greeks living in India. It is very interesting to note that the earliest extant representation of Krishna and his brother Balarama is found on the bronze coins of Greek king Agathocles

(c. 180–165 B.C.) who along with his brother Pantaleon ruled from Taxila over quite a large portion of Indian territory extending up to eastern Punjab.

Krishna was born to Devaki and Vasudeva of Yadava-Vrishni clan on the stormy midnight of Shravana Vadya Ashtami which generally falls in the month of August, in the dark prison cell of Mathura ruled over by his tyrant maternal uncle Kamsa.

The infant was smuggled out by father Vasudeva to Gokula by crossing turbulent Yamuna river flooded by torrential rain. He along with his brother Balarama grew in the house of cowherd chieftain Nanda. The playful and naughty child used to steal milk and butter from the houses of milkmaids and tease them. On one fragrant moonlit night of Sharada ritu dark-hued Krishna danced Ras with lovely cowherd girls fair as Champak flowers on the bank of river Yamuna sporting amorously with them.

The divine child killed several demons sent by king Kamsa to destroy him and ultimately killed the tyrant himself.

To save his clan from frequent attacks of Emperor Jarasandha, father-in-law of slain Kamsa, he migrated to Dwaraka. Here he performed many feats of bravery and romance and led a regal life.

During the swayamvara of princess Draupadi he was reunited with his cousins, the Pandavas, and that opened a new chapter in the political history of north India. The rivalry of Pandavas and their cousins known as Kauravas led to great Mahabharata war which left behind the trail of death and destruction.

Yadavas at Dwaraka too killed each other in drunken brawl which he could not stop. Saddened by the events Krishna in dejected mood started moving in the forests. One day while standing under the Ashvattha tree in a yogic posture he was hit by an arrow of a tribal hunter which caused his end.

Numerous events of Krishna's life were dramatised. His love with beautiful cowherd girl Radha became the theme of poetry, dance, drama, music, painting and sculpture.

Tracing the origin of Indian theatre E.P. Horrowitz wrote: 'The oldest Indian dramas, or rather colloquies, samvadas, were not composed in Sanskrit, but Prakrit. Indeed originally the Prakrit samvadas were mysteries too, either Krishna or Shiva acting and dancing principal part. Favourite episodes from Govinda's eventful life were the 'slaying of Kamsa the tyrant' and 'the binding of the heaven-storming titan'. Large crowds came to witness these open-air spectacles. The grand finale, the merry roundelay of the bright eyed Gopis, proved a special attraction. Rival worshippers flocked in equal number to the wanton bacchanals held in the honour of god Shiva. Vedic dialogues reflected the afterglow rather than the first morning flush of the rude representation, staged in the vulgar tongue, of Krishna's and Shiva's ancient mysteries. The Agra district is the holy land of Krishnaism. Shauraseni, the mediaeval speech of Agra populace, is frequently met with in Sanskrit plays.'

Bhasa was the first Sanskrit dramatist to portray Krishna's life through his plays, particularly the Balacharita. The tradition continued. Krishna is the source of a number of classical and folk dance and dance-drama forms.

The Krishna cult which is popularly known as Bhagavata sampradaya encouraged dramatic activities as a form of divine worship. In the eleventh canto of the Bhagavata Purana Krishna is shown enjoining his devotees to offer him dance, drama, music on festive occasions. He says: 'The faithful should sing and enact my story which is beautiful and auspicious.'

'The stories about my birth and life may be narrated. Joyous celebrations should be organised. Songs, dances, instrumental music should be offered to me on festive occasions in my temple.'

'When festival is organised for me food, songs and dances should be offered to me.'

'Organise my festivals, yatras, in regal manner arranging performances of music and dance.'

In the 12th century poet Jayadeva composed lyrical dance-drama Gita Govinda in Sanskrit. The inscription of Gajapati ruler of Orissa, Prataparudradeva, dated July 1499, enjoins that Gita Govinda and Gita Govinda alone should be enacted in the Jagannatha temple of Puri. This dance drama based on the love of Radha and Krishna immensely influenced the tradition of Indian theatre.

Many scholars contend that Surasena, the land of Krishna, is the home of the Indian drama. Sylvain Levi opines:

'The first document which positively attests the existence of dramatic representations of India associates the new art with the legend of Krishna. The association may have been a mere accident, yet it would not be difficult to give a rational justification for it. No other divinity deserves more to preside over the birth of the Indian drama than the young and brilliant hero, lover of Gopis, and vanquisher of demons. The cult of Krishna has been intimately associated with the history of the drama during long centuries. In the middle ages it gave to moribund theatre a new lease of life, and, in the present day, it gave birth to a new type of drama.'

Significantly playwright Bhasa calls Krishna the string holder, sutradhara, of eternal drama of life constantly evolving on the stage called universe.

KRISHNA ABHYUDAYAM

A mythological play written by Lokanatha Bhatta in the 17th century. Based on the story of the birth of Krishna the play was staged on the occasion of annual festival of Hastagirinatha at Kanchipuram.

KRISHNA ATTAM

According to a Puranic myth, Kerala is a narrow strip of land reclaimed from the sea by the legendary Brahmin warrior Parashurama, an incarnation of Vishnu-Krishna, for his own habitation. No wonder the cult of the Bhagavatas has flourished in the region since ancient times. The celebrated Trivandrum shrine of Padmanabha, where the Lord slumbers in yogic trance, is mentioned in a Tamil epic belonging to the second century. In this beautiful land, around the mid-seventeenth century, emerged a colourful dramatic form called *Krishna Attam*, based on the Krishna legend.

The Krishna cult in Kerala received impetus from the Alvar *bhakti* movement in the Tamil country between the sixth and the ninth centuries. King Kulashekhara of Malabar is counted among the Alvar saints who were great Krishna devotees. His collection of devotional hymns, *Mukunda Mala*, is often compared with Jayadeva's *Gita Govinda*. Keralite by birth, Adya Shankaracharya wrote lyrical *ashtakas* in praise of Lord Krishna. In his *Govindasataka*, he depicts various delightful sports of the cowherd Krishna. He composed these *ashtakas* at the behest of his mother who was a great devotee of Krishna. This shows that by the seventh century the Krishna cult had become quite popular in the region.

Many poems, epic in nature, have been written on the Krishna theme since the twelfth century, including *Srikrishna Vilasa* by Sukumara, *Srikrishna Vijaya* by Sankara, and *Krishna Gatha* by Cherussery. Poetic works like *Ras Krida* and *Gopi Kamoda* depict the erotic mysticism inherent in the cult of Krishna. Melapathur Narayan Bhattathiri's composition *Narayaniyam*, known as the gospel of Guruvayur, is considered as sacred as the *Bhagavata* itself. Bilvamangala's exquisitely beautiful work *Krishna Karnamrita*, known for its devotional flavour, had a deep influence on Chaitanya Mahaprabhu. He carried the work with him to Bengal. The medieval Keralan poetry made the Krishna lore popular among the masses.

Many diverse dance-drama forms have flourished in Kerala since ancient times. The histrionic skill of Chakyar, a traditional dancer-actor of the region, is described in *Silappadikaram*, a Tamil epic of the second century. These temple actors who trace their lineage to Suta, the narrator of *Mahabharata*, evolved a *Kutiyattam* style of presenting classical Sanskrit plays. The plays are still staged by the Chakyar men and the Nambyar women in the spacious temple theatres known as Koothambalams. It is significant to note that the *Kutiyattam* repertory includes Bhasa's *Balacharitam* which is the first extant Krishna *Leela* play of India. Usually through the enactment of this play the young Chakyar actors are initiated to the stage.

King Kulashekhara Varman of Mahodayapura who flourished in the tenth century made significant contributions to the *Kutiyattam* theatre of the Chakyars. It was he who first introduced the *Manipravalam* style of speech in Sanskrit theatre, to bring it closer to the local audience. This involved the explanation of Sanskrit and Prakrit dialogues by the *Vidushaka* (jester) in the Malayalam language. One of the two plays written by him is *Subhadradhananjaya* which is based on the Krishna theme. In this play we come across a clever, scheming Krishna who brings about the union of his sister Subhadra with his Pandava friend Arjuna against the wishes of his elder brother Balarama.

In the twelfth century, Jayadeva's musical opera, *Gita Govinda*, reached Kerala and became quite popular under the name *Ashtapadi Attam*. The sweet lyrics of Jayadeva were sung and enacted in the Vaishnava temples. This had a deep impact on the theatrical tradition of the region. In fact it is basically *Ashtapadi Attam* which inspired Manaveda, the Zamorin of Calicut, to evolve a new theatrical form based on the Krishna theme. However, like Jayadeva, he did not confine himself to the *Ras Leela* episodes only, but tried to dramatize the whole of the Krishna story. *Krishna Giti*, a cycle of eight Krishna plays written in Sanskrit by Manaveda, was successfully staged in 1650. The new theatrical form acquired the name *Krishna Attam* and became instantly popular.

The impact of the ancient *Kutiyattam* theatre of the Chakyars on the *Krishna Attam* is quite evident. The highly stylized mode of acting, colourful make-up and costumes and many other stage conventions of the earlier *Kutiyattam* theatre were adopted with some modifications by Manaveda while evolving his new theatrical form. However he introduced two important innovations which were later used in *Kathakali* as well. In *Kutiyattam* the actors deliver their own dialogues, but Manaveda entrusted that task to the chorus and made the actors concentrate more on the *abhinaya*. This, in a way, was necessary because of the dance oriented nature of the new form. There was no dancing as such in the earlier *Kutiyattam* theatre. Manaveda introduced a vigorous style of dancing which leaves the actor breathless and affects his speech, so the spoken word was taken up by the chorus. Manaveda dispensed with the extremely slow pace of the *Kutiyattam* theatre, and made *Krishna Attam* more racy and action oriented. A Chakyar actor picks up a single act of the play and performs it for several days. Manaveda avoided this and made *Krishna Attam* more crisp and precise. In *Kutiyattam* the *Vidushaka* occupies the most important position in the total scheme of the presentation. He strays from the actual text and takes the liberty of commenting with his characteristic oblique humour and sarcasm, not only on events in the play, but also on the contemporary social scene. No such character is introduced by Manaveda in *Krishna Attam*, maybe because of its avowedly religious nature.

The deep devotional flavour of the *Krishna Attam* can be explained by a legend associated with its origin. Manaveda once had a divine vision of the child Krishna. He saw the deity playing happily under the Ilanji tree in the premises of the Guruvayur temple. When he came out of the blissful mystic trance he found a colourful peacock feather fallen from the head-band of the cowherd Krishna. This mystic experience inspired Manaveda to compose his *Krishna Giti* which was dramatized as *Krishna Attam*. The legend further states that the beautiful peacock feather, received by Manaveda as a token of the Lord's grace, adorned the crown of the actor who played the role of Krishna in the opening performance. The sanctity of the performance is still maintained meticulously. Before starting the series of plays the actors observe a fast for a day to purify themselves. Devout members of the audience also observe a fast. The plays are performed as a votive offering to the Lord who is supposed to be present there, witnessing the *Leelas*.

Krishna Attam is a cycle of eight plays which are performed for eight consecutive nights. As it is not considered appropriate to end the drama cycle with the play *Swargarohana* in which Krishna's demise is shown, the next night again the first play of the cycle, *Avatharam*, is staged. This implies that Krishna is reincarnated again and again to protect his devotees from evil. The following is a brief synopsis of the plays of the *Krishna Attam* cycle.

1. *Avatharam*

   The Earth goddess prays sorrowfully to Brahma to relieve her from the tyranny of Kamsa. The marriage of Vasudeva and Devaki takes place. A divine voice foretells the death of Kamsa at the hands of their eighth child. Vasudeva pacifies Kamsa.

   Kamsa kills the first six babies born of Devaki. Ananta is conceived next. Vishnumaya enters Devaki's womb.

   Devaki conceives for the eighth time. Vishnu is born as Krishna. Vasudeva exchanges the child with Yashoda's new born girl. Kamsa enters angrily. When he tries to kill Yashoda's child taking her to be

Devaki's, by striking her against the rock, the child tells him that his enemy is safe elsewhere. Kamsa orders the killing of all the children.

Yashoda and the Gopis are happy that Krishna is born. Putana attains heaven. Krishna grows steadily. The Gopis complain to Yashoda about the theft of butter by the child. She scolds Krishna and consoles them.

2. *Kaliamardanam*
Yashoda sees all the worlds in Krishna's mouth. The naughty child is tied by Yashoda. *Arjuna Bhanjana Leela*. Krishna frees Nalakubara and Manigriva from a curse.

Krishna goes to Vrindavana. Krishna kills a demon who comes to Vrindavana in the guise of Baka. Agha who comes disguised as a snake is killed by Krishna. He rescues the cows and cowherds that had entered the snake's mouth.

Brahma praises Krishna.

The demon Dhenuka is killed by Balarama.

Krishna jumps into river Kalindi. The cobra Kalia becomes angry. While others are horrified Krishna dances on his hood.

Krishna steals away the clothes of the Gopis.

He tells Nandagopa to worship Govardhana instead of Indra.

3. *Ras Krida*
Krishna plays on the flute. The enchanted Gopis come to him. He sports with them.

Krishna elopes with Radha. The other Gopis go in search of him. They find Radha abandoned by Krishna because of her pride. They all go to the banks of the Yamuna and meditate. They shed all their pride and Krishna appears before them.

Ras dance by Krishna and the Gopis.

The Yaksha Shankhachuda takes away the Gopis who were with Balarama. Krishna follows him and kills him. Krishna gives 'Chudamani' which he takes from the Yaksha to Balarama.

4. *Kamsa Vadham*
The angry Kamsa tries to kill Vasudeva but Narada dissuades him. Vasudeva and Devaki are imprisoned by Kamsa.

Akrura, under orders from Kamsa, goes to Vrindavana to fetch Krishna and Balarama. The Gopis shed tears at their departure.

Armed with the teeth of Kuvalayapeeda, an elephant of Kamsa, they kill his wrestlers Chanura and Mushtika. Kamsa is also killed by Krishna. They free Vasudeva and Devaki.

5. *Swayamvaram*
As a tuition fee to their Guru Sandipani, Krishna and Balarama retrieve Sandipani's dead son from Yama, the god of death.

Kalayavana comes to fight with Krishna. In the chase Krishna tricks him and brings him before Muchakunda who reduces Kalayavana to ashes. Krishna appears before Muchakunda in his divine form with four arms.

Balarama weds Revati.

Rukmini who loves Krishna sends a messenger to Dwaraka to inform him of the intention of her brother to marry her off to Shishupala against her wishes.

Krishna takes away Rukmini and angers her brother Rukmi. He battles with Rukmi and humiliates him.

In search of 'Syamanthakam', a precious jewel, Krishna reaches the cave of Jambuvan. The defeated Jambuvan offers his daughter Jambavati to the victorious Krishna.

Krishna gives the jewel to Satrajit and marries his beautiful daughter Satyabhama. Satyabhama is enchanted by Krishna's subtle wit.

6. *Bana Yuddham*
With Satyabhama Krishna goes to battle with Narakasura. He kills the demon Mura. Then he has an encounter with Naraka. Krishna, hit by an arrow, swoons, Bhama continues the fight. Krishna recovers and kills Naraka.

Krishna does penance to please Shiva and gets his blessings. Narada informs Krishna about the imprisonment of his grandson Aniruddha by Bana. Krishna defeats Bana in battle and his protector Parama Shiva. Usha, Bana's daughter, marries Aniruddha.

7. *Vivida Vadham*
While Balarama is enjoying himself with wine and women, Vivida disturbs him. Balarama kills Vivida.

Krishna goes to Jarasandha with Bhima and Arjuna in the guise of Brahmins and appeals him to fight with any one of them. In the fight Bhima kills Jarasandha.

In the *Rajasuya* the Pandavas worship Krishna. Shishupala abuses Krishna and is killed by him.

The beginning of the Mahabharata war. Krishna narrates the *Gita* to Arjuna.

Sudama comes to Krishna who bestows on him immense wealth.

8. *Swargarohana*
Uddhava, who knows that the Yadavas are going to be destroyed because of the curse of sages, goes to Krishna who is about to ascend to heaven.

Krishna gives advice to Uddhava who returns to Badari.

Using the method of *yoga* Balarama abandons his body.

Jara shoots an arrow at Krishna by mistake. Krishna pardons the weeping hunter and grants him entry into heaven. Krishna's chariot-driver Daruka enters. Consoling him Krishna sends back Daruka.

Krishna turns himself into Mahavishnu.

The episode ends with Shri Vaikuntham in which songs in praise of Vishnu-Krishna are sung.

Nowadays *Krishna Attam* is mainly confined to the Guruvayur temple where it is performed as a votive offering to Lord Krishna, the presiding deity of the shrine. According to *Sthala Purana* of Guruvayur, Krishna enjoined Uddhava to rescue his idol from Dwaraka which was about to be submerged into the sea. This was done with the help of Guru and Vayu and the sacred idol was installed in the Parashuram Kshetra. The place became famous as Guruvayur and came to be known as the Dwaraka of south India. The temple has maintained its own *Krishna Attam* troupe which performs various Krishna plays in a majestic open-air concrete *mandapam* adjacent to the main shrine. The devotees arrange the performance of different plays as offerings in the hope of fulfilling their desires. For instance, a devotee who desires to beget a beautiful child offers the performance of *Avatharam* to the deity and the one who wants a handsome husband like Krishna offers the performance of *Swayamvaram*.

A second-floor corner room adjacent to the wall is turned into *Nepathya Griha* where all costumes, jewellery, masks and other make-up material are kept. Sitting on a mat the actors start their make-up and prepare themselves for the particular play they are enacting. Rice paste or *chutti*, charcoal powder, Indian blue, red arsenic and similar other indigenous dyes are used for the make-up. Glittering diadems and other ornaments are worn by the actors according to their roles. Characters like Brahma, Yama, Putana, Mura, Narakasura, Jambuvan wear painted masks. The bodily movements of the actors are so meaningfully choreographed that even the static, immobile masks worn by them come alive and start projecting various sentiments and emotions.

While the actors are busy doing their make-up, the chorus enter the place of performance with musical instruments and take their stand on the right side of a huge brass lamp. Then starts skilful playing of drums, called *Kelikayya*. *Krishna Attam* uses pure *Sopana Sangeetham*—a form of music evolved and preserved by the temple musicians of Kerala. The drumming announces the commencement of the play and the audience start gathering in the Mandapam. Then holding high a curtain in their hands, two persons appear on the scene. Behind the curtain four actors in the role of Gopis perform an invocatory dance while the chorus sing songs in the praise of the Lord. After the dance is over, the Gopis leave the place and the play proper begins. The important characters first dance behind the curtain and then appear from behind it in a majestic manner. The chorus sing the songs introducing the character while he is making his curtain-entry. Scene division is also indicated by the raising and removing of the curtain. When Lord Krishna enters, the fragrance of rose petals showered on him fills the whole atmosphere.

As stated earlier, the actors do not deliver their own dialogues but through dance and rich gesture language depict the meaning of the songs sung by the chorus. Apart from the dialogues of the characters the chorus sing the songs giving background information and maintain the story link between the various scenes actually enacted before the audience. The actors and the chorus together present the show to the viewers.

Except for a few wooden stools, no stage property as such is used in the performance. The audience and the performers are on the same floor level all the time. Two big brass oil lamps are lit to illuminate the acting arena. In *Kathakali* performances actors do not cross the lamps but *Krishna Attam* actors sometimes move beyond it.

Dances of Krishna are extremely graceful and enchanting. In the play *Ras Krida* he dances with Gopis in various beautiful formations. In *Kaliamardanam* a small wooden snake is projected from behind the half-raised curtain, and Krishna performs a vigorous dance before it, as if he is actually dancing on the serpent hood to subdue him by the forceful impact of his feet. There are many battle scenes in the *Krishna Attam* plays in which Krishna and Balarama encounter ferocious demons. These scenes are choreographed in a forceful (*Tandava*) style adopted from the ritualistic folk dances of the region. The technique of swift turns, whirls and jumps associated with a variety of dance-dramas particularly those belonging to the Bhagavati cult, were woven into the texture of *Krishna Attam*, lending it a unique grandeur. The Krishna theatre of Kerala is of course not devoid of the delightful *Lasya* aspect of dancing. It is particularly manifest in the play *Ras Krida* in which Krishna performs *Mallipu Chital*, the jasmine garland dance, with the Gopis. They dance in a circle, sometimes forming a circle within, displaying beautiful patterns.

KRISHNAMISRA YATI

Eleventh century author of the unique philosophical drama Prabodhachandrodaya which is a clever exposition of advaita vedanta system and lays stress on Vishnubhakti or devotion of Lord Vishnu.

Krishnamisra lived during the reign of Chandella king Kirtivarman whose capital city was Mahotsava nagara or Mahoba near temple city of Khajuraho. Krishnamisra was inspired to write the play by Gopala, a feudatory of king Kirtivarman, who helped him win the war against Chedi king Karna. Kirtivarman witnessed the drama in 1065 A.D. at Mahoba on the occasion of victory festival.

A legend says that Krishnamisra was great spiritual leader of the time and an ascetic. He wrote the play Prabodhachandrodaya to make one of his reluctant students study philosophy.

Some scholars believe, on the basis of internal evidence recorded in the play, that Krishnamisra originally belonged to Bihar who later migrated and settled in Mahoba.

KUCHIPUDI

The Kuchipudi emerged essentially as a classical dance-drama in the Andhra Pradesh around 17th century. The credit of evolving this dance-drama form is given to an ascetic named Siddhyendra Yogi who settled in the village Kuchipudi, composed a musical play Parijatapaharana, which became famous as Bhamakalapam, and got it enacted with the help of local artists in the premises of local temple of Ramalingeshvara.

As a classical art Kuchipudi follows Bharata's Natya Shastra and similar other works on dramaturgy.

Bhamakalapam is still a popular play in the Kuchipudi repertory. It is about a romantic altercation between two lovers—Satyabhama a young beauty proud of her looks and Krishna her naughty and playful husband.

Krishna visits the place of his young, very beautiful but proudish consort Satyabhama. Pointing at their reflected images in the mirror he mischievously asks who among them is more beautiful. Forgetting that she is speaking to lord of the universe, essence of all that is beautiful in the world, she declares herself to be more beautiful.

Pretended to be offended Krishna leaves her. Repentant Satyabhama writes a letter to Krishna humbly begging him to return. Krishna returns and the lovers are united.

There is a moral to this story. Pride and ego comes in the way of union with the divine.

The play has come down in several recensions. In some versions the concluding scene is a quarrel between two lovely queens of Krishna—Satyabhama and Rukmini. Krishna mediates and the drama ends on a happy note.

Subsequent authors wrote more plays for Kuchipudi stage. Plays such as Usha Parinayam, Prahlad Charitam, Mohini Rukmangada, Mohini Bhasmasura, Parvati Kalyanam, Alamelamanga Vilasam, Kalyana Srinivas are popular on Kuchipudi stage.

Elaborate Purvaranga is followed in which Vedic hymns are chanted, holy water is sprinkled on the stage, incense is burnt, Rangapuja is performed, flower offerings are made, jarjara is brought on the stage. However the most interesting part of the Purvaranga is the entry of elephant-headed god Ganesha. An actor wearing the elephant mask makes a curtain-entry and performs a dance. Enters Sutradhara and recites prayer songs in the honour of various deities.

Main characters make very dramatic entry introducing themselves through songs named as Praveshiki dhruva. Previously the characters used to sing their own songs and speak out their own dialogues but now this task is entrusted to a singer who sits with musical orchestra.

Jewellery and costumes are dazzling and beautiful, just suitable for mythological characters. The stage is simple, generally bare except a few chairs or a bench. Abhinaya is subtle and dance beautiful.

Kuchipudi in the beginning was male-oriented performance, even female roles were performed by male actors exhibiting beautifully intricacies of feminine coquetry. Gradually women joined the Kuchipudi troupes and today they are dominating the Kuchipudi scene. Kuchipudi evolved into solo performance also.

Kuchipudi evolved basically as an artistic product of Bhakti movement. Bhagavatamela Nataka of Tamil Nadu is its offshoot. A popular theatrical performance, Vithi Bhagavatam, grew out of Kuchipudi tradition.

KUMUDVATI PRAKARANA

A play mentioned in Padmaprabhrutakam, a Bhana by Shudraka. It was based on the love story of princess Kumudvati and a fisherman named Shurpaka. Kumudvati was passionately in love with the fisherman who ignored her. In the end the god of love, Kamadeva, made him fall in love of the princess. In the epic poem Saundarananda poet Ashvaghosha has referred to this popular folk tale by saying that daughter of king Senajita fell for a Chandala and Kumudvati for a fisherman. In his another poem Buddhacharita the name of the fisherman has been given as Shurpaka.

The play is lost to posterity but a few lines from it are quoted in the Bhana play Padmaprabhrutakam. Addressing the princess madly in love with the fisherman her nurse-maid says:

'O insane girl, your bosoms have not as yet grown nor line of hair has appeared on your soft stomach. You are still immature. Do not long for lover like mature young woman. Your female friends are teaching you wrong lessons. Why are you bent upon love-making? It seems you have matured before time.'

The name of the author of the play is not mentioned. It seems that the play was popular among the courtesans who used to stage it frequently.

KUNDAMALA

Six-act play based on the Uttarakanda of Ramayana by the 5th century playwright Dignaga. However some scholars attribute the authorship of this play to Veeranaga or Dhiranaga. The play starts with abandonment of Sita on the bank of river Ganga and ends with acceptance of Sita by Rama in Valmiki's hermitage and coronation of Lava and Kusha.

KUNDHEI NACHA

The glove puppet form in Orissa is known as Kundhei Nacha.The glove puppets are found mainly in Orissa and Kerala. These puppets are worn on hands, their heads and arms manipulated by the puppeteer with his fingers. The puppeteer sits in full view of audience and narrates his story in prose and verse with puppets illustrating its contents and characters.

Kundhei Nacha glove puppet troupe consists of a puppeteer and a drummer. There are only two puppets, one male and one female. The puppeteer sings songs and manipulates both the puppets. When he is manipulating one puppet the other is worn on his hand by the drummer who then will use his free hand to play on the drum. It is believed that the male-female puppets represent Krishna and Radha but they can also represent hero and heroine of the love song being sung by the puppeteer. Compositions of medieval Oriya poets, particularly depicting Radha-Krishna love, are sung by the puppeteer.

In this show the basic stress is on narration of the story, singing of songs, the puppets act as visual symbols illustrating the narration.

KURAVANJI

Dance-drama in Bharatanatyam mode that emerged in Tamil Nadu in the 18th century. In this dance-drama we see a Nayika pining for her divine or earthly lover. Suffering the pangs of separation she beautifully presents the vipralambha sringara or love-in-separation condition. A fortune teller, Kuravanji, appears on the scene. She consoles the Nayika and on the basis of her calculations she tells her that she will soon be united with her lover.

Kuravanji forms the part of Bharatanatyam repertory. It is believed that Kutrala Kuravanji by Thirukutarajappa Kaviyar is the oldest extant Kuravanji composition. About forty Kuravanji compositions are in the repertory of Bharatanatyam performers. Most popular among them is Sarabhoji Kuravanji in which the lover of beautiful Madanavalli is shown pining for the love of king Sarabhoji. Kuravanji presents excellent opportunity to the Bharatanatyam dancer to show her histrionic skill or abhinaya and various faces of woman's love.

KUSHILAVA

Actor, dancer, entertainer, ballad singer. Ku means bad and shila means character. Hence, it is believed by some scholars that as actors were known to be bad characters or men of bad character they were known as Kushilava.

Vatsyayana in his Kamasutra says that citizens should assemble in the temple of Saraswati and see the performances given by the Kushilavas. In his commentary Yashodhara explains the term Kushilava as nata-nartaka or actor-dancer.

The term Kushilava for class of actors occurs in the Mahabharata and Kautilya's Arthashastra.

Kautilya says that kushilava-karma or singing, dancing, acting is the task of shudra low caste people. He says that halls for recreation should not be constructed in countryside lest the entertainers such as nata, nartaka, vadaka, vagjivana and Kushilava would disturb the people busy in productive economic activity.

In the prologue of a number of plays such as Shudraka's Mricchakatika and Bhavabhuti's Malatimadhava actors are referred to as Kushilavas.

KUTIYATTAM

Traditional dramatic form of Kerala which specialises in the presentation of classical Sanskrit play in its own unique style.

It is believed that King Kulashekhara Varman of Kerala, who is identified with Bhaskara Ravi Varma, who ruled from 978 to 1036 A.D., with the help of a Brahmin scholar and poet Tolan created this form as we know it today. Community of actors known as Chakyars adopted it to theatre.

Chakyars and their histrionic skill find mention in the Tamil epic Silappadikaram ascribed to the second century A.D. It seems that during Chola period the art of Chakyars flourished in South India. A Tamil inscription of King Parakesarivarman alias Udaiyar Sri Rajendra Choladeva I records the gift of land by the great assembly of Kamaravallicaturavedimangalam to Sakkai (Chakyar) Marayan Vikramasolan for performing a dance Sakkai-kuttu thrice on each of the festivals–Markali-tiruvatirai and Vaikasi-tiruvatirai. The inscription is dated 1041 A.D. (SIE, No. 65 of 1914).

Yet another inscription (SIE, No. 250 of 1926) of Chola king Parakesarivarman registers a grant of gold and paddy to one Alaiyur Sakkai to enact three scenes of Sakkai-kuttu.

Kuttu is a solo performance by the Chakyar where he narrates mythological stories from epics, puranas and similar sacred works with angika abhinaya. Ancient Chakyars might have been solo-acting the scenes from Sanskrit plays like those of Bhasa. King Kulashekhara wrote two plays Tapatisamvarana and Subhadradhananjaya and staged them with the help of Chakyar artists.

We do not exactly know that initially these plays were performed by Chakyars. We get this information from a critique of Kutiyattam, Natankusha, written in the 15th century A.D. by a Brahmin scholar.

In the performance Nangiar women take female roles and Nambiar men play on musical instruments like big drum Mizhavu. Mani Madhava Chakyar writes: 'In some plays the entire role of the Nanid Sutradhara and part of responsibilities of Sthapana Sutradhara are performed by the Nambiar himself. He also enacts certain demonic roles, according to the demands of the occasion; however in proper Kuttu or Kutiyattam none except Chakyar, Nambiar and Nangiar are entitled to take role or even enter the scene of action' (Sangeet Natak, Nos. 111–114).

Acts from the plays of Bhasa, Harsha, Kalidasa, Shaktibhadra, Kulashekhara, Nilakantha, Mahendravikramavarman, Bodhayana are taken up for enactment. Such is the style of presentation that several days are needed for staging a single act from the play. Actor is not exactly bound by written text, he is free to bring in extraneous material related to the text. If a word 'water' occurs in the text the actor may wax eloquence on the subject water for hours together.

An actor can assume different roles in a scene without changing costumes or make-up or solo-perform the entire scene. His stylized speech delivery and acting style help in extending the period of performance.

The plays are performed in the temple theatres named as Kuttampalam. Kuttampalams at Vadakunnatha temple at Trichur, Bharata temple at Irinjalakuda and Krishna temple at Guruvayur are in good state of preservation. Elaborate rituals are performed before the enactment of plays in these theatres.

The characters that appear on the stage are classified in different types such as Paccha, Katti, Tadi, Minukku and Pazhukka. Make-up is very elaborate and colourful. Black, green, white, red are the colours mainly used. Dazzling headgears, jewellery and costumes help turn an actor into mythological character—divine or demonic.

Vidushaka plays major role in the performance. He freely uses Malayalam to explain the play to locals. For rendering a small monologue of Shandilya in the Bhagavadajjukam Vidushaka in his role takes several days.

Chakyars composed Attaprakaras and Karmadipikas—acting and production manuals—as guides to stage performance.

Musical instruments such as Mizhav, eddakka, kuzhithalam, kuzhal and sankhu are used for providing background music.

Kutiyattam is a very rich dramatic form with its own style, theatrical conventions, rituals and performative practices which are still alive in Kerala.

KUTTANIMATAM KAVYAM

Kuttanimata is a poetic composition of Damodaragupta who, according to the Rajatarangini of Kalhana, was the Chief Minister of Jayapida king of Kashmir who ruled from A.D. 779 to 813.

It reflects the life of cunning and crafty courtesans of Varanasi who exploit and fleece their customers in various ways. A courtesan Malati of Varanasi goes to an old and experienced Kuttani, a bawd, named Vikarala for professional advice. The poem is in the form of narration of Kuttani Vikarala.

In this poem Varanasi is described as a place where dramas of excellent playwrights, satkavikritarupaka, are frequently enacted. In one of the verses, 68, theatre or ranga attached to the house of courtesan or the part of courtesan's house where dance, drama and music performances are held is described. The poem says that shresthi, vanik, vita and kitava are the people who frequent these places of entertainment.

Since ancient times courtesans were custodians of dramatic arts. Vasantasena, a courtesan and heroine of Bhasa's play Charudatta, was an actress trained in dramatic arts. We find several inscriptional and literary references to prove that courtesans used to stage plays in temples, royal palaces, public theatres. They were well versed in dramatic compositions, particularly ones which excelled in Sringara rasa or erotic sentiment.

When Damodaragupta wrote his work in the eighth century same condition prevailed but probably courtesans had lost their interest in staging plays.

Speaking to prince Samarabhatta who along with his entourage visited the temple of Kashi Vishvanatha at Varanasi a Nrityacharya thus spoke to him—

'How could there be excellence in dramatic performance when knavish prostitutes play roles in it? These useless women spent their time either in love-making or drinking wine with their lovers. Even for a moment they do not leave the doors of their whore houses hoping that anytime some customer will arrive with fat purse. Even while standing on the stage if a wretched prostitute happens to know that some well acquainted customer has arrived at their house she would not hesitate to leave the theatre to meet him. How could there be grace in the performance given by the prostitutes involved with men and interested in drinking wine and meat all the time? However they do albeit reluctantly move their limbs to act in the production of the play Ratnavali by Sriharsha lest they would lose their means of livelihood.'

However, the Nrityacharya says, he has made them act well under his direction.

He then presents the performance of the first act of the play Ratnavali by the courtesans in the temple of Kashi Vishveshvara. There is a very elaborate description of this performance in the book.

Kuttanimatam Kavyam throws ample light on contemporary condition of Indian theatre as found in the city of Varanasi.

LALITMADHAV

A Sanskrit drama based on Radha-Krishna romance written by Rupa Goswami, disciple of Chaitanya Mahaprabhu, in the first half of the 16th century A.D. It was performed at the behest of Madhavi-Madhav temple on the bank of Radhakunda near Govardhana in Braj region. See Rupa Goswami.

LOKANANDA

A drama by Buddhist philosopher and poet of the 5th century A.D., Chandragomin, a Bengali by birth. Chinese traveller I-tsing, 7th century, has referred to him as a dramatist and Bodhisattva. The play has survived in its Tibeti translation.

MAANCH

Musical dance drama of Malva region of Madhya Pradesh with Ujjain as its centre.

Ujjain, one of the seven great cities of ancient India, and famous for its Mahakala temple, was a flourishing metropolis. It was a great centre of theatrical art and tradition says that it was here the plays of Kalidasa and Bhavabhuti were staged. In his Bhana play Padmaprabhrutakam describing the glory of the city Shudraka calls it a centre of performing arts such as singing, dancing, music, poetry and drama—drishyam shravyam geetam vadyam. He tells us that the courtesans of the city used to perform plays such as Kumudvati Prakarana under the direction of Natakacharyas. Banabhatta in his Kadambari has elaborately described the city and referred to the people proficient in Bharata's Natyashastra.

Maanch that evolved in Ujjain is a rather recent incarnation of musical dance drama tradition that flourished in north India.

In his work *A Memoir of Central India* published in the first quarter of 19th century Sir John Malcolm has referred to older dramatic tradition of the Malva region. He writes:

'The villages are also frequently visited by drolls or strolling players, many of the latter are very clever. The subject of the satire of their plays or rather farces which they represent is as often their mythological fables as the measures of their earthly rulers and governors. The figures of demi-god Hunoomann with his monkey face, Ganesha with his elephant head, and portly belly are brought on the stage to the great entertainment of the spectators. The incarnations of Hindu deities is the common topic with these players and frisking of the large fish which represents one of the principal incarnations of Vishnu always excites bursts of applause.'

Artists well versed in rich folk music and dance of Malva evolved the Maanch theatre. Maanch verse dramas are sung and danced out with occasional prose dialogues. Thematically Maanch plays are mostly woven round religious and mythological stories from epics and Puranas, lives of saints and great devotees, historical or semi-historical tales, folk romances. The plays basically provide rich fare of folk and classical music whatever may be the themes.

A wooden stage open on all sides is constructed for the performance. Musicians sit in the rear on the tek ka pat. The first person to appear on the stage is waterman, Bhisti, who sprinkles the performing arena with water. Then arrives Farrasan or sweepress who while singing sweeps the performing arena and spreads the carpet.

This particular portion of the preliminary is, according to scholar Dr. Shivkumar Mathur, taken from the ritual of ghost worship. Before asking the spirits to appear on the scene the expert in Hajarat Vidya or demonology asks the scavenger to clean the place, Bhisti to sprinkle the water and Farrasan to spread the carpet to accord the spirits royal welcome.

In the Rajasthani Kathaputali puppet show too at the beginning the Bhisti-Farrasan scene is enacted.

It seems that the practice of cleaning and making ready the place for holding royal court with the help of menials like Bhisti and Farrasan was prevalent in north India. Kathaputali performers, Hajarat vidya practitioners and Maanch gurus might have incorporated Bhisti-Farrasan act from this source.

After the stage is ready and swept clean all participating actors, all male, arrive on the stage and offer prayers to different deities. Bhairava is considered as presiding deity of Maanch. A boy in the guise of elephant-headed god Ganesha appears on the stage to give his blessings to the actors and musicians. Then performers are introduced to the audiences which is known as Salami. The procedure of Purvaranga mentioned above may vary from troupe to troupe.

After this play proper starts unfolding through songs, dances and music. Thousands of people assemble to witness or better listen to Maanch plays.

MADANABHUSHANA BHANA

One-act play in Bhana format by the 17th century writer Appa Dikshit hailing from village Kilayur near Tanjore. Known as Kavitarkika-Sarvabhauma he was court poet of king Shahaji of Tanjore. Apart from the Bhana play he authored poetic works such as Sringaramanjiri-Shahrajiya, Gaurimayur Champu and Achara-navanita.

The Bhana was performed in the dancing hall or Natya Shala of Gaurimayuranatha temple situated on the bank of river Kaveri on the occasion of Vasantotsava or Spring Festival.

The play depicts a day in the life of Vita named Madanabhushana and his meeting with several interesting characters such as courtesans, actors, dancers and palmists. His humorous encounters with men of religion such as Vaishnavas, Pauranikas and monks belonging to Ramanuja sect are well depicted. He then wanders in the locality of courtesans, Veshyavat, and flirts with them.

It is a fun-filled entertaining play.

MADHYAMAVYAYOGA

An interesting one-act play by Bhasa involving the Mahabharata characters—Ghatotkacha, Hidimba and Bhima—in an imaginary story weaved by him around them.

Pandava brothers, after losing their kingdom in deceptive game of dice they played with their crafty cousins, came to stay in a forest. As luck would have it one day an old Brahmin Keshavdas happened to pass through the same forest along with his wife and three sons.

Finding the family moving through the forest terrifying demon, Ghatotkacha, starts pursuing them. He wants them for the breakfast of her mother. After much discussion the unfortunate family decided to surrender the middle (madhyama in Sanskrit) son to the demon. With the permission of the demon he enters the forest in search of water to quench his thirst. When he fails to return quickly impatient demon starts calling after him and shouting his name Madhyama.

Bhima too was known as Madhyama. To find out who was calling him Bhima appears on the scene. After listening to their story Bhima assures them and picks fight with demon Ghatotkacha.

During the conversation with him Bhima comes to know that the demon is none else but his own son from Hidimba. But he continues to feign ignorance and indulge in wrestling.

Ultimately Bhima agrees to follow Ghatotkacha in the place of Brahmin lad to become the prey of his mother. When they together arrive at the place where the demoness was living she recognises her husband and then family reunion takes place. Heaving a sigh of relief the Brahmin family embarks on their onward journey free of fear.

The Mahabharata does mention the demoness Hidimba, her marriage with Bhima, and the son Ghatotkacha born to them and also the sojourn of the Pandavas in forest after losing their kingdom. But here in the play the story in which the epic characters are placed is invention of Bhasa, and not to be found in the epic. However excellent characterisation, interesting central conflict involving father and son, unexpected and suspenseful twists and turns of the story make the play very interesting.

Hidimba is deified and we find a beautiful temple raised in her honour near Manali in Himachal Pradesh. Near the temple the foot-prints of the demon-deity Hidimba are seen embossed on the stone.

To please her an offering of sheep is made to her by her devotees on special occasions. On the day of Vijaya Dashami or Dussehra a grand fair and festival of god Raghunathaji is held every year. The festival is not concluded till goddess Hidimba arrives on the scene.

MAHABHARATA

Great Indian epic which provided themes to a number of playwrights to compose their dramatic works since the time of Bhasa.

It is believed that based on earlier sources such as folk ballads and other floating literary and historical material, Vyasa several centuries before Christian era composed a work known as Jaya depicting the story of great Bharata war. It grew with time and by stages acquired present massive form around the fourth century A.D. Thus Jaya of yore subsequently became Mahabharata of today.

A famous Austrian scholar and Professor of Indology, Maurice Winternitz, amazed by its expanse wrote: 'In reality one can speak of the Mahabharata as an epic and as a poem only in a very restricted sense. Indeed, in a certain sense, the Mahabharata is not at all a poetic product, but rather an entire literature.'

Jean-Claude Carriere who wrote a script for Peter Brook's theatrical rendering of the Mahabharata calls it 'an immense epic poem' and says that 'the title can be understood as 'The Great History of the Bharatas'. But in an extended meaning Bharata means Hindu, and even more generally, man. So it can also be interpreted as 'The Great History of Mankind'.

When several centuries after Bhasa the director Peter Brook presented dramatised version of the epic for international audience it was hailed as 'theatrical event of the century'. Such is the dramatic potential of the epic.

Dramatisation of the epic must have started much earlier but we know of the tradition since the time of Bhasa. He wrote six plays based on the epic and one related to Krishna based on Krishna lore which found its place in Harivamsha, an appendix of Mahabharata.

After Bhasa we find Kalidasa writing a play based on the love story of Shakuntala and Dushyanta found in the epic under the title Abhijnana Shakuntala which is hailed as all time classic.

Sten Konow in his *Indian Drama* has mentioned several plays based on the epic story material. Prominent among them are Tapati-Samvarana by king Kulashekharavarman of the 10th century A.D., Chitrabharata of Kshemendra of the 11th century A.D., Parthaparakrama by Yuvaraj Prahladana of the 13th century A.D.

Venisamhara of Bhatta Narayana written in the 7th century A.D. is a well-known play based on the Mahabharata story of Bhima avenging the insult meted out to Draupadi in the Kaurava court. Kshemishvara in the 10th century A.D. wrote a play Naishadhananda based on the story of Nala-Damayanti found in the Mahabharata.

Around 16th century and after a number of dramatic forms such as Yakshagana, Kathakali, Terukuttu emerged in different languages in different parts of the country which frequently borrowed themes from the Mahabharata. Krishna lore found in the Mahabharata was elaborated in the Harivamsha Purana considered to be the appendix of the epic. Its popular appeal was further enhanced by the Bhagavata Purana. Life of Krishna and his lilas became the subject of a number of plays in Sanskrit and regional languages.

In the Mahabharata itself we find information about contemporary theatrical activity. It seems that shadow and puppet theatre was popular mode of entertainment at the time. The Mahabharata mentions a number of theatrical entertainers such as Natas, Nartakas, Rangavatarakas, Rupopajivanas, etc.

It is in the Mahabharata that ballad singer Suta, expert in Puranic lore, is called Sutradhara. This gave rise to the theory that drama evolved out of ballad singing and the ballad singer Suta became the Sutradhara of the Sanskrit drama.

It is significant to note that in the Sabhaparva of the epic the word Nataka meaning drama is clearly mentioned.

MAHAVRATA

A Vedic ritual full of singing, dancing, music and play acting. Reference to this festive ritual is made in various texts including Sankhyayana Aranyaka.

As a part of the ritual the hotri priest sits on a swing moving merrily to and fro. Various explanations are given of this ritual action. He swings up and while returning brings back with him all pleasures of heaven to earth. According to another theory his upswing indicates the upward growth of the crops in the field, however some say that the course of the swing in movement indicates the path of sun in the sky. It seems swinging, a joyous folk activity reflecting the gaiety of the favourable season, is turned into ritual with complex layers of symbolic meaning. In the north Indian festival of Teej which is celebrated in the rainy season the swings are suspended from the branches of the trees for girls to swing.

A hole is dug in the ground and covered with animal hide turning it into an earth drum. This drum is beaten with great gusto filling the atmosphere with a rhythmic boom. This is done to scare away evil spirits or announce the victory of the clan over enemies.

A mimic clash between a Shudra and an Arya over a white round piece of animal hide is staged. Archers shoot arrows at another piece piercing it in the process. This indicates the inclusion of sports in the ritual.

Singing merrily the girls dance around the sacrificial fire with pitchers full of water over their heads. Udgata and other sama singer sing while some women play on musical instruments with hundred strings. Some others play on a musical instrument named karkari.

Humorous dialogue ensues between a Brahmin and a Shudra. One praises the performer of the sacrifice and the other reviles him.

Ritual abuse is exchanged between a celibate student, Brahmachari, and a woman of bad character, Pumschali. The dialogue runs as follows:

The harlot must say: 'You who have misbehaved! Who have violated your vow of continence.'

The Brahmacharin must answer: 'Shame on you, depraved one! Harlot who washes for the village community, who washes man's member.'

> Sa bruyat duscaritina avakirnin iti; dhik tva jalmi pumscali gramasya-margani purushasya sisnapranejani iti (Sr. S. XI.3.9).

After this ritual copulation of a Magadha and a harlot takes place. Magadha is a professional bard and panegyrist.

It is believed by the scholars that Mahavrata was an ancient popular fertility ritual adopted by the Vedic priests. It shows how theatrical arts like dancing, singing, playing on musical instruments, recitation of dialogue and play acting form the part of a ritual. Some scholars are of the opinion that such rituals contributed to the evolution of drama proper.

MAHENDRAVIKRAMAVARMAN

Pallava king of Kanchi in South India ascribed to first half of the seventh century A.D. who wrote an interesting farce Mattavilasprahasana or A Farce of a Drunken Monk. This was probably the first Sanskrit dramatic work written in South India.

King Mahendravikramavarman is described as an able and versatile monarch, great in war and peace. He assumed several titles such as Mattavilasa, Vicitrachitta, Gunabhara and Shatrumalla. He was great builder and poet. Having interest in music he got musical exercise engraved on the stone in Kudimiyamalai or Pudukottai. He initially was a Jain who later converted himself to Shaivism.

Writing about the religious condition of South India historian K.A. Nilakantha Shastri says: 'Broadly stated, till about the close of the sixth century A.D. different religious sects lived together in admirable harmony. Vedic sacrifices, worship of primitive godlings with offerings of blood and toddy, the domestic rituals and temple worship of elite, Buddhism, Jainism all went on side by side. When Hiuen Tsang visited the south in A.D. 642, he noted with great regret that Buddhism was giving place to digambara Jainism. Reaction against Buddhism set in during the seventh century particularly in the Tamil country.'

In the Farce the playwright has made fun of followers of various sects such as Kapalika and Pashupata and made Buddhist monks butt of his ridicule.

Mattavilasprahasana throws flood of light on the practices of different religious sects and degeneration set in them.

MALATI MADHAVA

A romantic comedy in ten acts by eighth century playwright Bhavabhuti depicting the love story of brave and handsome Madhava and beautiful Malati set in the city of Padmavati, present-day Pawaya in North India.

Buddhist nun Kamandaki and her disciples play great role in bringing the lovers together. In the Kamasutra, Indian ars amoris, the role of female ascetics as go-between is underlined. According to Gonikaputra's quotation in the Kamasutra Bhikshuki, Kshapanika, Tapasi facilitate the meeting of lovers.

Go-between of various kinds are mentioned in the Kamasutra. The Nishrusthartha duti is one who takes upon herself the whole burden of the love business and arranges everything by the power of her own intellect. Nun Kamandaki plays this role very effectively in the play. Her skilful handling of the situations propels the plot.

Expressing his ideas about how the dramatic performance should be Bhavabhuti in the prologue says that it should be enlivened with profound display of aesthetic sentiments, bhumna rasanam gahanah prayoga, variegated and colourful story, chitrah katha, artful speech, vachi vidagdhata, display of good-heartedness, friendship and affection, sauhardahridyani vichestitani, daring action of lovers based on Kamasutra.

Bhavabhuti has adhered to all these ideas while writing his play. Apart from this

Kamasutra has a profound influence on the portrayal of love in this play. At places one feels that Bhavabhuti has just copied from Vatsyayana's great work.

After Bhasa's Avimaraka there is a very open reference to sexual fantasies in Bhavabhuti's Malati Madhava. He gives 'minute word-pictures of physical sensations during imagined sexual gratification of girls of noble families'. Heroine Malati experiences erotic dreams in which she experiences sexual gratification and shows its physical signs like sweating, uncontrolled trembling, etc.

In the name of variegated story Bhavabhuti has made the plot of the play complicated and contrived. Keith says that the plot, however interesting, is extremely badly knit together; the action is dependent upon accident to an absurd degree.

Malati Madhava betrays the influence of contemporary Tantric cults. In the fifth act of the play we see Madhava moving around in cemetery or burning ground full of ghosts, evil spirits, spectres of terrible and frightening appearances, selling human flesh. The ritual of selling human flesh, mahamansa, to evil spirits for certain gain was a common tantric rite of the time. This rite is mentioned in Bana's Harshacharita too.

In the same act we see Kapalika named Aghoraghanta and his female consort Kapalakundala performing tantric rituals in the temple of goddess Chamunda situated in the cemetery. As a culmination of the ritual they were making preparations for human sacrifice. Kapalakundala has attained the siddhi or supernatural power of flying into sky. They had brought heroine Malati to sacrifice her to the goddess but brave Madhava rescues her.

In the ninth act we meet another tantric Yogini named Saudamini who is well versed in tapa, tantra, mantra, yoga and abiyoga and has attained several supernatural powers and siddhis like Akarshani vidya and vidya of flying in the sky. As a disciple of Kamandaki she helps the lovers to unite.

As a poet Bhavabhuti excels at many places but fails as a dramatist as far as Malati Madhava is concerned.

MALAVIKAGNIMITRA

A delightful five-act romantic comedy by Kalidasa describing the love that blossomed between a palace beauty and king which reached its fruition after crossing several hurdles with the help of cleverly inventive and resourceful court jester. So ingenious is the court jester, Vidushaka, that he occupies central position and the plot virtually moves at his discretion. It is virtually Vidushaka's play. Some critics feel that 'of Kalidasa's three plays, the Malavikagnimitra is dramatically the best and least lyrical and probably the earliest.' Full of comic sentiment, hasya rasa, the play depicts a love intrigue of Shunga court.

Agnimitra, the hero of the play, is a historical personage, a scion of Shunga dynasty ruling from Vidisha. The Shunga dynasty was founded by Agnimitra's father Pushyamitra by overthrowing Maurya power. According to the Harshacharita of Banabhatta he slew the last Maurya king during military coup. In the later half of the second century B.C. Kalidasa in his play refers to another historical fact of Pushyamitra performing Ashvamedha Yajna or vedic horse sacrifice. A short Sanskrit inscription from Ayodhya mentions two Ashvamedhas performed by Senapati Pushyamitra and a relative of his who was perhaps ruling there as the viceroy of the Shungas.

Malavika, a beautiful Vidarbha princess, is the heroine of the play who was living in king's harem in disguise due to political misfortune that befell her branch of royal family. The play also refers to war between Vidarbha and Vidisha ending in the latter's victory and the recognition of the river Wardha as the boundary of two kingdoms.

The play also refers to the defeat of band of Yavanas who tried to capture the sacrificial horse of Pushyamitra on the right bank of river Sindhu, by Agnimitra's son Vasumitra. Patanjali attests to both the horse sacrifice and the Yavana invasion of Central India. Historians feel that the river Sindhu is probably Kali Sindhu, a tributary of the river Chambal flowing within hundred miles of Madhyamika which was besieged by Yavanas, or another Sindhu, a tributary of the Jamuna (*Advanced History of India*).

It is in the prologue that playwright Bhasa finds mention for the first time along with Saumillaka and Kaviputra as the famous dramatists of the past. Kalidasa describes himself as novice in the field, vartamana kavi, but requests the learned members of the audience to judge him by the merit of his work.

We are also informed that the play is being staged on the occasion of Vasantotsava or spring festival. No wonder romance and humour formed the core of the play.

In the beginning of the play we come to know that while chief queen Dharini was observing the recently made paintings by Chitralekhamacharya or master artist in the picture gallery of the palace king Agnimitra arrived there. His eyes fell on the figure of a beautiful girl standing by the side of the queen in a painting. On being enquired by the king his daughter tells him that she is Malavika. Observing that the king is attracted towards Malavika by seeing her painting cautious queen puts restrictions on her movements to put her out of sight of the king.

King requests jester Gautama to help him see Malavika in person. Jester cleverly provokes two masters of dance in the royal court to fight for superiority. Both are asked to present a disciple each to decide the matter. Beautiful Malavika is presented by one dance master as his disciple and she performs dance in front of the king and thus he sees the girl in painting in person. He instantly falls in love with dancing singing beauty and queen watches it helplessly.

A female ascetic, Pandita Kaushiki, is requested to act as judge to decide the merit of dancers. She is referred to as Pithamardika. Pithamarda is a person associated with the world of courtesans, dancing master who teaches courtesans, companion of the hero who helps him in his love affair, parasite, a kind of gogetter who moves in the company of citizens and courtesans, a pimp well versed in various fine and performing arts. Pithamardika is not a nice appellation for a female ascetic but Kamasutra of Vatsyayana prescribes the use of female ascetics as procuress.

As a judge of dance competition she asks the dance masters to bring their female disciples scantily draped, vigata nepathya, so that she could watch the dance movements of their lovely bodies. Nepathya means an ornament, decoration, costume of an actor or dancer, attire. Vigata means abstaining or desisting from. Vigata Nepathya means sans costume, attire. Body is the medium of the dance, heavy costume and make-up hinders the expression of body through gestures and postures, it obscures body language. Hence, says the judge of the dance, dancers should be presented scantily draped. Lovely sculptures of female dancers adorning the temples and monuments too are shown scantily draped.

Thus scantily draped Malavika, young and beautiful in limbs, is exposed to the gaze of the king already smitten by seeing her in painting. He found her more alluring than painting.

This gave an opportunity to Kalidasa to include the dance performance, titillating at that, in the drama. Before him we have seen Bhasa incorporating dance performance, Hallisaka, in his play Balacharita and in Pancharatra also.

The introduction of the characters of Natyacharyas and subsequent dance competition gave Kalidasa an opportunity to express his ideas and thoughts about the art of drama. Through his character Natyacharya Ganadasa he defines drama as ocular sacrifice, kratum chakshusham, pleasing to the gods. He further says that Lokacharita that is actions, doings, behaviour, deeds, adventures of the people emanate from three psychological factors, trigunas, known as raja, tama and sattva. In the Sankhya philosophy ingredients or constituents of Prakriti or nature, or chief qualities of all existing beings are three. They are sattva, rajas and tamas i.e. goodness, passion and darkness, or virtue, foulness and ignorance.

Sattva is quality of purity and goodness, good sense, wisdom, magnanimity, it is spiritual essence of mind. Raja is a quality of lofty passion, and tama is darkness of ignorance. These three qualities perpetuate and propel human action.

Human conduct and actions display various undercurrents of feelings and emotions which are called Rasas. Kalidasa says that human action is coloured with rasas.

Kalidasa says the Lokacharita or human conduct which emanates from three gunas and is coloured with rasas is the theme of the art of drama which pleases one and all without distinction. He echoes the definitions of drama provided by Bharata in his Natyashastra to certain extent but omits the Bharata's premise that drama is an imitation of life.

He also stresses the performative nature of science of drama by saying—prayogapradhanam hi natyashastram. He says drama is in reality its performance, performance is the drama.

In the third act we are informed that due to the mischief of the jester Gautama the chief queen Dharini fell down from the swing and hurt her feet, hence she had asked Malavika to perform the ritual of Ashoka dohada. It is believed that the tree of Ashoka when kicked by a beautiful girl starts blooming. Malavika arrives in the garden to perform the ritual. At the same time another queen of Agnimitra, young Iravati, fully drunk, too arrives in the pleasure garden with the intention of enjoying swinging with the king. However she finds the king flirting with Malavika. Drunken Iravati beats the king with her rashana or girdle. The frightened king falls at her feet to appease her but Iravati leaves in a huff.

It is Bhasa who for the first time brought drunken characters on the stage, all male, in his play Pratijnayaugandharayana to create humour. Kalidasa went a step ahead and brought a woman, a queen, in drunken state to amuse the audiences.

In her drunken state Iravati asks her maid if the adage that women look more alluring when drunk is true. Drinking was not uncommon among women in ancient India. They used to drink for fun, for enjoyment and for celebrating festive occasions like spring festival in company of their lovers. Several sculptures of drinking women testify to this fact.

It also was a common practice to fall at the feet of beloved to appease her. The Indian treatise on love, Kamasutra, too sanctions and approves this practice. In the one-act Bhana plays of Gupta period we see lovers falling at the feet of their beloveds or being kicked by them. One Bhana play Padataditakam is devoted to this theme. It is said in the play that like Ashoka a man too is aroused on being kicked by his angry beloved during love quarrel.

Swinging was the favourite pastime indulged in by the ancient Indians. Kamasutra says that swing should be suspended from the branch of the tree for the citizens to enjoy this pleasurable pastime. In the third act of the play Kalidasa describes the season of Vasanta or spring season. He has hence included in it the features of spring festivity such as drinking wine, swinging, and ritual of Ashoka dohada.

In the fourth act we are told that Malavika is kept behind bars in a dark cell as Iravati reported that she secretly met the king in the palace garden. Clever Vidushaka starts acting as if bitten by a serpent. To save his life queen Dharini gives her ring with figure of serpent embossed on it. With the help of the ring Vidushaka frees Malavika from the prison cell. The lovers then unite in the palace room called Samudragriha.

In the fifth and concluding act queen Dharini herself offers Malavika to the king knowing her royal birth as a Vidarbha princess and the play ends on a happy note.

Iravati describes the union of the king with Malavika as the result of the crafty moves of Vidushaka—iyamasya kamatantrasachivasya neetih. In this sense Malavikagnimitra is a Vidushaka's play.

MALLIKA MARUT

A ten-act play by 16th century playwright Uddandin, son of Ranganatha and Ranganba, and court poet of Zamorin of Calicut. The play depicts the love story of Mallika, daughter of Vidyadhara king's minister and Marut, son of the minister of the king of Kutala. The play is written in imitation of Bhavabhuti's celebrated drama Malati Madhava.

MANIPURI RAS

Classical dance, dance-drama style that emerged in Manipur in the 18th century A.D. under the impact of Vaishnava Bhakti cult.

In the 15th century, during the rule of King Kiyamba, Vaishnavism reached Manipur from Bengal. A temple dedicated to Vishnu was built and Keertan-Sankeertan singers started performing there. By 18th century Vaishnava culture with its cycle of social and religious festivals, customs and tradition became predominant in Manipur. Vaishnava rituals of devotional singing and dancing were held in the temples. Bhagavata Purana depicting the life of dark-hued cowherd Krishna became popular with Manipuri masses.

A Vaishnava myth regarding the origin of Manipur stated that this beautiful land was created by Shiva to dance the Ras with his consort Parvati. The myth says that Shiva had once approached Krishna because he wanted to see his beautiful Ras dance. He was only allowed to listen to Ras music and was asked to stand with his back to the Ras arena. Swayed by the music Shiva turned around but instantly everything vanished from his sight—Krishna, gopis and all. However Shiva remembered all the music. With the desire to dance to the tune of that music he created the land of Manipur.

A myth about Shiva attending the performance of Ras dance is prevalent in Vrindavan also. For that Shiva became cowherd girl and stood at the periphery of Ras circle. A temple of Gopishvar Mahadeva, or Shiva in the guise of cowherd girl, testifying this myth still stands in Vrindavan. In the evening the Shiva linga in the temple is covered with feminine cloths to show him as a gopi.

It was King Jaisingh, also known as Rajashri Bhagyachandra (A.D. 1763–1798) who evolved Nata Sankeertana and started the tradition of performing Raslila dance and dance-drama based on the Bhagavata Purana.

A myth says that he had a divine vision of Ras in a dream and converted it into reality. He made a beautiful image of Govindji and installed it in his palace. Ras dances devised by him were performed in its honour in which King's daughter, Princess Shija Lairoiba, enacted the role of Radha, consort of Krishna. It is believed that the first Ras was organised at Kanchipur on a specially constructed Ras Mandal near royal palace.

Theme of the Manipuri Ras is life of child Krishna in Braj region as depicted by the Bhagavata Purana.

The Krishna oriented Ras dances of Manipur are divided in two broad categories—Gopa Ras and Radha-Krishna Ras.

Gopa Ras is a beautiful dance-drama which unfolds in series of sequences various facets of Krishna's life in Vrajabhumi. Sage Narada is shown teaching Krishna and Balarama the art of tending cows. Then both the boys are shown playing the ball with their friends and enjoying themselves. After Kanduka krida they are shown killing two demons, Bakasura and Dhenukasura, sent by Kamsa to destroy them. The childhood pranks of Krishna including his stealing of butter, teasing cowherd girls fair as Champak flowers, breaking their pots of milk and binding Krishna to a stone mortar by Yashoda as a punishment for his naughty behaviour are the subjects of Ulukhal Ras.

The Radha-Krishna dance and dance-dramas of Manipur are extremely colourful and technically highly developed. Based on the Ras Panchadhyayi of the Bhagavata Purana they reveal various facets of the Radha-Krishna relationship taking recourse to very tender, graceful and flowing dance style.

Krishna appears in a blue dress with a peacock feathered diadem on his head. The cowherd girls wear red round skirts and glide softly on the stage. The colourful costumes, enchanting music, the soft lyrical movements of the dancers lend a dream-like quality to the whole performance.

In Vasanta ritu Krishna played Holi with Radha. This is the theme of Vasanta ras. In the Kunja ras Radha-Krishna abhisar or romantic dalliance is described. Maharas is most elaborate of Ras dances. In the Maharas the episode of Krishna dancing with Radha and cowherd girls on the bank of river Yamuna on one full-moon night of Sharada ritu is taken up for enactment.

In Manipuri Ras dances the story of child Krishna is unfolded through song, dialogue, music and dance in an atmosphere charged with devotion or Bhakti.

MATRIKA

Matrika means mother. Matrikas are mother goddesses. In Bhasa's play Charudatta and subsequently in Shudraka's Mricchakatika there is a reference to making food offering or bali to the matrikas at their shrine situated at crossroads. It seems that after worshipping Grihadevatas or divinities kept in the house citizens used to make food offering to Matrikas whose shrines were generally located at crossroads. Charudatta asks Vidushaka to go to the shrine of Matrikas with food offerings—krito maya grihadevatabhyo balih/ Gaccha twamapi chatushpathe matribhyo balimupahara.

On being asked by Vidushaka about the advantages of making such offerings Charudatta says that it is a part of daily routine of a householder. He further says that on being worshipped by penance, meditation, praise-words and food offering the deities remain pleased.

The tradition of worshipping mother goddesses dates back to several centuries. Terracotta figurines of mother goddesses some having the bird or animal-heads, some nude, some with children belonging to Indus valley period were found in excavations at different sites.

The tradition continued in different forms in later period. Mother goddesses are mentioned in the Vedic literature. Epics and Puranas contributed to the development of the cult of mother goddesses. Tantra literature upheld Shakti worship which evolved out of cult of mother goddesses.

Groups of mother goddesses having different numbers were worshipped. One such group of seven mother goddesses gained prominence and came to be known as Sapta Matrikas.

Mahabharata says that Matrikas dwell in the trees, in open spaces, in caves, in the cemetery, on mountains, waterfalls, more significantly at the meeting of crossroads. Among the list of Matrikas given in the epic one is named as chatuspatha-niketana (one who dwells at crossroads) and the other as chatushpatha rati (one fond of crossroads). Bhasa speaks of shrine of matrikas at crossroads.

Bhasa makes distinction of Grihadevata and Matrikas. Probably Matrikas were not worshipped in home shrine.

In the Natya Shastra Bharata uses the term matrika in his chapter on class dance. He says the sthanas, the charis and the nritta-hastas mentioned in the chapter are known as matrikas, the variation of which is called karanas (IV.61). In yet another verse in the same chapter Bharata says: The combined movement of hands and feet in dance is called karana. Two karanas will make one matrika, and two, three or four matrikas will make up one Angahara (IV.30–34).

In this sense matrika is mother-unit of the dance.

In the third chapter of Natya Shastra in the context of Rangapuja Bharata speaks of Natya Matrikas. It is not clear who these Natya Matrikas are. However in yet another verse he says bali or food should be offered to Brahmi and other Natya Matrikas. Probably he is referring to Sapta Matrikas—Brahmi, Maheshvari, Kaumari, Vaishnavi, Varahi, Aindri and Narasimhi.

Again in yet another verse he refers to Saraswati, Dhriti, Medha, Hri, Lakshmi, Mati, etc. as matarh or mothers.

In the same chapter Bharata speaks of Natya Kumaris as a group of goddesses connected with drama. But he offers no explanation as to who these Natya Kumaris are.

MATTAVILASPRAHASANA

Written by the seventh century Pallava king of Kanchi, Mahendravikramavarman, who assumed the funny title of Mattavilasa, this hilarious farce makes fun of followers of contemporary religious sects like Kapalika, Pashupata and Shakya and exposes shallowness of their beliefs.

The farce opens with the entry of drunken mendicant of Kapalika sect with his female consort equally drunk. Kapalika hails Shiva for showing the world the path of liberation or Moksha by resorting to drinking wine and enjoying the company of women. Deprecating Jain philosophy he says that though Jainas believe in the theory that karya is always in accordance with karana (cause and effect theory) they say that painful practices can lead to pleasure—dukshasya karyam sukha. How can painful practices of the Jainas like observing celibacy, plucking one's own hair one by one, wearing soiled cloths, not taking bath and eating according to rules lead to happiness or pleasure? he reasons. He is so disgusted at the mention of the Arhantas that he desires to wash his tongue with wine. And hence they both move around in the search of drinking den or pub.

They wander describing the glory of the city of Kanchi, singing the praise of wine and Kapalika way of life, comparing the sacred Yajnashala with pub in drunken state. Somewhere on the way they lose their kapal or begging bowl, which is their identity as Kapalika.

In this background appears a Buddhist monk. In his soliloquy he praises Buddha for allowing the monks to live in mansions, sleep in cosy beds, eat delicious food, drink sweet fruit juices. He wonders why the all merciful one did not grant them the permission to enjoy wine and women. He suspects that the old infirm monks of the order out of sheer jealousy must have removed relevant passages from the Pitaka rule book. Hence he vows to find out the original authentic Vinaya Pustakas.

When the Kapalika couple see the Buddhist monk moving around with begging bowl they think that the monk must have stolen their very own kapal. They start fighting. At this moment a Pashupata appears on the scene. He is in love with a maid-servant of a barber. Pashupata is sour with the Buddhist monk for he on several occasions tried to entice the beloved of Pashupata by showing her a coin under the cover of his garb as a cowherd will show fistful of grass to beckon a cow. So he too jumps in the fray. During the fight they make fun of tenets of each other's cults.

Kapalika accuses Buddha of abject plagiarism. He says that by borrowing from Vedanta, Upanishada and Mahabharata Buddha has filled his coffers hence he is in this respect more than Kharapata who wrote a treatise on the art of thievery, the Chaurashastra.

Kapalika offers wine to the monk. With great difficulty he resists the temptation of enjoying it. But on the pretext of lifting up the beautiful Kapalika woman who had fallen down during the fight he takes the chance of touching her.

Suddenly they see an insane person, Unmattaka, with kapal or begging bowl of the Kapalika in his hand. Unmattaka gives it to Kapalika and everything ends well.

By the way of this farce Mahendra-vikramavarman has intelligently exposed the hypocritical behaviour of followers of different contemporary religious sects.

Mattavilas is popular on Kutiyattam theatre of Kerala. In the Kottiyur temple only Mattavilas is performed during its annual festival.

In Vadakunnatha temple of Trichur too performances of Mattavilas are held.

MOHARAJAPARAJAYA

A Jain allegorical play written by Yashapala in early 12th century. It was staged at the Jain Kumaravihara temple at Tharad in Banaskantha district of Gujarat on the occasion of the car festival of Bhagavan Mahavira.

The play opens with benedictory verse in the honour of Jain Tirthankaras namely Rishabha, Parshva and Mahavira. The play describes the conversion of the Chalukya king of Gujarat, Kumarapala, to Jainism. Virtues—good, bad and evil—appear in human form. The play extols the virtues of Jain creed. In the conflict that ensues between the forces of good and evil the good vanquishes evil with the help of tenets of Jain philosophy.

Keith writes: 'An example of a Jain allegory of comparatively early date is afforded by Moharajaparajaya, the conquest of King Confusion, describing the conversion of the Chalukya king of Gujarat, Kumarapala, to Jainism, his prohibition of killing of animals, and his cessation from the practice of confiscating the property of persons dying without heirs in the realm, as a result of the efforts of the famous sage, Hemachandra....it has the merit of bringing vividly before us the activities of Jainism in its regulation of Kumarapala's kingdom, casting an interesting light on what is known from inscriptions and other sources of the history of Gujarat.'

MOHINI

Enchantress, female incarnation of Vishnu. Gods and demons churned the ocean for ambrosia, or Amrita, the elixir of life. When Amrita appeared from the sea the gods and demons fought over its possession. At that time Vishnu appeared in the form of enchantress, Mohini, and persuaded demons to allow the gods to partake of Amrita first. Thus Mohini deprived demons from having the Amrita.

There was a demon named Bhasmasura. By Brahma's grace he had a power of reducing anything to ashes by placing his hand on it. Vishnu appeared before him in the form of Mohini. When demon Bhasmasura requested her to be his consort she told her that if he would dance in her imitation she may consider his proposal. During her dance Mohini placed her hand on her head. When Bhasmasura did the same and placed his own hand on his own head he was burnt into ashes.

A classical dance of Kerala is known as Mohini Attam, the dance of the enchantress.

MOHINI ATTAM

Classical feminine dance style of Kerala fashioned on Bharata Natyam of Tamil country. According to a legend Mahavishnu took the form of an enchantress, Mohini, occasionally. Once after ambrosia or amrita emerged after churning the ocean Vishnu appeared in the form of beautiful enchantress to hoodwink demons. Again as Mohini he performed a beautiful dance to cast spell on indomitable Bhasmasura.

Mohini Attam is not an ancient dance form. However some scholars believe that it certainly was in vogue in the beginning of the 17th century.

However it acquired its present form quite recently. It is believed that it germinated in the court of Swati Tirunal Maharaja of Travancore. One Parameshvara Bhagavatar of Palghat was in his court as a musician. After the death of Maharaja he returned to Palghat and made the art popular there.

Mohini Attam is not a ritual art or one that flourished in temples. It is an art born in the court which more or less follows Bharatanatyam. It has incorporated certain mudras of Kathakali in its performative texture.

Costume and make-up is very simple. Colour of the saree is always white with a gold or contrasting border. She wears rose coloured or contrasting blouse. The hair tresses are weaved in a bun above the head. Ornaments are few and simple.

Essentially a solo dance of social diversion Mohini Attam enchants its audiences with easy grace and delightful moods.

MRICCHAKATIKA

Or Clay Cart is a distinctly unique ten-act dramatic composition by king Shudraka essentially based on a love story of a poor Brahmin youth and a rich and beautiful courtesan of Ujjain already dramatised by playwright Bhasa in four acts centuries earlier. Shudraka virtually lifted all the four acts of Bhasa's play, Charudatta, and reproduced them with some alteration and added to it six more acts of his own. Sylvain Levi informs us that one Nilakantha added one or two scenes at the end of the play as he thought that Shudraka has not suitably concluded the play. While extending the play Shudraka added a sub-plot of political intrigue to enrich its fabric.

The one-act Bhana plays portray the life of courtesans in its intricate details. Shudraka, it seems, is well acquainted with Bhana compositions. In fact, according to some scholars, he indeed wrote one Bhana play himself titled as Padmaprabhrutaka.

The play Padmaprabhrutaka is based on the love story of Muladeva and beautiful tender-aged courtesan Devasena. In Sanskrit literature Muladeva is mentioned as an Acharya of knaves and thieves who has written a treatise on thievery. In his Kadambari author Banabhatta has mentioned the Karnisutakatha and its characters Vipula and Shasha. The sub-plot of the love of a thief and a prostitute is found in Bhasa's Charudatta and Shudraka's Mricchakatika.

Rich courtesans falling in love with poor but handsome men forms the theme of many stories of the past. In Buddhist literature too such stories are found.

In ancient Buddhist work, Ashokavadana, there is a story of very rich and extremely beautiful courtesan of Mathura, Vasavadatta, whose fee per night was as high as five hundred gold coins, falling in love with incense-merchant Upgupta who later became the spiritual teacher of Emperor Ashoka. The tragic story however ends on a sad note.

There is controversy regarding the exact date of the play. However it seems that it was written sometime in Gupta era.

According to the prologue of the play the erudite king Shudraka among other things was said to be an expert in vaishiki kala. Vaishiki means harlotry. The play testifies to the fact that Shudraka indeed was well versed with the world of courtesans.

In the prologue it is said that there lived in the city of Avanti Ujjayani a brahmin trader, young and very poor, named Charudatta. In the same city there lived a courtesan named Vasantasena, as beautiful as the blooming Vasanta ritu or spring season, itself, who was attracted by the sterling qualities of Charudatta. The play, the prologue says, is based on their festive love-making, satsuratotsava, and portrays the nature of wicked people, vagaries of fate, error of justice, and turbulent political action.

When the play opens it is evening time, darkness gradually enveloping the city, people making food offering to mother goddesses at crossroads. It is the time when the principal street is crowded with courtesans, pimps and their attendants.

In the first scene we see the hero Charudatta in conversation with Vidushaka sadly lamenting over his state of poverty. Suddenly we see beautiful courtesan Vasantasena being pursued by Shakara and his associates Vita and Cheta, the pimps.

Shakara, a villain, is king's brother-in-law through one of his inferior wives, a foolish, frivolous, low and cruel man puffed with excessive pride and his connection with royalty. He represents the oppressive regime which is shown overthrown at the end of the play. Vita addresses him as Kaneliputra, a bastard, one whose mother was an unmarried woman, a concubine. Probably his sister too was the concubine of the king.

Taking advantage of the darkness of night Vasantasena enters the house of Charudatta in whose love she fell after she saw him in the garden attached to the temple of Kamadeva, the god of love. She keeps her gold ornaments with him on the pretext that she was being pursued for stealing them from her. Charudatta takes her safely to her house and returns. Here ends the first act.

In this act courtesan Vasantasena defines the nature of true love for the first time in Sanskrit dramatic literature. She says love cannot be forced upon anybody, good qualities in a person beget him love—gunah khalvanuragasya karanam, na punarbalatkarh.

In the second act we see a masseur turned gambler, Samvahaka, running for his life to escape from his fellow gamblers to whom he owed money. To hide himself he enters the mansion of Vasantasena.

On knowing that the Samvahaka once served her lover, Charudatta, Vasantasena pays off his debt. Samvahaka feels so humiliated that he vows to become a Buddhist monk.

In the third act we see the skill of thief Sharvilaka who enters the house of Charudatta in the dead of the night and decamps with jewellery kept by Vasantasena for safe keeping.

In the fourth act the thief Sharvilaka offers the stolen jewellery to Vasantasena without knowing that they belonged to her only to secure the freedom of his beloved Madanika serving in her house. Vasantasena generously frees her and keeps the jewellery.

Here Shudraka introduces his sub-plot of political intrigue which does not form the part of Bhasa's original work, Charudatta.

From behind the stage an announcement is made that nervous by the prophecy that dethroning the present king Palaka a cowherd youth Aryaka will become king, he is imprisoned.

After hearing the announcement Sharvilaka vows to make all efforts to free his friend Aryaka as minister Yaugandharayana made to free king Yudayana. Interestingly here is a veiled reference to Bhasa's play Pratijnayaugandharayana .

From the speech of Sharvilaka we come to know that the political revolt against king Palaka is being engineered by the people of lower strata of society suffering from oppressive regime, led by a cowherd youth.

After the departure of Sharvilaka enters Maitreya, jester friend of the hero, who is shown around the magnificent establishment of the courtesan Vasantasena. Maitreya is stunned by the opulence and luxurious grandeur of the place. Vidushaka tells Vasantasena that his master has lost her ornaments in gambling hence he has sent a diamond necklace, ratnavali, to compensate the loss. Naughty Vasantasena keeps the necklace and sends a message to Charudatta that she would be visiting him in the evening.

Bhasa's play ends after four acts. Next six acts are the original creation of Shudraka.

In the fifth act we see Vasantasena as Abhisarika Nayika moving through darkness of night to meet her lover Charudatta defying torrential rain. The act is full of lyrical description of rainy season and feelings of eager lovers poised to unite. Equally beautiful description of Varsha ritu or rainy season and Varsha Abhisar is found in the Bhana play Dhurta Vita Samvada by Ishvaradatta.

In the Kamasutra of Vatsyayana the young girl rushing to her lover on her own defying torrential rain is called durdinabhisarika. Vatsyayana says that if the cloth of visiting Nayika or girl in love is drenched in rain the lover should give her dry cloths and himself help her getting into them. In the play Charudatta too is shown observing this etiquette.

In the end of the act Vasantasena embraces Charudatta showing sringarabhava of intense passion and then both enter the house to make love.

Love takes back seat in the sixth and seventh acts and sub-plot of political intrigue has precedence over it. Aryaka who escapes the prison of king Palaka by mistake enters the bullock cart sent by Charudatta to fetch Vasantasena to the garden named Pushpakarandaka. On reaching the garden Charudatta assures Aryaka and allows him to escape.

Another interesting episode is described in the sixth act. Rohasena son of Charudatta appears on the stage with a toy cart of clay but starts demanding gold toy cart. Vasantasena gives all her gold ornaments to the boy and asks him to make gold toy cart.

In the eighth act we see Vasantasena falling in the hands of Shakara who tries to kill her as she refuses to submit to his passion. Taking her to be dead he leaves her. But she is unconscious only. The Samvahaka turned Buddhist monk saves her and takes her to his monastery.

In the ninth act we witness a court room drama. Shakara accuses Charudatta of murdering Vasantasena for her jewellery. Judge tries the case but refers it to the king who rules that Charudatta be hanged.

In the tenth and last act it is revealed that Vasantasena is alive and as a result of political revolution king Palaka is vanquished and in his place Aryaka has become a king. Charudatta unites with his wife and beloved Vasantasena.

Shudraka's Mricchakatika is considered as one of the masterpieces of Indian dramatic literature. Sylvain Levi writes that 'he remains with Kalidasa the greatest of dramatic poets of India.' Every character of Shudraka has distinct identity and individuality. He takes Bhasa's Charudatta to new heights by adding to it six acts of his own creation.

MRIGANKALEKHA

A natika by Vishvanatha Deva composed in 1607. It was enacted on the occasion of the festival of Kashivishvanatha. Kapurtilak, king of Kalinga, falls in love with Mrigankalekha, beautiful princess of Kamarupa. Demon Shankhapal tries to kidnap her by using his magical powers but Kapurtilak, the hero, with the help of a Yogini, takes her to his harem. However Shankhapal succeeds in kidnapping her and taking her to the temple of Kali. But hero Karpurtilak rescues her and in the end marries her.

MUDIYETTU

A ritualistic dramatic form of ancient origin associated with Bhadrakali cult prevalent in Kerala. Mudiyettu performances are held in the premises of Bhadrakali temples of Kerala as per Malayalam calendar month of Vrischikam which corresponds to November-December of the English calendar.

According to the myth the Demon Darika became very powerful after getting boons from Lord Brahma that he would not be defeated by man, demon or god. Out of blood drops that may drip from his wound in the battlefield thousands of Darikas would emerge to fight the enemies. Darika, armed with the boons, conquered the world and defeated even Indra, king of heaven. When his atrocities became intolerable gods requested Lord Shiva to contain the menace. From Shiva's fire-emitting third eye emerged goddess Bhadrakali to destroy Darika and his associate Danavendra. Nandikeshvara, Kooli and bloodthirsty Vetali joined the goddess. Vetali swallowed the blood dripping from Darika's wound before falling on the ground thus stopping the emergence of several Darikas. Bhadrakali fought a bloody battle with Darika and killed him.

Mudiyettu is dramatic rendering of this myth.

The ritual starts with drawing of the ferocious figure of Kali holding weapons in her several hands in the temple premises with coloured powders. Sometimes she is shown astride Vetali. This drawing is called Kalam and worshipped for several days with appropriate rituals. Songs are sung in the honour of the goddess and pujas are offered. Rituals over the priest wipes out the drawing, collects the used coloured powders and distributes it among devotees.

The Kalam ritual is followed by the enactment of Bhadrakali myth.

A well-lighted wick-lamp is placed in the performing arena and musical instruments are sounded. Two persons holding the curtain appear on the scene along with the chorus of singers and musicians who render invocation songs. With this ends the Purvaranga procedure.

Now the play proper begins. Lord Shiva standing on the high stool whose body below the waist is concealed behind the curtain appears on the scene. This gives the impression that he is positioned on the Kailasa mountain.

Now Narada, the divine sage, appears before him with a palm leaf in his hand on which misdeeds of Darika are recorded. Narada reads out the contents of the palm leaf to acquaint Shiva with Darika's atrocities. Shiva assures Narada that Darika will be destroyed soon.

Now demon Darika makes a majestic entry from behind the curtain which he lowers gradually. He shouts, jumps, whirls all over performing arena, even tramples over audiences in a show of strength. Finally he stands on a high stool signifying that he has conquered the world and holding an exalted position.

Now goddess Bhadrakali makes her curtain-entry in her majestic headgear and costume and challenges Darika. After a brief encounter Darika leaves the arena.

Now Kali is alone in the arena. She offers worship to the lamp placed there as a symbol of Shiva. With musicians, torch-bearers in attendance Kali circumambulates the temple accompanied by the devotees. In the end Kali returns to the performing arena.

Then enter two interesting characters—Koimbidar or Nandikeshvara and Kooli. Kooli is a kind of jester who makes people laugh by his antics and jokes. The drummers converse with Koimbidar who sings songs about the birth of Ganesha. This scene is introduced as a comic relief.

In the final scene people witness most ferocious battle Kali wages against Darika and Danavendra. The battle scene goes on for hours. At the end headgears of the demons are removed which symbolises the cutting of the heads of demons by Kali.

MUDRARAKSHASA

A seven-act play by Vishakhadatta full of political intrigue and action based on the life of Arya Chanakya the political mentor of Emperor Chandragupta Maurya who founded first empire of Indian History in the fourth century B.C.

The play written sometime during Gupta era is hailed as 'one of the great Sanskrit dramas' ever written. It portrays the ruthless political skill and acumen of one of the greatest Indian statesmen Arya Chanakya or Kautilya who is the author of all-time great work on polity, the Arthashastra.

After the fall of Nanda Empire Chandragupta Maurya ascended the throne of Pataliputra in Magadha. However, though the Nandas were vanquished, their clever minister Rakshasa survived the onslaught. Rakshasa was very faithful to the Nandas and virtually hated Chandragupta and his political mentor Chanakya. He continued his efforts to overthrow Chandragupta by consolidating his position with the help of friendly kings.

Chanakya knew the worth of Rakshasa and wanted him to become the minister of Chandragupta. This would have brought stability to Chandragupta. Hence Chanakya planned several moves to isolate Rakshasa and force him to accept Chandragupta as his master. In this the mudra or ring of Rakshasa was used by Chanakya very cleverly hence the play is named as Mudra-Rakshasa or Ring of Rakshasa. The play revolves round this theme.

Several historical personages including Chandragupta and Arya Chanakya are mentioned in the play but interestingly history is silent about Rakshasa as a minister of Nanda ruler.

Character of Chanakya as a key player of the drama is very well portrayed. Jester or Vidushaka, the stock character of Sanskrit drama, is not found in this play and it is practically devoid of female character of any significance.

MURARI

A playwright of repute who lived around the eighth century A.D. and wrote a play Anargharaghava based on Rama legend. He was the son of Vardhamana Bhatta and Tantumati. Nothing much is known about him. He has mentioned Mahishmati as a seat of Kalachuris. This led some scholars to speculate that he lived under the patronage of a prince of that dynasty at Mahishmati, present-day Mandhata on the bank of Narmada river.

NAGANANDA

A play in five acts on Buddhist theme by famous dramatist king Harsha of Kanauj. Ashvaghosha is the first playwright who wrote plays on Buddhist themes. Six centuries after him it was Harsha who worked on Buddhist theme and wrote a very popular play. A Chinese traveller I-Tsing who visited India after Harsha wrote:

'King Siladitya (Harsha) versified the story of Bodhisattva Jimutavahana (Lit. Cloud-borne) who surrendered himself in the place of a Naga. This version was set to music (Lit. string and pipe). He had it performed by a band accompanied by dancing and acting and thus popularised it in his time' *(Record of the Buddhist Religion*, pp. 163-64).

In the prologue of the play homage is paid to Buddha who firmly remained immersed in Samadhi despite onslaught of beautiful daughters of Mara. The Nandi verse says: 'Feigned is the trance; of what fair one dost thou think? Open thine eyes for a moment and gaze on us whom love doth drive mad. Protector art thou; save thou us. False is the compassion; could there be any man more pitiless than thou? May he, whom Mara's beauties thus addressed, the Buddha, the conqueror, protect you!'

Sutradhara tells us that the story of the play is related to Vidyadhara Jataka. In the first century A.D. poet Gunadhya wrote a great story book Brihatkatha which includes the stories of Vidyadharas. The book became popular and scholars started translating it in Sanskrit. In the 11th century Kshemendra's Brihatkathamanjiri and Somadeva's Kathasaritsagar appeared on the scene. In both these Sanskrit versions of Brihatkatha we find the story of Bodhisattva Jimutavahana. In 7th century Harsha, obviously, must have borrowed the theme from Gunadhya's original Brihatkatha in Paishachi language which later was lost to posterity but somehow survived in its Sanskrit versions.

Harsha retells the story of noble Vidyadhara prince Jimutavahana who sacrificed his life to save a Naga from the bird Garuda in dramatic form.

To make the play interesting Harsha begins the play with the love blossoming between noble Jimutavahana and beautiful daughter of Vidyadhara king Malayavati culminating in their marriage. He then goes on describing the drinking parties of Vidyadhara couples and as a comic interlude presents some drunken characters on the stage. Then Harsha portrays encounter of Naga, his mother and Jimutavahana and hero's resolve to stand in the place of Naga as a prey of Garuda. Ferocious Garuda attacks Jimutavahana but understands his mistake. Bodhisattva Jimutavahana preaches non-violence to killer bird and dies. Goddess Gauri appears on the scene and revives Jimutavahana.

Banabhatta in his Harshacharita has described how Harsha came under the influence of Buddhism. His brother and sister were ardent Hinayana Buddhists. 'In the honour of Hieun Tsang, Master of the Law, the king held a splendid assembly at Kanauj in March A.D. 640. This was attended by twenty tributary rajas, of whom were the king of Assam, Bhaskarbarman, from extreme east and Dhruvabhata from Balabhi from extreme west. There was a long concourse of Buddhists, Brahmins and Jains including a thousand learned monks from Nalanda. A golden image of the Buddha of the stature of king Harsha was installed in a tower 100 feet high and a smaller image, three feet in height, was carried in procession every day. It is said that the king carried in person the canopy upheld over the golden statuette of the Buddha. As the procession moved along, golden blossoms, pearls and other rare jems were scattered by the king on all sides in honour of the Three Jewels—the Buddha, Dharma and Sangha' (*Advanced History of India*, pp. 244–5).

In the prologue of the play the Sutradhara tells us that the play Nagananda was staged on the occasion of Indrotsava or festival held in the honour of god Indra. The play presented with singing, dancing and music became very popular and carried the message of non-violence which is central to Buddhist creed.

NAGARJUNAKONDA AMPHITHEATRE

In the year 1954 archaeologists excavated a quadrangular amphitheatre at the foot of the hill at Nagarjunakonda, an ancient Buddhist centre in Andhra Pradesh which formed part of Ishvaku dynasty.

Around the plain ground measuring about 54'6" x 45', leaving a wide passage to enter, there arose Cuddapah slab covered brick galleries, tier above tier. The structure was connected with the temple of Hariti on the top of the hill by the flight of steps.

A circular abacus part of a column was found at the centre of the quadrangle. Probably the capital of the column was used to place on it lamps to illuminate the arena in the night. The column acted as lamp-post.

A drain was located at the south-west corner for water to flow out. One of the benches bore a triratna and bow and arrow mark. Another stone bench had an inscription on it—kama shara or arrow of love. Also found in the arena was an inscribed pillar referring to putting up a perpetual endowment on the occasion of some utsava or festival. This is an enough indication to suggest that the arena was used to stage dance, drama, music performances on festive occasions, audiences watching from the galleries built around it.

Another interesting feature the archaeologists noticed about the structure was its perfect acoustics. One can very clearly hear the musical note struck in the arena by standing at the top of the flight of steps leading to the Hariti temple.

There seemed to be definite connection with the Hariti temple at the hill top and amphitheatre at its foot. This particular feature reminds us of Roman theatre temple, particularly that of Pompey where the altar of Venus was placed at the head of the auditorium.

An archaeologist opined that this stadium, only of its kind excavated so far, appears to have been constructed under foreign inspiration. One wonders whether the Yavanas who came to Western India in the first few centuries of Christian era and many of whom were converts to Buddhism, had conceived its construction in imitation of the classical models known to them.

We know that ancient Greeks celebrated their dramatic festivals in the holy precincts of Dionysus. Romans had their theatre temples. Such practices prevailed in India too.

As far as foreign influence some see on the construction of this amphitheatre we may note that evidence found in the Buddhist Jataka stories indicate that temporary open-air auditorium used to be raised by 'fixing the seats circle on circle, tier above tier' around the arena marked for the performers—cakkaticakke mankatimanke bandhimsu.

Ancient Buddhists were against theatrical entertainments but later playwrights like Ashvaghosha and Harsha wrote plays on Buddhist themes which were performed in Buddhist monasteries. Nagarjunakonda amphitheatre, ascribed to the later half of the third century A.D., was probably used to enact plays on Buddhist themes under the watchful eyes of goddess Hariti whose temple formed part of the amphitheatre complex.

It is very interesting to note that archaeologists found a figure of Dionysus, Greek god of wine, vegetation and theatre, carved on a stone slab at Nagarjunakonda. Roman terracotta figures and gold coins were excavated in the valley. There was maritime contact between Greco-Roman world and South India during early centuries of Christian era. Archaeologists feel that the plan of Nagarjunakonda amphitheatre was conceived by some foreign convert to Buddhism.

NANDI

Eulogium or praise of a deity, a kind of a blessing pronounced as a prologue to a drama.

According to Bharata the Sutradhara, director of the drama, recites Nandi as a part of Purvaranga or preliminaries performed before the actual commencement of the play.

Bharata has given a few specimens of Nandi:

1. Salutation to all the gods. Blesses be the twice-born class. Let the king and cows attain good health by his Soma-sacrifice.
2. Let there be an advancement of the cause of the Brahmins, and let their enemies be killed, and let the great king rule this earth together with all the seas.
3. Let this state prosper, and this theatre flourish and let the producer of the theatrical show attain virtues inspired by the Vedic knowledge.
4. Let playwright attain fame, and let this virtue increase, and by this kind of sacrifices let the god be always pleased (NS, Ghosh).

Generally we see playwrights composing Nandi in the honour of Lord Shiva. Nandi literally means joy. The eulogium which gives joy is Nandi, says Sahitya Darpana.

Panini in his Ashtadhyayi, written centuries before Bharata, mentions Nandi (III. 2.21) and for the singer of Nandi he used a term Nandikara.

NATA

Actor, dancer, mime, sometimes used to describe acrobats too.

NATAKA

One of the ten forms of drama mentioned by Bharata in his Natya Shastra.

The play which has its subject matter a well-known story, for hero a celebrated person of exalted nature and which describes the character of a person born in the line of royal seers, divine protection (for him), his many superhuman powers, and exploits such as success (in different undertakings), and amorous pastimes, which has suitable number of acts (anka) and introductory scenes (praveshaka) is called Nataka.

Behaviour of kings due to their joys and sorrows, when revealed by means of acts expressing in varied ways the psychological states (rasa), carrying many sentiments (bhava) is called a Nataka (NS: Ghosh). According to Bharata the Nataka and the Prakarana are made up of all the styles, vrittis. Number of acts should not be less than five and more than ten.

NATAKASHALA

Temple hall used for singing, dancing, music and dramatic enactment. There are a number of inscriptions which refer to Natakashala or Natyamandapa attached to the temples. Some of them are listed below.

Annual Report of Indian Epigraphy: 1921, No. 398: Tiruvadi, S. Arcot District, Tamil Nadu, Uttamacholadeva, year 14, Tamil. Records the gift of 96 sheep by Attaman Ayyaran alias Kandatol Gandappayyan of Pungunram for burning a perpetual lamp in the nataka-salai—mandapa erected by him in the temple.

Annual Report of Indian Epigraphy, 1925, No. 152: Tiruvaduturai, Tanjavur District, Tamil Nadu, Kulottungachola, year 46, Tamil. Registers a sale of land to the temple at the Tiruvaduturai by the assembly of Kottur alias Jayadara-chaturvedi-mangalam, a brahmadeya, which met in the temple of Eduttapada-Vinnagar-Alvar and a grant of 70 kasu by Rajadhiraj alias Rajendrasola-Anantpalar towards the taxes on the land, for the maintenance of a theatre called Nanavida Natakasalai in the temple.

Annual Report of Indian Epigraphy, 1945, No. F 9: Hire-Bendigeri, Dharwar District, Karnataka. In the characters of the 12th century, Kannada states that Goravabbeya Chattisetti caused to be constructed a natyasala for the temple of Svayambhu.

Annual Report of Indian Epigraphy, 1893, No. 534: Published in South Indian Inscriptions, Vol. V, No. 194, 11.6–7, Eluru,

West Godavari District, A.P. Saka 1155, Telugu. Refers to grant for whitewashing every year the temple mandapa and natyamandapa constructed by the donor, Malya-peggada, son of Sriman-mahapradhani Ananttana-peggada. The temple was of Mulasthana Sri Somesvara Mahadeva.

Annual Report of Indian Epigraphy, 1933–34, No. BK 20: Published in South Indian Inscriptions, Vol. XVIII, No. 117.1.22, Kaginelli, Dharwar District, Karnataka, 1121 A.D., Kannada. Refers to the construction of the temple of Kalesvaresa and a natyasala.

Annual Report of Indian Epigraphy, 1899, No. 361: Published in South Indian Inscriptions, Vol. VI, No. 1142, Simhachalam, Vishakhapatnam District, A.P. Saka 1190, Sanskrit and Telugu. It refers to the construction of mukhamandapa, natya mandapa and tiruchuttumalya in the temple of Narasimha on the order of the king Viranarasimha (in Simhachalam).

Annual Report of Indian Epigraphy, 1895, No. 154, Published in South Indian Inscriptions, Vol. V, No. 718, 11.34, Tamil. Tiruvidaimarudur, Tanjavur District, Tamil Nadu, Parekesari who took the head of the pandya, year 4. Mentions the nataksalai and stipulates that all the seven angas of the Ariya-kuttu should be danced in the temple.

NATA MANDIR

Dancing hall of Orissan temple. The fully evolved Orissan temples have four chambers. The first chamber Sri Mandir or Vimana is sanctum sanctorum in which the idols of the deities are kept and worshipped. The second chamber is called Jagamohana or assembly hall. Some of the early Orissan temples, like Parashurameshvar temple of Bhuvaneshvar, comprise these two chambers only. Some of the later temples too had initially these two chambers only but to them two more chambers were added. They were Nata Mandir, the dancing hall, and Bhoga Mandapa, the hall of offering. The best example of this development is the magnificent Lingaraj temple at Bhuvaneshvar. Now it has four chambers, Sri Mandir, Jagamohana, Nata Mandir and lastly the Bhoga Mandapa. The Jagannatha temple at Puri too evolved in the same manner—Nata Mandir and Bhoga Mandapa added to already existing Sri Mandir and Jagamohana. Nata Mandir is used to make offering of dance and music to temple deities placed in the Sri Mandir.

All these four chambers are joined together but the Nata Mandir of Sun Temple at some distance from the Jagamohana stands as an independent structure. It is in ruins, only the plinth and pillars surviving, covered with profusion of sculptures of dancers and musicians.

NATARAJA

Shiva as a supreme dancer; conceptualised in most dynamic and dramatic icon-type in South India infused with many dimensional rich symbolism.

Since ages Shiva is known as a cosmic dancer. Entire universe is manifestation of his dance representing movement and action of cosmic powers and forces. When performed in frenzied fury it unleashes the destructive energy that annihilates everything. Creation and destruction are twin aspects of his being.

The dance of Nataraja represents and symbolises five divine actions—shristi, sthiti, samhar, tirobhava and anugraha. When he dances the earth shakes and trembles by the impact of his feet, the majestic sweep of his hands throws celestial bodies in disarray, by the force of his whirling matted locks of hair heavens shudder. Seven types of Tandava he dances are sandhya tandava, kalika tandava, ananda tandava, tripura tandava, Gauri tandava, samhar tandava and Uma tandava.

Assuming terrible Bhairava form when he dances in burning ground all his ferocious attendant ganas whirl around him. In gentler mood he makes wife Gauri sit on the throne and dances before her displaying all his amours.

Puranas and literary works adore him with epithets such as Maha Shailusha, nartana-shila and natyopaharalubdha. The Mahabharata with great reverence describes the dance of jumping, yawning, laughing, singing, weeping Shiva.

The best tribute to Mahashailusha Shiva came from Acharya Nandikeshvara who in his Natyadarpana wrote:

Angikam bhuvanam yasya
Vachikam sarva vangmayam
Aharyam chandrataradi
Tam numah sattvikam Shivam.

'I bow before you 'Sattvika' Shiva whose 'angika' is entire universe, whose 'vachika' is entire literature and whose 'aharya' is glittering celestial bodies.'

Images of dancing Shiva are found since ancient times. One of the most majestic icons of dancing ithyphallic Shiva of early period is found adorning the facade of Vaital temple at Bhuvaneshvar, Orissa. Some of the Yogini temples in the country have in their centre the icons of dancing Shiva.

Most majestic temple dedicated to Nataraja Shiva is located at Chidambaram in Tamil Nadu. We find one hundred and eight dance postures, karanas, as described in the Natya Shastra sculpted on the temple. At Brihadeshvara Shiva temple at Tanjore Shiva himself is shown performing these Karanas.

In the first chapter of the Natya Shastra Bharata refers to the dance of Shiva full of actions, emotions and aesthetic sentiments—rasa-bhava-kriyatmaka. Bharata says that art of dance was Shiva's contribution to theatre.

Ritual worship of Shiva includes offerings of dance, music and drama. In his long poem Meghaduta Kalidasa has described the evening worship offered to Shiva at Mahakala temple at Ujjayani which included beautiful dances of the courtesans. Various inscriptions refer to dedication of devadasis to Shiva temples whose job was to dance before Lord's image.

In the plays of Kalidasa we find prayer songs in the honour of Shiva. However most majestic description of Shiva's dance is found in the Nandi of Vishakhadatta's play Mudrarakshasa. Here this dance is described as Dukkha Nritya.

We find references to Shiva-lila dramas in literary works. Shiva is considered as presiding deity of classical dance form, the Bharatanatyam.

NATASUTRA

A manual for actors mentioned in the Ashtadhyayi of Panini. Shilalin and Krishashva were the authors of Natasutra, the work now lost to posterity.

Exact time of Panini is not known but most of the scholars tend to place him sometime between the 7th and 5th century B.C. He was born in the city of Shalatura in Gandhara. This city is identified with Lahur, a small town north-west of Ohind, in the angle of river Kabul meeting the river Sindhu or Indus. In the 7th century A.D. Chinese traveller Yuan Chwang visited this city wherein he found the statue of Panini raised in his honour.

Ashtadhyayi is the work of Sanskrit grammar. Here we find numerous musical instruments mentioned. Panini knew the term Nandi and the singer of Nandi, the Nandikara. Nandi is a prayer song sung at the beginning of the performance of the drama. He also mentions the words like actor, nata, dancer, nartaka, singer, gathaka, dance, nritya and dramatic acting, natya. His sutra pramada sammadau harshe suggests that he knew about musical opera too.

The composition of Nata Sutra or Manual for Actors presupposes flourishing dramatic activity. Probably drama proper was in existence during the time of Panini.

NATI

Actress, dancer, courtesan. Generally appears in the prologue of Sanskrit play as a wife of Sutradhara.

Vatsyayana in his Kamasutra categorises Nati as a courtesan. Explaining the word commentator Yashodhara says that Nati is rangayoshita or woman of the stage. In this sense she is referred to as rangopajivani or one who depends on stage performance for her livelihood.

We are told in the Kamasutra that once to appreciate the dance performance of a Nati, the general of Pandya king, Naradeva, tried to touch her in the fit of passion. Accidentally his powerful hand hit the eye of performing Nati and it got damaged for ever. Commentator Yashodhara gives her name as Chitralekha—rajakule nati chitralekha.

In the Gatha Saptashati, a collection of Maharashtri Prakrit folk verses belonging to the first century A.D., there is a mention of a Nati who has applied the make-up of Haritala over her face—haritalamanditamukhi nati.

In yet another verse there is an indirect reference to female performer on the stage. It says that female best suited for love-making is one who has just returned from the stage after giving a performance—rangottirna. Nati is already defined as rangayoshita or woman of the stage.

In Patanjali's Mahabhashya she is referred to as Natasya stree—wife of Nata or woman belonging to Nata community. When Nata women go to stage people naughtily ask them 'to whom to whom you belong' and they reply, 'to you to you!'—Natanam striyo rangam gata yo yah prcchati kasya yuyam kasya yuyam iti tam tam tva tva ity ahuh.

Son of an actress is known as Nateraka. In the Bhana play Padmaprabhrutakam Nateraka Darduraka, disciple of drama director Natakacharya Gandharvadatta is mentioned.

As a wife of Sutradhara the Nati appears in the prologue of some Sanskrit plays, sometimes she sings some song or converses with Sutradhara, or gives an indication that she too is going to act in the play they are speaking about.

NATIKA

One of the ten forms of drama mentioned by Bharata in his Natya Shastra.

Plot should be invented, original, hero a king, contain incidents related to music or affairs of the harem. Its chief features being four acts, abundance of female characters, graceful gestures as its soul, well arranged constituents, many dances, songs and recitations and love's enjoyment. The Natika should be known also to contain a display of royal manners, a fit of anger and its pacification, and to have the hero, his queen, the female messengers and attendants as its dramatis personae (NS: Ghosh).

NATYACHARYA

Teacher of dramatic arts. Since ancient times there existed a guru-centred system of imparting education in dramatic arts including singing, dancing, playing on musical instruments and play acting. We find references to manuals or text-books, Nata Sutras, written for the same purpose in ancient literary works. Panini speaks of Nata Sutras, Bhasa refers to Natya Shastra, the treatises lost to posterity. However Bharata's work on dramaturgy has survived the vagaries of time.

In Bhasa's play Charudatta the courtesan Vasantasena is described as one educated in theatrical arts hence expert in voice modulation—esha rangapraveshena kalanam chaiva shikshyaya, swarantarena daksha.

Ganikas or courtesans were specially trained in dramatic arts. In the Ganikadhyaksha Prakarana of his Arthashastra author Kautilya says that the state should provide for the livelihood of teachers who train courtesans in dramatic arts including the reading of dramatic texts—pathya and natyakshara.

In the Kamasutra it is said that courtesans should learn sixtyfour arts which include singing, dancing, playing on musical instruments and visual enactment of dramatic legends, stories—nataka akyayika darshanam. There were teachers to teach these dramatic arts variously referred to as Natyacharyas or Nrityacharyas.

In the Bhana plays of the early Gupta period Natacharyas whose job was to teach courtesans are mentioned. In the Bhana play

Padmaprabhrutakam by Shudraka there is a mention of Natakacharya named Gandharvadatta. We are informed that Natakacharya has asked his disciple Darduraka to take the copy of the play Kumudvati to courtesan Devasena as she is playing a role of a heroine in it. Though unwell out of respect for the Natakacharya courtesan Kumudvati accepts the copy of the play. This indicates that courtesans used to learn play acting at the feet of Natakacharyas.

In Kalidasa's play Malavikagnimitra appear two Natyacharyas, Ganadasa and Haradatta, who are employed in the royal court to educate and train the women of seraglio in dramatic arts. Ganadasa says that those who teach just for the sake of money are not more than shopkeepers selling knowledge for price—jnanapanyam vanijam.

In the Kuttanimatam kavya we come across a very strict Nartanacharya who makes his disciple labour very hard. Mother of a girl who was receiving training from this particular Nartanacharya sends a message to him not to put her daughter to severe physical strain as she is very young and tender in limbs.

In the same work we meet a Nrityacharya who directed and staged the first act of the play Ratnavali by Harsha in the temple of Kashi Vishveshvara of Varanasi.

In the Kathasaritsagara we meet a dance master, Labdhavara, who seduces the queen, his disciple, and elopes with her. This reminds us of Arjuna, hero of the epic Mahabharata, who under the guise of Brihannala taught dance to princess Uttara, daughter of king Virata, and treated her as her own daughter.

In ancient Buddhist literature teachers of theatrical arts are mentioned. In Gamani Samyutta we meet a dance master named Talaputa who discussed the nature of dramatic arts with Lord Buddha himself. In the Ashokavadana there occurs a story of Natyacharya of Dakshinapatha who staged a Bauddha Nataka, play based on the theme of the life of Buddha, in which he played the role of Buddha.

A number of inscriptions mention dance masters attached to temples to teach dance and drama to temple girls. In sculptural panels attached to temples dance masters are shown training the female disciples. Natyacharyas and Nrityacharyas played key role in imparting the training of dramatic arts since ancient times.

NATYA SHASTRA

Great encyclopaedic work of ancient origin ascribed to Bharata. The scholars ascribe it to the period between the 2nd century B.C. and 2nd century A.D.

The tradition of writing works on dramaturgy precedes Bharata. Grammarian Panini in his Ashtadhyayi, ascribed to the 6th–7th century B.C., refers to a short manual for actors, Natasutra, written by Shilali and Krishashva.

In the fourth century B.C. playwright Bhasa in his play Avimaraka makes a reference to Natya Shastra. Boasting about his profound scholarship the Vidushaka or jester says that there is a Natya Shastra named Ramayana, asti Ramayanam nama natyashastra, and he has read full five stanzas from it before the passing of a year.

It is not clear to which Natya Shastra reference is made here. It may or may not be the work of Bharata having similar title.

Bharata too mentions the names of the scholars like Dhurtila, Shandilya, Vatsya and Kohala who wrote before him.

Bharata in his Natya Shastra did not take the credit of writing it. He says that it was Brahma who created the Natya Veda and handed over to him for putting it to practice.

Probably Bharata by assimilating the contents of earlier works on dramaturgy created his own Natya Shastra. Some scholars feel that the Natya Shastra as is available to us is not the original work of Bharata. Like Mahabharata the original Natya Shastra of Bharata continued to grow thanks to the later writers who by their contributions inflated its text.

Some scholars take Bharata as a clan of actors and ascribe Natya Shastra as a work formulated by this clan and not by one person named as Bharata.

Whatever may be the case the Natya Shastra exerted profound influence on the entire gamut of Sanskrit dramatic literature, and its production technique.

Natya Shastra as is available to us contains thirtyseven chapters and is written in mixed prose and verse form. It deals with several topics related to dramaturgy as the origin and history of dramatic art, construction of playhouses, procedure of play production, acting, dance and music, costumes and make-up, rules of prosody, diction of a play, construction of plot, rules on use of languages, various kinds of plays, sentiments and emotions found in drama, the rasa siddhanta or theory about aesthetics of drama, various styles of presentation, dramatis personae, audiences, etc. It is a profound work with great magnitude covering every aspect of dramatic art.

At the end of the tenth century A.D. Kashmiri scholar Abhinavagupta wrote a commentary on the Natya Shastra under the title Abhinava Bharati and carried forward the tradition of Bharata.

In the works like Abhinava Bharati, Sangitaratnakara, Natyalakshana Ratnakosha names of several authorities on dramaturgy like Udbhata, Lollata, Shankuka, Matrigupta, Subandhu, Nakhakutta are mentioned However their works are lost to posterity.

In the tenth century A.D. a new style of staging Sanskrit plays, known as Kutiyattam, evolved in Kerala. It differed from Natya Shastra style of dramatic production.

However a number of dance, dance-drama forms that emerged from time to time followed the Natya Shastra tradition and presentation techniques. Natya Shastra still very much dominates the field of classical dance and dance-drama forms prevalent in India.

NATYA VEDA

The science of dramaturgy. After Kritayuga came Tretayuga. People were afflicted with jealousy, anger, lust and greed and gave themselves to sensual pleasures, gramya dharma, that diluted their happiness with sorrow. Disturbed by this development in the Jambudwipa gods led by Indra approached Brahma and humbly requested him to create a pleasurable diversion accessible to all the people, sarvavarnikam. They requested him to devise a purposeful entertainment, kridaniyaka, which is audible as well as visible, drishyam sravyam chayadhavet. They pleaded with him to create the fifth Veda, panchama veda.

Considering their request Brahma went into deep meditation with the intention of creating the fifth Veda, the Natya Veda, the repository of historical legends. He desired to create Veda reflective of all future actions of the people, sarvakarmanudarshakam, and conducive to dharma, artha and yasha (right conduct, wealth and fame). He desired to enrich it with the essence of all sciences and make it repository of all arts, sarvashastratha sampannam sarva shilpa pradarshakam.

With this resolve Lord Brahma remembered all the four Vedas. From the Rig Veda he culled text pathya, from the Sama Veda song and music, gita, from Yajurveda he took acting, abhinaya and from Atharva Veda the aesthetic sentiments or rasa.

After creating the Natya Veda Lord Brahma gave it to Indra. Pleading his inability to put it into practice he gave it to sage Bharata, the legendary harbinger of Indian theatre.

NAUTANKI

An operatic folk drama of North India full of singing, dancing and music.

Nautanki evolved out of earlier Swang tradition that was prevalent in northern part of the country. Saint poet of Varanasi, Kabir, frequently mentions Swang Tamasha as a dramatic form of folk entertainment. At one place he has caustically said that during religious discourses people go to sleep but when there is a performance of Swang Tamasha they keep wide awake and sleep, even for a moment, does not overtake them.

This testifies to the popularity of Swang theatre as a mode of folk entertainment.

Famous Sufi poet Malik Muhammad Jayasi wrote an epic Padmavat in the first half of the 16th century in which he has referred to the folk drama, Swang.

The 17th century Hindi poet Sabalsingh Chauhan in his Mahabharata wrote: Kahu nrityakari nachi gave kahu nataki Swang dikhave.

In 1883 Captain R.C. Temple published his famous work *The Legends of Punjab* in which he has given the texts of three Swang plays. According to him these Swang plays were annually performed during Holi festival at Jagadhari in the Ambala district of Punjab.

The Swang tradition of folk entertainment spread to other parts of the country such as Rajasthan, Punjab, Uttar Pradesh, Madhya Pradesh and evolved under different generic names assimilating local influences.

In 19th century Nawab Wajid Ali Shah, ruler of Avadha, borrowing from earlier forms such as Ras, Swang, created his own style of musical dance drama named as Rahas. It deeply influenced local folk and traditional dramatic forms.

In Hathras-Kanpur region the swang tradition took the form of Nautanki. This operatic form full of singing and dancing started entertaining people by staging love stories such as of Gabru and Jamal. It is said that the story of princess Nautanki became so popular that this newly evolved musical theatre became famous as Nautanki.

Initially Nautanki was purely a play in verse but later prose dialogues too were incorporated in its performance. To begin with Nautanki employed only male actors, female roles too were enacted by male performers. Gradually women too joined the Nautanki troupes. It later came under the influence of Parsi theatre and became more loud and showy.

Nautanki plays are based on mythological legends, medieval love-stories, lives of saints and social reformers, historical tales. During India's freedom struggle plays were written to inspire people to rise against British rule, some of which were even proscribed by the administration. On the story of Jaliyanwalabag massacre a Nautanki play Khune Nahak was written by Srikrishna Pahelwan of Kanpur. Plays were written on the lives of revolutionaries like Bhagatsingh.

Nautanki troupes came up in other cities like Lucknow and Jhansi and regions including Braj became the centre of Nautanki art. Nakkara is the principal musical instrument of Nautanki performance. It is employed in a very dramatic manner.

After the inclusion of erotic, and sometimes even obscene, songs and dances in Nautanki performances it fell into disrepute.

During festivals like Holi and rural fairs Nautanki performances are staged. Traditional Nautanki provides rich fare of folk and classical music.

NAVARANGA

A pillared dancing hall with circular dance floor in front of sanctum sanctorum of the medieval Jain temple. Navarangas are seen in the Jain temples of Karnataka, particularly at Halebid. The 12th century Jain temples of Halebid have magnificent images of Tirthankaras. It is said that Shantala, queen of king Vishnuvardhana, used to perform dance in these temples having beautiful Navarangas.

Queen Shantala is described in an inscription (EC, Vol. V, BI 58) as a 'jewelled lamp in the house of Bharatagama (Natyashastra), a hand-jewel in all manners of dancing and Sarasvati in singing.' Some Hindu temples like the Channakeshava temple at Belur have circular dance floors for dance performances.

NAYAKA

Principal male character of the drama around whom the plot revolves.

Nayaka word is derived from the verbal root 'ni' which means to lead. In this sense he is the lead character of the play, model of all virtues and embodiment of good qualities. There indeed are a very few lead characters who differ from this model.

Four types of heroes are mentioned in the works on dramaturgy. They are:

1. Dhirodatta: Courageous, firm, noble and sublime. Example: Bhagavan Ramachandra.
2. Dhiroddhata: Courageous, firm, noble but haughty, impudent. Example: Bhima.
3. Dhiralalita: Courageous, firm, noble, he is soft by nature. He is fond of fine arts, dancing, singing, music and pleasure loving. Example: Vatsaraja in Ratnavali Nataka.
4. Dhiraprashanta: Courageous, firm, noble he is sacrificing by nature and usually a Brahmin. Example: Madhava in Malati Madhava.

The following four categories of Nayaka are based on his attitude towards Nayika or heroine:

Anukula: Agreeable, friendly, kind, obliging and faithful to beloved or Nayika.

Dakshina: Pleasing, clever, dexterous. Man of many women but loves them equally well.

Grishta: A Nayaka who does not feel ashamed even when rebuked, remains carefree and unrepentant even after being caught by wrong foot, goes on telling lies even after his mistakes are pointed out is called Grishta.

Shatha: False, deceitful, cheat, fraudulent. A lover who pretends affection for one female while his heart is fixed on another.

One more category of Uttama, Madhyama and Adhama is added to this. Uttama is best, madhyama is middling and adhama a lowly character.

Theorists have imagined a great variety of heroes. There are ten main and ten subsidiary forms of drama. Each type has its own kind of hero. For instance Nataka needs celebrated hero of exalted nature, Ihamriga, says Bharata, should have divine hero, Prahasana has a rogue as a hero, Prasthana needs slaves as hero and heroine, Uttapya has four heroes, person of lower position is the hero of Prenkhana, Vilasika has person of low standing as hero.

NAYIKA

The principal female character in the play, heroine. Woman who leads the man on the path of love.

She can be anybody—a nymph, deity, princess, courtesan or commoner—but she is always beautiful, full of feminine graces, said to be twentyeight in number, including radiance of youth, sweetness, gay, frolicsome, playfulness.

There can be play without heroine such as Mudrarakshasa or one totally devoted to describing beauty and graces of heroine scenes after scenes like Karpuramanjiri of Rajashekhara. There is at least one minor form of drama, uparupaka, named Bhanika in which hero is shown inferior to heroine. In Bhanika hero is manda or idle, sluggish, weak, lazy and dull but the heroine is udatta or sublime, illustrious.

There are ten main forms of drama and eighteen minor ones. Each one has its own kind of heroine.

Interestingly no woman is ever presented as a vamp or principal villainous character in the traditional Indian drama, except probably for Kaikeyi, the step-mother of Rama, prince of Ayodhya.

Indian theorists and poets took great delight and interest in describing the Nayikas whose number runs into hundreds. Nayikas of Kamasutras and Natyashastras are different. In the works on erotica we find Nayikas categorised into Kanya, Punarbhu, Veshya or Mrigi, Badava, Padmini, Chitrini, Hastini and Shankhini.

In the works on dramaturgy three basic types of Nayikas are Swiya, Anya and Sadharani. Swiya is Nayaka's own wife, Anya is daughter or wife of another person and Sadharani is courtesan.

There are three more categories—Mugdha, Madhya and Pragalbha.

Mugdha Nayika is a tender aged girl standing on the threshold of youth, young inexperienced beauty, innocent of art of coquetry, hesitant to make love, very shy and always blushing, coy.

Madhya or middling Nayika is one who is in the prime of her youth, given to the pleasures of love overcoming shyness. She enjoys variety in love-making, vichitrasurata. She is grown up sexually and physically and pines for love.

Pragalbha is a mature woman, very passionate, expert in all kinds of love-making or samastaratakovida and one whose lover is won by aggressive sexual overtures and is obedient to her.

Various sub-divisions of these main types are found described in works on poetics.

However the Ashtanayikas or eight heroines of Natyashastra are very famous and they are portrayed in dance and drama. They are:

1. Vasakasajja (A heroine dressed up for union): A woman who in eager expectation of love's pleasure decorates herself joyfully when the conjugal union is due is Vasakasajja Nayika.
2. Virahotkanthita (A heroine distressed by separation): A woman whose beloved one does not turn up on account of his preoccupation with many other engagements and makes her afflicted with sadness by his not coming is Virahotkanthita Nayika.
3. Swadhinabhartrika (A heroine having her husband in subjugation): A woman whose lover captivated by her pleasing qualities as well as intense pleasure of love (surata) from her stays by his side is Swadhinabhartrika Nayika.
4. Kalahantarita (A heroine separated from her lover by quarrel): When woman is impatient for her lover having gone away due to a quarrel or jealousy, and not returning is Kalahantarita Nayika.
5. Khandita (One enraged with her lover): A woman whose beloved one, due to attachment for another female, does not come for conjugal union is Khandita Nayika.
6. Vipralabdha (A deceived heroine): When lover does not come to such a woman (i.e. Khandita) for a certain reason even when after he had met her and made a tryst is a Vipralabdha Nayika.
7. Proshitabhartrika (A heroine with a sojourning husband): A woman whose beloved one is living abroad on account of serious duties and who has the ends of her hair scattered is Proshitabhartrika Nayika.
8. Abhisarika (A heroine moving towards her lover): A woman who due to love or lust is attracted to her lover and gives up modesty for going out to meet him is Abhisarika Nayika (NS: Ghosh).

All the Nayikas except Proshitabhartrika are beautifully portrayed at one place in the musical opera, the Gitagovinda. Most poetic and dramatic description of Abhisarika Nayika is found in the play Mricchakatika.

We find all these Nayikas portrayed beautifully in various schools of miniature painting.

NEPATHYA

Also known as Aharyabhinaya means costumes, make-up, stage property, setting related to the production of drama. Bharata says that Nepathya is of four kinds:

1. Model work—Pusta
2. Decoration—Alamkara
3. Painting of limbs—Angarachana
4. Living Creatures—Sanjiva

Stage property and setting which include raising of hills, palaces on the stage or making of objects like carriages, armours, banner-staffs, artificial elephants out of mat, cloth, and similar material are discussed by Bharata.

He also speaks of mechanical devices, yantra, used on the stage probably for trick scenes such as showing characters flying through the sky, descending from heaven, etc.

Under Alamkara Bharata discusses various kinds of ornaments for different parts of the body, garlands and drapery. He advises drama director not to use too many ornaments for they will cause fatigue to actors and hinder their movements. Instead of ornaments of pure gold Bharata advises the use of artificial jewellery made of lac inlaid slightly with jewels.

As far as Angarachana is concerned Bharata says that black, blue, yellow and red are original or natural colours and there are derivatives from these primary colours and also minor colours. They should be used for painting the limbs and make-up.

Bharata then goes on to discuss costumes, mainly of three kinds viz. red, white and variegated coming from different marts. He also speaks of soiled cloths used for lunatics, intoxicated persons and persons struck with calamity.

He then tells us how to make masks, different kinds of wigs, limbs, crowns, weapons which in fact should come under pusta. Under Sanjiva he speaks of bringing living animals on the stage. Other minor accessories demanded by the art of theatre are termed as upakaranas.

Bharata says that the object accessories required for the dramatic production should be made out of light material such as grass, mat, lac, cloth, beeswax, wood, leather, sliced bamboo, palm-products, etc.

We get glimpses of the Nepathya griha in Rajashekhara's play Karpuramanjiri. Looking at the preparations going on in the tiring room the Sutradhara says that actors are busy making the costumes ready, some are making garlands while others are seen spreading around the masks, some with brushes in the pots of colours to decorate the limbs.

In the prologue of the play Malati Madhava by Bhavabhuti the Sutradhara asks his assistant to tell the Kushilavas or actors to wear coloured make-up—Varnika Parigraha.

In Bhasa's play Pratimanataka there is a reference to Sangitashala attached to the palace of Dasharatha having Nepathyagriha attached to it. We are told that Rava is the Nepathya-rakshika or keeper of this tiring room where different kinds of objects such as ashokapatra and costumes made of barks of the tree were stored for the use of actors.

In the Harivamsha Purana there is a description of enactment of drama on the occasion of Kalotsava in the capital of demon king Vajranabha. The Yadavas, the Purana says, who presented the play Rambhabhisara appeared in proper costumes and make-up, baddhanepathya, on the stage appropriate to their roles.

In Kalidasa's play Malavikagnimitra Pandita Kaushika asks the dance masters to bring their disciples for dance competition devoid of make-up and heavy costume—vigata nepathya.

In the prologue of the play Ratnavali by Harsha the Sutradhara says that as soon as the decoration of the stage, nepathyarachana, is ready I shall stage the play.

However Bharata says 'if you have expertise to create palaces, hills on the stage, make models of elephants, horses, carriage it is well and good but better option is their existence should be established by symbolic gestures, body movements, acting' (NS, XX: 41–42).

NISHUMBHA NRITYA

A terrible dance of fierce goddess Chamunda which she performs in the court of Lord Shiva.

We find majestic description of Nishumbha Nritya in the eighth century playwright Bhavabhuti's drama Malati Madhava.

By the impact of the footsteps of the dancing goddess the universe starts trembling, sparks of fire lit her yellow eyes and when she whirls her head looks like a wooden wheel of fire. The black serpents worn by the goddess around her arms as amulets get terribly disturbed and start vomiting poison. When her outspread arms touch the mountains during dancing they get uprooted and start flying around. When the goddess wearing the garland of skulls around her neck and donning the costume made of elephant hide starts dancing her attendant fiends, ghosts, evil spirits start howling in terrible voice applauding her performance.

Worship of such a terrible goddess formed the part of tantric rituals which Aghoraghanta and his consort Kapalakundala are shown performing in the play.

After praising the dance of the goddess the tantric couple too performs ritual dance to appease the deity.

OBSCENITY

Defining obscenity, or ashlila, the Sahitya Darpana says that conversation, discourse, dialogue or dramatic entertainment which opens with amorous topic involving talk about sexual intercourse or love making may be described as obscene or ashlila—surataarambhago-shthydavashlilatvam. Double entendres with sexual innuendos too are considered obscene by Vishvanatha.

Kautilya too in his Arthashastra prohibits performing artists from speaking about, or making fun of, copulation of men and women.

Sanskrit dramatic literature is not totally free from obscenity as defined by Sahitya Darpana. Surata or sexual intercourse finds mention in some plays.

For instance in Bhasa's Avimaraka we find hero Avimaraka contemplating how amorous feelings and gestures would make the face of the heroine look beautiful during the course of love-making or surata—Kathannu suratantaraprachuravi-bhramam tad bhavet.

In Bhavabhuti's Malati Madhava we find 'minute word-pictures of physical sensations during imagined sexual gratification of two girls of noble families.'

In the prologue of the play Mricchakatikam the Sutradhara bluntly says that the play depicts the festival of love-making—satsuratotsava—of Charudatta and Vasantasena. In the Mahanataka of Hanumat we find trace of obscenity in description of romance of Rama and Sita.

In the musical opera, the Gita Govinda, there is very erotic description of love-making. In the opening of the poem it is said that it was written for the people curious to know about art of love-making—ratikalasukutuhalam.

A number of Bhana and Prahasana plays contain obscene passages. It is believed that ritual use of obscenity, abuses, lascivious words effectively drives away evil spirits. In the Himachal Pradesh in the ritualistic dramas such as Rakas Khel obscene songs, dialogues are included to drive away evil spirits.

Obscenity is found in fertility rituals and festivals. In the festival of Holi obscene gestures, songs, dialogues and performances, dramatic skits are freely enacted. Obscenity is found in songs and dialogues of some of the folk dramatic forms like Tamasha and Nautanki. Double entendres with sexual innuendos are common to these forms of great rustic charm. Bharata allows Vidushaka to evoke laughter by uttering obscene words—ashlilabhasita (NS: 13.141).

ODISSI

Graceful, lyrical and sculpturesque classical dance style of Orissa.

Dance tradition in Orissa dates back to several centuries. Bharata in second century B.C. refers to a dance style Odra-Magadhi that flourished in Orissa along with other neighbouring region.

Jain monarch of Orissa, Kharavela, in his famous Hathigumpha inscription incised in the natural ceiling of a natural cavern on Udayagiri hill near Bhuvaneshvar and datable to the second century B.C., refers to himself as Gandharva veda budho or expert in dramatic arts and music. The inscription also refers to festivals organised by him which were full of dancing, music, play-acting—dampa nata gita vedita samadasanahi utsav samaj kara panahi cha kidapayati nagarim.

Jain caves, particularly Rani Gumpha cave in Udayagiri, are famous for their dance scenes sculpted in them. In fact the Rani Gumpha cave is identified as an open air theatre. Dance panels in Rani Gumpha cave are considered as earliest evidence of classical dance in India.

Inscriptional evidence indicates that at least since 10th century A.D. Devadasi girls were consecrated to temples. Their job was to dance before the idols of temple deities. Dancing halls or Nata Mandapas were added to temples. In the 12th century Jayadeva composed his immortal opera Gita Govinda which Devadasis started performing in the Jagannatha temple at Puri.

In the inscription of July 1499 Gajapati ruler of Orissa Prataparudradeva by a royal decree enjoined the temple administration to perform Gita Govinda opera every day in the Jagannatha temple at Puri. The inscription states:

'Dancing (nat) should be performed at the Bhoga time of the Elder Thakur (Balarama) and Gita Govinda Thakur (Jagannatha). The dancing should be held from the end of the evening Dhupa to the time of Bada singar (bed-time) Dhupa. The batch (dancing girls) of Bada Thakur, the fixed female dancers of Kapileshvara Thakur, the old batch, the Telangi batch, all will learn no other song than Gita Govinda of Bada Thakur. They will not sing any other song. No other kind of dancing should be performed before the God. Besides dancing there are four Vaishnava singers, they should sing only Gita Govinda. Hearing in one tone from them, those who are ignorant will learn the Gita Govinda song. The superintendent who knowingly allows other song to be sung, and other dance to be performed rebels against Jagannatha.'

Dancing girls were there in the service of Jagannatha at least since 12th century. According to temple chronicle, Madala Panji, the son of Chodagangadeva, Gajarajadeva II (1170–1194 A.D.) consecrated twenty dancing girls to serve Jagannatha at his Puri temple.

Devadasi girls in Orissa were known as Mahari. Some of them known as Nachuni or dancers and Gauni or singers were entrusted with the task of dancing and singing in the temple. They were assisted by male musicians who played on different musical instruments such as Veena and Pakhawaj. The duty of Mahari known as Samparada Niyoga was to dance during various deva-yatras or processions. Maharis were settled around Jagannatha temple.

In the 16th century Gotipua dancers emerged on the scene. Gotipua boy will don a female attire and dance which apart from graceful movements is known for its supple acrobatic feats, Bandha Nritya.

Since 15th century a number of treatises on dance and music were written in Orissa codifying the local artistic traditions, prominent among them being Abhinayachandrika by Maheswara Mohapatra and Natya Manorama by Raghunatha Rath.

Earlier record of dance postures and mudras is there in the form of dance sculptures found embellishing Orissan temples since ancient times.

The word Odissi applied to classical dance evolved locally in Orissa is derived from the term Odra Nritya found in the Abhinayachandrika. The revival of this ancient art preserved by Maharis and Gotipuas, recorded by the authors of treatises such as Abhinayachandrika and sculptors of innumerable dance-sculptures adorning Orissan temples took place quite recently.

For abhinaya the compositions of Oriya poets including Gita Govinda of Jayadeva, mostly depicting Radha-Krishna love are taken up by dancers.

In general the Odissi dance performance starts with Mangalacharana comprised of a number of small items to invoke various deities including Ganesha. Then a pure dance item of immense charm Batu Nritya is performed. After Pallavi the Abhinaya starts in which lyrical compositions of poets are danced out with appropriate gestures and movements. The concluding item is Moksha Nata depicting pure dance.

OJA PALI

Semi-dramatic form of story telling full of singing, dancing and music that is prevalent in Assam.

Oja-pali is a group of singers and dancers. Oja, the leader of the party, is the main singer-narrator and Palis his assistants. Daina-pali is the chief assistant of the Oja among Palis.

There are two kinds of Oja-pali, one which takes the Manasa story for narration and the other which narrates stories from epics and Puranas. The first kind of Oja-pali is known as Sukandanni and the other as Vyah-gowa.

Manasa is a serpent goddess who has a great following in Assam. Sukavi Narayana has narrated the story of Manasa in his Assamese Padmapurana composed in verse form. The story is divided into three Khandas—Deva Khanda, Baniya Khanda and Bhatiyali Khanda. The Oja-pali party narrates this story for over several days.

The Oja stands in the forefront of the line of Palis behind him or they all stand in a single line with Oja at the centre. The performance opens with the singing of prayer songs in the praise of different deities. After the Purvaranga is open the Oja starts narrating the story using dance and music. He enacts different roles in the course of his narrative and at times converses with the Daina Pali. They all dance in different intricate patterns.

Vyah-gowa adopts similar performative style but the stories he takes up are from Assamese versions of epics and Puranas. He too assumes different roles while narrating the story. For instance if he is narrating Kamsa Vadha Prasanga he will alternatively enact the roles of Kamsa, Krishna, Balarama, Chanura, Mushtika, etc.

According to Daityari Thakur the Oja-pali parties were employed by Mahapurusha Shankardeva for chanting devotional prayers. It is said that he used the performative techniques of Oja-pali while evolving his Ankia Nat drama, particularly its Purvaranga. The character of Sutradhara which appears in the Ankia Nat is fashioned on the character of Oja.

PADATADITAKAM

A Bhana play written by Mahakavi Shyamilaka around 4th-5th century A.D. The venue of the play is Sarvabhauma Nagar or Ujjain and in all mock seriousness it discusses the issue of a courtesan kicking the head of her lover in fury and its implications in social, ethical, moral, legal terms.

Bhana is an one-act, one-actor burlesque in the form of a monologue. An actor in the guise of Vita, a pimp, appears on the stage and describes during his wanderings the scenes, events, happenings and merrily converses with different people in humorous and sometimes in satirical tone as if they are there in front of him.

We come to know from the narration of Vita that the chief courtesans of Saurashtra, Madanasena, in anger kicked the head of her lover Taundikoki Vishnunaga, a Brahmin well versed in grammar and law and on the top of it a high ranking government officer.

In the Vesha, or geisha quarter, such incident is never treated seriously. On the contrary lover receives the kick of his beloved as a favour done to him by his playful mistress. The shapely leg of the beautiful courtesan painted with red lac and adorned with belled-anklets chiming musically is compared with the flag-staff of Cupid, the god of love.

But stupid Vishnunaga took it otherwise and started fuming and fretting in anger. How could a mere prostitute hit the head of a Brahmin, ritually sanctified by the priests, by her feet? Vishnunaga blew the issue out of proportion.

He thinks he had committed a great sin in receiving the kick of a prostitute on his head. He rushes to elderly Brahmins to take their advice on the ways by which he could atone for his sin. Brahmins laugh at him but in all seriousness tell him that though they had studied the dharmashastras or religious law books by Manu, Yama, Vashishtha, Gautam, Bharadwaj, Shankha, Likhita, Apastamba, Harita, Pracheta, Devala, Vriddhagargya, etc., they really could not suggest the ways of redemption of such a sin as it is not mentioned anywhere in their law books. They advised him to approach the Vita-sabha or assembly of Vitas as Vitas are expert in matters related to Vesha.

Ultimately Vishnunaga presents himself before the assembly of Vitas who really enjoy the situation but treat the issue with mock seriousness. Vitas one after other rise and pronounce conflicting verdicts. Ultimately the chief of the assembly of the Vitas, Vitamahattara Bhattijimuta, pronounces his judgement. Henceforth he says, no beautiful girl ever arrange the hair of Vishnunaga with her hands adorned with bangles, delicate like the stalk of lotus, sparkling with jem-studded rings and he should move around with dry dishevelled hair.

And, he further pronounced, beautiful Madanasenika, eyes rolling due to intoxication caused by drinking wine, should oblige me by placing her feet, coloured with red lac and adorned with anklets, on my head, jealous Vishnunaga watching it helplessly.

Between the incident of Vishnunaga receiving the kick from his beloved and the organising the assembly of Vitas which decides the mode of his atonement, the Vita meets several persons.

One among them was Cahuksha Bhagavata Amatya Vishnudasa, a magistrate famous for dozing during the court trials like a bull in the market place and who was involve with a courtesan Anangasena.

When he enters the Vesha he sees drunkard Bhashpa singing and dancing with glass of wine in his hands. Then he sees old courtesan Saranigupta circumambulating the sacred flag of Kama, Makarayashti, planted in the courtyard of Kamadevayatana. He also meets Harishchandra, the medicine man, and some painters painting the flag of the temple of Kamadeva, a Buddhist monk in love with courtesan Radhika, his own beloved courtesan Surasenasundari, etc.

Vita refers to courtesans from different countries who have settled in the Vesha of Ujjain including Sinhalika from Lanka and Yavani Karpuraturishta from Yavana country, and customers like Indraswami who were particularly interested in girls from foreign countries.

In this Bhana we find beautiful description of the city of Ujjain and its magnificent vesha crowded with lovely courtesans. Several musical instruments like Saptatantri Veen, kansyapatra, venu are mentioned and also the performances of dance, drama and music, and boisterous drinking parties. Yaksha worship was very much in vogue. Shrine of Purnabhadra Yaksha is mentioned. A stocky character is referred to as Vesh-vithi-yaksha. There is a reference to the shrine of Ganga and Yamuna. Bhana as a dramatic form is defined as an eka-nata-nataka or one-actor play.

From this Bhana we get information about cultural and social life of early Gupta era.

PADMAPRABHRUTAKAM

An exhilarating burlesque by Shudraka, fourth-fifth century A.D. in the mode of Bhana, based on the love adventures of Karniputra, his romantic and amorous overtures with beautiful, tender aged courtesans with the help of his Vita friend. Ujjain is the venue of the play.

Bhana is one-act one-actor burlesque in the form of a monologue. An actor in the guise of Vita a pimp appears on the stage and describes during his wanderings the scenes, events, happenings and merrily converses with different people as if they are there in front of him.

When play opens we see Vita named Shastra standing there. It is vasanta ritu. Vita in his style describes the ambience of joyous season conducive to love, then goes on describing the glory of the city of Ujjain.

He tells us that Karniputra is mad after delicate sixteen-year-old beauty, Devasena, younger sister of his beloved Devadatta, standing on the threshold of youth, full of childish charm. He has been entrusted with the task of finding out if Devasena too is favourably inclined towards him.

Vita describes Karniputra as expert in many shastras and arts and techniques of seducing girls—vyutpannayuvatikamat-antrasutradhara.

Karniputra, known by other names such as Muladeva, Mulabhadra, Kalankur, is a popular character of the Indian story literature. Banabhatta in his Kadambari has mentioned three characters of the story

Karnisuta, Vipula and Shasha—karnisutakatheva sannihitavipulachala shashopagata cha.

He was Acharya of thieves and knaves and said to have written a treatise on thievery, Steyasutta.

On his way wandering on the Rajamarga, principal street, of the city Vita meets interesting characters such as so-called poet Katyayana, Pithamarda named Darduraka and pimp of courtesan Vipala who was once a favourite girl of Karniputra. After indulging in talk with them and grammarian Dattakalashi he proceeds further and bumps into Pavitraka, son of a magistrate, who calls himself Vaishnava Bhagavata but is involved with an ordinary prostitute Varunika, daughter of Mattakashini. After teasing him the Vita reaches Pushpavithi or street moving through flower market.

Here he meets with Mridangavasulaka who is described as purana-nataka-vita which may mean old Vita who used to act in plays, moving around trying to conceal his old age by colouring his hair black. A little further he sees one Shaishilaka trying to conceal himself behind the pillar of the gambling hall, dyutasabha.

Vita confronts him with the story he heard that when lovelorn Malatika, daughter of garland-maker's daughter, sent to Shaishilaka a female Buddhist nun, Shakyabhikshuki, as her messenger he tried to seduce her without waiting for Malatika.

Vita enjoys Shaishilaka's reply that it is not advisable to leave the happiness at hand for the vague hope of enjoyment in future. It is interesting to note that this line in the play is borrowed from the verse in the Shantiparva of the Mahabharata.

When Shaishilaka tells him that when the nun protested he let her go Vita remarks that it happened like ending the act of the play without drumming. It seems that in ancient India it was the practice to bring the act of the play to close by drumming.

Vita then enters the locality of courtesans, Vesha, proper. The first person he meets here is crook Buddhist monk Sanghilaka living in the local monastery—dharmaranyanivasi Sanghilako nama dushta shakya bhikshu—moving in brown-red robes. He addresses him as the devil of the monastery—viharvetal—wandering like an owl during daytime. He exclaims: 'O, how pious is the Buddhist order, Buddhashashana, that it is continued to be worshipped and respected day by day despite such rogue monks who tonsure their heads without understanding its significance.'

After ridiculing him Vita moves forward. And lo his eyes fall on beautiful daughter of Vasantavati, Vanarajika, bedecked with flowers descending the steps of the temple of Kamadeva, god of love, after offering worship to him. Giving her compliments Vita stands at the gate of courtesan Tambulsena's house. At the time she was enjoying love making with Irim, probably a Greek-Hermes. She rushes towards the door to stop him from entering the house. He describes various signs of love-making adorning her lovely body and she blushes profusely. He teases her for enjoying sexual intercourse in the afternoon.

After meeting Kumudvati, suffering the separation from her lover Mauryakumar Chandrodaya, he moves forward and sees lovely courtesan Priyanguyashtika playing with ball. Vita beautifully describes the ball-game and dance-like movements of young Priyanguyashtika revealing the beauty of her supple person.

After meeting two more courtesans Vita reaches the house of Devadatta. Here he comes across disciple of Natakacharya named Gandharvadatta, Darduraka, a son of an actress—nateraka, who had been to Devasena to give her the copy of the text of drama Kumudvati Prakarana. Devasena was selected to play the lead role in the play.

Vita sees young Devasena in the garden of the house. She is shown suffering from the pangs of separation. Vita with his skilfull persuasive talk makes her give her consent to meet Karniputra and leaves the place happily after accomplishing his task.

Padma means lotus and prabhrita is gift. Vita asks Devasena to send her lover a lotus as a gift. Here lotus symbolises young courtesan herself and her surata or love-making will constitute lovely present for her lover.

The Bhana is full of humour, wit, sarcasm and revels in erotic sentiment.

PANCHAMA VEDA

The fifth Veda. Traditionally the number of Vedas is four. They are Rig, Sama, Atharva and Yajur. Lord Brahma created an additional Veda, the Natya Veda, expounding the knowledge of dramaturgy, by culling the elements from the existing four Vedas. He named it as Panchama Veda or fifth Veda (see Natya Veda).

PANCHARATRA

A three-act play by Bhasa based on the Virat Parva of the Mahabharata. Pandavas are in exile and have gone underground to save themselves from detection. Prince Duryodhana performs a Yajna and in a generous mood asks Guru Drona to express his wish which, the prince says, would be fulfilled. Drona asks him to return the share of Puru kingdom to Pandavas which they had lost in the game of dice. Duryodhana says that if he could locate the Pandavas in five nights or Pancha ratra he will do the bidding of his Guru.

In the second act we see Kauravas attacking Virat's cowpen and capital and their defeat at the hands of Pandavas in disguise. This act includes a dance by cowherd boys and girls performed by them in the cowpen of Virat which reminds us of the similar dance in Bhasa's another play Balacharita.

In the third act Duryodhana says he would return Pandavas' half share of the kingdom as promised to Guru Drona as they were detected before the stipulated time frame of Pancha ratra or five nights.

In the first act of the play Bhasa has introduced a chorus of three Brahmins which describes the glory of Duryodhana's Yajna. In the beginning all the three Brahmins speak in unison, then they speak individually, then again they speak in unison and then individually— the cycle goes on. Bhasa is the first and only Sanskrit dramatist who has included a chorus in the play. Chorus in a dramatic play is very much a part of Greek drama. However Bhasa's chorus seems to be the relic of a style of ballet singing practised in the past, rather than it being an imitation of Greek theatrical tradition.

PANDAVANI

Pandava means sons of Pandu, five heroes of the epic Mahabharata. Vani means several things such as speech, music, choir of musicians and singers, praise, laudation, literary composition. In essence Pandavani means narration of the Pandava of Mahabharata story through song, music, dance, mime and speech. It is a single person performance popular in the tribal central India.

Holding in his hand a stringed musical instrument studded with jingle-bells, tamboora, and in the other castanets of Kartal the tribal Pandavani singer alternates between verse and prose speech one complementing the other, story condensing in the song and song extending into story.

While narrating the story, standing or sitting, the Pandavani ballad singer assumes alternatively different roles of the characters in the story and creates drama.

The performance starts with Vandana or invocatory songs in the honour of several deities and ends with prayers offered to Krishna. In between stories from Mahabharata are narrated. A performance lasts for four or five hours and for days together performances are repeated to narrate the entire epic.

Of all the Pandava heroes Bhima is the most favourite of the Pandavani singers. Bhima's wife was an Adivasi forest girl, hence the Adivasi Pandavani singers feel affinity for him.

Pandavani singer is assisted by musicians—a harmonium player and a drummer.

While narrating the Pandava story the imaginative ballad singer weaves into its fabric numerous interesting folk tales and stories to entertain his audience.

The only stage property is the musical instrument tamboora in the hand of singer. When he is enacting the role of Bhima it acts as his mace; when he is in the role of Arjuna it is his bow. Adivasi Pandavani singer enthrals his audiences for hours by narrating the stories from Mahabharata through verse and prose, through dance and mime.

PARIJATAMANJIRI NATIKA

An interesting romantic drama with four acts found engraved on stone slabs at Dhar in Madhya Pradesh. Dhar was the ancient capital of Paramara rulers of Malva. The dramatic inscription was found at the Bhoja Shala—Kamal Maula Mosque—at Dhar. The slab of black stone, five feet eight inches by five feet, upon which this dramatic inscription is engraved was attached to the northern wall of the principal mehrab in the mosque with the writing turned inside.

It was taken out in November 1903. It contained first two acts of the play. Next two acts must have been engraved on similar other stone slab which is missing. This means only first two acts of this Natika have survived the vagaries of time.

The title of the Natika engraved on stone is given as Parijatamanjiri or Vijayashri. It was composed by Rajaguru Madana whose family hailed from Gauda or Bengal. He was the preceptor of the king Arjunavarman, the 13th century Paramara ruler of Dhar.

The inscription reveals that this panegyric, prashasti, was engraved by the artist or shilpin named Ramadeva, the son of excellent sculptor or rupakara named Sikha. This is the first and only Sanskrit play found engraved on stone.

It is interesting to note that dramatic inscription is termed as panegyric. Hence scholars feel that it was composed and engraved in the lifetime of the prince whom it celebrated—Arjunavarma a Paramara king of Dhar, descendant of Emperor Bhoja. Arjunavarma is the hero of the play whose heroic and romantic exploits form its theme. Probably it was for the first time a romantic comedy was composed by a playwright with his living patron king as its hero.

According to the prologue the first performance of the drama took place in the temple of goddess Saraswati on the occasion of spring festival, Vasantotsava. Vatsyayana in his Kamasutra refers to the tradition of staging plays in the temple of Saraswati, goddess of learning and arts.

The title of the first act is the spring festival or vasantotsava. It describes the king watching it from the top of his palace in the company of the jester, the queen and her maid.

The title of the second act is reflecting ear ring or tadanka darpana. Here we see the king accompanied by jester witnessing the marriage of mango tree to a spring creeper, a ceremony performed by the queen in the pleasure garden, lilodyanam or pramadodyanama, of the palace. It is also watched by young and beautiful heroine of the play Parijatamanjiri from behind the tree. King sees her reflection in the ear-ring of the queen and he is overjoyed. Suspicious queen leaves him in anger. King gets an opportunity to talk with his new found love. The love talk is interrupted by a messenger of the queen. King rushes to pacify the angry queen and heroine too departs threatening suicide.

Commenting on the story Prof. E. Hultzsch in his article in Epigraphia Indica, Vol. VIII states:

'As the hero of the drama was a living and reigning king, it is unlikely that the chief persons that appear on the stage together with him were pure invention of the poet. It would have been a poor panegyric that made Arjunavarman move among fictitious characters. Hence I believe that, as stated in the drama, the chief queen was actually named Sarvakala and that Parijatamanjiri or Vijayashri happened to be Arjunavarman's favourite at the time when the drama was composed. Her miraculous appearance and her fanciful connection with the vanquished king of Gujarat may have been suggested to the poet by her real name. They could not fail to please the king and his mistress, and could perhaps be risked all the more easily because the lady was not of royal blood, but owed her elevation only to her personal charm.'

Probably it was for the first time the real lifetime romance of the living patron king was dramatised and staged before him.

PASHUPATA

An ancient tantric Shaiva sect known for its weird ritualistic practices. Pashupata ascetics appear in the plays like Mattavilasprahasana by king Mahendravikramavarman of Kanchi.

Pashu means animal. Shiva is known as Pashupati or Lord of animals. In Vedic literature all living beings are termed as Pashu.

Pashupatas are mentioned in the Anushashana Parva of the epic Mahabharata as ash-smeared, weird, nude mendicants holding begging bowls of clay in their hands, wandering all over aimlessly desiring nothing.

In the first or second century A.D. there lived in Gujarat an ascetic named Lakulisha who is considered principal apostle of Pashupata sect. Varahamihira in the sixth and Hieun Tsang in the seventh century have referred to the Pashupatas.

Pashupatas are enjoined to deliberately behave in weird manner like laughing loudly, making animal sounds, dancing as if hit by paralysis, talking nonsense, exhibiting the signs of lust at the sight of youthful women. Figures of ascetics making exhibitionistic gestures showing their state of desire embellishing medieval temples are identified as those of Pashupata initiates.

Pashupatas flourished in medieval period. They became rich and influential. In the Kuttanimata kavya there is a reference to a Pashupata Acharya named Bhavashuddha who built Dhavalagriha, most magnificent mansion in the city of Varanasi, for a courtesan named Anangadevi. In yet another verse a courtesan mischievously taunts another courtesan that by establishing relationship with Pashupatacharya she too has become super nun or acharini.

In the farce Mattavilasprahasana we come across a Pashupata named Babhrukalpa who mediates in the quarrel between a Buddhist monk and Kapalika. He is sour with the Buddhist monk as he tried to entice his beloved, a maid-servant in the house of a barber, by showing her a coin under the cover of his robe as a cowherd will show a fistful of grass to beckon a cow.

PATIYANI

Ritualistic masked dance generally performed at Bhadrakali temples in central Kerala. According to legend even after killing the demon Darika the fury of Bhadrakali did not subside. To make her laugh several masked dancers appeared before her, the sight of whom calmed her.

Patiyani masks are quite grotesque and made of lumpy pods of arecanut trees. The masks are painted and embellished with tender palm leaves.

The masked dancers represent various deities. Vigorous Patiyani dancers are quite spectacular and awe-inspiring.

PATRA

Literally means drinking vessel. An actor playing a role in the play is called Patra, as he like drinking vessel carries the rasa to audiences. Bharata in the Natya Shastra defines the qualities of patra or actor. He says: 'Intelligence, strength, physical beauty (buddhi-sattva-swarupa), knowledge of time and tempo (layatalajnata), proper age, curiosity (kutuhalam), knowledge of psychological states and sentiments (rasabhavajnata), acquisition (of knowledge of arts), (their) retention, vocal music prompted by dance, suppression of stage fright, and enthusiasm will be the requisite qualities of the actor (patra).'

Speaking about the blemishes of the actor which come in the way of success of the play Bharata says:

'Unnaturalness (in acting), wrong movements (of the actors), unsuitability of a role (to an actor), loss of memory (of the actors), speaking other words (those which are not in the play), (actor's) cry of distress, want of proper hand movements, falling off the crown and other ornaments, defects in playing the drums, shyness of speech, laughing or crying too much, etc. during his performance' (NS: Ghosh).

PAVA KOOTHU

Glove puppet theatre of Kerala is known as Pava Koothu. Kerala glove puppets are ornate, colourful and resemble the characters on Kathakali stage. Kathakali plays are known as Atta Kathas. The Atta Kathas are taken up for visual presentation through puppets.

A big brass lamp is lit for illumination behind which sits the chief puppeteer and his chorus. The chief puppeteer wears two glove puppets on his two hands and when more than two characters are to be presented his other companions join him by wearing puppets on their hands. Thus the show continues. In this form basic stress is on the narration of the story, the Atta Kathas. The puppets on hands are used to illustrate the narration.

PEOPLE—ULTIMATE DESTINATION

Ultimate destination of drama is people, says Bharata. In his definitions of dramatic art 'the people' or Lok occupies central position because Bharata feels that Lok is the theme of dramatic art. In the end of the 26th chapter of the Natya Shastra he says:

'The events related to people in their different conditions, Lokasya ya varta nanavasthantaratmika, should be included in the play by those who are well versed in the Canons of Drama or Natya Veda.

Whatever Shastras, laws, arts and activities connected with human practice, may be produced as drama.'

Bharata feels that it is not possible to be all-encompassing for the Shastra to cover all human activity. He says:

'Rules regarding the feelings and activities of the world, movable as well as immovable, cannot be formulated and ascertained exhaustively by Shastras.

The people have different dispositions, and on their dispositions drama rests. Hence playwrights and producers (prayokta) should take the people as their ultimate authority as regards the rules of arts' (NS: Ghosh).

PISHACHA

Malevolent evil spirit having hideous, repellent, frightening form. Bloodthirsty Pishachas inhabit dark places and haunt burning grounds. In the Vedic literature they are mentioned along with Rakshasas and Asuras. In the Rig Veda the word Pishachi occurs. In the Atharva Veda they are described as kravyada or the eaters of the raw flesh. The later Vedic people knew the works known as Pishacha Veda or Pishacha Vidya.

According to mythology in the beginning Brahma created eighteen Prajapatis, Yakshas, Gandharvas and Pishachas. Puranas say that Pishachas were born to Kashyapa and his wife Krodhavasha.

Pishachas are mentioned in epics and Puranas as human race. Gunadhya wrote a great story book in Paishachi language named Brihatkatha which had influenced the dramatic works. The book is lost to posterity, however Sanskrit versions of it like Brihatkathamanjiri of Kshemendra, Kathasaritsagar by Pandit Somadeva and Brihatkathashlokasangraha by Budhaswami have survived the vagaries of time.

In the Shastras eight kinds of marriages are mentioned. One of them is Paishacha vivaha or marriage by rape. When a girl who is fast asleep, or under the influence of liquor or unconscious is raped it is called Paishachi vivaha.

In the ancient times before the commencement of actual play a number of preliminaries used to be performed. Together they were known as Purvaranga. Bharata in his Natya Shastra has described the Purvaranga procedures in detail. A number of items in the Purvaranga used to be performed to appease various deities and malevolent spirits. In the playhouse the task of protecting Mattavarini raised on the stage was entrusted to Bhutas, Yakshas, Guhyakas and Pishachas. Bharata prescribes rituals to appease Pishachas and similar other spirits.

In his chapter on Costumes and Make-up Bharata says that Pishachas should be painted dark blue in colour.

In his chapter on Harmonious Representation he has described Pishacha type of woman. He says:

'A woman who has more or less the usual number of fingers, is merciless during sexual acts, has habit of roaming in gardens and fields, and of terrifying children, is treacherous, speaks with a double entendre, behaves abominably during sexual acts, has a hairy body and loud voice, and is fond of spirituous liquor and sexual indulgence, is said to have a nature of a Pishacha' (NS: XXIV.113–4).

The 8th century playwright Bhavabhuti wrote a romantic drama in ten acts titled as Malati Madhava. It was for the first time performed on the occasion of the annual fair of Bhagavan Kalapriyanatha of Ujjain. In the fifth act of the play there is a terrible description of crematorium and bloodthirsty, flesh eating Pishachas roaming around. Pishachas are defined as flesh eating or raw flesh eating evil spirits—pishitam mansamashnatiti pishachah. The fifth act establishes this fact. In this act hero Madhava enters the stage with raw human flesh in his hand to sell it to the Pishachas. He in his long soliloquy describes awe-inspiring, flesh eating, blood drinking terrible Pishachas and their consorts.

The quaint practice of selling Mahamas or human flesh to evil spirits is mentioned in the third chapter of Banabhatta's Harshacharita. It is said that tantric Bhairavacharya used to sell human flesh to Pishachas and obtain from them precious stones like Mainashila. This terrible ritual used to be performed to cure a person of his illness. In the fifth chapter of Harshacharita Banabhatta has described various terrible Shakta rituals performed to rid the king Prabhakaravardhan of his fatal illness, one of which was selling of human flesh by the princes to evil spirits—apartra prakashanarapatikumarkriyamana mahamasavikrayaprakra-mam. In the sixth chapter of the book it is said that one Kumarasena was killed by Vetala while he was trying to sell human flesh during the festival dedicated to Mahakala Shiva.

Bhavabhuti mentions this custom in his play Malati Madhava though he did not specify which favour hero Madhava was seeking from the Pishachas.

PITHAMARDA

Kamasutra of Vatsyayana defines Pithamarda as 'a man without wealth, alone in the world whose property consists of a few articles like mallika, phenaka and kashaya, who comes from a good country, and who is skilled in all the arts; and by teaching these arts is received in the company of citizens and in the abode of public women.'

It is interesting to note that in the play Malavikagnimitra of Kalidasa a female ascetic Pandita Kaushiki who acts as a judge of a dance competition is called Pithamardika.

PLAYHOUSE

See PREKSHAGRIHA.

PLAY WITHIN A PLAY

An interesting technique of inserting a brief dramatic spectacle, a play within the play, has been resorted to by some Sanskrit dramatists. In the parlance of Sahitya Darpana we may term it as Garbhanka, an act within the womb of an act. In Harsha's play Priyadarshika's third act we find the example of play within a play.

Bhavabhuti continued the tradition of inserting a play within a play in his play Uttararamacharita. In the seventh act of the play we are told that a play directed by Bharatamuni and enacted by apsaras or nymphs is going to be enacted. The play within the play shows pathetic plight of Sita after her abandonment.

In the Sahitya Darpana the play Sita-swayamvara within the play Balaramayana by Rajashekhara is referred to as an example of the garbhanka. We find this garbhanka in the third act of the play:

'Ravana is still in the grip of amorous melancholy. In order to distract him his ministers organise a dramatic performance. The celestial troupe directed by Kohala will stage a play, the Swayamvara of Sita, composed by Bharata. In this play within the play, Garbhanka, Rama and Lakshmana, led by Vishvamitra, arrive at the court of Janaka. They are received by Janaka, Shatananda, Sita and her friend Hemaprabha. Rama falls in love with Sita. The competition starts, the competitors being called one by one by female door-keeper. When Rama's turn comes, he breaks the bow and all rush to congratulate him. At this point Ravana bursts out in a fit of jealousy. Prahasta tries in vain to pacify him. The play has to be discontinued' (*Theatre of India*).

In the fifth act of the same play a puppet play within a play is introduced. Here two wooden puppets representing Sita and her friend with parrots hidden in their mouths who are trained to recite their dialogues are brought on the stage.

In the sixth act of the play Janakiparinaya by Ramabhadra Dikshita we see Ravana's ministers asking Ushanas to produce a play with the help of Apsaras and the play thus conceived is staged before him to tell him that Sugriva has concluded an alliance with Rama to attack him so he should make necessary preparations.

Yet another example of the play within a play is found in the drama Chaitanyachandrodaya.

PLOT

Plot of the drama is called itivritta or vastu. The main story inherent in the plot of the drama is called adhikarika vastu and subsidiary one is called prasangika vastu.

The plot develops in five stages. They are known as Avasthas. Avasthas are five:

Arambha: Beginning of the story.

Prayatna: Effort to achieve the aim, striving to attain the objective.

Prapti-sambhava or Praptyasa: Hope or possibility of attainment of the objective of the hero.

Niyatapti: The certainty of the success brought about by the removal of obstacles is in view.

Phalaprapti or Phalayoga: Attainment of desired object.

The five elements of the plot are called Arthaprakriti. They are seed (bija), vital drop (bindu), episode (pataka) and action (karya).

Also connected with the plot are five joints or Sandhis. They are:

Mukha sandhi: where the germ is deposited and rasa is introduced. Pratimukha sandhi: the germ shows its first manifestation. Garbha: things become clearer, attainment of the object appears possible, but not definite. Vimarsha: aim for which endeavour is made is imperilled by doubt. Nirvahana: all threads meet together, realisation of aim follows.

PRABODHACHANDRODAYA

An allegorical play based on Advaita Vedanta philosophy by the eleventh century ascetic Krishnamisra Yati. It was staged at Mahoba as a part of the victory festival organised to celebrate the victory of Chandella king Kirtivarman over Chedi king of Benaras named Karna. Kirtivarman witnessed the play in 1065 A.D.

The tradition of introduction of allegorical characters representing abstract concepts dates back to Bhasa's play Balacharita. Buddhist scholar Ashvaghosha too wrote an allegorical play which has survived in fragmentary form. Sylvain Levi describes the play as the 'masterpiece of the genre'.

The play it seems was inspired by the Vishnu Purana which contains near similar story with allegorical characters.

The play depicts beautifully the conflict between the forces of good and evil. The evil forces are represented by characters like Dambha or Deceit, Moha or Illusion, Lobha or Greed, Kama or Lust, Mada or Arrogance, Himsa or Violence, etc. And the forces of good have characters like Vishnubhakti or Devotion to Lord Vishnu, Dharma or Righteousness, Upanishad or Sacred Lore, Shraddha or Faith, etc. In the conflict between virtue and vice the virtue led by Vishnu Bhakti emerged victorious.

In the third act of the play there is an interesting interlude in which we see monks representing Jainism and Buddhism respectively clashing with an ascetic of Kapalika sect who believed in the hedonic tantric philosophy involving drinking wine, eating meat and enjoying the company of women. The dispute is settled in favour of Kapalika when Jain and Buddhist monks are embraced by voluptuous and beautiful Kapalini. The monks get convinced that real saukhya and moksha or pleasure and liberation can be achieved by joining Kapalika sect. They request the Kapalika to initiate them in Mahabhairavanushashana. Kapalika performs the ritual of initiation by uttering mantras and making the monks drink wine. Intoxicated monks then perform drunken dance.

Chandellas patronised temple building activity at Khajuraho. Profusion of erotic sculptures is found in early 11th century temples including Kandariya Mahadeva. Post-Kandariya temples at Khajuraho are less sexually oriented. Some scholars believe that this change occurred due to 'protest against sex so pronouncedly expressed in the work of court dramatist Krishnamisra.' But as scholars pointed out even Krishnamisra who wrote an anti-sex play Prabodhachandrodaya was not free from tantric influence totally. Probably Krishnamisra was compelled to depict eroticism to underline contemporary reality against which he led a crusade.

Following Krishnamisra a number of playwrights took to writing allegorical plays. Even Jain playwrights were inspired to write allegorical plays like Moharajaparajaya. The play Moharajaparajaya was written by Yashapala in the first half of the 13th century. As pointed out by Keith the play was performed on the occasion of the festival of the idol of Mahavira at the Kumaravihara or the temple erected by Kumarapala at Tharapadra, where the author seems to have been governor or resident.

But no play of this genre written after Prabodhachandrodaya could match its merits.

PRABUDDHARAUHINEYA

A Jain play in six acts by the 13th century playwright Ramabhadra Muni, pupil of Jayaprabha Suri. It was staged on the occasion of the yatra festival of Adishvar Jinalaya of Jalore. The hero of the play Rauhineya was a famous thief and contemporary of Mahavira. The play portrays how the bandit became prabuddha or wise under the Jain influence.

PRACHANDAPANDAVA

Also known as Balamahabharata is a play by the 10th century playwright Rajashekhara. Only two acts of the play are available. In the first act the story of Draupadi Swayamvara or marriage of Draupadi is portrayed. In the second available act we see Yudhisthira and Duryodhana indulging in the game of dice in which Yudhisthira is defeated and is exiled with his brothers and wife Draupadi.

PRAHASANA

Prahasa means to burst into laughter, to laugh at, mock, deride, ridicule. Prahasana is a form of drama intended to provoke laughter, farce, burlesque, stage show full of humour, wit, satire and irony. Bharata says Prahasana is of two types, pure (shuddha) and mixed (sankeerna).

Bharata says: 'The Prahasana is known as pure when it contains comic disputations of Shaiva gurus (Bhagavat), ascetics, Bhikshus, Shrotriya Brahmins, and others, and abounds in jocular remarks by persons of low class.

The Prahasana is called mixed in which courtesans, servants, eunuchs, Vitas and Dhurtas and unchaste women appear with their immodest appearance, dress and movements. Some popular type of scandal or incident of hypocrisy should be introduced in the Prahasana through the disputations of Dhurtas and Vitas' (NS: Ghosh).

In the Natya Shastra there is a very interesting legend about the origin of the Prahasana. It is said once intoxicated by the knowledge of the Natya Veda or dramatic art they possessed sons of Bharata started making fun of the people by staging Prahasanas full of humour and laughter—sarva lokah prahasanairbadhyante hasyasanshraye. These Prahasanas were full of sexual innuendos, obscenity—gramyadharma, fraudulent behaviour—durachara—and a number of things not socially acceptable. This angered the sages and due to their curse sons of Bharata were dispelled from the heaven.

Generally the Prahasana is an one-act play but two-act Prahasana plays too are found. Ganika or prostitute is generally a heroine of the Prahasana and a number of characters including hypocritic ascetics, their disciples vie for her attention. Some of the Prahasanas are frankly obscene but there are a few Prahasanas which contain delightful humour. Mattavilasprahasana written by Raja Mahendravikrama, Pallava king of Kanchi belonging to the seventh century A.D., is earliest surviving example of Prahasana. Number of Prahasanas written after him is quite large.

PRAKARANA

One of the ten forms of drama mentioned by Bharata in his Natya Shastra.

The play in which the writer prakrute (devises) by his own intellect an original plot with its hero and works up its elaboration is called Prakarana. When a playwright constitutes a play of marvellous qualities with original seed, and hero not coming out of Rishi's works is called Prakarana. It does not have exalted hero, characters of gods, story of king's enjoyment and plot construction and rasa same as that of Nataka. It should include characters such as slaves, vitas, head of the bankers' guild, should contain incidents arising from the attendance of courtesans as well as exploits of depraved woman of good family. Number of acts should be not less than five and more than ten. All styles are included (NS: Ghosh).

PRASANNARAGHAVA

A ten-act play based on Rama story by the 13th century playwright Jayadeva, popularly known as Piyushavarsha. Born at Kundina in Vidarbha his father's name was Mahadeva and mother's Sumitra. Apart from writing a play he wrote a treatise on poetics named Chandraloka. The play opens with the scene of Sita Swayamvara and ends with triumphant return of Rama to Ayodhya after killing Ravana, the demon king of Lanka.

PRASHNIKA

Person or persons expert in dramatic arts. There was a tradition in ancient times to refer dispute, if any, regarding merit of the performance of an individual actor or dancer, or dramatic show to Prashnika or a jury of Prashnikas.

Bharata in his Natya Shastra states: 'If there be any controversy (Sangharsha) (about the performance of individual actors) the following are the Prashnikas (Assessors): an expert in sacrifice (yajna), an actor (nartaka), a prosodist, a grammarian, a king, an archer, painter, a courtesan, a musician (gandharva) and a king's officer (raj sevaka).

Such an instance is found in the Bhana play of Gupta era, Padataditakam, by Shyamilaka.

According to the play once Harishudra of Vidarbha, a high ranking government officer, went to the house of Draunalika, Veshyadhyaksha Pratihar, to attend dance-drama performance, preksha, on invitation.

It was the turn of Mayurasena, the courtesan from Sinhala Dwipa, to perform dance.

Musicians started playing on musical instruments in the beginning. Then Devatamangal or ritual worship to different deities was performed. Then singing beautifully the dancer Mayurasena started performing.

Laska Upachandra who was a knowledgeable person started finding fault in her dance under the influence of liquor. Members of the audience supported him. But Harishudra spoke in the favour of Mayurasena. The dispute was referred to Prashnika. He on the basis of shastras gave the decision that Harishudra was right.

PRATIJNAYAUGANDHARAYANA

A four-act play of Bhasa based on the Udayana story which is the part of ancient folklore. It revolves round the episode of capturing of king Udayana of Vatsa country with its capital at Kaushambi by the soldiers of king Mahasena of Ujjayani, and his eloping with the daughter of Mahasena, Vasavadatta, courtesy clever stratagem planned by his prime minister, Yaugandharayana.

Interestingly the king Udayana and princess never appear on the stage. The central character of the drama is minister Yaugandharayana who is shown busy planning the escape of his master.

Udayana is captured by the enemy by a clever strategy. An artificial effigy of an elephant is kept half camouflaged in the forest with a posse of soldiers concealed in its stomach. During his hunting expedition Udayana goes near the elephant. The soldiers pour out of the stomach of the effigy of the elephant. This reminds us of the story of Trojan horse, a gigantic hollow wooden horse, with Greek soldiers concealed in it, used during the Trojan war.

Yaugandharayana enters enemy capital in the guise of Unmattaka, a mentally deranged person, along with his associates and plans the escape of his master. When he comes to know that Udayana has fallen in love with the princess Vasavadatta he becomes terribly upset and expresses his disapproval and deprecates king's weakness for women.

In the next act we meet Gatrasevak, fully drunk assistant of the elephant. He creates lot of humour.

In the play there is a mention of the shrine of Yakshini in Ujjayani. She is respectfully addressed as Bhagavati Yakshini. This reference points at the prevalence of Yaksha cult at Bhasa's time.

Yaugandharayana's strategy works and Udayana makes good his escape with princess Vasavadatta.

PRATIMANATAKA

Seven-act play by Bhasa based on the epic Ramayana. It covers the Rama story from the cancellation of his coronation and his proceeding to forest with his brother Lakshmana and wife Sita to return of the hero to Ayodhya and his coronation after fourteen years of exile.

The title of the play is based on the reference to a building named Pratimagriha in the third act. Pratimagriha was the place where human-sized images, Pratimas, of the deceased kings of Ishvaku dynasty, were served by a priest named Devakulik.

At a place called Mat, near Mathura, archaeologists excavated a relic of ruined structure from where the stone images of the kings were recovered. According to inscription found there the structure was known as Devakula. This Devakula had the images of Kushana kings, some of which are now kept in the Mathura Museum. Most prominent of these royal images is that of Emperor Kanishka. That means the Devakula of Mat can be ascribed to early centuries of the Christian era.

PRATINAYAKA

Villain. A character in the play who constitutes an important evil agency in the plot. Defining Pratinayaka the Sahitya Darpana says: Dhiroddhata papakari vyasani pratinayakah. As an example he mentions Ravana in the story of Rama.

According to definition he is brave but proud, haughty and violent. He is sinful, addicted to vice, attached to evil passion. Shakara of Mricchakatika is the best example of vicious villain, pratinayaka.

PRATISHIRSHA

Pratishirsha is the term used by Bharata for mask. Devised by the primitive shamans as a ritualistic object to identify themselves with the spirits, supernatural powers, the secular, festive and theatrical use of the mask was later development. However once it arrived in the green room it became integral part of theatrical performances.

In prehistoric cave paintings located at different sites including ones at Bhimbetka, Lakhajoar, Jaora, Pachmarhi and Kathotia we find naked figures of spirit impersonators, wizards, dancers mostly wearing animal or bird masks.

At Mohenjodaro shallow masks of baked clay were excavated which archaeologists believe were used as votive offering. A big clay mask datable to 4th-3rd century B.C. was found in the excavation conducted at Chirand in Bihar. It was identified as an actor's mask.

It was Bharata who has written about the mask as theatrical accessory and how to make them.

Bharata says:

'Different masks (prati-shirsha) are to be used for gods and men according to their habitation, birth and age. Hair and eyes (of masks) of Rakshasas, Danavas and Daityas (demons) should be of tawny colour, and they should have tawny moustaches. The ministers, armour-bearers, leaders of merchants' guild, and priests should have masks with a piece of cloth tied around the head like turban. And the masks of generals and the crown prince should be provided with a small crown and such should be done in the case of high royal officer, Mahamatra. The masks of ghosts, lunatics, goblins, spiritual aspirants, ascetics should have long hair.'

Bharata also tells how to make masks. He writes:

'One should prepare with proper care and measurement the Pati (cloth) for making the head. The Pati should be made by using Bilva-paste on cloth. Masks should be made with ashes or husks of paddy being mixed with Bilva-paste, or some watery form of it, after covering these with cloth smeared with the thick Bilva-paste. The Pati, thus prepared, should neither be too thick nor too thin, and neither should be made too soft. After getting the Pati dried up by fire or the sun, one should pierce holes in it according to rules, by means of sharp instrument, and these holes should be made after dividing it into two equal halves. In the Pati thus prepared an opening, six Angulis long and one Anguli wide, should be made according to one's own measures, in the form of forehead, and it should have two angles at two ends. Then the opening, two Angulis long and one and half Anguli wide, should be made for the cheeks, and after this has been made for cheeks, other openings are to be made for ears. The opening for the ears being three Angulis long, the same should be the length for the opening of the mouth, and afterwards symmetrical neck should be made equal to twelve Angulis. So much about the rules for the cutting of the openings in the Pati for covering the head. On this are to be placed various forms of crowns set with many kinds of jewels and decorated with different kinds of designs.'

Pratishirshas are mentioned in the prologue of Rajashekhara's play Karpuramanjiri. He has also mentioned some masked dances in the play.

In Indian classical, traditional and folk dramatic forms a variety of masks are used—some use face masks, some full body masks and some mask-like make-up. All the characters appearing in some varieties of Chhau dance-drama use masks. Mask-like make-up is the special feature of Kathakali and similar dance-dramas of South India. All-masked dramatic performances of ritualistic nature are performed in the Buddhist Lama monasteries located in Himalayan region.

There are interesting stories about prowess and supernatural energy shown by actors wearing Hanuman mask in Ramlila and lion-god Narasimha mask in Prahlad Natakam of Orissa and Bhagavatamela Nataka of Melattur in Tamil Nadu. In Karnataka ritualistic Ghost dance dramas are performed in which masks are used. It is believed that the Bhuta spirit possesses the actor-dancer who wears the Bhuta mask, obliterating thin line between theatre and ritual.

PREKSHA

Drama, dramatic performance, show, spectacle. In the Brahma-Gala-Sutta of the Digha Nikaya there is a list of amusements in which you find the term Preksha for dramatic shows. Buddha felt that theatrical arts being sensuous create confusion in the minds of the people. He says:

'Whereas some recluses and Brahmanas, while living on the food provided by the faithful, continue addicted to visiting shows (visuka dassanam; the Sinhalese render it viparita darsana), that is to say:

1. nauch dances (nakkam)
2. singing of songs (gitam)
3. instrumental music (vaditam)
4. shows at fairs (pekkham)
5. ballad recitation (akkhanam)
6. hand music (panissaram)
7. chanting of bards (vetalam)
8. tam tam playing (kumbha-thunam)
9. fairy scenes (sobhanagarakam)
10. acrobatic feats of kandalas (Kandala-vamsa-dhopanam)
11. combats of elephants, horses, buffaloes, bulls, goats, cocks and quails
12. bouts of quarter staff, boxing, wrestling

13-16. sham fights, roll calls, manoeuvres, reviews

Gotama the recluse holds himself aloof from such games and recreations' (*Dialogues of the Buddha*).

In this exhaustive list of amusements after dancing, singing and music comes dramatic enactments—preksha or pekkham.

In Kautilya's Arthashastra the word preksha is used frequently in the sense of dramatic performance. He made it mandatory for people to contribute their share for arranging dramatic shows—preksha. He says: 'One who does not contribute one's share for organising stage show, preksha, shall not witness it with one's people. If one listens to, or witnesses it, secretly one shall perforce give a double share.'

He further says that City Police should not arrest on suspicion a person found moving in the night if he explains that he had gone to attend dramatic show, preksha.

The dramatic shows given by the men are termed by Kautilya as Purusha Preksha and by female artists as Stree Preksha. Women were required to seek permission of elders to go to see these shows.

The entertainment tax imposed on the artists and actors of other countries performing in the state is called Preksha vetana.

Bharata too in his Natya Shastra uses the word Preksha for dramatic performance, preksha-griha for theatre hall and prekshaka for audience.

Kamasutra too uses the term preksha and its derivative prekshanaka in the sense of dramatic performance. He says that woman falls for a man who, among other things, is fond of dramatic shows, prekshanaka. He says lover should sit by the side of his beloved while watching a dramatic performance, prekshanaka, and try to touch her and flirt with her. When people are engrossed in watching dramatic performance, prekshanaka vyaprute, he should slip away with her and make love to her.

PREKSHAGRIHA

Or Natyamandapa means theatre constructed for performing plays. In his Natya Shastra Bharata has devoted one full chapter describing different types of playhouses, their architectural features, ground plans, measurements, and interior decoration.

Bharata mentions three types of theatres: oblong (vikrishta), square (chaturasra) and triangular (tryasra). They are all available in three sizes large, medium and small.

Bharata prefers medium size playhouse because he says that in a big playhouse the visibility of expressions on the face of actors gets diminished, their dialogues too are not quite audible. Medium sized oblong theatre is generally preferred.

On a good piece of land an area 64 x 32 measures should be marked. It should be divided into two equal parts of 32 x 32 each. One of this is marked for auditorium and the other for the stage.

Now the stage area is divided into two equal parts of 16 x 32 each. The back portion is your tiring or make-up room, Nepathya Griha. The front portion is again divided into two equal parts of 8 x 32 measures, ranga-pitha and ranga-shirsha, where dramatic action takes place.

Bharata says on each side of the stage should be built mattavarinis and this should be furnished with four pillars and should be equal in length to the stage, and its plinth should be a cubit and half high.

The tiring room should be provided with two doors for actors to enter the performing arena.

No example of ancient Prekshagriha has survived the vagaries of time. We find many ideas of Bharata incorporated in the plan of Kerala temple theatres, Koothambalams.

In Jain literature we find elaborate descriptions of theatre halls known as prekshagriha mandapa. One such theatre hall is mentioned in the Jain work Rayapasenia sutta. It says:

'The theatre hall was supported by many columns and was furnished with large altars, arches, and shalabhanjika figures; it was decorated with ihamiga, was fitted with a mechanism to show the moving figures of the pair of Vidyadharas, had hundreds of figures decorating it, had many domes, was decorated with flags and bells, was well plastered and bore the palm impression inside and outside. Its gate had sandal pitchers and arches, and there were flowers, garlands, perfumes and incense and the ceiling was decorated with lotus creepers. In the centre of the hall was a stage which had a jewelled seat in the centre. On that there was a throne having discs, lions, feet, tops, the body and the joints' (*Life in Ancient India*, p. 188).

In another Jain Prakrit work, Tiloyapannatti, we find a description of a theatre hall with thirtytwo platforms on which thirtytwo dancers danced singing songs. In Bhagavata Jinasenacharya's Adipurana two theatre halls are mentioned.

In the works like Manasara we find theatre halls mentioned.

In ancient literary works we find the words ranga, samajvata, sangitashala, nrityashala, sabha indicating the existence of theatre halls for performing dance, drama and music.

In the bottom story of the Rani Gumpha cave in Udayagiri hill near Bhubaneshwar in Orissa belonging to the second century B.C. there is a relief carved in stone showing a dancer performing on the stage, which is a structure with four pillars and a roof supported by them.

A fragment of a running frieze showing a dance scene and belonging to the second century B.C. was excavated at Mathura. It is now kept in Lucknow Museum. Here we see a dancer performing under a hut-like structure, roof supported by four pillars, and people sitting in front of it in open.

In Bhasa's Pratimanataka there occur two terms related to Prekshagriha—ranga and nepathya. Ranga means stage proper used by actors for presenting a play and nepathya is tiring room behind the ranga used by actors for doing make-up, etc. and storing material required for the play-production. This indicates that Prekshagriha having these two units and, though not mentioned explicitly, an auditorium in front of it, was in existence at around 4th century B.C.

PRIYADARSHIKA

A four-act play in Natika form by the seventh century playwright king Harsha of Kanauj based on the love story of Vatsaraja Udayana and princess Priyadarshika, beautiful daughter of Maharaja Dhridavarma.

Maharaja Dhridavarma desires to give his daughter in marriage to Vatsaraja Udayana hence he rejects the marriage proposal of king of Kalinga. Angered by this king of Kalinga attacks Dhridavarma and puts him behind bars. However princess Priyadarshika escapes and reaches the capital of Udayana. She disguises as Aranyaka and starts living in the royal seraglio as a maid of queen Vasavadatta. Udayana falls in love with this beautiful young girl of his harem. Queen Vasavadatta puts hurdles in the fruition of their love but when she comes to know that Aranyaka is none else but princess Priyadarshika she gladly agrees for marriage alliance.

Harsha has inserted 'a play within a play' technique in the third act of the play. Here in the court of Vatsaraja a play based on the theme of marriage of Udayana and Vasavadatta is shown enacted. In this play king Udayana himself plays the role of Udayana and the role of Vasavadatta is played by the newly arrived harem beauty Aranyaka.

The story of the play is borrowed from Gunadhya's Brihatkatha. We find deep influence of Kalidasa's Malavikagnimitra on the play.

PULINDA DANCE

Pulinda is a barbarous tribe. Pulinda dance is mentioned by the tenth century playwright Rajashekhara in his play Karpuramanjiri. He says that women as dark as ink or collyrium, masikajjalaka lakaya, eyes as sharp as bows, wearing the costume of Pulinda women bedecked with peacock feathers dance gracefully to amuse the people.

PUPPET THEATRE TRADITION

So ancient is the puppet theatre tradition of India that it is universally known as the Home of Puppet Theatre. Puppet theatre is mentioned in a number of ancient Indian literary works including epics, Puranas and plays.

In the ancient Buddhist work Therigatha there is a reference to puppet theatre. Included in this work are the Gathas or verses composed by nuns of the Buddhist order who were direct disciples of Bhagavan Buddha. Hence we may say that they reflect the social conditions of Buddha's times.

In this collection there is a composition related to the story of theri or Buddhist nun named Subha who was very beautiful. Once a youthful libertine of Rajagaha tried to seduce this gazelle-eyed beauty with long drawn eye-lashes, offering her many presents including fine diaphanous gear of Banaras. While telling him about the impermanence of physical beauty Subha referred to dancing doll of puppet show. She said:

'O, I have seen it—a puppet, well painted, with new wooden spindles, cunningly fastened with strings and with pins—diversely dancing.

But if the strings and pins be all drawn out and loosened and scattered,

So that the puppet is made non-existent and broken in pieces

Which of the parts wilt thou choose and appoint for thy heart's rest and solace?

O, thou are blind: thou chasest a sham deluded by the puppet shows' (*Psalms of the Early Buddhists*).

Here we get interesting information about string puppet show of about sixth century B.C. Different body parts of the dancing doll made of wood are assembled and pinned together and painted. This colourful puppet was made to dance with the help of the strings manipulated by the puppeteer.

In the Mahabharata there are a number of references to puppets manipulated by strings. These references are known as puppet similes. More than once Mahabharata compares a person in the hands of fate or gods with string manipulated puppet in the hands of puppeteer. At different places it says:

'Like a wooden doll manipulated by the strings, sutraprota darumayiva yosha, man plays in the hands of the fate, paraprayuktah purusho vichestate.'

In the Shantiparva of the epic there occurs a term rupopajivanam which is explained by commentator Nilakantha to mean the artists of shadow theatre shows.

In the literary works we find references to mechanical devices and male and female automata capable of entertaining the people.

In the Samarangana Sutradhara by the 11th century Paramara king of Malva there is a chapter on mechanical contrivances, yantras. These mechanical dolls were capable of singing, dancing, playing on musical instruments, presenting various dramatic episodes, play acting.

In the Kathasaritsagara it is said that Somaprabha, daughter of Asura architect Maya, presented a basketful of mechanical dolls capable of performing various acts to her friend, princess Kalingasena.

In Sriharsha's Naishadhiya Charitam there occurs a description of statues of Kama and Rati which would give out erotic sighs and sounds during love making.

It was a different kind of puppet theatre.

We have an interesting example of puppet show being made the part of drama proper. In the 10th century dramatist Rajashekhara's play Balaramayana such an experiment was made. In the fifth act of the play titled as Unmatta Dashanana two life-size wooden dolls representing Sita and her maid Sindurika are brought on the stage and made to enter into dialogue with an actor assuming the role of Ravana. These dolls were made by yantrakara or mechanic named Visharada to deceive Ravana we are informed.

The show involving human actor and puppet is termed in the Kamasutra of Vatsyayana as panchalanunayanam. This may mean human actor imitating the movements of a doll performing on the stage for the entertainment of audiences.

Sutra means strings. String holder of the puppet show is called Sutradhara. In Sanskrit drama Sutradhara appears at the beginning of the play. This led to an interesting theory that human theatre has its origin in puppet theatre.

A number of Sanskrit plays are termed as Chayanataka or text for performing shadow plays. However some prominent scholars do not agree with this interpretation of the term chayanataka and say that this category of Sanskrit dramatic compositions is unknown to theorists of dramatic genre.

However a reference to shadow theatre is found in the 13th century Sanskrit play Ullagharaghava. The following conversation between two characters—Vrukamukha and Karpatika—is found in the play:

Vrukamukha: Friend, the images of Rama and Lakshmana that I carry in my heart I have depicted in this picture for the pleasure of my lord. Please have a look at it. (He gives him pictures, patrapatta.)

Karpatika: (Taking it and looking at it) Well done great man well done: They are beautifully painted according to the convention of shadow theatre.

This goes to show the antiquity of different forms of puppet theatre in India. Even today we find thriving puppet theatre in the country. For instance there are string puppet theatre forms such as Kathaputali of Rajasthan, Sakhi Kundhei of Orissa, Gombeyatta of Mysore, Bomalattam of Tamil Nadu, rod puppet form like Putul Nauch of West Bengal, shadow puppet forms like Ravan-chhaya of Orissa, Tolpava Koothu of Kerala, Tholu Bomalata of Andhra Pradesh, Togalu Gombe Atta of Mysore and glove puppet form like Kundhei Nacha of Orissa and Pava Koothu of Kerala.

Puppetry may be divided into two categories. In the first category we have the kind of puppets which can perform various difficult movements, acrobatic feats and there is less stress on story element. In the second category the puppets or their shadows across the screen are used to illustrate the narrative of the story which is more important part of the show.

PURANA

Pura means before, hence Purana means legends, stories—historical as well as mythological—which belong to past. Nirukta defines Purana as literature, even though belonging to olden times, is ever new, ever fresh—pura navam bhavati. Vayu Purana says the literature that contains ancient traditional stories is Purana. Skanda Purana states that Purana is the soul of Vedas—atma puranam vedanam.

The word Purana is found in the Atharvaveda which says from God emanated Richa, sam, chanda, Purana along with Yajurveda. Manusmriti says that on the occasion of Pitri Shraddha, rituals performed to appease ancestors, one should listen to Dharmashastras, Vedas, Akhyanas, Itihasa and Puranas.

Shatapatha Brahmana says that 'Itihasa is the Veda, Purana is the Veda.' It enumerates five great sacrifices one should perform. They are sacrifice to beings, the sacrifice to men, the sacrifice to fathers, sacrifice to gods, sacrifice to Brahman. As a sacrifice to Brahman, the Shatapatha Brahmana enjoins that as a part of Vedas one should study various forms of literature. It says:

And, verily the precepts (anusasanani), the sciences (vidyas), dialogues (vakovakyam), the traditional myths and legends (Itihasa-Purana) and Narasamshi Gathas are honey offerings to gods; whosoever, knowing this, studies day by day the precepts, the sciences, the dialogue, the traditional myths and legends, and Narasamshi Gathas for his lesson, satisfies the god with honey offerings (SBE, Vol. 44, p. 98).

Purana literature was known to Vedic people. But ancient purana works of Vedic period are lost to posterity. According to a legend it was Vyasa who later created eighteen Puranas which are known as Adipuranas or Mahapuranas. Eighteen Mahapuranas are as follows:

> Brahma, Padma, Vishnu, Shiva, Bhagavata, Naradiya, Markandeya, Agni, Bhavishya, Brahmavaivarta, Linga, Varaha, Skanda, Vaman, Kurma, Matsya, Garuda and Brahmanda.

There are eighteen more works which are known as Upapuranas. However the actual number of minor Puranas exceeds this number.

Puranas contain lot of historical, social and cultural information but basically they contain numerous stories, legends, tales and are religious in nature. We also find in them information about various fine, plastic and performing arts. The stories of a number of dramatic works are taken from Puranas.

PURURAVA-URVASHI SAMVADA

In the Rig Veda we find some hymns in monologue, dialogue and chorus form having story elements. It is believed that these pieces were dramatically rendered during Yajna ceremonies and rituals. They are described as 'rudimentary dramas' from which Sanskrit theatre sprang.

Pururava-Urvashi samvada is one of the most dramatic of Rig Vedic dramatic hymns. Pururava was the king of Puru dynasty and Urvashi a nymph. Centuries later the great Indian dramatist wrote a play Vikramorvashiya with Pururava-Urvashi love as its theme.

Rig Vedic dramatic dialogue hymn recording the story, in part, of king Pururavas and nymph Urvashi is very interesting. The context of this hymn can be explained with the help of the Shatapatha Brahmana. We will here first quote the context of the story from the Brahmana, then give the text of dialogue between two lovers as recorded in the Rig Veda and then conclude the story by again quoting the Brahmana. The Shatapatha Brahmana says:

> The nymph Urvashi loved Pururavas, the son of Ila. When she wedded him, she said, 'Thrice a day shalt thou embrace me; but do not lie with me against my will, and let me not see thee naked, for such is the way to behave to us women.'
>
> She then dwelt with him a long time, and was even with child of him, so long she dwelt with him. Then the Gandharvas said to one another, 'For a long time, indeed, has this Urvashi dwelt among men; devise ye some means how she may come back to us.' Now an ewe with two lambs was tied to her coach; Gandharvas then carried off one of the lambs.
>
> 'Alas', she cried, 'they are taking away my darling, as if I were where there is no hero and no man!' They carried off the second, and she spake in the selfsame manner.
>
> He then thought within himself, 'How can that be (a place) without a hero and without a man where I am?' And naked as he was, he sprang up after them: too long he deemed it that he should put on his garments. Then the Gandharvas produced a flash of lightning, and she beheld him naked even as by daylight. Then, indeed, she vanished. Wailing with sorrow he wandered all over Kurukshetra. Now there is a lotus-lake there called Anyatahplaksha. He walked along its bank; and there nymphs were swimming about in the shape of swans.
>
> And she (Urvashi) recognised him, said, 'This is the man with whom I have dwelt.' They then said, 'Let us appear to him!' 'So be it!', she replied; and they appeared to him.

He then recognised her and implored:

Pururavas: Ho indignant wife, with mind (relenting), stay a while, let us now exchange a discourse. These, our secret thoughts, whilst unspoken, did not yield us happiness even at the last day.

Urvashi: What can we accomplish through such discourse? I have passed away from thee like the first of the dawns. Return, Pururavas, to thy dwelling. I am as hard to catch as the wind.

Pururavas: The arrow is not to be cast from the quiver for glory. I am no longer the impetuous despoiler of cattle (of the enemy), nor their hundredfold (riches). My prowess having lost its strength, (my might) no longer flashes forth; (my warriors) the terrifiers (of the foe) hear not my shout in battle.

Urvashi: If, Ushas, this Urvashi, offering food and wealth to her father-in-law, loves (her husband), she has repaired from the neighbouring house to her husband's home, where she loved [her lord], being delighted night and day by his embrace.

Thrice a day, Pururavas, hast thou embraced me, thou hast loved me without a rival; I have followed thee to thy dwelling, thou, hero, hast been the sovereign of my person.

Pururavas: Sujurni, Shreni, Sumna-api, Hradechakshus, Granthini, and the swift moving (Urvashi who arrived) they, decorated and purple-tinted, did not go first, they lowed like milch-kine for protection.

Urvashi: As soon as he was born the wives (of the gods) surrounded him, the spontaneously flowing rivers nourished him, for the gods reared thee, Pururavas, for the mighty conflict, for the slaughter of the Dasyus.

Pururavas: When, becoming their companion, (Pururavas) the mortal associated with these immortal (nymphs) who had abandoned their bodies, they fled from me like a timid doe, like horses harnessed to a chariot.

When a mortal mixing with these immortal nymphs has conversed with them with words and actions, they becoming ducks do not show their bodies, like playful horses champing (the bit).

(Urvashi) who shone like a flashing lightning, bringing me the desirable dews (of heaven, has appeared); a son able in act and friendly to man has been born; (Urvashi) has prolonged my lengthened existence.

Urvashi: Thou hast been born thus to protect the earth; thou hast deposited this vigour in me; knowing (the future) I have instructed thee (what to do) every day; thou hast not listened to me; why dost now address me, neglectful (of my instructions)?

Pururavas: When shall a son (born of thee) claim me as a father, and crying shed a tear on recognising (me)? What son shall sever husband and wife who are of one mind, now that the fire shines upon your husband's parents?

Urvashi: Let me reply, (thy son) will shed tears, crying out and calling aloud when the expected auspicious time arrives; I will send thee that (child) which is thine in me, depart to thy house, thou canst not, simpleton, detain me.

Pururavas: (Thy husband) who sports with thee may not depart, never to return, (depart) to proceed to a distant region. Either let him sleep upon the lap of Nirriti or let the swift-moving wolves devour him.

Urvashi: Die not Pururavas, fall not; let not hideous wolves devour thee. Female friendship does not exist, their hearts are the hearts of jackals.

When changed in form I wandered amongst the mortals, I dwelt (with them) for four delightful years. I ate once a day a small quantity of butter; satisfied with that now I depart.

Pururavas: I, Vashistha, giver of the dwellings, bring under subjugation Urvashi who fills the firmament (with lustre) and measures out a rain. May (Pururavas), bestower of auspicious rites, abide near thee; come back—my heart is burning.

Urvashi: These gods said to thee, O son of Ila, since thou are indeed subject to death, let thy progeny propitiate thy gods with oblations, thou shalt rejoice (with me) in heaven.

(Rig. 10.8.5)

Then her heart took pity on him. She said, 'Come here the last night of the year from now: then shalt thou lie with me for one night, and then this son of thine will have been born.' He came there on the last night of the year and lo, there stood a golden palace! They then said to him only this (word), 'Enter!' and then they made her go to him.

She then said 'Tomorrow morning the Gandharvas will grant thee a boon, and thou must make thy choice.' He said, 'Choose thou for me!' She replied, 'Say let me be one of yourself!' In the morning the Gandharvas granted him a boon; and he said, 'Let me be one of yourself!'

They said: 'Surely there is not among men that holy form of fire by sacrificing wherein one would become one of ourselves.' They put fire into the pan and gave it to him saying, 'By sacrificing therewith thou shalt become one of ourselves.' He took it (the fire) and his boy, and went on his way home. He then deposited the fire in the forest, and went to the village with the boy alone. (He came back and thought) 'Here I am back'; and lo! it had disappeared! What had been the fire was an Asvattha tree (Ficus religiosa) and what had been the pan was a Sami tree (Mimosa suma). He then returned to Gandharvas.

They said, 'Cook for a whole year a mess of rice sufficient for four persons, and taking each time four logs from the Asvattha tree oint them with ghee, and put them on the fire with verses containing the words 'log' and 'ghee'. The fire which shalt result therefrom will be that very fire (which is required).'

They said, 'But that is recondite (esoteric), as it were. Make thyself rather an upper arani (churning stick for producing fire) of Asvattha wood and lower arani of Sami wood: the fire which shalt result therefrom will be that fire.'

They said, 'But that also is, as it were, recondite. Make thyself rather an upper arani of Asvattha wood and a lower arani of Asvattha wood: the fire which shalt result therefrom will be that fire.'

He then made himself an upper arani of Asvattha wood and a lower arani of Asvattha wood; and the fire which resulted therefrom was that very fire: by offering therewith he became one of the Gandharvas.

(*Sacred Books of the East*, Vol. XLIV, pp. 68–74)

PURVARANGA

Preliminaries to be performed on the stage before the actual commencement of the play are collectively known as Purvaranga. Some of the preliminaries are to be performed behind the curtain and some after removing it.

Procedure of Purvaranga is very elaborate. Bharata in his Natya Shastra has described the sequence of this procedure in detail.

In the beginning musical instruments are tuned and adjusted, singers take their place, rituals to appease different deities are performed. Vidushaka, Sutradhara and his attendants—pariprashvakas—perform trigata or three men's talk, Nandi is sung. After their exit Sthapaka enters and starts prastavana or prologue procedure in which name of the playwright, theme of the play and similar other relevant information is given.

Bharata says that if the producer of the play will perform the preliminaries according to rules laid down, nothing inauspicious will happen to him and after his death will reach the heavenly region.

PUTUL NAUCH

The popular rod-puppet theatre form of West Bengal is known as Putul Nauch, the dance of the dolls. The puppet mounted on a pole is manipulated from below by the puppeteer with the help of the strings in his hands. A bamboo-made hub is tied firmly to the waist of the puppeteer on which a rod with a puppet mounted on it is placed.

A six feet screen is raised behind which the puppeteer hide themselves and manipulate the puppets hoisted on the rods. Audiences did not see the puppeteers who sing, recite dialogues and transfer movements to the puppets on the rods. Mythological themes are taken up for enactment. However with the popularity of the Jatra theatre the puppeteers have adopted the themes of Jatra plays for exhibition through their pole-mounted dancing dolls. The tradition of rod-puppetry has survived only in the state of West Bengal.

RADHA

Fair and lovely cowherd girl of pastoral Vraj, love-companion of dark-hued Krishna, immortalised by the 12th century poet Jayadeva through his musical opera Gita Govinda and deified by scriptures Radha has profound influence on Indian art and literature, dance and drama.

Her origin is shrouded in mystery. Major literary works including Mahabharata, Vishnu Purana, Harivamsha and Bhagavata do not refer to Radha as a part of Krishna's early life. She is for the first time mentioned in a verse found in the collection of Maharashtri Prakrit folk poems by king Hal Satavahana, the Gatha Saptashati, ascribed to the first or second century A.D. In this beautiful verse Radha's love relationship with Krishna is hinted at delicately.

This is followed by stray references to her here and there everytime highlighting her amorous relationship with Krishna. Shudraka mentions her in his play Mricchakatika. In the late tenth century inscriptions of Vakpati Munja, Paramara ruler of Malwa, Krishna is described as 'sick with the pain of Radha's desertation'. Separation and union of the cowherd lovers seems to be central theme of these early references which Jayadeva elaborated in his operatic poem. Jayadeva portrayed Krishna as dramatic hero, Nayaka, and Radha as dramatic heroine, Nayika, passing through various stages of love and intense passion, alternating between separation and union.

It seems that a few centuries before Jayadeva appeared on the scene Radha found her place in dramatic literature. In the eleventh century Ramachandra-Gunachandra in their treatise on drama, Natya Darpana, have mentioned a play based on the Radha-Krishna theme, Radhavipralambha, by one Bhejjala.

Radhavipralambha has been described as a Rasakanka—one-act play based on Ras theme. When a Nayika, dramatic heroine, is separated from the Nayaka, dramatic hero, it is called vipralambha shringara or love in separation. The title of the play indicates that it was about Radha's separation from Krishna and their ultimate union culminating into amorous Ras dance. Scholars ascribe playwright Bhejjala to the tenth century A.D. Jayadeva certainly had a predecessor. As a play Radhavipralambha is lost to posterity, we cannot say about how much influence Bhejjala exerted on Jayadeva.

Another writer of the same period, Sagarnandi, in his work on dramaturgy Natak-lakshana-ratnakosha mentions a play titled as Radha which too is lost to posterity. The only clue the title of the play gives to us is that it was about Radha and predictably about her love for Krishna. However the mention of the plays like Radha and Radhavipralambha points at the fact that well before Jayadeva there were playwrights who made Radha heroine of their dramas. However the credit of making Radha famous goes to Jayadeva, and to his musical opera Gita Govinda.

In the sixteenth century Rupa Goswami, disciple of Chaitanya Mahaprabhu, who had settled in the Braj region wrote three plays—Vidagdha Madhav, Lalit Madhav and Danakelikaumudi—with Radha as their Nayika or heroine.

Around the same time there arose a folk theatre form in the region which became famous as Raslila. Radha occupied premier position in the Raslila plays which are still enacted in the Braj region. Manipuri Ras is another dramatic form prevalent in the state of Manipur which revolves round Radha. Classical dance forms like Kathak and Odissi prominently portray Radha as Nayika. In the Karnataka there emerged a folk theatre form Radhana Ata in imitation of Marathi folk theatre form Tamasha which gives considerable importance to Radha as a consort of Krishna.

Around fifth-sixth century A.D. Radha, a simple cowherd girl of Gatha Saptashati, was elevated to the position of a goddess. In the Panchatantra she is described as an incarnation of goddess Lakshmi. The Puranic works like Devi Bhagavata and Brahmavaivarta Purana contributed significantly to this belief. Various cults that flourished in Bengal and Brajabhumi accepted Radha as goddess. She is seen as hladini shakti or blissful energy of Krishna. She is also called Prakriti and Maya that is nature incarnate and mysterious power of illusion. At Barasana in Mathura district a magnificent temple was built on a hill in her honour. However, generally the dramatic literature laid stress on her human personality and portrayed her as Krishna's playful companion, beloved and a model devotee. Sometimes her divine status too is underlined as is seen in the operatic Raslila plays of North India.

RADHAVIPRALAMBHA

In the Natya Darpana written by Ramachandra-Gunachandra in the eleventh century a play named Radhavipralambha is mentioned. It is described as Rasakanka or one-act play based on the theme of Ras dance. According to Puranic literature Ras was a dance performed by Krishna with beautiful cowherd girls on the bank of river Yamuna on the autumnal full moon night. The name of the poet who wrote this play is given as Bhejjala. When a Nayika or heroine is separated from the Nayaka or hero it is called Vipralambha shringara or love in separation. As the title suggests the separation of Radha from Krishna must have been the main theme. As the happy ending is the rule of Sanskrit drama in the end the poet must have shown union of Radha and Krishna. A verse from the play has been quoted by Abhinavagupta in his work Abhinavabharati written around the end of the tenth century. The drama is lost to posterity. However it underlines the fact that before Jayadeva wrote his opera Gita Govinda in 12th century plays were written on the theme at least during the 10th century A.D.

RAJASHEKHARA

A 10th century poet, writer and dramatist. He wrote three Sanskrit plays—Balaramayana, Balamahabharata or Prachanda Pandava and Viddhashalabhanjika. He also wrote a sattaka play in Prakrit named Karpuramanjiri. He belonged to Maharashtra and was grandson of poet Akaljalada and son of Durdak. The name of his mother was Sheelavati.

He was a Yayavar Brahmin who married a beautiful girl Avantisundari of Chauhan kshatriya family. Avantisundari was a scholar herself and on her request he wrote and staged his lovely Prakrit play, Karpuramanjiri.

Rajashekhara was in the court of king Mahendrapal of Kanauj who ruled from 890 to 908 A.D. He was also the guru of his son Mahipal who ruled up to 940 A.D. after his father.

Rajashekhara is famous for his work on poetics, Kavyamimansa.

RAMABHYUDAYAM

A chaya nataka with two acts by 15th century playwright Vyasa Sriramadeva. In the first act fire-ordeal of Sita is described and in the second we see Rama returning to Ayodhya and his coronation.

RAMANATTAM

In the 17th century the ruler or Zamorin of the principality of Calicut composed a Sanskrit dramatic epic known as Krishnagiti. It described Krishna's life from his birth to final ascent to heaven. It was presented as a cycle of eight plays with the help of dancers, actors, musicians about 1650 A.D. in the Guruvayur temple. The performers appeared in colourful make-up, masks and costumes and danced out the songs sung in the background without uttering a word themselves. The performance came to be known as Krishnattam.

It is said that Vira Kerala Varma, the chieftain of the principality of Kottarakara who was also known as Kottarakara Thampuran requested the Zamorin to send his troupe of Krishnattam to perform in his capital. The request was refused as Krishnattam was intended to be performed in the Guruvayur temple only.

Incensed by this refusal Kottarakara Thampuran wrote Ramayana cycle of eight plays and got them staged. The plays were written in local Malayalam language. They became famous as Ramanattam. This happened sometime between A.D. 1660 and 1680.

It is believed that Kottarakara Thampuran selected the performers from the boys trained in Kalari gymnasium. Gradually the thematic base of Ramanattam got broadened and stories from the Mahabharata, Bhagavata and other Puranas were too taken up for enactment. And thus Ramanattam evolved into a new form named as Kathakali.

RAMAYANA

In ancient time there lived in Ayodhya, a capital city of Kosala, a noble prince of Ikshvaku dynasty whose story became very popular in Aryavarta. From the floating mass of Rama story in its various versions in the form of Gathas, ballads, legends, accounts recorded in works known as Itihasas and Puranas poet Valmiki culled material to write an epic, the Ramayana.

When exactly Valmiki wrote his magnum opus is not known but it certainly existed before Buddha. Though we find traces of Rama story in Buddhist and Jain literature taken from different traditions, it was Valmiki's version which became popular and came to be known as authentic.

With the passing of time, it is believed, the original work of Valmiki grew in size due to literary material added to it from time to time. Some scholars are of the opinion that entire Balakanda at the beginning of the epic and the Uttarakanda at the end are later interpolations.

It is believed that recitation of epics exerted strong influence on the development. In fact the recitation of ancient ballads, gathas on the one hand gave rise to epics and on the other to drama.

The tradition of borrowing themes from epics for composing dramas is quite old. Ramayana too attracted the attention of playwrights at least since 5th-4th century B.C. Bhasa, the first extant Sanskrit playwright belonging to the period, wrote two Ramayana-based plays—Abhisheka and Pratima. Interestingly we do not find the influence of Balakanda and Uttarakanda which are considered as later interpolations, on Bhasa's plays. Both the plays end with the coronation of Rama. The scholars believe that the original Ramayana of Valmiki too ended with Rama's coronation.

In the Harivamsha Purana which was composed around third century A.D. there is a description of a play based on the epic Ramayana—Ramayana mahakavyamu-ddishya natakam—enacted by Bhadra and his troupe.

It showed how the god Vishnu assumed the human form to destroy the demon king Ravana. The story of sage Rishyashringa was enacted. It showed how Dasharatha with the help of Lomapada invited Rishyashringa with his wife Shanta to perform horse sacrifice. The roles of Rama, Lakshmana, Shatrughna and Bharata as well as Rishyashringa and Shanta were assumed by actors resembling epic characters.

Rishyashringa episode and Horse sacrifice of Dasharatha are mentioned in the Balakanda. We may conclude that by the third century or so Balakanda was added to original Ramayana.

In the fifth century A.D. playwright Dignaga wrote a play in six acts, Kundamala, based on Uttarakanda of Ramayana. This indicates that Uttarakanda was added to original Ramayana sometime between the 3rd and 5th centuries A.D.

In the eighth century Bhavabhuti wrote two excellent Rama plays—Mahaviracharita and Uttararamacharita. His patron king Yashovarman wrote a Ramayana-based play Ramabhyudaya which is lost to posterity.

In the eighth century Murari wrote his Rama-drama named as Anargharaghava and Shaktibhadra his Ashcharya Chudamani. In the ninth century Hastimalla wrote Maithilikalyana and in the tenth Rajashekhara wrote his Balaramayana.

The tradition of writing Rama plays continued in following centuries. Some of the better known Rama plays are Mahanataka or Hanumannatak by Hanumanta, Prasannaraghava by Jayadeva, Dutangada by Subhata, Unmattaraghava by Bhaskar, Janakiparinaya by Dixit.

Several Rama plays are mentioned in the works on poetics and dramaturgy but they are lost to posterity. Manuscript libraries all over the country contain unpublished manuscripts of Rama-plays.

K.P. Narayana Pisharoti in his article in Sangeet Natak (No. 111-114) refers to an ancient interesting tradition of combining three Ramayana plays—Pratima and Abhisheka by Bhasa and Ashcharyachudamani by Shaktibhadra—and presenting them together for months by Chakyar actors on Kutiyattam stage of Kerala; altogether there are twentyone acts.

The Ramacharitamanas written by Goswami Tulasidas became more popular than the Sanskrit Valmiki Ramayana on which it is based in north India. It gave rise to new dramatic tradition of enacting Rama story which came to be known as Ramlila. The Ramlila cycle of plays are staged in the month of Ashvin concluding on the Dussehra day.

In the Valmiki Ramayana itself several dramatic arts are mentioned frequently. Professional theatre artists like nata, nartaka, kushilava, shailusha are referred to in the epic. When Rama was exiled he wanted Sita to live in Ayodhya under the care of her in-laws. Angry Sita retorted by saying that like a Shailusha Rama wants to give me to others—Shailusha eva mam Rama parebhyo datumicchati. This throws light on morality of Shailusha community. No wonder actors were known as jayajiva or living off on the income of wives.

The terms like Vadhu-natak-sangha and Nata-nartak-sangha found in the epic suggest that there were companies of professional entertainers. Such companies are referred to in the Buddhist literature too.

In the Ayodhya kanda of the epic there is a clear reference to drama proper. The epic says that the friends of prince Bharata entertained him with stories, instrumental music and humorous plays—Natakanyapare smahur hasyani vividhani cha.

In the same Kanda there occurs a term vyamishraka which the commentators have explained as a multilingual play, the play containing different languages including Prakrits—prakritadi bhasha samisrita natakadishu.

At one place Valmiki describes Rama, the hero of his epical composition, as Vaiharikanam shilpanam jnata or one who is expert in various arts of entertainment. In ancient times all fine arts including dancing, singing, acting were covered by the term shilpa. The poet wants to indicate that Rama was adept in theatrical arts.

RAMLILA

A dramatic form depicting the life of Rama, epic hero and prince of Ayodhya, as depicted in the Ramacharitamanas, a popular work in Avadhi by saint-poet Tulasidas (1532–1623 A.D.).

According to tradition it was poet Tulasidas himself who dramatised his epic poem based on Valmiki's Ramayana and started Ramlila performance at Assi Ghat on river Ganga in Varanasi.

As a culmination of lila performances it is believed that Tulasidas created a Jhanki or tableau vivant of coronation of Rama on the day of Sharad Purnima, five days after navaratra of Durga, on the Assi Ghat. The followers of Tulasidas belonging to Tulsi Mandir or Tulsidas ka akhada are continuing this tradition.

Gradually the tradition of staging Ramlila spread to other parts of North India and today, around Vijayadashami day, Ramlila plays are enacted with great fervour all over the northern part of the country in varying formats.

Ramlila is performed as a cycle of plays spreading over several days. Episodes related to Rama's life up to his coronation are divided into smaller segments and they are taken up for enactment in the form of cyclic performance.

Generally speaking the Ramayana story from the birth of Rama to his coronation after his return from exile is taken up for cyclic presentation. Processions, tableaux, burning of the effigies of Ravana, Kumbhakarna and Meghanada on Vijayadashami day form part of Ramlila performances.

Basically there are two styles of Ramlila performance. In the first importance is given to the recitation of the epic Ramacharitamanas and actors in the guise of Ramayana characters illustrate the recitation by their presence, very little acting, dialogues if any are just very brief. In the other style proper plays with dialogues and action based on the epic are enacted. Ramlila in some places is presented as musical dance-drama. In fact Ramlila is performed in a number of formats.

Sometimes the locales of Ramayana are marked on ground extending over a few kilometres. Every day the lila is performed on a new locale. Famous Ramlila of Ramnagar near Varanasi has adopted the style of shifting locales. It runs for thirtyone days, from Bhadrapada shukla chaturdashi to Ashvin shukla chaturdashi, moving from one place to another. Tableaux, processions, burning of the effigies of demons form part of this spectacular Ramlila celebration.

Every city has its own custom, tradition of performing Ramlila. The traditional form of Ramlila enactments can be seen in cities like Varanasi, Prayag and Mathura.

Delhi is emerging as a great centre of Ramlila celebration. Ramlila is enacted at different places in Delhi on a very grand scale with pomp and show.

Traditionally child actors are employed to enact Ramlila plays. After they don the costumes they are treated as divinities.

In a book, *Benares Illustrated in a Series of Drawings* by James Princeps, published in 1831, there is a description of Ramlila celebration. It gives us an idea as to how Ramlila used to be enacted and celebrated about hundred and seventy years ago.

In the book *The Great Indian Epics* by John Campbell Oman there is a description of the Ramlila procession he saw in the year 1884 in Lahore. He writes:

'Days before the time fixed for the Dasahra festival, men, done up like monkeys and attended by drummers, may be seen in the bazaars collecting money for the fair, at which the more striking leading incidents of the epic are annually performed, part by part, in a rude pantomimic fashion. Sometimes the opening scene is a great marriage procession. One such, on an unusually large scale, was got up in Lahore in 1884, at the expense of certain rich bankers. This motley and gigantic procession was made up of very heterogeneous elements. Several camels led the way; some bulky elephants put in an appearance, and a great number of mounted men, on good cavalry horses, gave dignity to the procession. Three or four well filled carriages, gaily decorated with tinsel, flowers and coloured cloths, had the honour of accommodating the friends of Rama. A few huge litters, each borne aloft on the shoulders of sixteen or twenty bearers, were conspicuous objects in the throng. On some of these sat men personating the gods and goddesses of India in all their grotesqueness; on others squatted favourite female singers with their attendant minstrels, who delighted the audience with their grace and vocal performances. Imitation artillery armed with explosive bombs, dancers, mountebanks, musicians, and an innumerable crowd of ordinary citizens on foot, raised noise and dust enough to gratify the most pleasure-seeking Indian mob. The hero, Rama, and his inseparable brother, were dragged along on wooden horses, placed on a wheeled platform. There they sat, side by side, holding tiny bows and arrows in their hands, in a most ridiculous way, while the less important mythological personages, divine or other, came along in carriages or litters.'

Even today a similar grand procession is taken out every day during Ramlila celebration in Old Delhi from Esplanade Road to Ramlila ground which includes horses, elephants, camels and floats with tableaux vivants mounted on them.

There is no other such a majestic and grand dramatic festival as Ramlila elsewhere in the world.

RANGA

The word Ranga is frequently used in ancient literature as a place for public amusement or for dramatic exhibition, stage, arena, any place of public assembly, theatre or playhouse.

Ayoghara Jataka refers to a juggler performing in the ranga. An open-air theatre used to be made by raising wooden scaffoldings around the performing arena. Seats circle upon circle, tier above tier were raised around the place of public amusement —chakkatichakke manchatimanche bandhimsu—the Jatakas say.

In the Kullavagga portion of the Buddhist Vinaya texts is recorded the story of the wicked and shameless bhikkus, followers of Assagi and Punabbasu living on Kita hill. They used to visit ranga or theatre halls, spread their robes and ask the beautiful dancers to dance on it by saying: 'Here you may dance, sister'— Rangamajjhe pi sanghati patharitva, nacchaki evam vadanti igha bhagini nacchasu.

Patanjali in his Mahabhashya refers to naughty and mischievous spectators who would visit the place of public amusement, ranga, and provocatively ask the dancers, natanam striya: 'Whom do you belong to? Whom do you belong to?' And they would get an equally naughty reply—'To you! To you!'— Natanam striyo rangam gata yo yah prcchati kasya yuyam kasya yuyam iti iti tam tam tva tva ity ahuh (VI.I.2).

In the Ganikadhyaksha prakarana the persons earning their livelihood by performing on theatre are called rangopajivin. In Bhasa's play Charudattam beautiful Ganika Vasantasena is described as adept in the art of entering the theatre, ranga, and thus expert in voice modulation— rangapraveshena kalanam chaiva shikshaya, swarantarena daksha.

Bharata has used the word Purvaranga for the rituals preceding the actual commencement of the drama. A verse in the Gatha Saptashati terms the foreplay preceding the actual act of love-making as ratinataka purvaranga—prologue of drama of sexual union.

RANGADEVATA

Goddess of stage or theatre. Acharya Nandikeshvara in his 12th century work Abhinaya Darpana refers to Rangadevata as a presiding deity of the stage.

The Acharya says the dancer before wearing make-up should first offer worship to Vighnesha or Ganesha and Shiva as well as to sky and the earth. After worshipping musical instruments bowing before Guru she should obtain his permission to start doing make-up.

After completing the make-up she should offer prayer to the presiding deity of stage. She should say:

'O the bestower of good fortune on the clan of actors, creator of Bhava, Rasa and Ananda, one who enchant the world by her skill in arts grant me success and prosperity.'

Thus praising the Rangadevata she should scatter flowers on the stage.

This procedure is described as Purvaranga by Acharya Nandikeshvara. It is necessary for a dancer to perform this procedure before starting actual dance performance.

RANGAPUJA

Consecration of Natyagriha or playhouse with appropriate rituals is called Rangapuja. It was considered necessary to perform Rangapuja immediately after constructing a playhouse. During Rangapuja various deities are invoked, all musical instruments are worshipped and puja is offered to Jarjara, an auspicious bamboo pole with five knots. Different kinds of foodstuff are offered to different deities according to their liking by uttering mantras. Deities are offered milk, honey and sweets and demons as well as evil spirits are propitiated with meat, wine and various kinds of liquors.

Homa is performed with suitable mantras. A pitcher full of water is placed on the stage. The hero and the dancers and musical instruments are sprinkled with sacred water. Benediction for the success of dramatic performance is uttered praying the mothers such as Saraswati, Dhriti, Medha, Hri, Lakshmi, Smriti, etc.

Then the water pitcher is broken by the director of drama, the entire playhouse is illuminated. Drama director runs around the playhouse with torch in his hand roaring, jumping and enacts a mock fight on the stage. Wounds caused during fight are considered as a good omen.

It is believed that if the auditorium is consecrated with proper ritual it will bring good luck to all and ensure smooth sailing for dramatic performance.

RANI GUMPHA AMPHITHEATRE

Udayagiri and Khandagiri are two beautiful hills near Bhubaneshvar in Orissa which are famous for Jain caves of great antiquity. Located in the Udayagiri hill is a magnificent double-storied rock-cut cave with a large courtyard belonging to the second century B.C. having the appearance of an amphitheatre. Famous as Rani Gumpha local tradition claims it to be a place used for staging dramatic performances, music concerts, public shows involving singing and dancing. In the nearby Hathigumpha cave there is an inscription of Emperor Kharavela of Kalinga belonging to the second century B.C. The inscription describes him as Gandharva-veda-budho or one well versed in the arts of dance, drama and music. The line five of the inscription states that he organised a festival, utsava samaja, full of singing, dancing and dramatic enactments for citizens, dapa-nata-gita-vadita samdamsan-ahi utsava-samaja-karapanahi cha kidapayai nagarim (Epigraphia Indica, Vol. XX, p. 87), presumably in the hills of Khandagiri-Udayagiri. It is believed that this Utsava-samaja was held in the Rani Gumpha or at least it inherited the tradition of celebrating such theatrical festivals.

Describing the Gumpha Percy Brown says:

'This 'abbey church' is a double-storied production with its cells arranged around three sides of an open courtyard, the fourth side comprising the frontal approach. A broad terrace, projected from the upper story, was originally supported on structural pillars, either of wood or stone, and these formed the verandah of the ground floor. A stairway cut in the rock at the side gave access to this upper terrace on one face of which there is a spacious throne with arms, a foot-rest, evidently a seat of honour of the abbot or other high dignitary. While the general arrangement of the cells indicates that most of them were for accommodation of monks, there are several supplementary echambers and recesses evidently devised for special purposes connected with the ritual, either as robing rooms or for preparation of offerings. In addition there are rooms for storing sacred vessels and vestments, with a place for the custodian or sacristan.

That the open courtyard and its overlooking terraces were specially designed for some spectacular kind of ceremonial seems fairly clear and a clue to the form it took is also provided. For around the walls of upper story there is a long frieze containing figure in a series of connected episodes of a distinctly dramatic character. As the same scenes are repeated in parts, in one or more viharas on this site, they evidently represent some vivid epic in the heroic age of the people.

It may therefore be inferred that this arrangement of courtyard and terraces forming the Rani Gumpha constituted an open-air theatre in which scenes depicted in the sculptural friezes around it were brought to life by being performed on festive occasions as a kind of passion play, in the same way that the so called devil-dances are enacted in the monastery (gumpha) quadrangles of Tibet.

If so, the peculiar formation of the gumpha is at once explained, and its various parts fall into their proper place. Moreover, it is not difficult to picture the courtyard occupied by the actors in this drama, while seated on the terraces, like an amphitheatre, with the high priest enthroned in the central position, with closely grouped background of spectators, the whole forming a brilliant and moving pageant amidst the dark encircling groves' (*Indian Architecture: Buddhist and Hindu*, 1976, pp. 29–30).

In the space between the doors of the cells some stories are carved in relief. In one of the friezes we see a fight between shield and sword wielding man and woman and then man carrying the woman away in his arms as if she is a war trophy. According to marriage custom of Joang tribe of Orissa the bridegroom's marriage party goes to the house of the bride and dances with sword and shield and takes away the bride as if won in the war. Maybe the friezes reflect this custom, maybe it is a depiction of some local story.

There is yet another interesting frieze in which we see a king pursuing the frightened deers with bow and arrow in his hands. In the next scene related with it we see him standing before a girl sitting on the branch of a tree who is by her gesture asking him to stop hunting the harmless animals. Some scholars consider it to be the depiction of the episode of hunt of king Dushyanta and his encounter with Shakuntala. Shakuntala story is depicted in the Mahabharata, in Kalidasa's play Abhijnana Shakuntalam and its Buddhist version is found in the Katthahari Jataka. We may take this frieze as an artist's representation of Shakuntala story.

In the bottom storey corridor carved in relief between the doors of the cells is an interesting dance scene. Here a female dancer is seen dancing under a canopy with a musical orchestra in attendance. This is one of the earliest dance scenes found sculpted in Indian art.

All this indicates that the Rani Gumpha amphitheatre must have been used for staging dramatic performances full of dancing, singing, music and play acting.

RASASADANA BHANA

One-act play in Bhana format by Yuvaraja of Kerala. He is ascribed to the 15th-16th century on the basis of the style and diction of the play. It presents in monologue experiences of the Vita, narrator of the play, which he gets during his wanderings. Giving the outline of the story Konow says: 'Vita, at the command of his friend Mandaraka, has taken upon himself the task of taking care of his wife Chandanamala. He follows her to the temple and goes with her for stroll, where they fall at the head of a raging elephant. Then he brings her home and himself goes to his own lady-friend, with whom he converses cheerfully. Then he goes out again, chats with the young people, gives them advice, arranges secret unions, accepts the invitation of some young maidens of different towns to call on them as quickly as possible, describes the life on the streets and finally returns to Chandanamala, with whom his friend Mandaraka has been united in the meantime.'

We find in this Bhana beautiful songs describing the beauty of nature and female form.

RASA THEORY

Related to the aesthetic experience of dramatic art Rasa theory was first expounded by Bharata in his Natya Shastra. Rasa is a thing which can be tasted, any object of taste is called Rasa. The basic sentiments found in the drama which can be tasted or relished, as one would relish delicious food, aesthetically are called rasas. Bharata calls them as natya-rasa also. Eight in number they are:

1. Erotic—shringara
2. Comic—hasya
3. Pathetic—karuna
4. Furious—raudra
5. Heroic—veera
6. Terrible—bhayanaka
7. Odious—bibhatsa
8. Marvellous—adbhuta

These rasas, says Bharata, evolve out of eight durable emotive states, known as Sthayibhavas. They are:

1. Love—rati
2. Mirth—hasa
3. Sorrow—shoka
4. Anger—krodha
5. Energy—utsaha
6. Terror—bhaya
7. Jugupsa—disgust
8. Astonishment—vismaya

Now the question arises as to how these eight durable emotive states, sthayibhavas, graduate into rasa. Bharata has given a formula for that. He says:

Vibhavanubhavavyabhicharisanyo-gadrasanishpatti.

This is called rasa-sutra. It means when vibhava, anubhava and vyabhichari bhava unite with sthayibhavas the result is rasa.

Vyabhichari bhavas are fleeting emotions. They are thirtythree in number and are as follows:

discouragement, weakness, apprehension, envy, intoxication, weariness, indolence, depression, anxiety, distraction, recollection, contentment, shame, inconstancy, joy, agitation, stupor, arrogance, despair, impatience, sleep, epilepsy, dreaming, awakening, indignation, dissimulation, cruelty, assurance, sickness, insanity, death, fright and deliberation.

Vibhava includes dramatis personae and the environment they are put in. Vibhava is of two kinds: Alambana and Uddipana. Alambana is dramatis personae, people as a seat of emotions and Uddipana is outer environment which excites emotions, feelings, sentiments.

Anubhava means physical expression of these emotions—permanent or fleeting—visible to viewer, acting in the case of drama.

According to Indian tradition as reflected in the Natya Shastra entire universe is the theme of the drama. The universe is comprised of two things—man and his environment. They are found described in poetry or drama as alambana vibhava and uddipana vibhava. The characters in the play like the hero, the heroine, the villain are alambana vibhavas and external environment as Vasanta ritu which excites feelings is uddipana vibhava.

Bhavas are of two kinds sthayi and vyabhichari that is permanent and fleeting, temporary. These bhavas find expression through physical gestures and movements. As these physical expressions follow the bhavas or emotions stirred in the minds of dramatis personae they are known as anubhavas. In short anubhava means acting.

When vibhava, anubhava and vyabhichari unite with sthayi bhavas, rasa emerges for audiences to relish.

The rasa theory of Bharata was subjected to various interpretations by later theorists.

Bharata has explained in detail the sthayibhava, vibhava, anubhava and sancharibhava of each rasa. For instance he has explained the Raudra or Furious sentiment as follows:

Sthayi bhava—krodha
Vibhava—naughty men
Vyabhichari bhavas—determination, energy, indignation, restlessness, fury, perspiration, trembling, etc.
Anubhavas—red eyes, knitting of eyebrows, biting of the lips, etc.

(NS: Ghosh)

Bharata has given symbolic colours to each rasa and has also mentioned their presiding deities:

Shringara	Shyam	Vishnu
Hasya	Sita	Pramatha
Karuna	Kapota	Yama
Raudra	Rakta	Rudra
Veera	Gaura	Mahendra
Bhayanaka	Krishna	Kaladeva
Bibhatsa	Nila	Mahakala
Adbhuta	Pita	Brahma

RASIKAVINODA

A play in Trotaka form by 17th century playwright of Gujarat, Kamalakarabhatta. The play is based on the life of Gokulesha, grandson of Vallabhacharya, and his variety of Vaishnava religion and philosophy.

RASLILA

Musical dance-drama based on Krishna theme which emerged in the 16th century in the pastoral Braj region on the bank of river Yamuna with Mathura, Vrindavan and region around Govardhana-Barasana as its main centres.

Devastated by Muslim invasion the culturally rich region of Braj started recuperating in the 16th century. Temples were built, old cultural and religious traditions were revived, association of Krishna myth with various locales in the region was rediscovered, sacred and secular literature and poetry blossomed with renewed vigour. In this atmosphere of regeneration an interesting Krishnite dramatic form rich with dance, music, poetry evolved in the region which became famous as Raslila.

Ras is the dance performed by dark-hued Krishna with beautiful cowherd girls of Braj, fair as Champak flowers, on the white sands of river Yamuna on one fragrant autumnal full moon night. The dance finds mention in a number of Puranas, dramas, poetic works written from time to time. Bhagavata Purana devotes full five chapters, known as Raspanchadhyayi, to narrate the story of Ras.

Lila means divine sports or acts of Krishna like killing several demons, lifting up mountain Govardhana on his little finger, stealing butter from the houses of cowherd girls and romancing beautiful Radha.

Operatic Raslila plays through dance, music and poetry create delightful vision of

Krishna's Ras and lilas. Rather than a play the traditionalists consider it as a sacred ritual perpetuating sentiment of Bhakti or devotion to Krishna.

Brahmin by caste the practitioners of this performing art are known as Rasdharis. An enterprising Rasdhari floats a Raslila troupe, known as Rasmandali, recruits children to play different roles and trains them in dance and music. He is called Swami. He selects beautiful poetic compositions in Brajaboli and weaves them into a story revolving round Krishna lila. Thus he formulates basic text of the play. Several such plays revolving round several lila themes are composed for enactment.

Child actors is the significant feature of the Raslila opera. All the main roles such as that of Krishna, Radha, Sakhis, cowherd boys, etc., are played by child actors. Once they attain puberty they are out. All female roles are played by male children. Women are not allowed on Ras stage.

At the beginning the Swami appears on the stage with his musicians, offers prayers to different deities and constantly remaining on the scene conducts entire proceedings of the play. It is he who narrates Krishna story with the help of child actors and musicians in his orchestra.

The stage is very simple, a performing arena provided with a small throne for divinities, Radha and Krishna, to sit on it. The performance is divided into two parts. The opening part is known as Ras which is followed by another part known as lila.

When the curtain is removed we see Radha and Krishna sitting on the throne attended by Sakhis, female friends of Radha, standing in two rows facing each other. They offer 'arati' and 'puja' to divine couple. Then Krishna gets down from the throne and requests Radha to descend the throne and dance with him. Thus starts Nitya Ras —Radha, Krishna and Sakhis dancing in different alluring formations.

After the Nitya Ras the lila portion starts. It is dramatisation of some interesting episode from Krishna's life, particularly related to his childhood stay in Brajbhumi. The dialogues are in prose and verse, with humour evoked by a jester character, Mansukha. Poetic compositions set to folk and classical tunes and ragas, dances set to tala and laya enrich audio-visual fabric of the lila plays.

It seems that Raslila evolved gradually to reach the present-day format. Probably it started with singing of songs related to Krishna's Ras by smooth-faced boys donning the costumes of cowherd girls. Gradually dancing might have been introduced with Radha and Krishna as principal characters. Lastly the lila portion that is dramatisation of episodes from Krishna's childhood life in Braj might have been added to it.

Krishna drama in Brajbhumi took different formats like Vanajatra processional theatre and Budhi lila series of plays performed at different locales around Barasana, Chiksauli, Uchagaon in the form of dramatic village fairs.

Raslila plays are performed all over the year but essentially they form part of Janmashtami and Holi festivals which fall respectively in the months of August and March.

Some nineteenth century British writers have described the Ras Lila theatre of the northern region in detail, which gives us a fairly good idea of the Ras performances of the time. Captain Thomas Deur Broughton, who attended the Janmashtami festival at the Sindhia camp in the year 1809, has left a graphic record of the event which is included in his book *Letters from a Maratha Camp during the Year 1809*. In a letter dated 8 September he writes:

> The tent in which we were received was about one hundred and fifty feet long, divided lengthwise into three compartments by a double row of posts ornamented with coloured paper, and to each of which was affixed a score of candles. At the further end was a stage raised about two feet from the ground and made to represent like a kind of Gothic hall, with pillars and arches highly painted and gilded. This is called Sungasun or throne in the centre of which was placed Phool Dhol...in which lay the image of Bal Govind... The centre space of the tent was left open for the dancers and those on either side filled up to the level of the stage...Candles were lighted...After one or two sets of Nauch girls had performed, the Rahus-d'harees who were seated at the upper end of the tent on a kind of raised sofa...came forward. They were boys, always Brahmuns who are educated at Muttra for this purpose. Parties of them travel about at this season, to perform at different Hindoo courts in India; that now in the camp consists of four besides musicians...The eldest represented Kunya, the youngest his beloved Radha and the other two her youthful companions. The performance was a kind of ballet, descriptive of sports of this amorous and inconstant but interesting deity with Gopees during which they sang stanzas...in the language of Brij.
>
> I have procured the copies of some of the songs performed...The first is supposed to be a dialogue between Kunya and one of the Gopees who returned to him, after a former visit, sooner than he expected. The second contains a description of the effect caused in the bosoms of the Muttra maids by the sound of the pipe of their darling shepherd and a dialogue between them and Jasooda in consequence of their interview with him in the groves of Madhuban.

After this Captain Broughton gives a fine translation of the dialogue that transpired between Krishna and a Gopi:

> *Kunya:* Again my fair one!—hast thou purchased me?...
> *Gopee:* Think'st thou uncalled I boldly came?...
> Ah, see!...
> The gathering clouds, dear youth, invite to love.
> *Kunya:* How could a frame so soft, such dangers prove?
> While e'en thy pretty self was lost in the night, how see thy way?
> *Gopee:* The lightning gleamed so bright!
> *Kunya:* O'er broken roads, through mire and tangling thorn,

Thy tender limbs must ache, thy feet be torn?

Gopee: Steps light and firm will weariest way overcome.

Kunya: Yet dark's the night; and thou wert all alone.

Gopee: No my soul's Lord! for love was with me still. Pointed my path and warded every ill!

KUBIT

The pipe is heard of Nundh's sweet boy;
The Goalins hearts beat high with joy;
To the cool woods in crowds they speed;
Nor danger fear, nor toil they heed;
And if by chance the youth they spy,
Away go prudence, modesty;
They gaze, by his bright beauties burned,
And swoon,—their pails are overturned!
Jasooda!—listen to our prayer;
Thy son's audacious frolics hear!
To Brindavan we went our way—
He seized our arms, and bade us stay...
Lady! our cheeks with shame were red;
Like modest girls away we fled...
In vain we have milked, in vain we have churned
For he—our pails has overturned...

Commenting upon the performance Captain Broughton further states: 'Both the dancing and the singing of the Rahus-d'harees was far superior to that of common performers, their attitudes were exceedingly graceful and their voices were never raised beyond the natural pitch. The dresses were appropriate and elegant, specially that of Kunya who wore a brilliant sun upon his head, and a quantity of superb jewels around his neck and breasts; all of which, as well as the dresses of the other boys, were furnished from the wardrobe of Muha Raj.'

The author also refers to *Jhanki* that is a dramatic scene freezed in time, a tableau, by the boys performing the Ras play: 'After the dances were over, they exhibited in group representations of the most celebrated statues of Krishna and his relatives, with an accuracy and steadiness quite surprising in such children.'

Colonel James Tod in his *Annals and Antiquities of Rajasthan* not only describes the Ras performance but also tries to explain its metaphysics: 'In the mystic dance, the Rasmandel, yet imitated on the annual festival sacred to sun god Heri, He is represented with a radiant crown in dancing attitude playing on a flute to the nymphs encircling him...each holding a musical instrument. These nymphs are called non-ragini, from Raga, a mode of song over which each presides, and no-rasa, or nine passions excited by powers of harmony. On the festival of the nine passions excited by powers of harmony. On the festival of the Jenum, or "birth-day", there is a scenic representation of Kaniya and Gopies when are rehearsed in mellifluous accents of ionic land of Vaij, the songs of Jydeva, as addressed by Kuniya to Radha and her companions.'

RAS LILAGRIHA

Raja Mansingh Tomar, the great 15th century patron of music and dance, constructed unique open-air theatre at village Barai-Panihal near Gwalior to stage dance, drama, music performances. Writing about it in Gazetteer of the Gwalior State, Captain Luard says: 'There is an old theatre known as Ras Lilagriha with traces of ruined rooms built around a circular open ground lined at intervals with lamp-posts surmounted with small cupolas resembling in style the cupolas of Man Mandir of Gwalior fort.'

Locally known as Racch this is a very interesting open-air theatre structure. When we look at it from outside we see a circular bastioned fortification having three entrances. When we enter it we see this circular fortification lined with a number of rooms with flat roof. In the centre of the area covered by the fortification there is a spacious circular dancing floor with a stone pillar in its centre. On the periphery of the dance floor, slightly raised from the ground surrounding it, stand eight leaning towers and in between four platforms with cupolas. It is believed that the towers leaning towards dance floor were used for placing lights on them to illuminate the dancing floor in the night. The four platforms with cupolas were for the musicians.

This open-air theatre was situated on the bank of a water reservoir known as kridasarovara.

The entire structure is now in ruins and the kridasarovara has gone dry. Exactly what kinds of performances used to take place in this remote open-air Racch is not known. However if the name of this theatre is any indication of the concerts held there we may say that it was built for performing Ras dances associated with the cult of Krishna.

RAS MANDAL

Circular dance floors mostly built with clay, or bricks and mortar, found in the Braj region on the bank of river Yamuna and used for staging Raslila performances. Some Ras Mandals are provided with small thrones for Radha and Krishna, the principal dramatis personae of the Raslila. Some Ras Mandals are provided with roof too supported by pillars.

It is believed that earliest Ras Mandal was built in clay by Hita Harivamsha, the founder of Radhavallabha Sampradaya, at Govindghat in Vrindavan in 1543. Later it was subjected to many changes and renovations. Today it is a structure with high plinth provided with a circular dancing arena and a throne within it. It has a roof supported by pillars. The whole structure is attached to a small temple of Radha. Raslila performances are held here regularly.

RASO

Medieval poetic compositions particularly found in Rajasthan for singing or enacting in Jain temples.

Jains made significant contribution to Indian theatrical tradition. The Rayapaseniya Sutta has described thirtytwo types of drama including one portraying the life of Tirthankara Mahavira from his birth to Nirvana.

In the 11th century Anahilapattan in Gujarat was the great centre of Jain culture. Acharya Hemachandra was a famous Jain scholar of the time. His disciple Ramachandra in collaboration of yet another scholar Gunachandra wrote an exhaustive treatise on dramaturgy named Natya Darpana.

It is said that a Jain monk Asadabhuti wrote a play on the life of Emperor Bharata, son of Rishabhadeva. Staged for the first time in Pataliputra it so powerfully advocated the philosophy of asceticism that after witnessing it many kings abandoned their kingdoms. Fearing that no warrior would be left to rule the earth if this trend continued, the play was destroyed.

A number of plays such as Chandralekhavijaya Prakarana by Devachandra, Prabuddharauhaneya by Ramabhadramuni, pupil of Jayaprabha Suri, Moharajaparajaya by Yashapala were written for staging them during Jain temple festivals.

In 12th-13th century Rajasthan became a major centre of Jain theatrical activities. Musical compositions known as Raso or Ras were written on Jain themes for singing or enacting in temples. They depicted the stories of Jain apostles, saints and ideal devotees with great religious fervour. Religious Ras plays such as Gayasukumar Ras, Nemi Ras and Bharat Bahubali Ras were quite popular.

The plays were considered sacred and performed as an offering to Jain Tirthankaras and divinities. Witnessing these plays was considered as pious act. For instance Revantgiri Ras says that 'whosoever will enthusiastically enact this Ras play of Sri Vijayasena Suri will be blessed by Jina Neminatha and goddess Ambika will fulfil all his desires.' However this tradition was stopped due to the opposition of certain section of the sect.

RATNAVALI

A four-act play by Harsha who lived in the seventh century A.D. It is based on the love story of king Udayana of Vatsa country and princess Ratnavali of Sinhala or Sri Lanka.

Udayana cycle of stories are popular in India since ancient times and are referred to in Pali and Buddhist literature. Udayana stories were included in the Brihatkatha of Gunadhya. They are referred to in Kautilya's Arthashastra and Patanjali's Mahabhashya. In his poem Meghaduta poet Kalidasa says that old people in the Avanti region are very well versed with Udayana katha—Udayanakathakovidagramavriddha. In Shudraka's Mricchakatika king Udayana and his minister Yaugandharayana are mentioned.

Udayana story, it seems, was popular with playwrights. Bhasa wrote two plays—Swapnavasavadatta and Pratijna Yaugandharayana—based on Udayana story. Harsha too wrote two plays with Udayana as their hero.

In the first act of the play there is elaborate description of Vasantotsava or Madanamahotsava dedicated to Kamadeva or god of love. This Dionysian festival full of drunken revelry, dance, music, fun and frolic is well portrayed. The Kuttanimatam kavya by Damodaragupta records that this particular act was staged by the courtesans of Varanasi in the temple of Kashi Vishvanatha.

In the fourth act of the play a magic show finds place. A scene of palace harem catching fire and king entering it to save heroine also adds action to the proceedings of the act though later it is proved that the fire was the illusion created by the magician.

Crossing several hurdles and the opposition of the queen Vasavadatta the lovers unite in the end. It seems that this play is written by Harsha under the influence of Kalidasa whom he follows in many places. Ratnavali is a love story told delightfully.

RAVAN CHHAYA

A popular shadow theatre form of Orissa. Rama story became quite popular in the region after Sarala Das translated the epic Ramayana in Oriya language in the 15th century. However the Ravan Chhaya artists use the Vichitra Ramayana by Vishvanatha Khuntia, a medieval Oriya poet. The puppets made of deer skin are quite small and without any joints. Many props such as trees, chariots, mountains are made and their shadows are obtained on the screen to create a setting for the scene.

The moving shadows on the screen illustrate the narration of Rama story quite dramatically.

RITU VASANTA

Brilliant, sparkling, spring season of the year, comprising the months of Chaitra and Vaishakha or from the middle of March to that of May. Joyous festive Vasanta ritu is favourite of Indian poets and dramatists.

Season or ritu is comprised of two months. According to Indian calendar there are six ritus or seasons in a year. They are Vasanta, Grishma, Varsha, Sharad, Hemanta and Shishira.

The months each ritu covers are as follows:

Vasanta:	Chaitra and Vaishakha (Spring)
Grishma:	Jeshtha and Ashadha (Hot season)
Varsha:	Shravan and Bhadrapada (Rainy season)
Sharad:	Ashvin and Kartik (Autumn)
Hemanta:	Margashirsha and Pausha (Winter)
Shishira:	Magha and Phalguna (Cool season)

Vasanta Panchami heralds the arrival of Vasanta. According to Indian calendar it falls on Magha shudda panchami. Though Vasanta proper commences much later in the month of Chaitra, all the signs of Vasanta ritu start appearing from mid-Magha. It is believed that Kama, the god of love, was born on the day of Vasanta Panchami so also the goddess of learning and arts, Saraswati.

In ancient times seasons were personified, addressed in Mantras and worshipped by libations. In the Vedic literature Year is likened to a bird whose head is Vasanta, Grishma and Sharad left and right wings, Hemanta middle part and Varsha tail. When only five seasons are mentioned Hemanta includes Shishira.

Kalidasa in his celebrated poem Ritusamhara has described the beauty and ambience of different seasons and their influence on the human love-life. We find similar description of the Ritus in the Bhana play Dhurtavitasamvada by Ishvaradatta.

Poems depicting the natural ambience of the seasons and months, and their influence on human beings, particularly lovers separated from each other, are found written in many languages. Such poems constituted the literary genre known as Barahmasa. Barahmasa poems have inspired artists of various schools of miniature paintings.

The beauty and ambience of Vasanta ritu is found described in a number of Sanskrit plays. The joyous portrayals of Vasanta related festivals and rituals also form part of the plays. From the prologues of these plays we come to know that a number of dramatic performances were held during this season.

Kalidasa's romantic comedy Malavikagnimitra was staged on the occasion of Vasantotsava. He has described the natural beauty of the season in the play and also the ritual of Ashoka dohada which is performed during spring. Kalidasa has also shown how women drink during the season and aspire to enjoy swinging with their lovers.

The beautiful heroine of the play Mricchakatika by Shudraka is named after this lovely season. She is Vasantasena, as beautiful as the Vasanta ritu itself—vasantashobheva vasantasena. The names of her attendants are Pallavaka and Parabhrutika. Pallavaka signifies new delicate leaves that sprout on the branches of the trees during the season of Vasanta. Parabhrutika means the bird koyal or cuckoo whose music is heard in Vasanta ritu in particular. In the first act of the play we see her being pursued by Vita and Shakara. When she calls out the names of her attendants for help Shakara retorts that what of Pallavaka or Parabhrutika she may call entire Vasanta ritu for help but nobody would be able to save her from his clutches.

Shudraka's Vasantasena is the beauty of Vasanta ritu personified.

Sriharsha's play Ratnavali was staged on the occasion of Vasantotsava. In the play we find beautiful description of Madanotsava which is celebrated during Vasanta ritu. The ritual of Kama worship too is described in detail. Kama, the god of love, is specially worshipped during spring season.

Shudraka's Bhana play Padmaprabhrutakam was staged during Vasanta ritu. The play opens with beautiful description of the joyous season. Vararuchi's Ubhayabhisarika too was staged during Vasanta.

Sanskrit dramatic literature carries within itself the fragrance of Vasanta, the joyous season of spring.

RUPA GOSWAMI

Prominent disciple of Chaitanya Mahaprabhu, author of the plays Vidagdhamadhav, Lalitmadhav and Danakelikaumudi, and a work on dramaturgy, Nataka Chandrika. Among his many works Bhakti Rasamrita Sindhu and Ujjavalnilamani stand out prominently for codifying the aesthetics of Krishna Bhakti.

Ancestors of Rupa Goswami were Brahmins from Karnataka. Some of them came and settled in Bengal at the end of 14th century. Rupa was born in 1488 A.D. and died in 1591 A.D.

Rupa and his brother Sanatana were in the employ of Husenshah of Gauda as ministers and were known as Davir Khas and Sakar Mallik. At Ramkeli, the capital city of the Shah, they came in contact with Chaitanya Mahaprabhu and leaving their high positions they became his ardent disciples, and took to Radha-Krishna worship.

Ultimately they settled in Vraj region of North India and were responsible for the cultural renaissance along with other Goswamis of the sect including Jiva, Gopal Bhatta, Raghunatha Das, Raghunatha Bhatta, Krishnadas Kaviraja and Narayanabhatta. Together they were known as Shat-goswamis or six goswamis.

Apart from writing they helped locating and reviving numerous holy places in the region, virtually establishing the geography of Krishna myth. They encouraged temple building activity and promoted theatrical arts.

Rupa Goswami found an ancient image of Govind Deva at a place called Goma tilla in Vrindavan. He arranged for its worship at Brahmákunda of the city. Later encouraged by him Raja Mansingh built a magnificent temple at Vrindavan for housing this image.

The one-act Danakelikaumudi, described as Bhanika, was written by Rupa in 1505 A.D. before he came in contact with Chaitanya Mahaprabhu. Vidagdhamadhav was composed in 1532 A.D. and Lalitmadhav in 1537 A.D. These plays are based on Radha-Krishna lila and shringar is the main rasa of all the three compositions. The play Vidagdhamadhav was performed at Keshi tirtha in Vrindavan and Lalitmadhav at the east of the Madhavi-Madhav temple on the bank of Radhakunda near Govardhana. It is believed that these plays were translated in Braj bhasha too.

SAMAVAKARA

One of the ten types of drama mentioned by Bharata in his Natya Shastra.

The Samavakara should have the exploits of gods and asuras as its subject matter and one of them as its well known and exalted hero and it is to consist of three. It should include deception, excitement and love in their three varieties and as many as twelve dramatis personae, and deals with their joys and sorrows.

Three kinds of excitements: such as being due to battle, flood, story and fire, elephant at large, siege of a city.

Three kinds of love: in relation to duty, dharma, wealth (artha) and sexual passion (kama) (NS: Ghosh).

SAMVADASUKTA

There are certain hymns in the Rig Veda like Pururava-Urvashi Samvada which are known as Samvada Suktas or Akhyana Suktas and are in dialogue form, some even in monologue and chorus form. It is believed that these dramatic compositions were enacted at the time of Yajna or fire sacrifice as mystery plays and contained the seed of further evolution of dramatic art (see AKHYANA).

SANSKRIT DRAMA

Sanskrit drama is very precious and significant cultural heritage of the world whose history spreads over several centuries. Though we do not know exactly how and when it originated and evolved in initial stages, the chronology of its progress through time, one thing is certain that it is an ancient art that came into being and matured in the Indian sub-continent.

The first Sanskrit playwright whose works have survived the vagaries of time is Bhasa who is placed in the fifth-fourth century B.C. He was probably on the scene to witness the glory and decline of Nandas of Pataliputra, invasion of Alexander and the rise of Mauryan Empire in Magadha which subsequently spread to other parts of India, though his plays do not record these contemporary events or their impact on Indian life as such. He mainly relied on Indian epics, the Ramayana and Mahabharata, for thematic material. He refers to his patron king as Rajasimha who is identified with the founder of Maurya Empire, Chandragupta, by some scholars.

Bhasa wrote thirteen plays in different formats—from one-act plays to full-fledged dramas with ten acts. This is the sure indication of the fact that the tradition of writing plays for dramatic performances must have started much earlier.

A number of theories were propounded by the scholars about the possible origin of the Sanskrit drama.

Vedas are considered as most ancient works in Sanskrit language. Apart from religious overtones they are the living records of social, cultural and political life of ancient Indians. Nobody knows when they were composed but according to one modest estimation they appeared on the scene sometime around 1500 B.C.

Vedas being the most ancient works in Sanskrit available the scholars tried to seek the origin of Sanskrit drama in these works.

In the Rig Veda there are certain hymns in dialogue form with story element. They are known as Akhyana Suktas or Samvada Suktas. Scholars believe that Vedic priests used to enact these dialogues at the time of Yajna, fire sacrifice purported to appease gods by making them offerings. Sanskrit drama originated in such enactments of the dialogue hymns.

According to another theory the Sanskrit drama originated in Vedic rituals, some of which are very dramatic, full of theatrical elements, dance, drama, music, playing on musical instruments, play acting. Scholars feel that these rituals were responsible for the emergence of Sanskrit drama proper.

According to another set of scholars the Sanskrit drama evolved out of the singing of ballads, hero-lauds and recitation of epics like the Ramayana and the Mahabharata by Sutas, Magadhas, Kushilavas. The ancient style of dramatic narration has survived in a few plays of Bhasa in the form of choruses. Sanskrit drama evolved out of such recitations.

Some scholars try to trace the origin of Sanskrit drama to ancient folk theatre. They point at the Prakrit passages in Sanskrit drama to prove their theory. Pischel thinks that India is a home of puppet theatre and from puppet play emerged the Sanskrit drama.

There is a group of scholars who think that Greek drama is the source of the origin of Sanskrit drama. Greek drama reached India with Alexander the Great which inspired the locals to create a drama of their own in Sanskrit language, they contend.

Sanskrit drama is totally of indigenous origin—various factors including Vedic ritual and cult dramas, local traditions of dance, music and folk entertainments, epic recitations, religious festivals contributing to its evolution.

Bhasa is the first extant dramatist placed in the fifth-fourth century B.C. who wrote thirteen dramas. After a couple of centuries we come across Ashvaghosha who wrote his plays on Buddhist themes around second century A.D. Fragments of his plays have survived. After yet another long gap Kalidasa appears on the scene with his three dramas in fourth-fifth century A.D.

Vishakhadatta and Shudraka wrote their celebrated plays Mudrarakshasa and Mricchakatikam during Gupta period. In the eighth century Harsha and Bhavabhuti wrote their plays.

The south Indian tradition of writing plays in Sanskrit started with the farce Mattavilas Prahasana by king Mahendravikramavarman of Pallava dynasty who ruled from Kanchi in the 7th century A.D.

In the eleventh century Krishnamisra Yati wrote his famous allegorical play Prabodhachandrodaya. In the sixteenth century Rupa Goswami wrote three plays on Krishna theme in Vrindavan. A number of prominent playwrights like Bhatta Narayana, Rajashekhara, Murari wrote in the intervening period.

We know of several writers who wrote plays in Sanskrit including the prominent ones mentioned above. In the 12th century Jayadeva wrote a musical opera Gita Govinda in Sanskrit which gave new direction to Indian theatre.

At the end of the tenth century A.D. king Kulashekhara Perumal of Kerala evolved a regional style of staging classical Sanskrit plays with the help of his friend Tolen and traditional Chakyar actors and named it as Kutiyattam. The plays were enacted in the temple theatres known as Kuttampalams. Even today the plays of Sanskrit dramatists like Bhasa are enacted in Kutiyattam style in the temple theatre of Kerala.

SARASWATI

Goddess of learning, wisdom, speech who revealed language and writing to mankind. She is source of literature, oral and written, and patroness of arts and music. An interesting image of Saraswati was excavated at Mathura with inscription carved on it. According to the inscription on the image of Kushana period it is evident that she was worshipped by the dancers also.

In a verse she is described as a graceful woman as fair as moonlight, snow and kunda flowers, wearing sparkling cloths, sitting on a white lotus, holding Veena in her hands. She is also described as riding a peacock and rarely a lion.

A female figure standing on the lotus flower and holding Veena in her hand is found adorning railing of the Bharhut stupa. She has been identified with goddess Saraswati. We start getting Saraswati images from the Gupta period. Since 12th century we find her marble images. Her images are found in South India too. A few images of dancing Saraswati too are found. Rarely we find images showing Saraswati and Brahma in a close embrace.

In his Natya Shastra sage Bharata has mentioned Saraswati quite frequently. He says that it was Saraswati who gave visibility and audibility to drama—sravyatvam prekshaniyasya dadau devi Saraswati. He describes her as the consort of Hari or Vishnu. He propitiates her with the mantra—O the goddess of gods, the very blessed one, the dear wife of Hari, accept this my offering consecrated by the mantra. The offering of payasa of milk is made to her. Along with other deities she occupies a place in circular Yantra designed to protect the theatre hall. She has been entrusted with the task of protecting the actress enacting the role of heroine in the play from the evil spirits.

In the Kamasutra of Vatsyayana it is said that once in a month or so an assembly of citizens should be convened in the temple of Saraswati to witness the performance of Kushilavas—actors, dancers, singers, etc.—and the next day they should be rewarded suitably. If their performances are liked they may be retained for repeat show the following day. The commentary Jayamangala of Yashodhara defines Kushilavas as nata nartaka. He says that on the occasions like Ganesha chaturthi, Saraswati panchami, Shiva ashtami, etc. such performances should be held in the temple of Saraswati, she being the goddess of Vidya and Kala.

Dhar, a town near Mhow in the Madhya Pradesh, was once the capital of Paramara kings of Malva. In 1903 an inscription was found in the local Kamal Maula Mosque which once was a structure named Bhoja Shala having a statue of Saraswati in it. The inscription on black stone is nothing but first two acts of the play Parijatamanjiri or Vijayashri written by Rajaguru Madana, a Gauda Brahmin. The inscription mentions two such slabs but one has not been located.

The play eulogises king Arjunavarman who ruled Dhar in early 13th century. The opening line of the play specifically mentions that it was performed in the temple of Saraswati—Sharadadevyah sadmani.

The inscription confirms that there was a tradition of staging dance, drama, music performances in the temple of Saraswati as said by Vatsyayana in his Kamasutra.

SATRIYA DANCE

A classical dance of Assam that evolved in the Satra or Vaishnava monasteries around 15th-16th century A.D.

Since ancient times Assam is known for its excellence in the arts of music and dance. Bharata refers to classical dance style prevalent in eastern region including pragjotisha or Assam as Odra-Magadhi. In a poetic copper-plate inscription of 9th century ruler of Assam, King Vanamalavarman the boats trembling on the waves of river Brahmaputra are likened to dancing women agitated at the approach of men dancers. A 12th century Kalika Purana describes many ritualistic and secular dances.

Devadasi tradition reached Assam also and Shaiva and later Vaishnava temples had Devadasi dancing girls to entertain the presiding deities of the temples.

Oja-pali performances devised to narrate the story of serpent goddess Manasa of Vaishnava lore from Assamese versions of epics and Puranas were full of dance, drama and music. Some Oja ballad singers tell that they use a dance-treatise named Tauryatrika-sara.

Scholars believed that they might be referring to the Natya Shastra of Bharata or Abhinayadarpana of Acharya Nandikeshvara.

It was in the 15th century Mahapurusha Shankardeva evolved a dramatic form which became famous as Ankia Nat. Dance and music form integral part of the Ankia dramas. Shankardeva choreographed beautiful dances for the Sutradhara and other characters such as Krishna, cowherd girls. All his experiments were conducted in the Vaishnava monasteries, Satra, hence they came to be known as Satriya dances.

New forms such as Raser nach, Nadu-Bhangi, Chali nach, Yuddhar nach, Bahar nach, Apsara-bhangi, dhemali dance, etc. came into being mostly through dramatic performances of Ankia Nat.

A treatise on hand gestures Hasta-muktavali written by Shubhankara kavi was found in Anuiati Satra. It is ascribed to the 16th century A.D. Scholars have found that the main tenets of the art are based on the work of Bharata who is twice mentioned in the Hastamuktavali. This work contributed significantly towards the evolution of Satriya dance.

SAUGANDHIKAHARANA

A Prekshanaka form of the play by Vishvanatha, a 14th century writer, whose patron king was Prataparudradeva, Kakatiya ruler of Varangal in South India. It depicts the story of Bhima procuring lotus flowers from Kubera's water-tank for Draupadi after defeating Yakshas guarding them.

SHAILALAKA

Actor, nata. In Panini's work on grammar, Ashtadhyayi, there is a mention of Natasutra or manual of actors by Shilalin and Krishashva. Scholars believe that Shailalakas were actors belonging to Shailalin school of performers.

Patanjali tells us that Shailalins were natas—shailalino natah. In an inscription ascribed to first or second century A.D. found at Mathura this class of actors is mentioned. The inscription says:

'Success! in the year (illegible), on the fifth, on the aforementioned (date) at the shrine of the blessed Dadhikarna, Lord of Serpents, a stone slab was set up by the boys headed by Nandabals, the sons of those actors (shailalakas) of Mathura who were being praised as Chandaka Brothers. May the merit of this gift be for their parents, preferably; may it be for the welfare and happiness of all beings' (Epigraphia Indica, 1(1892), 371–93).

Explaining the term Chandaka Brothers, chandaka bhratrika, of the inscription Norvin Hein says that Chandraka means lunar. The actors mentioned in the inscription were famous as Lunar Brothers because they performed the roles of the pair who are Lunar Brothers par excellence: Samkarshana and Krishna. Hein further says that Vaishnava literature makes a great point of the lunar descent of these two.

According to him this leads to the conclusion that some kind of dramatic form depicting the lives of Krishna and Balarama

(Samkarshana) was prevalent during early centuries of Christian era at Mathura.

This is one of the earliest inscriptions mentioning actors.

SHAILUSHA

Actor, dancer, singer, entertainer Shailusha is mentioned in the Vedic literature. Taittiriya Brahmana says for singing a Suta and for dancing a Shailusha (iii.4.2). Although the Vedic and Puranic tradition associates Suta with music and Shailusha with dancing the Vajasaneyi Samhita (30.6) says that Suta is for dancing and Shailusha for singing—nrittaya sutam gitaya shailusham.

At one place in the epic Ramayana Sita says like a Shailusha Rama wants to give me to others—Shailusha iva mam Rama parebhyo datumicchyami. This statement throws light on the morality of actor class. Due to this practice of offering one's wife to others actors in the ancient India were known as Jayajiva.

In a number of plays the actors are referred to as Shailushas. For instance the Sutradhara of the play Venisamhara of Narayana Bhatta calls his actors as shailushas and asks them to get prepared for staging the play.

Nataraja Shiva, the supreme dancer, is called Mahashailusha.

SHALABHANJIKA

The Shalabhanjika, or woman and tree motif, is found in Indian art since second century B.C. It was favourite of medieval sculptors too. Early appearance of this beautiful fertility motif can be traced to Bharhut, Sanchi stupa monuments. Here beautiful women are shown entwined with trees, many of them in diaphanous garments frankly exposing their provocative charms. Yakshi at the east gate of Sanchi holding a branch of a tree is one of the enchanting examples of the genre. Yakshi embracing a tree at Bharhut is named as Chulakoka devata.

Exact origin of this lovely sculptural motif is not known but on one Indus seal we see a tree sprouting from the womb of a woman. Mother of Buddha gave birth to him in standing position while holding the branch of Sala tree by hand. Some scholars consider this as an origin of the motif. The belief that touch of a beautiful woman can bring a tree to immediate flowering may be behind this motif. It can be a relic of old fertility festival which connects fertility to women and vegetation.

Shalabhanjika figures became ornamentation of religious monuments, palaces and other buildings. Bharata in the second chapter of his Natya Shastra speaks of decorating the theatre with Shalabhanjika figure and painting the walls with erotic drawings.

A 10th century Sanskrit playwright wrote a drama named Viddhashalabhanjika which was produced for Kalachuri king Yuvaraja Keyuravarsha of Tripuri. The hero of the play king Vidyadharamalla sees a beautiful girl in his dream and is fascinated by her. Next day he sees her again in his picture gallery but in a sculptured form of a Shalabhanjika.

SHANKHA PARABHAVA

A historical play in Vyayoga format by 13th century playwright Harihara. It describes the real life historical event of war between prince Shankha, son of King Sindhuraj of Lata or Gujarat and Vastupal able minister of king Veeradhaval of Chalukya dynasty of Patan.

In fact the play itself was staged as a part of victory celebration ordered by minister Vastupal who is referred to in the play as Vasantapal.

In the beginning of the play we are informed that on receiving the information that prince Shankha is making preparations for war Vastupal throws a challenge to him.

War starts. It is described by the characters of the play standing on the stage.

In the end we are informed that Shankha or Sangramsingh is defeated.

Citizens then celebrate the victory by singing, dancing and music and offering worship to local goddess Ekallavira. And with this the play ends.

SHRIKRISHNA-BHAKTI-CHANDRIKA

A play based on religious philosophy of different sects by 16th century playwright Anantadeva.

In the beginning the followers of Shaiva and Vaishnava sects clash over the superiority of their respective godheads. Abhedadarshi Mahavaishnava appears on the stage to tell them that Shiva and Vishnu are one and the same. Then Tarkik, Shabdik and Mimansaka start forward to tell them the devotion to Krishna is the best way to achieve liberation. All of them agree and turn Krishna devotees.

Anantadeva has used the medium of drama to preach the efficacy of devotion to Krishna.

SHRINGARABHUSHAN BHANA

A Bhana play by 15th century playwright Vamanabhattabana who was court poet of king Vemabhupala, also known as Veera Narayana, of Trilinga country. The hero of the play, a Vita, describes his experiences while moving in the locality of courtesans. Here he meets beautiful courtesans, men fighting among themselves to possess them, sees wrestling bouts, cock fights and other entertaining games such as kanduka krida or the ball game. In this Bhana we hear beautiful description of Vasanta-ritu or spring season.

SHRINGARATILAK BHANA

A Bhana play by the 17th century playwright of Kanchipuram, Varadacharya who is also known as Ammalacharya. It is a love story of Vita named Bhujangashekhar and courtesan Hemangi. Vita moves in the locality of courtesans, meets various people, witnesses the magic show and the performance of snake charmer and in the end unites with his beloved Hemangi.

SHUDRAKA

A royal playwright who adopted Bhasa's Charudattam and developed it into one of the finest dramas of Sanskrit language, the Mricchakatikam. He is also the author of Bhana play Padmaprabhrutakam based on the love story of master thief Acharya Muladeva and courtesan Devadatta.

In the prologue of the play Mricchakatikam we find some interesting information about Shudraka. He was a very handsome king having face like full moon, large eyes like those of Chakora bird, gait of an elephant, best among the warrior clan and a poet of repute. He was fond of war, wrestling, had a profound knowledge of Vedas, and a penance performing ruler of the earth.

By the grace of Shiva his eyes penetrated the darkness of ignorance and acquired the proficiency in arts, the science dealing with courtesans—vaishiki and skill of riding the elephant. He had a profound knowledge of Rig Veda, Sama Veda and mathematics and performed the Ashvamedha Yajna. After enjoying long life of hundred years and ten days, leaving his kingdom to his son, he entered into fire.

We are clueless about which country he ruled and at what time. The prologue is silent about these vital details.

We find a number of Shudrakas mentioned in various works. In the Skanda Purana there is a mention of king Shudraka. Scholars take him to be Simuk, the first king of Andhra dynasty. Bhagavata Purana says that the first Andhra king was a shudra, probably hence was known as Shudraka.

Dandi in his Avantisundarikatha and Vamana in his Kavyalankarsutravritti have mentioned Shudraka. Vamana in the eighth century A.D. speaks about dramatic composition of Shudraka—shudrakadirachiteshu prabandheshu—and quotes a line from Mricchakatikam.

In Kadambari Banabhatta says that Vidisha was the capital of Shudraka. In the Vetalpanchavimshati the capital of Shudraka was said to be Vardhaman and Somadeva in his Kathasaritsagar said it was Shobhavati. Kashmiri historian Kalhana too has mentioned Shudraka by name. But this only goes to prove that there were a number of kings who were known as Shudraka.

A few more works too mention king Shudraka but who among them was Shudraka, author of Mricchakatikam, is difficult to deduce.

So complicated and vexed is the issue of the identity of king Shudraka of Mricchakatikam that a scholar like Keith goes up to an extent of saying that Shudraka was merely a legendary person, really clearly mythical, whose name was used by the real playwright who created Mricchakatikam out of Bhasa's Charudattam to conceal his real identity.

The seventh century poet Dandi in his Kavyadarsha had quoted a verse from the first act of Mricchakatikam. Vamana in the eighth century has quoted not only a line from the play but mentioned the name of Shudraka. This goes to show that Shudraka must have lived before seventh century A.D.

The earliest known plays, including Padmaprabhrutakam of Shudraka, appeared in the Gupta era say the scholars. Shudraka might have written Mricchakatikam and Padmaprabhrutakam after Kalidasa in the fifth century A.D.

SHYAMILAKA

Author of the exhilarating Bhana play Padataditakam. He describes himself as a son of Udichya kavi Vishveshvaradatta. Udichya means northern region, the country to the north and west of river Saraswati. Some scholars take him to be a Kashmiri poet. He has beautifully described the Sarvabhauma-nagar or city of Ujjain in this play. Whatever may be the place of his birth he seems to have settled in the city of Ujjain.

Abhinavagupta in 10th century and Kshemendra in 11th century have mentioned him in their works. Hence some scholars place him in 9th-10th century A.D. However some others ascribe him to 4th-5th century A.D. on the basis of internal evidence of the play.

SITABENGA CAVE THEATRE

On the Ramgarh hill in the erstwhile Sarguja state of Madhya Pradesh there is a cave named Sitabenga. Considering the structure of the cave and an inscription therein some scholars declared it to be 'an Indian theatre of third century B.C.' Describing it T. Bloch wrote:

'In front of the entrance of the cave was a row of benches arranged in terraces in the shape of a crescent...which would be suitable as benches to seat an audience watching a play or similar performance acted in front of them...There is sufficient space in front of the small rock-cut amphitheatre for the erection of a stage, and the benches themselves might have easily seated fifty or more spectators.

The interior forms an oblong, 46 x 26 feet. Along three sides run broad rock-cut seats, 2-1/2 feet high and 7 feet wide, slightly terraced by lowering the front a few inches. The ground near the entrance is somewhat lower than the corners of the seats. The most important feature is however two holes cut into the floor at the entrance. They were evidently made to hold wooden posts, to which a curtain was fastened to shut out the cold air of the winter nights when the audiences retired to the interior. At such times the spectators would be seated along the broad benches and the dancing party would perform in front of the curtain that closed the door.

That the plan of the small amphitheatre in front of the cave with the hemispherical rows of rock-cut seats rising in terraces above each other and with the pathways between them arranged somewhat like concentric circles and radiants, resembled the plan of the Greek theatre cannot be overlooked' (*Archaeological Survey of India Report*, 1903–4).

The inscription found in the cave in its English translation reads:

'Poets venerable by nature kindle the heart, who....At the spring festival of the vernal full moon, when frolics and music abound, people tie garlands thick with jasmine flowers around their necks.'

T. Bloch says that the great festival of vernal full moon night in the Phalguna, the modern Holi, is still called dol jata or swing festival in Bengal. In ancient times Holi was part of Vasantotsava the occasion for poetry recitation, fun, frolic, singing, dancing and play acting. Considering the theatre-like structure of the cave and the inscription therein T. Bloch thinks that it was not certainly used by ascetics but it was the place where poetry was recited, love songs sung and theatrical scenes acted.

In India there was an ancient tradition of organising of mountain top fun-filled festivities full of dancing, singing and play acting. In Buddhist literature such festivities were called Giragga Samagga. Monks were prohibited from attending them. In the Hathigumpha cave inscription of Emperor Kharavela of Kalinga belonging to the second century B.C., there is reference to Samaj festival organised by him on the Udayagiri-Khandagiri hills near Bhuvaneshvar which was full of singing, dancing and play acting. In the epics Ramayana and Mahabharata festivities on hill top are mentioned.

On the same Ramgarh hill there is yet another cave named Jogimara. The inscription therein in English translation reads as follows:

> Sutanuka by name
> a devadasi
> Sutanuka by name, a devadasi
> The excellent among the young men loved her
> Devadinna by name, skilled in sculpture.

Devadinna is described in the inscription as lupadakhe. This word has been translated by some scholars as shadow puppet artist. They think that two holes cut at the entrance of the Sitabenga cave were there to put in them two poles to tie a screen of white cloth across for shadow theatre performance.

The tradition of using caves as theatre is very old. Bharata in his Natya Shastra says that theatre building should be made like a mountain cave—shailaguhakaro. By this probably he was referring to the tradition of cave theatre which was in vogue before free-standing theatre buildings came into existence.

STAGE CRAFT

See NEPATHYA.

STREE PREKSHA

Stree means woman and preksha means a dramatic performance. By Stree Preksha we mean all-women dramatic performance.

In ancient India male actors used to enact male roles and female actresses female roles. This is evident from the legend recorded in the Natya Shastra that for enacting female roles Brahma created Apsaras or Nymphs from his mind. It was admitted that graceful style, kaishiki, can not be practised properly by men hence they needed women to participate in dramatic performance along with men.

However Kautilya in his Arthashastra points at yet another tradition of all-male dramatic performance, Purusha Preksha, and all-female dramatic performance, Stree Preksha.

Kautilya says: If a woman without a permission from her husband ventures out in the day time to see a dramatic performance by women, Stree Preksha, a fine of six panas should be recovered from her. A fine of twelve panas should be imposed if she attends all-male dramatic performance, Purusha Preksha, under the similar condition. Double amount should be imposed as a fine if she does the same things in night (Artha. 3.3).

In the Ramayana there is a reference to Vadhu Nataka Sangha which means all female dramatic troupe.

On the Prasenjit pillar of the Bharhut stupa a musical opera by all-women dramatic cast is sculpted. In the Kuttanimatam kavyam by Damodaragupta, ascribed to the eighth century A.D., there is a reference to the enactment of the first act of Ratnavali, a play by Harsha, by the Varansi all by themselves.

In the prologue of the play Malati Madhava by Bhavabhuti addressing the Sutradhara, a male, Nata the actor, another male, says that as Sutradhara has prepared to play the role of old Buddhist female monk Kamandaki, he, the actor, has also prepared himself to play the role of Avalokita, female disciple of Kamandaki. Here is an example of male actors playing the female roles. Probably Malati Madhava was performed by all-men dramatic troupe.

SUTA

Balladeer, singer, narrator of epics and Puranas, also charioteer and according to some texts architect who measures land with the help of thread.

We find Suta mentioned in Vedic literature. Sometimes he is described as singer and sometimes dancer. Probably in ancient times he was both. He would sing and dance too, translating the contents of the song or ballad into appropriate movements, gestures, mudras. However in later period he is mainly seen as a narrator of epics and Puranas. In fact the epic Mahabharata came down to us through Suta tradition. Vyasa after composing the Mahabharata revealed it to his son Shuka, five Dharmacharyas and Suta named Lomaharshana. Son of Suta Lomaharshana, Sauti Ugrashrava, obtained the knowledge of the epic from one of the Dharmacharyas, Vaishampayana. In the process Sutas included numerous stories into original text of the epic known as Jaya. Jaya became Bharata and then Mahabharata due to the contribution of Sutas.

In the Taittiriya Brahmana we find a verse which says—Gitaya sutam nrittaya shailusham, which means Suta would sing and shailusha, the actor, would perform and through his dance interpret the textual contents of Suta's narration into a visual presentation with the help of dance and abhinaya or acting.

According to yet another Vedic text, the Shatapatha Brahmana, for dancing a lute player, hand clapper and flute player would provide a musical support. If we consider this as a composite performance it would mean:

> Suta would sing or narrate a story
> Shailusha the actor would visually interpret the contents of the story through dance movements and abhinaya
> Lute player, hand clapper and flute player would provide musical support.

This performance gave rise to drama proper. In Sanskrit drama Suta became sutradhara who appears in the beginning of the play, delineates the story line and disappears leaving the prayoga or actual performance to actors—shailushas, natas or kushilavas who would deliver dialogue too.

In the Adiparva of the Mahabharata we are told that when Serpent sacrifice of king Janamejaya was to commence there appeared on the scene a Suta. He is thus described:

> Sthapati buddhi-sampanna sutradhara
> suta pauranika (Adi. 51.15-16).

Suta who was intelligent and expert in Puranic lore was an architect too and in this capacity he is called Sutradhara. In the context of drama too he retained his appellation as Sutradhara in the sense of string-holder of the stage performance.

It seems that in the process of evolution the Suta transferred the task of delivering dialogues and carrying on the story to shailushas or actors. In the Sanskrit theatre we see Suta-Sutradhara disappears after introduction and actors take over from him from there.

This is how, according to one theory, drama evolved out of ballad singing.

SUTRADHARA

Sutra means string. In the parlance of drama Sutradhara is the person holding the strings of dramatic performance in his hands, drama director, or a principal actor who superintends the whole performance of drama. Sometimes he is referred to as Stage Manager also.

Some scholars believe that originally this term belonged to puppet theatre. Sutradhara is a person who holds sutra or strings attached to the puppets at other end to manipulate them. Prevalence of this term in drama proper gave rise to the theory that in India human drama emanated from puppet theatre.

The other theory is that the Suta, ancient ballad singer and narrator of epics, became Sutradhara of drama as the ballad singing and recitation of epics, in the course of time, evolved into drama.

In the Mahabharata (Adiparva 51.15) Suta is actually referred to as Sutradhara. Ancient Sutas used to perform several duties apart from being Pauranikas or narrators of Puranic lore. As an architect, Sthapati, he used to hold suta or string for land measurements. In this capacity he was addressed as Sutradhara-Sthapatir buddhisampanno vastu-vidya-visharadh itybravit Sutradharah suto pauranikastada.

In figurative sense Sutradhara Suta became the architect of dramatic performance.

The elaborate preliminaries to be performed before the actual commencement of the play are collectively known as Purvaranga. According to Bharata during purvaranga the Sutradhara along with his two assistants holding golden pitcher and Jarjara respectively should appear on the stage in white cloths, perform certain rituals, offer puja to various deities, sing Nandi and take exit from the stage.

Then, says Bharata, the Sthapaka should enter and inform the audiences about the play, its theme, its author, etc.

However it seems that this elaborate procedure was seldom adhered to. As is evident from the texts of the plays the Sutradhara used to appear on the stage, sing Nandi, enter into conversation with his wife Nati or assistants, Pariparshvakas, and inform the audiences about the play. After his exit the play proper would begin.

SWAPNAVASAVADATTA

A six-act play by master dramatist Bhasa portraying with rare sensitivity ethereal love a king felt for his presumably dead queen. Swapnavasavadatta or Dream of Vasavadatta is considered as the masterpiece of first extant Sanskrit playwright.

Though Bhasa was mentioned by Kalidasa and Bana none mentioned the names of his plays. It was the tenth century poet, writer and playwright Rajashekhara who was the first to mention a play of Bhasa, the Swapnavasavadatta. To assert its excellence and timelessness he wrote that Bhasa's plays were subjected to fire ordeal and only Swapnavasavadatta survived.

Acharya Abhinavagupta in his commentary on Natya Shastra has mentioned the play. Ramachandra-Gunachandra in their Natya Darpana, Sharadatanaya in his Bhavaprakasha, Bhojadeva in his Shringarprakasha referred to it.

When T. Ganapati Shastri found a codex of manuscripts of texts of dramas in Kerala there was a copy of Swapnavasavadatta in it. It helped the scholar to state that all the plays in the codex belonged to none else but Bhasa, because of several similarities between the style of Vasavadatta and other plays discovered.

The basic storyline is simple. Astrologers make a prophesy that the luck of king Udayana will shine after he is married to princess Padmavati of Magadha. Fully knowing that till queen Vasavadatta is alive Udayana will never agree to marry the Magadha princess a rumour is floated that Vasavadatta and king's minister Yaugandharayana have perished in a fire. Yaugandharayana entrusts Vasavadatta in disguise to princess Padmavati who later gets married to handsome Udayana. Vasavadatta gets several opportunities to overhear the king expressing his undiminished love for her which saddens and delights her heart. One day mistaking a person sleeping in a bed in Samudragriha for Princess Padmavati, Vasavadatta disguised as Avantika sleeps by her side embracing her. In fact the person sleeping in the bed was none else but king Udayana himself. In his sleep he calls out for Vasavadatta. Recognising his voice startled Vasavadatta gets up but continues responding to his dream-talk for a while and then moves out swiftly. The king instinctively feels that Vasavadatta is alive and he comes out of the state of slumber and sits up in the bed. But Vidushaka, king's jester friend, reminds him of harsh reality that queen is dead. The jester says the king might have seen the harem girl Avantisundari who is a Yakshi. By Yakshi he means enchantress with supernatural power. It was Vasavadatta who was living with Padmavati as Avantisundari. Swapna means dream and Vasavadatta the heroine of the play. Swapna-Vasavadatta means dream of Vasavadatta. The scene in which Udayana thinks he has seen Vasavadatta in dream is the source of the title of the play. The purpose of spreading the rumour of Vasavadatta's death was to prepare the king psychologically for marrying Padmavati. As it was accomplished both Yaugandharayana and Vasavadatta appear before the king in the field.

The play is considered the best among the creations of Bhasa.

SWARUPA

God in his own form or shape that is how the word Swarupa is taken in the parlance of some of the miracle plays of North India such as Raslila and Ramlila. The child actors playing the divine roles such as Radha, Krishna and Sakhis in the Raslila or that of Rama, Sita, Lakshmana, Hanuman in Ramlila are known as Swarupa. Once the actors appear in such roles the audiences treat them as if they are divinities themselves.

TALA MADDALE

A unique semi-dramatic form of narrating mythological stories picked up from epics, Puranas and similar sacred works prevalent in Karnataka in medieval period.

The reference to this form is made in an inscription of 1556 A.D. found at Lakshminarayana temple in Kurugod in the Bellary District of Karnataka. It records the endowment of the land as a financial support for arranging Tala Maddale Seva in the temple.

In this Seva the chief narrator, Bhagavata, along with his band of musicians sits at the head of two rows of narrators, known as Arthadharis, sitting face to face. Arthadharis assume different roles in the story to be narrated.

Bhagavata starts the performance by offering prayers to different deities. After that he starts singing the story. Taking cue from him the Arthadharis converse among themselves in prose and verse as per the roles they have assumed.

Suppose the story is about Krishna and Pandavas. The roles of Krishna and five Pandava brothers are distributed among the Arthadharis. When during the course of narration Bhagavata refers to Krishna the Arthadhari who has taken upon himself the task of assuming the role of Krishna starts delivering his speech. Then the Arthadari assuming the role of Arjuna would likewise enter into dialogue with him.

Arthadharis do not wear make-up, nor do they stand up during the performance, but they do use some hand gestures and facial expressions.

This performance, in a way, may be described as a link between ballad singing and drama proper.

The performance is known as Tala Maddale because in it the musical instrument Tala, small brass cymbals, and Maddale, a small drum, are used.

TAMASHA

Evolving itself from earlier forms of folk entertainment the musical theatre of Tamasha emerged in Western Maharashtra in the later Peshava period of Maratha history. We start hearing about Tamasha performance more frequently in the later half of the 18th century. It came of age in early 19th century under the patronage of Peshava Bajirao II and is still popular in Maratha country.

It seems that initially Tamasha started as a form of titillating entertainment full of provocative singing and dancing. The class of poets known as Shahir composed songs for Tamasha performances. Though these poetic compositions had different themes the popular ones were those which celebrated love as a subject. Tamasha performances since then are famous for their romantic love songs, songs even highly erotic.

Tamasha troupe consisted of a Shahir who is a main singer and usually a composer himself, dancers, musicians and a jester character named Songadya. Initially tender aged boys in the female garb, nachya, used to dance in Tamasha. Later women too joined as dancers and singers. Dholaki, turtune, harmonium are the principal musical instruments to which Sarangi too can be added.

The Tamasha performance starts with the singing of Gana. Gana means songs sung in the honour of Ganesha. Songs in the praise of other deities too are sung in the beginning.

Then the songs called Gaulan are presented. Gaulan means cowherd girl. These songs are about Krishna, cowherd Gopa girls and their flirtatious encounters on the bank of river Yamuna. We see cowherd girls led by Radha with milk pots on their heads proceeding to Mathura market. The group is waylaid by Krishna and his friends who ask the cowherd girls to give them milk. Krishna's mischievous jester companion Pendya clashes with Mavashibai the old cowherd woman. Cowherd girls dance, sing and request Krishna to allow them to go. Humorous conversation takes place between two groups—one led by Krishna and the other by Radha.

Shahir plays the role of Krishna and female dancers of the troupe appear as Radha and her friends. Songadya becomes Pendya and a senior male performer appears as Mavashibai, covering his head with saree

After this small skit is over the programme of Lavani singing and dancing starts. Tamasha girls draped in nine yard sarees perform provocative dances singing romantic Lavani songs. This is the core of the Tamasha performance which goes for hours.

Then a small dramatic performance called Vag is staged. Musical Tamasha play is called Vag. It contains songs and prose dialogues. Around 1865 a Tamasha artist Umaji Savlajkar and his associate Babaji Mang wrote a first Vag play Mohana Batava. Inspired by him a number of other writers too wrote Vag plays for Tamasha. Rasya and Shringara are two main sentiments which find place in Vag plays.

Tamasha performance confined only to singing and dancing out Lavani songs is known as Sangit bari. Sometimes Vag is staged as an independent programme.

Tamasha is still a popular form of entertainment in rural as well as urban Maharashtra.

TERRUKUTTU

A vibrant folk dramatic form full of singing, dancing, music which evolved in South India in the 18th century A.D. Mahabharata based cycle of Terrukuttu plays were performed in Karnataka, Kerala and particularly in Tamil Nadu as a part of Draupadi Amman Festival which is celebrated in the month of Chaitra (April-May).

Draupadi, wife of Pandava heroes, is deified in South India. We find shrines raised in her honour. During her festival which traditionally runs for 18 days Mahabharata story is narrated through three different performances.

One performance is prasangam or religious discourse depicting Mahabharata story which is held in the temple itself. Second performance is in the form of a processional theatre. A procession is taken out and as its part dramatic enactment is held. For instance take the example of the enactment of the episode of Baka Vadha or Killing of Demon Baka. An actor in the guise of Bhima as a Brahmin sits on a bullock cart which is led by a music band, melam, through the village lanes. Another actor in the guise of demon Baka leaps and jumps in a demonic fury around the cart. En route the cart stops at the houses of the villagers who offer rice and sweets for Baka's consumption. When the procession reaches back to the temple instead of giving the food thus collected to Baka hungry Bhima himself starts eating it. This leads to angry verbal exchanges between Baka and Bhima leading to big fight. In the end Baka is killed by Bhima.

The third performance is staging of Mahabharata based Terrukuttu play in the night.

Terrukuttu is traditionally an open-air street corner theatre which requires just a square piece of plain land as a stage. Four poles are fixed at four corners to support roof made of cloth. In the name of stage property there are a few stools for actors to sit.

Actors are all male, female roles are performed by male impersonators. Make-up and costumes are colourful, gaudy and dazzling. Headgears of different sizes and shapes are used by the characters according to their status. Ornaments made of light wood are decorated with gilt paper and glass pieces. Masks are used for characters such as Narasimha, man-lion incarnation of Vishnu. All the performers invariably wear tinkling anklets on their feet.

Orchestra of musicians and singers sit at the back of the stage. Mridangam, mukha veen, cymbals and harmonium are the musical instruments pressed into service.

The performance begins with Malakattu that is playing on musical instruments. Invocatory songs are sung in the honour of various deities including Ganesha.

After this is over there appears on the stage a character named Kattiyakkaran who is Sutradhara and jester rolled into one. Sometimes as his companion a buffoon named Komali is also seen with him. In his introductory speech he gives the context of the episode to be enacted on the day, its summary, and other relevant information. He is ever present on the stage, participates in dramatic action, speaks to audience, links different episodes with his commentary.

After the ritual of patra-pravesham is over the play proper begins.

The script of the play is nothing but a few songs and chants handed down from generation to generation of performance through mostly oral and at times written tradition. The actors know their songs and chants by heart. They expand the contents of these songs and chants extempore during the performance in the form of prose speeches and dialogues.

The acting, dancing and physical movements of the actors are very forceful, energetic and vigorous. The singing and orchestration is high pitched. It is a high voltage folk drama in high key.

Though primarily associated with depiction of Mahabharata, the Terrukuttu performers take stories also from other epics, sacred and mythological works such as Ramayana, Bhagavata and other Puranas for enactment. Apart from Draupadi Amman festival they are performed on a number of other occasions too.

For instance the play Karna Mokshyam is performed as a part of Tithi or Kurumati Puja held on the eighth or tenth day after the death of an elderly person in the family for the deliverance of his soul. After the day-long rituals held in the honour of the dead the play Karna Mokshyam is enacted as an extended ritual.

When in the play Karna is shown dying of his wounds he would ask Krishna standing in front of him to grant Moksha to the deceased person also.

On the conclusion of the last play of the Terrukuttu cycle held on the occasion of Draupadi Amman festival the actors playing the roles of Bhima and Duryodhana go to the field outside the village where mud effigy of Duryodhana is lying. Then there ensues the mock fight between Bhima and Duryodhana. In the end Bhima smashes the thigh of the mud effigy of Duryodhana with his mace as a grand finale.

TEYYAM

Ancient ritualistic performance of Kerala essentially related to the cult of spirit worship.

Teyyam performers in their grotesque and awe-inspiring make-up and costume represent deified ancestors, heroes, folk and tribal mother goddesses, deities of various diseases, persons who have died prematurely or had unnatural death, individuals who became prey to social injustice and cruelty, deified animals and forces of nature, anyone whose memory the society wanted to cherish through myth and ritual by glorifying them.

The stories about Teyyams are sung, danced out, dramatised and enacted during ritualistic festivals associated with their rural shrines.

Teyyam costumes, make-up and dances have influenced the evolution of more advanced theatre forms of Kerala such as Kathakali.

THEATRE OF THE GHOSTS

The relics of primitive cult of ghost worship have survived in the Dakshina Kannada district of Karnataka having a long coastline. It is inhabited by Tulu speaking people of Dravidian stock. There are a number of ghost or Bhuta shrines in the region where worship is offered to spirits by the devotees.

Some of the Bhutas worshipped in the shrines are of totemistic origin with faces of animals such as tigers, bulls, pigs, cats. Some represent serpent spirits, some primitive ferocious mother goddesses and some heroes died in tragic circumstances. Under the Brahmanic influence some Puranic deities also crept in Bhuta pantheon along with terrible Ganas or attendants of Shiva, Lord of Cremation Ground. Heterogeneous conglomeration of Bhuta pantheon represents different social and cultural strata of local population.

The task of these Bhutas is to protect their devotees from calamities natural and man-made, punish the sinners and reward the meritorious ones. They hold courts to settle disputes through impersonators or ones whom they possess, and make prophecies.

Annually festivals are organised in the honour of Bhutas of different shrines as per local traditions and customs. The performance given by the ghost-impersonator may be described as a 'drama in ritual framework' or simply as ritual drama. The Bhuta dance-drama has all ingredients of theatrical enactment such as impersonation, dance, music, make-up, mask, speech, dialogue, costume. Sometimes the assistant spirit who accompanies the main Bhuta impersonator provokes humour by his action and pranks. Frenzied dance of Bhuta-impersonator wearing ferocious masks or make-up and colourful costume presents a thrilling dramatic spectacle.

To appease snake-spirits a spectacular ritual drama called Nagamandala is performed. Auspicious and magical drawings are made on floor with coloured powders to represent the world of serpents. Then as a part of rituals a ballet-like dance is enacted by two persons—patri who is possessed by serpent deity and naga Kannike a serpent maiden—in the background of crescending music. The songs are sung by naga Kannike in the praise of serpent spirit to which patri responds appropriately.

In Kerala too performance in the honour of serpent deities like sarpakalam and sarpatullal are organised with elaborate details.

There are narrative ballads, paaddana, woven round the myths and legends about the origin of the spirits, their supernatural powers, their heroic deeds which form part of ghost-drama.

Bhuta cult and dramatic practices inherent in it have very ancient origin. Bharata in his Natyashastra prescribes various rituals to appease spirits and fiends. Dima is one of the ten forms of drama described by Bharata. He says that ghostly spirits like Asuras, Rakshasas, Bhutas, Yakshas and Nagas appear in the Dima kind of drama. In the chapter on Make-up and Costume Bharata says that Bhutas, Nagas are of different colours and Pishachas should be painted with dark blue colour. He further says Bhutas or Ghosts are known to be of various colours. They are dwarfs with odd faces and many have faces of boars, rams, buffaloes and deer as well.

In the Purana a goddess named Bhutamata or Mother Ghost is mentioned. A festival known as Bhutamatrimahotsava used to be celebrated in her honour in the month of Vaishakha. Jayasenapati in his Nrityaratnavali written in the 13th century mentions this festival. In the Prabhasakhanda of Skandapurana it is said that during the festival of Bhutamata dramatic performances used to take place in the night.

People used to worship Bhutamata to save themselves from the wrath of evil spirits such as Bhuta, Preta, Dakini, Shakini, Pishacha and Rakshasa. This festival with dramatic rituals and dance was particularly popular during seventh to thirteenth centuries.

Bhuta worship is found in Kerala also. The ritualistic Bhuta theatre in Kerala is known as Teyyam. In Himachal Pradesh ritualistic demon plays known as Phagali and Rakas Khel are enacted to drive away evil spirits. In the courtyards of Buddhist Lama monasteries masked devil dances are performed.

THEORY OF IMITATION

While defining drama Bharata says that it is an imitation, anukarana, of situations, actions, conduct, emotional states of people. It is actor who does the imitation and acting is his mode of imitation. Later theorists like Dhananjaya, author of Dasharupaka, Sharadatanaya, author of Bhavaprakasha also accepted the theory that drama is an imitation of universe by actors.

It is interesting to note that ancient Greeks too have used the term imitation while explaining the nature of dramatic art. Plato (427–347 B.C.) in his *Republik* refers to imitation skill of the actors. He says that they are so clever that they can imitate everything.

Aristotle (384–322 B.C.) well-known pupil of Plato in his *Poetics* speaking about the imitation in the context of poetry and dramatic arts says: 'Object of imitation is men in action. Tragedy is an action. Even dancing imitates character, emotion and action. Epic poetry and tragedy, comedy also, dithyrambic poetry and the music of the flute and of the lyre in most of their forms are all in their general conception modes of imitation.'

It was Kalidasa who dropped the concept of imitation while defining the nature of drama. In his play Malavikagnimitra, he says conduct of the people governed by three gunas (raja, tama, sattva) is the concern of drama which caters to the people of different tastes by showing different rasas.

THOLU BOMMALATTA

A shadow puppet theatre of Andhra Pradesh is known as Tholu Bommalatta. Tholu means leather and Bommalatta means puppet dance. The leather puppets made for this form are quite large and have joints at shoulders, elbows, knees and sometimes at wrists and neck also. They are also brightly coloured. Stories from the Ramayana and the Mahabharata are presented on the screen by Tholu Bommalatta artists.

Annual Report of Indian Epigraphy, 1938, No. 216 and also p. 111, Chidipiralla, Cuddapah district, Saka 1501, Telugu. This record refers to the endowment of the village Chadupurela as sarvamanya by a certain Candramayya to one Pedacittayya for the performance of screen-dramas (tera-natakam). The donor who probably was a local chieftain appears to have been himself an art-connoisseur and adept in the art of shadow puppetry as indicated by his appellations such as Bommalata-Rayitau and Bommalata-Amritakavai.

TIME FOR PERFORMANCE

Bharata has formulated certain rules regarding the time best suited for enacting plays. According to him certain time of the day is suitable for staging certain kind of play. He says forenoon, mid-day and afternoon is a day time and performances held in the evening, the midnight and at dawn belong to night. It seems he is not much in favour of night shows. He says:

'The performance which is pleasant to ear and is based on the tale of virtue (Dharmakhyankritam) should be held in the forenoon.

That which is rich in instrumental music, includes the story of strength and energy (Sattvotthanaguneryuktam) and carries the chance of abundant success should be performed in the afternoon.

That which relates to the graceful style, kaishiki vritti, the erotic sentiment, shringararasa, and is full of vocal and instrumental music should be performed in the evening (Pradosha kal).

The drama which relates to the magnanimity of the hero, and contains mostly pathetic sentiment, karunaprayamevacha, should be performed in the morning, and it will scare away sleep.

The drama should not be performed in the midnight or at the time of Sandhya prayer or of taking meals.

Thus after looking into the time, place and basis (plot) of the play one should bring about its production according to the psychological conditions, yatha bhavam yatha rasam, it contains' (NS: Ghosh).

However Bharata says that 'when the patron (lit. master) orders, the time and place are not to be taken into consideration, and performance should be held without any hesitation.

TOGALU GOMBE ATTA

In the Mysore region of Karnataka a shadow theatre form Togalu Gombe Atta is quite popular. Togalu means leather, gombe means puppet and atta means drama. Mysore puppets are well painted and beautiful, small compared to Andhra leather puppets. Stories from the Ramayana and Mahabharata are shown on the screen with the help of colourful leather puppets. Krishna legend is particularly popular. Sometimes to depict small two or more characters are the parts of single leather sheet.

TOLPAVA KOOTHU

The shadow puppet theatre of Kerala is known as Tolpava Koothu. Tol means leather, pava means puppet and koothu means drama. This leather puppet show depicts the Rama story from his birth to coronation based on Tamil Ramayana by poet Kamban. It is performed in the specially constructed stage called Koothu madam. Koothu madam has big white screen stretched taut in its front on which the dark shadows of flat leather puppets made of deer skin are obtained with the help of row of lamps placed behind. Each puppet has one jointed hand which is manipulated by the puppeteer to give it an action during conversation. The Rama story is screened for seven to twentyone days as desired by the temple authorities.

The legend says that once upon a time Lord Shiva created goddess Bhadrakali to destroy a powerful demon named Darika who was tormenting the three worlds. Goddess Bhadrakali annihilated the demon in a fierce battle. She fought with him exactly when Rama fought with demon Ravana and killed him. This deprived the goddess of the pleasure of witnessing the Rama-Ravana yuddha. Hence, for her benefit, entire Rama story including his fight with Ravana is re-enacted in the form of shadow puppet show.

Tolpava Koothu is an offering made to the goddess Bhadrakali and actually is a part of temple ritual. A number of rituals precede and succeed the performance of the shadow play. For instance the lamps required for the show are lit from the big brass lamp in the temple to establish a ritual link between the temple and the Koothu madam. The ritual differs from temple to temple. Generally a temple oracle, velicchapadu, after circumambulating the temple in a spectacular manner proceeds towards Koothu madam to bless the performers. G. Venu writes that in rich temples the coming of the velicchapadu itself is made into an occasion to celebrate. For example, at the Pailur temple of Kollengode where the distance to be covered to reach the Koothu madam is about two hundred metres the procession of velicchapadu is a spectacular affair. He arrives in a regal style accompanied by caparisoned elephants, music, fireworks and surrounded by devotees moves towards Koothu madam taking not less than two hours to reach his destination.

In some temples a day after the episode of the killing of Ravana is shadowed feast is held in the temple and a grand festival of Rama's coronation takes place. The puppets of Rama, Sita, etc. are taken in a grand procession.

The shadows of various characters on the screen are basically used to illustrate the recitation of the story. K. Bharata Iyer writes: 'A wave of expectant enthusiasm sweeps over the audiences before whom the stirring drama, a battle of wits, is to be staged by the story tellers with their masterly eloquence, making the night ring with their well modulated voices. By sheer power of his magnetic eloquence the story teller invests the stage with extraordinary dramatic power. The puppets become dynamic, though their movements are few and restricted, and they seem to pulsate with a strange stylised energy. The illusion is effectively created by the gripping power of the story teller. Here acting and make-up are reduced to a shadow, the stage entirely depends upon vachikabhinaya, the power of spoken word uttered by the disciplined voice.'

TRIPURADAHA

A play, Dima, mentioned in the Natya Shastra based on the story of burning of three cities by Shiva, staged in Himalayan region along with yet another play Amrita Manthana composed by Brahma.

Story of Tripuradaha is a part of Puranic lore. According to a legend the Asura architect Maya created three cities of gold, silver and iron that could move at will in sky, on earth or in water. These cities inhabited by Asuras were destroyed by Shiva by shooting an arrow. This story formed the basis of the play.

UBHAYABHISARIKA

A hilarious Bhana play by Vararuchi who lived around 4th-5th century A.D. Pataliputra is the venue of the play.

Bhana is a one-act, one-actor burlesque in the form of monologue. An actor in the guise of Vita, a pimp, appears on the stage and describes during his wanderings the scenes, events, happenings and merrily converses with different people in humorous and sometimes in satirical tone as if they are there in front of him.

After a brief prologue Vita appears on the stage and begins his narration by describing the beauty of Vasanta ritu. He then tells us about the quarrel that took place between Kuberadatta, son of Shresthi Sagaradatta, and courtesan Narayanadatta.

It thus happened. When courtesan Madanasena was presenting a musical opera or sangitaka named Madanaradhana in the temple of Bhagavan Narayana Vishnu, Kuberadatta praised her for her performance. This angered Narayanadatta who too was playing a role in the drama. Poor Kuberadatta fell at the feet of Narayanadatta but she refused to relent.

Vita says that the task of reuniting the estranged lovers is entrusted to him by Kuberadatta hence he is moving out in the direction of his beloved's house in the locality of courtesans via rajamarga or principal street of the city.

Moving on the rajamarga Vita describes the glory of the city of Pataliputra.

First of all his fall on young and beautiful courtesan Anangadatta, daughter of Charanadasi, sporting on her body the signs of vigorous love-making. She tells Vita that she is coming from the house of Nagadatta, son of Mahamatra, after spending a night there. Vita points out that the riches of Nagadatta were a thing of the past and under the circumstance her continued liaison with him refuting the advice of her greedy mother was against the nature of courtesans. However he congratulates her for her selfless love.

This reminds us of rich courtesan Vasantasena of the play Mricchakatika who loved poor Brahmin Charudatta against the wishes of her mother.

Vita then meets Madhavasena, daughter of Vishnudatta, moving away speedily from her pursuing family members to avoid being pushed on the lover she does not desire. She was coming from the house of Samudradatta, son of Dhanadatta Sarthavaha, after spending a night there.

Vita understood her problem. Samudradatta was undesired lover. She faked her love for him and did not participate in foreplay or love making whole-heartedly during the night.

Vita says to her that lovers may or may not be of your liking it is the duty of the courtesan to arouse passion in them and earn money. And this is what shastra says.

This is exactly how the Vita of Mricchakatika advises courtesan Vasantasena when she refuses to yield to the advances of her undesired lover, Shakara.

After her departure he bumps into a female monk of Vaishika school of philosophy Parivrajika Vilaskaundine sporting distinct signs of love-making. She very easily defeats Vita in talk and he appreciates her erudition.

He then comes across Ramasena, mother of young courtesan Charanadasi, who is moving towards the house of once rich but now defunct trader Dhanika to bring her daughter back home on the pretext of she being needed for a dramatic performance.

As he moves forward he sees a eunuch named Sukumarika. It is for the first time a eunuch is mentioned in the dramatic work and made fun of. Vita says when lovers embrace breasts do not come in its way, nor she becomes pregnant as pregnancy is enemy of good looks and youthfulness. Also she does not suffer from menses every month. Hence her company is not less than an uninterrupted festival of love.

In the Kamasutra of Vatsyayana there is a chapter giving information about making love with eunuch.

The Vita sees Dhanamitra, son of Parthaka Sarthavaha, moving in a pathetic condition after squandering his entire wealth on courtesans, particularly Ratisena. Ratisena's mother now refuses the permission to poor Dhanamitra to see her. He requests Vita to do something and unite him with his love, Ratisena.

After him he meets beautiful courtesan Priyangusena. She profusely thanks Vita for getting invited to the palace of king Apratihatashashana Kusumapurapurandara or Emperor Kumaragupta to present a sangitaka or musical opera, Purandara Vijaya, along with courtesan Devadatta.

Appreciating her acting skill the Vita refers to abhinaya of four kinds, hastaprachar of thirtytwo types, eye movements of eighteen types (thirtysix types are mentioned in the Natya Shastra), sthanas of six types, three gatis, exhibiting his profound knowledge of dramaturgy.

Vita comes to know that Narayanadatta has patched up with Kuberadatta. After meeting them Vita returns home a happy man.

The play is named Ubhayabhisarika because both of them meet as estranged lovers, both of them decide to meet one another on their own, propelled by passion arousing season of Vasanta.

ULLAGHARAGHAVA

An eight-act play by the 13th century playwright Someshvara based on Rama story. It starts with the Sita Swayamvara and ends with the return of Rama after killing Ravana to Ayodhya.

UNMATTARAGHAVA

A play by the 15th century playwright Virupakshadeva based on the Rama story. During his sojourn in forest Ram goes after a deer to catch him. Sita on hearing the cries of Rama sends Lakshmana to his succour. On their return they find Sita missing. Rama suffers from intense sorrow and wails for Sita. Lakshmana goes out in her search, strikes friendship with monkey-king Sugriva, kills his brother Vali and by attacking Lanka rescues Sita and brings her to Rama suffering from her separation.

UNMATTARAGHAVA

A Prekshanaka variety of drama by the 14th century playwright Bhaskara based on Rama story. Sita, wife of Rama, goes to collect flowers in a garden and suddenly disappears without leaving a trace. When Rama comes to know about this on his return from the hunting expedition he virtually becomes mad, unmatta, hit by love's sorrow and pain of separation. Agastya rishi appears on the scene with Sita. He tells Rama that as she entered into prohibited land cursed by Durvasa she turned into a female deer. Rama is filled with joy when he unites with Sita again.

URUBHANGA

A tragic one-act play by Bhasa describing poignantly the last painful moments of ill-fated Kaurava prince Duryodhana lying on the battlefield of Kurukshetra with a broken thigh waiting for death.

Villain in life and hero in death Duryodhana is one of the prime characters of the epic Mahabharata. Son of a blind king of Hastinapura he virtually ruled over Puru kingdom. Throughout his life he intensely hated his cousins, the Pandavas, and made several efforts to destroy them. His refusal to concede the share of Puru kingdom to his cousins led to disastrous Mahabharata war. In his Arthashastra Kautilya too ascribes the same reason for Duryodhana's downfall.

In a game of dice the Pandavas staked their beautiful wife, Draupadi, and lost her to their adversaries the Kauravas. The Kauravas dragged her to their court and insulted her in various ways. Duryodhana patted his thighs and asked her to sit on his lap. Furious Bhima then and there vowed to smash the thigh of the villain.

And at the end of Mahabharata war Bhima fulfilled his vow without mercy and left him broken-thighed on the battlefield. Bhasa picks up the thread from here and further describes the agony of dying Duryodhana, the fallen hero.

Bhasa's Duryodhana admits that his downfall was the result of his greed—apartoshasya phalam.

Interestingly the play opens with the entry of the chorus of three soldiers. The chorus is an interesting dramatic ploy basically found in the ancient Greek plays. Bhasa is the first and last of the Sanskrit dramatists who introduced chorus in his plays. They discharge similar functions as ones in Greek plays. Can we call it an influence of Greek theatre?

The chorus in Bhasa's play can best be described as the relics of ancient Indian style of narration, ballad singing by the group of performers like Kushilavas, retained by Bhasa's play stand on the threshold of the transition from ballad singing to theatre proper. After all dramatic performance is nothing but multi-headed story telling.

The three members of the chorus, all soldiers, speak in unison and individually also. Initially they speak in unison, then split and speak individually, then again speak in unison and then again split to make individual statements and the cycle goes on.

The chorus describes the ghory scene of the Bharata battlefield, the devastation caused by the war, suffering of the warriors involved. Then they describe the mace fight between Duryodhana and Bhima going on in the presence of Krishna, Balarama and Vidura, Bhima smashing the thigh of Duryodhana and wounding him fatally, leaving him on the battlefield to die in pain and humiliation.

After the exit of the chorus Balarama, elder brother of Krishna and guru of Duryodhana, appears on the stage vowing vengeance as Bhima in contravention of the rules of mace-fight hit Duryodhana below the belt. We see Duryodhana crawling on the stage due to his broken thigh.

As they were speaking old parents, wives and son of Duryodhana come searching for him. There occurs a family union under strange circumstances. There ensues pathetic scenes.

The fallen hero advises his son to serve the Pandavas, obey the orders of Kunti and treat Draupadi as his mother and end the terrible cycle of revenge and counter-revenge.

But this was not to be. Enters vengeanceful and angry Ashvatthama, son of guru Drona killed treacherously by the Pandavas, and shouts revenge. He oints Durjaya, Duryodhana's son, as the next king and promises Duryodhana that he will avenge the injustice done to Duryodhana.

On the threshold of death Duryodhana suffers from hallucinations and dies a hero's death on the battlefield of Kurukshetra, beautiful apsaras standing around to take him to heaven.

The play is described as one and only tragedy found in the Sanskrit dramatic literature. Bhasa follows the format of Utsritikanka type of play later described by Bharata as one of the ten forms of drama. The custom of Sati is mentioned in the play.

Vagaries of fate is the central theme of the play. Crowns crumble, fortunes vanish, kingdoms lost all due to fate, the all-powerful unseen force that controls human life without mercy. It is called Kal. Ashvatthama says that it was the all-pervading Kal who ultimately brought about the downfall of king Duryodhana who ruled over vast empire and commanded largest army on the earth.

Duryodhana is deified in the Himalayan region of Uttaranchal where temples are raised in his honour. Urubhanga is considered as one of the best plays of Bhasa.

UTSRISTIKANKA

One of the forms of drama mentioned by Bharata in the Natya Shastra.

The plot should be well known, but it may sometimes be otherwise furnished with male characters who are not divine. It should abound in pathetic sentiment, it will treat women's lamentations and despondent utterances at the time when battle and violent fighting has ceased, it should include bewildering movements of mourners, and it should be devoid of grand, energetic and graceful styles and its plot should relate to one's fall (NS: Ghosh).

VANA JATRA

Perambulation of a number of sacred places, woods, groves, ponds, wells, hills and temples connected with the legend of Krishna in Brajbhumi in a fixed order by the group of devotees is known as Vana Jatra. The singing and dancing pilgrims walk from one sacred place to another in the day, at night, camp at convenient place and continue their journey again in the morning. The Jatra is spread over several days. Generally Jatra starts from Mathura after the Janmashtami festival is over. Vana Jatra pilgrims trail conducted every year by Radha Vallabha sect is very famous and lasts for more than a month.

It is believed that the tradition of Vana Jatra was started by Narayanabhatta belonging to Chaitanya sect in the mid-16th century. He wrote a book Vrajabhaktivilasa which formed the basis of Vanajatra—pilgrim's trail.

A number of references to him in Bhakti literature underline his contribution to the evolution of Raslila theatre. He started a unique tradition of staging Raslila plays at the stations on the pilgrimage trail.

It was rediscovered on which place Krishna performed which lila in Vraj-bhumi. On its way when the Jatra would reach that place a Raslila play based on the legend associated with it will be enacted. For instance at a place in Vrindavan where Krishna is known to have subdued ferocious cobra Kaliya the Kaliyadaman Raslila play will be enacted. Krishna is known to have killed Kamsa at Mathura hence when Vana Jatra would reach Mathura Kamsavadha lila will be enacted. At Uchagaon Chandravali lila will be performed and at Gokul the Janma lila. Thus if there are forty halts on pilgrim's trails forty lila plays depicting the legends associated with those forty places or stations will be enacted by the Rasmandali accompanying the Jatra.

Due to association of lila enactments en route the Vana Jatra turns into processional theatre.

In the second half of the 19th century F.S. Growse, then collector of Mathura, wrote a book *Mathura: A District Memoir* in which he has mentioned about Ras theatre of Braj and Vanajatra. He states:

'Till the close of the 16th century, except in the neighbourhood of the one great thoroughfare, there was only here and there a scattered hamlet in the midst of unreclaimed woodland. The Vaishnava cult then first developed into its present form under the influence of Rupa and Sanatana, the celebrated Bengali Gosains of Brinda-ban; and it is not improbable that they were the authors of Brahma Vaivarta Purana, the recognised Sanskrit authority for all the modern local legends. It was their disciple Narayan Bhatt, who first established the Ban-jatra and Ras-lila, and it was from him that every lake and grove in circuit of Braj received a distinctive name, in addition to some seven or eight spots which alone are mentioned in earlier Puranas. In the course of time, small villages sprang up in the neighbourhood of different shrines bearing the same name with them, though perhaps in a slightly modified form. Thus Khadiraban, or 'acacia grove', gives its name to the village of Khaira; and the anjan pokhar, on whose green bank Krishna pencilled his lady's eyebrows with anjan, gave its name to the village of Ajnokh, occasionally written in greater length Ajnokhari. Similarly when Krishna's home was fixed at Nand-gaon and Radha's at Barasana, a grove half way between the two hills was fancifully selected as a spot where the youthful couple used to meet to enjoy the delights of love. There a temple was built with the title of Radha Raman, the village that grew up under its walls was called Sanket, that is 'place of assignation'.

Thus gradually Krishna myth was given a geography and location by creative Goswamis of Chaitanya sect, and these locations were connected by a pilgrim's trail—Vanajatra.'

Growse further writes:

'As the anniversary of Krishna's birth is kept in the month of Bhadon...a series of melas is held at different woods where the Ras-lila is celebrated. This is an unwritten religious drama, which represents the most popular incidents in the life of Krishna, and thus corresponds very closely with the miracle plays of mediaeval Christendom. The complete series of representations extends over a month or more, and each scene being acted on the very spot with which the original event is traditionally connected.

The marriage scene, as performed at Sanket, is the only one that I had the fortune to witness: with a garden-terrace as a stage, a grey stone temple for background, the bright moon over head, and an occasional flambeau that shot a flickering gleam over the central tableau framed in its deep border of intent and sympathizing faces, the spectacle was pretty one and was marked with the absence of anything even verging upon indecorum. The local Gosain, whom he acknowledges as his spiritual director, organises all the arrangements through one of the Rasdharis, who collects the troupe (or mandali as it is called) of the singers and musicians, and himself takes the chief part in the performance, declaiming in set recitative with the mandali for chorus, while the children who impersonate Radha and Krishna act only in dumb show.'

Vanajatra is a unique processional theatre of Braja-bhumi.

VARARUCHI

Author of the Bhana play Ubhayabhisarika. Scholars differ about the identity of Vararuchi. Some consider him to be a contemporary of Panini and author of Kanthabharana and Charumati. Some place him between Panini and Patanjali, ancient Indian grammarians of pre-Christian era, and some in the Gupta era.

Legend about Vararuchi is found in the Kathasaritsagara. Originally an attendant of Shiva he took birth in a poor Brahmin family of Kaushambi and saw many ups and downs in life. It was he who narrated the story of seven Vidyadharas to a Pishacha named Kanabhuti. Kanabhuti in turn narrated this long story to Gunadhya who wrote a book in Paishachi language, Brihatkatha, which has survived in the form of some Sanskrit translations. According to legend this Vararuchi was contemporary of last Nanda emperor of Pataliputra and lived during the reign of Chandragupta Maurya.

Vararuchi is famous as a grammarian in Indian literature. However some scholars consider him to be contemporary of Gupta rulers Chandragupta II and Kumaragupta.

It seems that Vararuchi, the author of the Bhana play Ubhayabhisarika, is different from Vararuchi the grammarian. He in his Bhana refers to Emperor Kumaragupta of Pataliputra as Apratihatashashana Kusumapura-Purandara. This places him in the 4th-5th century A.D.

VATASAVITRI FESTIVAL

A tenth century playwright Rajashekhara in his play Karpuramanjiri mentions the festival named Vatasavitri Mahotsava which was celebrated by women with various kinds of dances including Charchari, dandaras, tribal Pulinda dance and awe-inspiring ghost-mask dance. Women danced playing on various musical instruments.

Vatasavitri festival is mentioned in various Puranas including Padma, Skanda, Agni, and also in Chaturvarga Chintamani of Hemadri. Traditionally it is observed on the full moon day of Jaistha or Jaistha Purnima which falls in May-June of the English calendar.

According to the legend in the epic Mahabharata a pious woman Savitri made Yama, the god of death, to return the life of her dead husband, Satyavana, on this day.

On the day women worship a banyan or Vata tree. Puranas enjoin women to observe fast, sing and dance around the banyan tree and pray for the long life of their husbands.

VATSARAJA

12th-13th century playwright, minister at the court of Chandella king Paramardideva of Kalanjara and his son Trailokyavarmadeva. His contribution to Sanskrit dramatic literature is unique in the sense that he composed his works in not much used formats such as Ihamriga, Samavakara and Dima. His plays in these formats are the only surviving examples of the genres.

He wrote six plays.

His Kiratarjuniyavyayoga is a one-act play in Vyayoga format based on the epic Kiratarjuniya by Bharavi. In this play the fight between Shiva in the guise of Kirata hunter and Pandava archer Arjuna is portrayed beautifully.

Karpuracharita Bhana and Hasyachudamani Prahasana are humorous one-act plays in Bhana and Prahasana format. The first play is the story of cheat and knave gambler Karpuraka and the other is about a fake guru Jnanarashi and his Kevali vidya by which, he claims, he could detect the lost property.

In Tripuradaha dima he has portrayed the mythical story of the burning of Tripuras by Shiva.

Rukminiharana Ihamriga is the only extant example of Ihamriga form of drama. It is based on the story of Krishna's marriage with Rukmini.

Samudramanthana Samavakara depicts the story of churning of the ocean by gods and demons. It is the only extant example of the Samavakara form of drama.

The names of Tripuradaha dima and Samudramanthana Samavakara are mentioned by Bharata in his Natya Shastra. But these works are lost to posterity. Taking cue from Bharata playwright Vatsaraja wrote his own dima and samavakara plays with the same titles.

After Bhasa it is Vatsaraja who composed plays in a number of dramatic forms in large number.

VATSYAYANA

The author of the world-famous treatise on love, the Kamasutra. Indian tradition refers to him as Maharshi, the great rishi. Rishi means revealer of sacred text, a sage, a man old in wisdom, saint or ascetic, a man exuding spiritual knowledge.

Dharma, Artha, Kama and Moksha are considered as four goals of life or purusharthas. Vatsyayana chose Kama which means love, lust, passion and sensual pleasure which is basic to human existence as the subject of his meditation.

Concluding the Kamasutra he wrote: 'This treatise is written by me by observing strict celibacy and entering into spiritual trance concentrating on the subject, tadetad brahmacharyena parena cha samadhina, for the welfare of entire society. For that I have studied the works of earlier authorities on the subject and their practical utilisation in life.'

A celibate ascetic writing about the science of love is in itself quite an unusual thing, having no parallel in the history of literature. Probably the Maharshi needed to be celibate to be perfectly objective in approaching his subject.

Nothing is known about this great sage except a few words he wrote about himself in his work. That gave rise to lot of speculation and confusion about his real identity.

In the Vasavadatta written by Subandhu and also in the commentary on the Kamasutra the name of the author of Kamasutra is given as Mallanaga. Scholars believe that Mallanaga became famous as Vatsyayana which can be his gotra or sect name.

Vatsyayana in his work mentions the name of king Kuntala Satakarni who existed in the first century A.D. This helps us to fix upper limit of the work. Mallanaga's Kamasutra is mentioned in Subandhu's fifth century work Vasavadatta. While describing a mountain Subandhu says it was filled with elephants and was fragrant with the perfumes of the jungles just as Kamasutra written by Mallanaga contains the delight and enjoyment of mistresses—Kamasutravinyasa iva Mallanagaghatitakantarasambodah.

This leads us to conclude that Vatsyayana wrote his work sometime between first and fifth century A.D.

In his work Vatsyayana refers to a number of purvacharyas or scholar-thinkers who wrote on the subject. This indicates that there existed a number of works on the subject belonging to pre-Vatsyayana date. It seems that the work of Dattaka dealing with harlotry, an erotica he wrote for the courtesans of Pataliputra, remained in vogue till Gupta period as he is mentioned in some Bhana plays of the era.

Later in the medieval period a number of works on erotics were written. They include Nagarasarvasvam by Padmashri, a Mahayana Buddhist, Ratirahasya by Pandit Kokkoka, Panchasayaka by Jyotishvara, a Jain author, Ratimanjiri by Jayadeva, Anangaranga by Kalyanamalla, Kandarpa-chudamani by Virabhadradeva and Kamasamuha by Ananta. But no work could surpass the Kamasutra of Vatsyayana.

Scholars believe that Vatsyayana lived in western or south India and wrote his masterpiece in the third century A.D.

VENISAMHARA

A six-act play by the seventh century playwright Bhatta Narayana based on the story of Mahabharata war.

Draupadi, the chief queen of Pandava brothers, was dragged in the Kaurava court by her hair and efforts were made to disrobe her. Draupadi vowed that till her insult is avenged she will not braid her hair.

The play shows how Pandavas, particularly Bhima, avenged the insult heaped on Draupadi by killing Dussashana and Duryodhana on the battlefield of Kurukshetra.

Veṇisamhara means binding together of hair. In the final act we see Bhima tying the hair of Draupadi into a braid.

Bhasa was the first playwright who wrote plays depicting the episodes related to the theatre of terrible Bharata war. Centuries after Bhasa it was Bhatta Narayana who wrote an extensive play covering various episodes related to the Bharata war. Full of heroic sentiment Venisamhara became very popular. The play opens with the failure of the peace-mission of Krishna and ends with the fall of Duryodhana. Keith says that the style of the play is clear and not lacking either in force or dignity. The popularity of the play can be gauged from the fact that a number of passages from the play were mentioned by the writers on poetics in their works.

VERY FIRST THEATRICAL SPECTACLE

According to a legend recorded in the Natya Shastra after learning the technique of dramatic enactment Bharata went to Lord Brahma. Brahma told him to put his knowledge of Natya Veda into practice during the Festival of Indra's Flagstaff, Sriman Mahendrasya Dhwajamahotsava, which was fast approaching. Accordingly Bharata presented his first dramatic spectacle with great enthusiasm. The performance commenced with the singing of Nandi, prayer song, with eight stanzas based on Vedic lore.

Then Bharata presented the imitation of the recently fought war between demons and gods in which gods became victorious. The performance was full of angry exclamations of the gods and running asunder, panic, agitation, flight (on the part of demons), weapon fight and wrestling (leading to the victory of gods).

This must have been an open-air violent spectacle, dialogues (if any) confined to verbal challenges and counter-challenges. The performance, it seems, was confined to recreating a war scene showing gods and demons engaged in wrestling and some of them fighting with weapons. It was all action and practically no speech, it seems.

It will be interesting to compare this performance with the Naga war dances described by Loomis Havemeyer (see Hunt Drama).

VIDAGDHAMADHAV

A seven-act Sanskrit drama based on Radha-Krishna romance written in the first half of the 16th century by Rupa Goswami, disciple of Chaitanya Mahaprabhu. The play was enacted at Keshi tirtha in Vrindavan. See RUPA GOSWAMI.

VIDDHASHALABHANJIKA

A romantic four-act play by 10th century playwright Rajashekhara based on the love story of king Vidyadharamalla and Mrigankavali, beautiful daughter of Lata king Chandravarman. Interesting part of the play is that the heroine Mrigankavali lives in the court of the hero Vidyadharamalla in the guise of a boy. This creates lot of fun and confusion. In the end the hero is married to Mrigankavali and yet another princess named Kuvalayamala, daughter of Kuntala.

The play takes its name from a statue, Shalabhanjika, in the king's palace. In the first act of the play king Vidyadharamalla sees in his dream a young and beautiful girl putting a pearl necklace around his neck. After awakening he finds the statue, Shalabhanjika, resembling the dream-girl in his palace. Thus the title of the play Viddhashalabhanjika.

VIDUSHAKA

A jester, wag, buffoon, jocose, companion and confidant of the hero of the play whose business is to excite mirth in person and attire, and help him get his object of love.

Defining the appearance of Vidushaka a verse in the Natya Shastra says: Vamano danturah kubjo dwijanma vikritananan/ khalatij pingalakshascha sanvidheyo vidushakah. 'A Brahmin, ludicrous alike in dress, speech and behaviour he is a misshapen dwarf, baldheaded, with projecting teeth and red eyes (Keith).'

Speaking about the gait of the jester the Natya Shastra says: 'The jester will have the gait consisting of simple laughable steps with feet raised high (and put forward). And his gait relates to three kinds of laughter: laughter due to limbs, due to words and due to costume and make-up. Of these the ugly big teeth, bald head, hunch on the back, lameness, and distorted face will be causing laughter due to limbs. When he walks like a crane looking up and looking down with wide strides, this too becomes an object of laughter due to limbs.

Talking incoherently, meaninglessly, garrulously and uttering obscene words are to be known as (causing) laughter due to words.

A person covered with tattered cloths or skin, or smeared with ink (or lamp-black), ashes or yellow ochre will be (causing) laughter due to costume and make-up. Hence the (jester) after considering the character (he is to represent) should carefully (lit. essentially) assume (one or more of) these states' (XIII.137–146).

The Natya Shastra further says that he should carry a crooked stick, kutilaka or kutila, in his hand. In the Mathura Museum there is a pillar adorned with the sculpture of nati or actress. On the medallion above the sculpture there is a scene showing Vidushaka with kutilaka in his hand regaling his audiences, by his speech and action. In the fresco in cave no. 1 at Ajanta showing a royal couple watching a dance performance, we see Vidushaka with his protruding teeth sitting at the feet of the king.

Vishvanatha in the Sahitya Darpana says that Vidushaka is named after some flower or season like Vasanta, enjoys quarrel and making other people quarrel, makes people laugh with his actions, body, costume and language, and never loses the sight of his aim that is obtaining delicious food.

According to Bhavaprakasha Vidushaka is dear to queen and her female attendants, he does not eye money or woman, mediates between king and his beloved, by his action sometimes he separates them and sometimes unites them.

We find Vidushaka in the plays of Bhasa, Ashvaghosha, Kalidasa and many others. But he is not found in the plays of Bhavabhuti and Vishakhadatta. Vidushaka occupies key position in the play Malavikagnimitra of Kalidasa, he virtually runs the show.

In various folk and traditional dramatic forms we find Vidushaka present under different names.

Humour was the most important part of theatrical entertainment. Some scholars believe that Nata was originally a figure of mirth. It was believed that 'a player who on the stage or in the arena makes people laugh and delights them with truth and falsehood, on dissolution of body after death is reborn in the company of laughing devas.'

In the Vedic literature there are references to fun makers. One such fun maker mentioned in the Rig Veda (IX. 112.4) is upamantrin who is defined by Sayana as coaxing pleasure-companion who wants fun making for creating laughter. Upamantrin used to be attached to royal courts.

In Vajasaneyi Samhita and Taittiriya Brahmana occurs the word Kari meaning a jester 'walking abnormally like one who goes dancing, as it were.' His job was to entertain common citizens.

During the excavations at Mohenjodaro statuettes of dwarfs were found by the archaeologists. Mackay says probably Indus people used to keep dwarfs for amusement as in Egypt. Indian tradition considers dwarf an object of amusement. The Shukla Yajurveda in the 10th verse of its 30th book says that a dwarf is an object of amusement.

In the Natya Shastra the dwarfish attendants of Shiva, Pramatha Ganas, are considered as the presiding deities of Hasya Rasa or the sentiment of humour. The jester or Vidushaka of the Natya Shastra is dwarf or vamana.

In the Kamasutra it is said that 'a Vidushaka (also called a Vaihasika, i.e. one who provokes laughter) is a person only acquainted with some of the arts, who is a jester, and who is trusted by all.' It further says that along with Vita and Pithamarda the fun making Vidushaka too is employed in the matters of quarrels and reconciliations between citizens and courtesans.

Some scholars believe that the 'Vidushaka is an old figure of the popular stage, which the classical drama has borrowed from the popular dramas of the wandering dancers and mimes.'

However, as we have seen, the professional jesters existed outside the world of drama, and they were employed by the citizens to entertain them and used as conduit between them and courtesans. Finding them fascinating drama might have adopted them.

VIDYADHARA

Semi-divine beings having magical powers. They change form at will and move through the sky. They marry and interact with humans and are kind and helping. In Jain and Buddhist mythology and in Brihatkatha there are numerous stories of Vidyadharas. They are lustful and fond of women and wine. There are a number of clans of Vidyadharas having their own kings and kingdoms. Flying Vidyadharas are sculpted in Indian art as a part of entourage of principal deities like Vishnu and Shiva.

In Bhasa's play Avimaraka Vidyadhara appears along with his consort to save hero from committing suicide. He gives a magic ring to hero which helps him to get invisible. In his Abhisheka Nataka a chorus of three Vidyadharas appears in the sixth act to describe the war between Rama and Ravana.

The hero of Harsha's play Nagananda, Jimutavahana, is the Vidyadhara prince.

In Kalidasa's play Vikramorvashiya we are informed that when beautiful nymph Urvashi went to mountain Gandhamadana with her lover Pururava to enjoy the pleasures of love he stared at Vidyadhara beauty Udayavati. Angry and jealous Urvashi entered the forest called Kumarvana to run away from Pururava. Entry of women in Kumarvana belonging to Kartikeya, a celibate son of Shiva, was strictly prohibited. As Urvashi entered the forest she turned into a creeper.

VIKRAMORVASHIYA

Or Urvashi Won by Valour is a five-act play of Kalidasa depicting the love story of nymph Urvashi and king Pururava. The enchanting story of self-willed nymph Urvashi and lovelorn king Pururava is found in the Rig Veda for the first time. Shatapatha Brahmana elaborates upon it and the later Puranas present their own versions. Kalidasa, it seems, relied more on Puranic account of origin of Urvashi from the thigh or uru of sage Narayana and her kidnapping by demon Keshi, etc.

King Pururava rescues Urvashi who is kidnapped by demon Keshi. She falls in love with the king and the king too is enchanted by her youth and beauty. Nymph Urvashi moving invisibly writes a love letter on the palm leaf expressing her love. However it falls in the hand of the queen who becomes angry. King falls at her feet, the ritual practised by Indian lovers to appease their beloveds when they are angry, but in vain. Ultimately queen relents and permits the king to unite with the nymph.

We are informed that Bharata produced a play Lakshmi Swayamvara in the court of Indra. Urvashi who played the role of Lakshmi instead of mentioning the name of Purushottama or Vishnu as the object of her love took the name of Pururava. Bharata cursed her for the slip and expells her from heaven. However Indra grants her permission to live with her mortal lover Pururava.

In Kalidasa's Abhijnana Shakuntalam heroine Shakuntala, a daughter of nymph, is cursed by sage Durvasa. In Vikramorvashiya heroine Urvashi is subjected to a curse. At a number of places the influence of Abhijnana Shakuntalam is seen on the plot of Vikramorvashiyam.

Kalidasa is probably the first playwright to mention Bharata, celebrated author of the Natya Shastra, for the first time. The Natya Shastra mentions a play Amritamanthana staged by Bharata in the heaven. The basic story of Amritamanthana and Lakshmi Swayamvara is the same. This points at the fact that Kalidasa knew Bharata and his work very well.

Before Kalidasa the playwright Bhasa too mentions a work called Natya Shastra. In his play Avimaraka the jester Vidushaka boasting about his eruditon says that he had read five verses of the Natya Shastra named Ramayana. We are not sure to which Natya Shastra Bhasa is referring to. He does not mention the name of Bharata in this context.

Urvashi starts living with Pururava. We are informed that one day Urvashi took Pururava to mountain Gandhamadana to enjoy love-making. Kalidasa says making love in such environment is real love making—sa nama sambhogo yastadrishesh-upradeshesu.

While moving on the bank of river Mandakini Urvashi notices the king looking intently at a Vidyadhara beauty, Udayavati. Leaving him in huff she entered a forest named Kumarvana and turned into a creeper as women were not allowed to enter it.

Lovelorn king starts moving in the forest in search of Urvashi in delirium like a lunatic. His long soliloquy is very poetic and lyrical expressing intense and deep-felt pangs of separation, and considered as the best example of vipralambha shringara. In the northern manuscripts of the play a number of lyrical apabhramsha songs are put in the mouth of the lovelorn king with the direction to their mode of singing. If they are authentic and genuine compositions by playwright we may say that Kalidasa is the first playwright who has introduced Apabhramsha songs as a novel experiment.

With the help of magical Sangamaniya mani the king locates Urvashi who regains her human form again.

In the last act the king is united with his young son also and the play ends on a happy note. The play, probably the last work of Kalidasa, may be described as good poetry but it cannot be said to be a good work of drama.

VILLAIN

A character in the play who constitutes an important evil agency in the plot. See PRATINAYAKA.

VISHAKHADATTA

Sanskrit playwright, author of the plays Mudrarakshasa and Devi Chandragupta, ascribed to 4th-5th century A.D. The play Mudrarakshasa is based on the life of Arya Chanakya, the political mentor of Emperor Chandragupta Maurya of Pataliputra, belonging to fourth century B.C.

The play Devi Chandragupta is lost to posterity but a few excerpts from this play are found in Natya Darpana and Shringarprakasha. The play was based on the story of love affair of Chandragupta of Gupta dynasty and Dhruvaswamini.

In the prologue of the play Mudrarakshasa the playwright describes himself as the grandson of Samant Vateshvardatta and son of Maharaja Bhaskardatta. In some manuscripts instead of Bhaskardatta name of Pruthu is mentioned. Identity of these persons has not been clearly established as yet.

In the concluding verse of the play Mudrarakshasa the name of the patron king of the playwright is mentioned as Parthiva Chandragupta and in some manuscripts instead the names of Dantivarma, Avantivarma and Rantivarma are found mentioned.

Some scholars believe that Parthiva Chandragupta was none else but Emperor Chandragupta Second of Gupta dynasty and the play was possibly performed at Pataliputra, the capital of the Guptas, in 4th-5th century A.D.

However some scholars consider him to be associated with Maukhari king Avantivarma whose son had married the sister of king Harsha. This places the playwright at the end of the sixth century A.D.

It is believed that the word Rantivarma is just a corrupt form of Avantivarma. History knows of one Pallava king Dantivarma and also Rashtrakuta king of the same name. There was one more Dantivarma who was the king of Lata country.

However it is generally believed that he belonged to Gupta era and most probably associated with Emperor Chandragupta Second and thus was contemporary of Kalidasa.

VISHNU

A Vedic deity who later grew in stature and occupied significant position in Hindu pantheon by forming a trinity with Brahma and Shiva. Vishnu means all-pervasive. However the scholars like Louis Renou consider the origin of the name Vishnu as obscure and possibly non-Aryan. In the Rig Veda a few hymns are dedicated to him. The term shipivista ascribed to him, according to some scholars, points at his phallic origin. In the Rig Veda he is referred to as Vishnurgopa, Vishnu the cowherd, which connects him to his major incarnation, Sri Krishna. In the Brahmana works he is equated with Yajna—Yajno vai Vishnu. However it was epic Mahabharata which increased the importance of Vishnu and rich mythology grew around him.

According to mythology Vishnu took several incarnations. The Bhagavata Purana says: 'Just as from an inexhaustible lake thousands of streams flow on all sides, so also from the Hari, sum of all reality, come forth countless incarnations. The seers, lawgivers, the gods, the human races, the lords of progeny, all are parts of him.'

However some of his incarnations are more famous which according to the Gita Govinda are ten. They are Meena (fish), Kacchapa (tortoise), Sukara (boar), Narahari (man-lion, Nrisimha), Vamana (dwarf), Bhrigupati (axeman brahmin, Parashurama), Rama (prince of Ayodhya), Haladhara (Balarama—ploughman), Buddha, and Kalki. Jayadeva contends that they are all forms of Krishna who is considered as Vishnu himself!

Function of Brahma is to preserve, of Vishnu to sustain and of Shiva to annihilate, thus together they move the wheel of existence.

From the first century B.C. we start getting the images of Vishnu which were made at Mathura and region around in imitation of Yaksha images. With the passage of time more and more images in different attitudes were made, temples too were raised in his honour. In popular imagination he is a deity with four hands, holding in them conch, disk, mace and lotus respectively. Lakshmi, the goddess of wealth, is his wife. He resides in Vaikuntha loka or in milky ocean where he sleeps on the coils of serpent Shesha, Lakshmi massaging his feet. From his navel springs a lotus flower on which Brahma sits in meditation. The bird Garuda is his vehicle.

In his play Dutaghatotkacha playwright Bhasa offers prayers to Narayana Vishnu by saying that he is the string holder, Sutradhara, of life cycle constantly being enacted in all the three worlds from beginning to end.

Bharata has mentioned Vishnu several times in his Natya Shastra. Shringar or erotic sentiment is considered as a prime sentiment or rasa that pervades dramatic literature. Vishnu is the presiding deity of Shringar rasa.

A myth recorded in the Natya Shastra says that Vrittis or styles emerged when Vishnu fought with demons Madhu and Kaitabha. When the Lord engaged the demons in verbal duel there emerged Bharati (verbal) style, when he fought with them in strength (sattva) taking bow in his hand the Sattvati vritti (grand style) emerged, when the god moved sportively exhibiting various postures, angaharas, tying the knot (shikha) of hair on his head the Kaishiki (graceful) style emerged, when he struck various charis during the combat the Arabhati (energetic) style emerged.

The themes of several dramas were taken from Vaishnava mythology, particularly related to Vishnu's Rama and Krishna incarnations.

VITA

The character of Vita appears in a number of dramas. Kamasutra of Vatsyayana defines Vita as 'a man who has enjoyed the pleasures of fortune, who is possessed of good qualities, who has his wife with him, and who is honoured in the assembly of citizens and in the abodes of public women, and lives on their means and on them.'

Sahitya Darpana describes him as a voluptuary who has squandered his wealth on sensuous pleasures, who is knave, knower of arts, expert in dealing with courtesans, a man with sweet tongue and fond of literary-cultural–artistic meetings—goshthis.

Sometimes he appears as a companion of the hero, sometimes of the courtesan. He is a man of liaison. In the play Mricchakatika the Vitas have played significant role.

However there is a genre of drama named Bhana. It is one-act, one-actor drama. Single character appears on the stage and the play is nothing but his humorous narration. This character is nobody else but Vita.

The colourful character of Vita is revealed in the corpus of Bhana plays. There are many references to Vita and his activities in the Kuttanimata kavya of Damodaragupta. He was the part of Vesha-culture. We find him mentioned in a number of medieval literary works.

VITHI

One of the ten forms of drama mentioned by Bharata in his Natya Shastra.

Vithi should have one act and is to be acted by two persons or one. And it is to include characters of the superior, the middling or the inferior type, it may contain any of the sentiments and it may be of thirteen types (NS: Ghosh).

VITHI BHAGAVATAM

An offshoot of Kuchipudi dance-drama tradition the Vithi Bhagavatam or Natakam flourished in some parts of Andhra Pradesh towards the end of 19th century.

Some artist families well versed in Natya Shastra tradition migrated from Kuchipudi to other parts of Andhra Pradesh. Siddhendra Yogi refused to allow female performers to enact roles in the dance-drama he evolved in the Kuchipudi village. However the Gurus who migrated from Kuchipudi did not observe this constraint. They did not mind training female disciples.

Dr. Sunil Kothari writes: 'The female artists, generally from courtesan families, expert in sadir nauch, solo dance were trained by the Bharatamvaru in their repertory. By crossing the features of these two the form Vithi Bhagavatam was evolved. Independent of the Kuchipudi dancers and their troupes, the female dancers popularised Vithi Bhagavatam. Bharatamvarus instructed the Kalavantalu or courtesans into sustained Bhagavata lore.'

In Vithi Bhagavatam a female dancer gives a solo performance attended by the musicians playing on pakhavaj, violin and harmonium. The Vithi Bhagavatam performances were generally held during temple festivals.

Eastern style of Vithi Natakam is known as Turpubani Vithi Natakam.

VRITTI

Four constituent styles of drama. These are Bharati, Sattvati Kaishiki and Arabhati.

A legend regarding the emergence of Vrittis is recorded in the Natya Shastra. Once two demons Madhu and Kaitabha puffed with the pride about their strength challenged Lord Vishnu for fight. Lord fought with them with words, actions, movements and from those emanated four Vrittis.

Bharata explains that the Vrittis are made repository of various psychological states and sentiments—nanabhavarasashraya, words and gestures being their chief characteristics.

Bharata connects four vrittis with four Vedas. He says: Bharati vritti is from Rig Veda, Sattvati from Yajurveda, Kaishiki from Samaveda and Arabhati from Atharvaveda.

Bharati vritti or verbal style basically concerns itself with words and speeches. Bharata says: 'The style which is to be applied by the male characters and not by females and which gives prominent place to speeches made in Sanskrit, is used by eponymous Bharatas (actors) is bharati (verbal).' Bharati is suited to all sentiments—vrittih sarvatra bharati. There are four varieties of Bharati vritti.

Sattvati vritti or the grand style according to Bharata 'is the style endowed with the quality of the spirits (sattva), the Nyayas, proper metres and has exuberance of joy and suppression of state of sorrow. Related to plays expressing the spirit (sattva) the grand style is known to consist of representation by words and gestures. It is to contain sentiments such as Heroic and Marvellous and the Furious (Veera, Adbhuta and Raudra) and to the small extent the Pathetic and Erotic; the characters in it should be mostly majestic and defying one another. There are four varieties of this style.'

Kaishiki or graceful style, according to Bharata, 'is specially interesting on account of charming costumes worn by dramatis personae mostly women, and in which many kinds of dancing and singing is included, and the themes acted are practices of love and are connected with its enjoyment. It has four varieties.'

Arabhati or energetic style according to Bharata 'includes mostly the qualities of the bold person (arabhata) such as speaking many words (probably during altercation or verbal duel), deception, bragging, falsehood. There is representation of mosel work (pusta), falling down, jumping, crossing over, piercing, deeds of magic and conjuration, and varied types of fighting. It has four varieties.'

Bharata says 'the styles in the Erotic and Comic sentiments (shringare chaiva hasye cha) should be Kaishiki, and in Heroic and Marvellous (Veera and Adbhuta) it should be Sattvati. And in the Terrible, the Odious, and the Furious sentiments (Bhayanaka, Bibhatsa and Raudra) one should use Arabhati.' Though it is believed that Bharati is suited for all the sentiments Bharata says it is applicable to Pathetic and Marvellous (Karuna, Adbhuta) sentiments.

Sahitya Darpana says that these four Vrittis can be termed as mothers of all kinds of dramas—sarvanatyasya matrikah. It says that vrittis are related to the performance (vyapara) of dramatis personae like the Nayaka or hero, etc. in the drama.

Bharata speaks of ten kinds of play. Here he tells us which vritti is suited to which kind of play. For instance:

Utsristikanka should be devoid of grand, energetic and graceful styles.

Dima is to be carefully made in the grand and energetic style and is to have many psychological states to support it.

Nataka and Prakarana are to be made up of all styles, vrittis and remaining eight kinds of play should avoid graceful style.

Bharata in his chapter on Dasharupa-vidhanam says that 'styles or vrittis are traditionally known as the constituent elements of all dramatic works—sarveshameva kavyanam matrika vrittayah smrita. Variety of plays come into existence due to variety of styles.'

VYAYOGA

Vyayoga should have one well-known hero, a small number of female characters and event spread over one day. It should have one act, royal sage as its hero and not a divine personage, should include battle, personal combat, challenge and angry conflict exciting sentiment as its basis (NS: Ghosh).

WORKS ON DRAMATURGY

The tradition of writing books on drama and dramatic arts dates back to several centuries. Earliest known work on the subject is Natasutra by Shilali and Krishashva which is lost to posterity. Bhasa in one of his plays refers to a work titled as Natya Shastra but does not mention the name of its author.

Natya Shastra of Bharata which is placed between the second century B.C. and second century A.D. is the oldest surviving work on the subject. In his work Bharata refers to a number of authorities on the subject including Dhurtila, Shandilya, Vatsya and Kohala.

Some of the major works on dramaturgy that appeared after Bharata's Natya Shastra are:

Bharat Kosha by Mahendra Vikram (7th century A.D.), Abhinavabharati, a commentary on Natya Shastra, by Abhinavagupta (10th century A.D.), Dasharupaka by Dhananjaya (10th century A.D.), Avaloka vritti, a commentary on Dasharupaka, by Dhanika (10th century A.D.), Natakalakshana Ratnakosha by Sagarnandi (11th century A.D.), Natyadarpana by Ramachandra and Gunachandra (12th century A.D.), Bhavaprakasha by Sharadatanaya (12th century A.D.), Abhinayadarpana by Nandikeshvara (12th–13th century A.D.), Natakaparibhasha by Simhabhupala (14th century A.D.), Nrityadhyaya by Ashokamalla (14th century A.D.), Nrityaratnakosha by Kumbhakarna (14th century A.D.), Natakachandrika by Rupa Goswami (15th century A.D.) and Natyapradeepa by Sundar Mishra (17th century A.D.).

Apart from these works drama as a subject is discussed in a number of works such as Kavyaprakasha by Mammata, Rasarnavasudhakara by Simhabhupal, Shringarprakasha and Saraswatikanthabharana by Bhoja, Prataparudrayashobhushan by Vidyanatha and Sahityadarpana by Vishvanatha.

YAJNAPHALA

A seven-act play based on the Balakanda of Ramayana. Some scholars are of the opinion that it was written by Bhasa, however some think that it is simply written in imitation of Bhasa's style. It starts with the birth of Rama and his brothers and ends with Sita Swayamvara.

YAKSHA

Handsome semi-divine beings, Yakshas, and their beautiful female consorts, Yakshinis, are mentioned in the Indian literary works since ancient times and there are numerous Yaksha-related stories revealing their malevolent and benevolent traits. Awe-inspiring, marvellous and mysterious Yakshas were feared and loved by the people of ancient India. They were worshipped with the offerings of meat, wine, flowers, incense and above all with dance, music and dramatic enactments. Yaksha cult dates back to hoary antiquity, certainly pre-Vedic in its origin.

In the third act of Bhasa's play Pratijnayaugandharayana based on Udayana cycle of stories there is a reference to Yaksha cult prevalent during 5th-4th century B.C. We are informed that young and beautiful princess of Ujjayani, Vasavadatta, on the day of Kalashtami went to offer worship at the stead of Bhagavati Yakshini, Bhaavadiye jakkhiniye tthanam.

Kalashtami is the name of the eighth day of the dark fortnight of the month. Probably there prevailed a custom of worshipping Yakshini on that day. Now-a-days the deities of Shaiva pantheon like Mahakala, Bhairava are worshipped on this ashtami.

Initially the sthana or stead of Yaksha was not more than a plain raised platform made of clay, brick or stone with a triangular stone slab, pindi, Ayagapatta, or pujashila, placed on it, situated under the canopy of sky or tree.

Since about fourth century B.C. massive stone images of Yakshas and Yakshis were sculpted. Most famous of these ancient Yaksha images was one found at Parkham near Mathura. This standing image measuring about 8′ 9″, according to inscription on it, is of Yaksha Manibhadra. Among free-standing Yakshini images one found during excavation at Didargunj at Patna is extremely beautiful. Yakshini image found at Besnagar is also quite alluring. They heralded an era of stone sculpture in India.

We do not know the exact nature of 'sthana' mentioned in the Bhasa's play. Bhasa is placed in 5th-4th century B.C. Probably the tradition of making massive Yaksha images started during his time. It is significant to note that the princess herself used to worship Yakshini of Ujjayani regularly, such was the influence of Yaksha cult during the period. The influence lingered for centuries. In the Bhana play of Gupta period, Padataditakam, there is a mention of a crossroad named after Yaksha Purnabhadra—Purnabhadra sringataka. Probably there was a shrine of Purnabhadra Yaksha nearby in Ujjayani.

Beautiful Yakshini images are found adorning ancient Buddhist monuments. Yakshini images of the gateways of Sanchi stupa are very alluring, some of them frankly nude or in diaphanous cloths. Yakshini images found attached to railing pillars which were excavated at various sites in Mathura are sensuous and evocative.

According to an ancient story, with their magical powers Yakshinis used to raise beautiful pavilions in the forest or desert land and entertain the travelling merchants with singing and dancing, and regale them with wines. After they were asleep the Yakshinis would devour them in the dead of night.

Lustful Yakshas used to possess young and beautiful girls and enjoy them carnally. Numerous Yaksha myths, legends and stories are found strewn in literary works.

Bharata in his Natya Shastra has recognised the contribution of Yakshas made to the evolution of dramatic art. He has prescribed rituals to appease them. The task of protecting the foundation of the stage in the theatre hall is entrusted to the Yakshas. Bharata while describing various kinds of group dance formations, or pindibandhas, speaks of Yakshi pindibandha that please god of wealth Dhanada or Kubera. Kubera is the chief of Yakshas.

While describing various types of women Bharata speaks of woman of Yakshini type. He says: 'A woman who sweats during sleep, loves quiet rest in bed or seat, is very intelligent, fearless and fond of wine, sweet scent and meat, takes delight in seeing the beloved one after a long time, feels gratitude to him, does not sleep for a long time is said to have a nature of a Yakshi.'

In playwright Kalidasa's long poem Meghaduta or Cloud Messenger there is a very romantic description of Alaka, city of Yakshas, and music, dance, wine loving Yakshinis. Vasavadatta's Yakshini shrine was in Ujjayani so was the Purnabhadra sringataka of Padataditakam. No wonder Kalidasa who wrote about beautiful Yakshinis of Alakapuri too belonged to Ujjayani.

In the later literature there are references to the shrines or temples raised in the honour of Yakshas. All kinds of performing artists used to flock these shrines in large number. Near the city of Champa, says a Jain work Aupapatika Sutra, there was a shrine of Yaksha Purnabhadra which was haunted by actors, dancers, rope walkers, wrestlers, boxers, jesters, jumpers, reciters, ballad singers, story tellers, pole dancers, picture showmen, pipers, lute players and minstrels.

According to yet another Jain work there was a shrine dedicated to Yaksha Sutanjana in the South India where a play relating the story of that Yaksha used to be enacted. The tutelary Yaksha of Vaishali too was offered dance, song and music to appease him.

In the South India there flourished a dance drama named Yakshagana which is still enacted in Karnataka region.

In the Kamasutra of Vatsyayana there is a mention of a festival known as Yaksharatri. Yashodhara in his commentary describes it as sukharatri or night of pleasure when people used to indulge in gambling near Yaksha stead. In the Mahaban in Braj region a fair known as Jakhaiyaka Mela is held in the month of Magha. It is believed that it is a relic of Jakkha or Yaksha Maha of ancient times.

YAKSHAGANA

Vibrant and colourful operatic folk dramatic form full of singing, dancing and music that evolved in Malnad region of Karnataka in early 16th century.

Yakshagana was a system of music prevalent in medieval Karnataka. Since twelfth century the equivalent terms such as ekkalagana or ekkedigaru started appearing in Kannada literature. This system of music was adopted by the devotees of Bhagavata cult while evolving a theatre revolving round the Vaishnava mythical themes, hence the new form came to be known as Yakshagana.

There were certain ritualistic and folk dramatic performances which used locally evolved dance forms. They were adopted by Yakshagana. Scholars have found similarities between ritualistic dance performance called Nagamandala and Yakshagana as far as pattern of dance is concerned.

The Bhuta cult or cult of spirit worship flourished in the coastal Karnataka since ancient times. Dramatic festivals are held at the Bhuta Sthanas or ghost shrines to propitiate the spirits. The ritual drama performed there contains elements such as music, songs, dancing, costumes, make-up, masks, story, dialogue. It seems that these spirit rituals greatly influenced the Yakshagana theatre.

Yakshagana plays in verse form are known as Prasangas. The mythological stories from works such as Mahabharata,

Ramayana, Bhagavata Purana are borrowed for writing Yakshagana verse plays. Prose dialogues are improvised by the actors during the performance itself taking cue from the verse recitation by the Bhagavata.

Bhagavata is a pivot around which the performance revolves hence he is known as Prathama Vesha or prime character. He along with his chorus of singers and musicians remains on the stage from the beginning to the end of the performance. It is he who sings the play and taking cue from him the actors deliver impromptu prose dialogues. It is as if he is presenting the story with the help of actors with whom he enters into conversation at times.

The Yakshagana stage is very simple, a square piece of land in open field. Four bamboo poles are fixed at four corners which support the cloth roof above. A wooden platform is there for Bhagavata and his chorus of singers and musicians to sit. The stage is known as Chowk. It is virtually bare of stage-property except for a couple of chairs.

Some distance from the performing arena there is a make-up space known as Chowki.

Yakshagana make-up is very elaborate and colourful and costumes impressive. Divine characters really look elegant and divine and demonic ones ferocious and awe-inspiring. There are multiple of mythological, human and animal characters that appear on the stage with their faces coloured appropriately.

The most colourful and elaborate make-up is worn by the demonic characters. They are known as Bannada vesha, banna meaning colour in Kannada. The demonic Rakshasa or villainous characters look terrifying in their multi-coloured facial make-up, high headgears, dazzling jewellery and colourful costumes. Led by the men holding oil-torches they sometimes come from a distance to the stage in a majestic procession shouting, dancing, jumping in frenzy.

Some rituals are conducted in the make-up room and worship is offered to various deities including Ganesha before actors move to stage.

The Bhagavata and his chorus arrive first on the stage from the make-up room in a procession led by musicians playing on their instruments. A jester carries the idol of Ganesha with him. Puja is offered to Ganesha on the stage.

Purvaranga or preliminaries of the Yakshagana are very elaborate. It contains items such as dances of Konnagis, Bhagavata's Sabhalakshana vivechana, dances of two male characters known as Balagopala and of two female characters identified as Rukmini and Satyabhama, humorous encounter of jesters and Bhagavata. Vaddolaga is a preliminary entry procedure of the characters appearing in the play. Vaddolaga or curtain-entry of ferocious demonic characters is always very spectacular.

After the preliminaries are over Bhagavata starts unfolding the story with the help of the actors. Bhagavata first sings a song, character on the stage performs a dance expressing its contents through his movements, then taking cue from the song sung he breaks into prose dialogue or speech elaborating upon its meaning. Through song-dance-speech sequences the story moves to its end.

After that the Bhagavata sings mangala or benediction, performs aarati ritual and returns to Chowki with the performers.

Kalaga that is battle and kalyana that is marriage of the mythological characters are popular themes. Most of the Yakshagana plays or prasangas due to their preoccupation with battle and marriage themes are replete with heroic, furious and shringara rasas with some sprinkling of comics. Battle sequences choreographed in Yakshagana style are really spectacular.

YAMA-YAMI SAMVADA

In the Rig Veda we find some hymns in monologue, dialogue and chorus form having story element. One such hymn is Yama-Yami Samvada. It is believed that these pieces were dramatically rendered during Yajna ceremonies and rituals. They are also described as 'rudimentary dramas' from which Sanskrit theatre sprang. Here is one illustration of Rig Vedic dialogue hymn in the form of Yama-Yami Samvada.

Yama is the first ancestor and Yami his twin sister. According to one interpretation here Yami is imploring her brother to have intercourse with her for the continuity of human race. L.v. Schroeder puts forth a theory that this Rig Vedic Hymn in a dialogue form is but a part of big fertility cult drama of Yama and Yami in which Yami finally makes Yama submit to her wishes. He feels that the verses in the second act of the play being of phallic nature might have been edited out by the compilers of the Rig Veda. Winternitz also feels that this hymn is only a torso though an excellent work of art (*A Hist. of Ind. Lit.*, p. 97). He says: "whether this torso is to be explained through the loss of an introductory and concluding prose legend according to an Akhyana theory or through the loss of the second and the most important act according to the conception of the same as a drama cannot be settled" (*ISD*, p. 16). The composer of the hymn has portrayed the characters of both Yama and Yami and conflict of human passions in a remarkable dramatic manner is certain. One cannot deny the possibility of culminating the cult drama into some kind of fertility ritual which certainly is no taboo to Vedic people. Thus runs the text of the hymn:

Yami: I invite you, Yama, my bosom friend, to intimate friendship. May Prajapati bestow an offspring for the sake of thee becoming the father of a son to be born to us.

Yama: Thy friend long not for a friendship in which a kinswoman is treated as one of a different family. The hero sons of the great Asura (are) upholders of heaven, they can see from afar.

Yami: The immortals take pleasure in (a union) like this which is forbidden to every mortal. Let thy mind then concur with mine, and as the progenitor (of all) was the husband (of his daughter Saraswati), do thou enjoy my person.

Yama: We have not done what was done formerly; for how can we who speak truth, utter now that which is untrue? Gandharva (the sun) was in the watery (firmament), and the water was his bride. She is our common parent, hence, our near affinity.

Yami: The divine omniform generator Twashtri, the progenitor, made us two husband and wife, even in the womb; none frustrate his undertaking; earth and heaven are conscious of our (union).

Yama: Who knows anything of this (his) first day (of existence)? Who hath beheld it? Who has ever revealed it? The dwelling of Mitra and of Varuna is vast. What sayest thou, who punishest men with hell?

Yami: The desire of Yama hath approached me, Yami, to lie with me in the same bed; I will abandon my person as a wife to her husband; let us exert ourselves in union like the two wheels of a chariot.

Yama: The spies of the Gods, which wander upon the earth, never stop, never close their eyes. Associate quickly, distractress, with some other than me, and exert yourself in union like two wheels of a chariot.

Yami: To him (Yama) let every worshipper sacrifice both day and night, on him let the eye of the sun repeatedly rise, (for him may) the kindred pair (day and night) unite with heaven and earth. Yami bears patiently Yama's unbrotherly (refusal).

Yama: The subsequent ages will come when sisters will choose one who is not a brother (as a husband); therefore, auspicious one, choose another husband than me, make thine arm a pillow for thy mate.

Yami: Is he a brother whose sister has no Lord? Is she a sister (whose brother) misfortune approaches? Overcome by desire, I strongly urge this one request; unite thy person with mine.

Yama: I will not unite my person with thine; they call him who approaches a sister a sinner. Enjoy pleasure with some other than me; thy brother, auspicious one, has no such desire.

Yami: Alas, Yama, thou art feeble; we understand not thy mind or thy heart. Some other female embraces thee as a girth a horse or as a creeper a tree.

Yama: Do thou, Yami, embrace another; and let another embrace thee as a creeper a tree; seek his affection, let him seek thine, and make a happy union.

(Rig. 10.1.10)

Winternitz describes this hymn as "valuable fragment of the ancient art of narration" and recognises the fact that these speeches are full of dramatic power (*A Hist. of Ind. Lit.*, pp. 95–96).

YOGINIVALAYANARTANAKELI

In the tenth century playwright Rajashekhara's Karpuramanjiri a playful circular dance of Yoginis is referred to. It is called yogini-valaya-nartana-keli. Describing the dance Rajashekhara says that on the background of musical chimes of small bells of the anklets, singing beautifully on laya and tala, women danced in a circular formation like Yoginis dance.

The word Yogini is explained variously. Yogini means female taken to yogic practices, one who follows the path of Yoga, female counterpart of Yogi. Female Yoginis are depicted in miniature paintings of different schools.

Also Yoginis are human females who participate in tantric Chakra puja rites along with their male consorts which involves partaking of fish, meat, parched grain, liquor and sexual intercourse. She is also called Bhairavi. Chakra puja means rites performed by the participants in circular formation.

Again Yoginis are those human females who indulge in esoteric rituals on Sriparvata in the Andhra Pradesh. It is believed that since 6th century A.D. Sriparvata, modern Srishailam, became centre of tantric cult of Kapalikas. Saudamini possessed the power of flying in the sky.

Another female ascetic belonging to Kapalika cult, Kapalakundala, too is mentioned in the play. She too is shown possessing the power of flying through sky. It seems she too belonged to Yogini category.

In the works like Kathasaritsagara and Rajatarangini the cluster of Yoginis is mentioned as Yogini-chakra. Chakra means wheel-like circular formation.

There are certain goddesses, generally sixtyfour in number, who are referred to as Yoginis. Their temples are generally circular. Circular Yogini temples at Hirapur and Ranipur-Jharial in Orissa are very famous. Equally famous is circular Yogini temple at Bhedaghat, probably ancient Bhairavaghat, on river Narmada.

The 'circle' is closely associated with the Yoginis. No wonder the dance formation of Yoginis, as described by Rajashekhara, is circular—valaya-nartana.

Probably women attired as Yoginis might have been dancing in circular formation wearing anklets studded with small bells, singing songs, in imitation of the same tantric ritual.

YUKTIPRABODHAM

Written by the Jainacharya Meghavijaya Gani in the 17th century as an allegorical play to establish the superiority of Jain philosophy.

SELECT BIBLIOGRAPHY

Agrawala, V.S.: Bharatiya Kala, Prithvi Prakashan, 1966.

Baird, Bil: The Art of Puppet, Macmillan Company, 1965.

Benegal, Som: A Panorama of Theatre in India, Popular Prakashan, 1968.

Bhavanani, Enakshi: The Dance in India, Taraporewala, 1965.

Bowers, Faubion: Theatre in the East, Thomas Nelson & Sons, 1956.

Brockett, Oscar G.: History of the Theatre, Allyn and Bacon, 1969.

Byrski, Christopher M.: Concert of Ancient Indian Theatre, Munshiram Manoharlal, 1974.

Cheney, Sheldon: Theatre—Three Thousand Years of Drama, Acting and Stage, Vision Mayflower, 1952.

Das Gupta, H.C.: History of Indian Stage, Vol. I to VI.

Gairola, Vachaspati: Bharatiya Natya Parampara Aur Abhinayadarpana, Samvartika Prakashan, 1967.

Gargi, Balavant: Theatre in India, Theatre Arts Books, 1962.

Ghosh, Manomohan: Natya Shastra, Manisha Granthalaya, 1967.

Hein, Norvin: The Miracle Plays of Mathura, Oxford University Press, 1972.

Horrowitz, E.P.: The Indian Theatre, Benjamin Bloom, 1969.

Joshi, N.P.: Bharatiya Murtishastra, Maharashtra Vidyapitha Grantha Nirmiti Mandal, 1979.

Keith, A.B.: The Sanskrit Drama, Oxford University Press, 1924.

Ketkar, Godavari: Bharatiya Natyashastra, Popular Prakashan, 1963.

Khokar, Mohan: Traditions of Indian Classical Dance, Clarion Books, 1979.

Konow, Sten: The Indian Drama, General Printers and Publishers, 1969.

Kothari, Sunil: Kuchipudi, Abhinav, 2000.

Kunjuni Raja: Kuttiyattam, Sangeet Natak Akademi, 1964.

Levi, Sylvain: The Theatre of India, Vol. I & II, Writers Workshop, 1978.

Mathur, J.C.: Drama in Rural India, ICCR, 1964.

Neog, Maheshvar: Satriya Dances, Publication Board, Assam, 1975.

Motichandra & Agrawala, V.S.: Chaturbhani, Hindi Grantha Ratnakar, 1959.

Nicoll, Allardyce: The Development of the Theatre, George G. Harrap & Co., 1966.

Pani, Jivan: Living Dolls, Publications Division, 1987.

Pani, Jivan: Ravan Chhaya, Sangeet Natak Akademi, 1987.

Rangacharya, Adya: Drama in Sanskrit Literature, Popular, 1967.

Rangacharya, Adya: Introduction to Bharata's Natyashastra, Popular, 1966.

Sahadev, Manjula: Sanskrit Natakon Me Ram, Vimal Prakashan, 1979.

Sharma, Veerabala: Sanskrit Me Ekanki Rupak, M.H.G. Akademi, 1972.

Shekhar, I.: Sanskrit Drama, Munshiram Manoharlal, 1977.

Subhedar, Sunil: Natya Darshan, Sahitya Sangh, 1981.

Tarlekar, G.H.: Studies in Natyashastra, Motilal Banarsidass, 1975.

Upadhyaya, U.P. and Smt. Sushila: Bhuta Worship, Regional Resources Centre for Folk Performing Arts, 1984.

Varadpande, M.L.: Traditions of Indian Theatre, Abhinav, 1979.

Varadpande, M.L.: The Critique of Indian Theatre (Edited with Dr. Sunil Subhedar), Unique Publications, 1981.

Varadpande, M.L.: Ancient Indian and Indo-Greek Theatre, Abhinav, 1981.

Varadpande, M.L.: Krishna Theatre in India, Abhinav, 1982.

Varadpande, M.L.: Religion and Theatre, Abhinav, 1983.

Varadpande, M.L.: Invitation to Indian Theatre, Arnold Heinemann, 1987.

Varadpande, M.L. : Mahabharata in Performance, Clarion Books, 1990.

Varadpande, M.L: History of Indian Theatre, Vol. I, II, III, Abhinav, 1987, 1992, 2003.

Varnekar, S.B.: Sanskrit Vangmaya Kosha, Vol. I & II, Bharatiya Bhasha Parishad, 1988.

Wells, H.G.: Classical Drama of India, Asia Publishing House, 1963.

Yajnik, R.K.: Indian Theatre, Allen & Unwin, 1939.